TEMPTED BY THE BILLIONAIRE NEXT DOOR

THERESE BEHARRIE

A BACHELOR, A BOSS AND A BABY

RACHEL LEE

MILLS & BOON

First Published in Great Britain 2018
by Mills & Boon, an imprint of HarperCollinsPublishers,
1 London Bridge Street, London, SE1 9GF

Tempted by the Billionaire Next Door © 2018 Therese Beharrie
A Bachelor, a Boss and a Baby © 2018 Susan Civil Brown

ISBN: 978-0-263-26494-4

38-0518

MIX
Paper from
responsible sources
FSC™ C007454

FSC
www.fsc.org

This book is produced from independently certified FSC™ paper to ensure responsible forest management.

For more information visit: www.harpercollins.co.uk/green

Printed and bound in Spain
by CPI, Barcelona

TEMPTED BY
THE BILLIONAIRE
NEXT DOOR

THERESE BEHARRIE

For Grant, my best friend.

And Jenny, for taking the squirming, questing and searching journey of friendship with me. I can't imagine doing this without you.

CHAPTER ONE

JESSICA STEYN HADN'T deliberately sought out the half-naked man who'd entertained her over the last week. But she couldn't deny that watching him had fast become her new favourite hobby.

She watched as he bent over to pick up another stack of logs—watched as the muscles of his naked back rippled, the lightest sheen of sweat defining them even more—and conceded that it was *definitely* top-notch entertainment.

Guilt poked at her, but she ignored it. It wasn't *her* fault that he wasn't wearing a shirt. Nor was it her fault that he'd made a routine of cutting up the trees in his yard. Every day at noon he emerged from the house—wearing an old T-shirt that inevitably got tossed aside about five minutes into his task—and hacked the trunks he'd cut down the day before into logs. He then placed them in a pile, before carrying them over to an enclosed area where he'd set them down and start all over again.

So, ever since she'd noticed there *was* a routine, every day at noon she would settle in front of the window that overlooked his property to enjoy the show.

Thank goodness she'd discovered him, she thought as he gulped down a bottle of water. Water that dribbled over his chin, creating an enticing path down the column of his throat, between his pecs and the impressive ridges of his abs. Her heart rate immediately skyrocketed, and she thought that maybe *she* needed a glass of water, too.

He was a pretty decent distraction in an otherwise boring day. Now that her friend and boss, Anja, was away with her husband, Chet, on business, Jess's days were mostly free. Apart from watching Mr Sexy-Next-Door.

And, of course, thinking about the child she carried.

Before her mind could take that detour—about how this child made Jess feel as if her life was actually worth something for the first time—she thought about how annoyed she was with Anja for not telling her that there *was* a Mr Sexy-Next-Door.

She'd been helping Anja manage her yoga studio for almost two years now, and this was the first time Jess had seen him. Though, to be fair, it was also the first time Jess had stayed at Anja's house for longer than a few days. But she still expected Anja to tell her about the man. Perhaps not as her boss, but as her friend.

And definitely as her *best* friend.

But all thoughts of that vanished when the top log of the stack Mr Sexy had set down started to roll. He'd already turned away, so didn't see the snowball effect of that one log. Jess pushed out of her chair, a wordless cry of warning on her lips, but it was too late. The logs had rolled under his feet and she watched in horror as he fell to the ground, twisting his body so that he landed on his hip.

Before she knew it, she was out of the front door. She had to turn back when she realised she hadn't locked the house and, after she did, she ran as fast as her swollen body would allow to her temporary neighbour's house. She said a silent prayer of thanks when she found his gate open and then she was kneeling beside him, her hands running over the chest she'd admired only minutes before.

She ignored how the grooves of his muscles, his abs, felt beneath her hands and focused on identifying whether anything was broken. She realised that he'd turned over onto his back then, but it only made her pause for a second. Then her hands were on his ankles, his calves, but, before she could feel his thighs or hips, two large hands gripped her wrists.

'I'm not opposed to having a beautiful woman run her hands over me, but maybe we should leave that particular area for when we know each other better.'

Jess felt her face burn and quickly pulled back. But her balance was off and she landed on her butt. Her hand immediately went to her stomach, but she dropped it just as quickly. Not because his eyes had followed the gesture, and the way the interest there had cooled reminded her of the dismissive looks her parents had used to give her, but because she was fairly certain the baby was fine. She hadn't fallen very hard. Though she really had to remember that pregnancy had made her clumsy.

'I'm assuming that response means you didn't knock your head on the way down.' She debated not saying anything else, but she knew she would worry if she didn't ask. 'Are you okay?'

'Yeah, I guess so. Well, as okay as you can be when someone witnesses a couple of logs trip you.' He moved to push up to his forearms, but she crawled forward and set a hand on his chest, pushing him back down.

'You should stay still until we're sure you're really fine.'

'I *am* sure. I'm fine.'

Realising he was the stubborn sort, Jess pressed a hand against his hip and nodded when he winced. 'You're not fine. I'm calling an ambulance.'

Before she could move to her feet, he grabbed her wrist again. This time, she felt the heat of his hand on her arm. Felt the callused bumps at the base of his fingers rub against her skin. She wasn't sure why it sent a flush through her body, but she stilled and then gently pulled her arm out of his grip.

His expression didn't change, though something in his eyes flickered. 'I really am fine. I'll probably have a bruise on my hip tomorrow—and my ego will probably need to be resuscitated since it was murdered so cruelly—but I promise you, I'm fine.'

He sat up then, and she let him. 'Besides,' he continued with a smile that made the flush in her body go hotter, 'if I'm not fine, maybe you'll come to my rescue again.'

'Unlikely,' she replied, ignoring the way her lips wanted to curve at his words. 'I just happened to be looking out of my window when you fell.'

It sounded legitimate, she thought, and almost patted herself on the back when she saw he'd bought her excuse. Good thing, too. She wasn't sure how she could explain the real reason she'd seen him.

'I appreciate you wanting to help me. Are you a doctor?'

'No.'

'Nurse?'

She shook her head.

'So, you just ran over when you saw me fall without any medical skills whatsoever?'

'I was a lifeguard when I was a teenager.' A choice her parents had disapproved of heartily. Funny how they'd chosen to be interested in something so insignificant when they'd ignored everything else in her life. When they'd ignored *her*. 'I have first-aid experience, and falls were the first thing they taught us to deal with.'

'I stand corrected.' His smile was more genuine now, less cocky, and yet it had the same effect on her body.

Or maybe it was the fact that he still didn't have a shirt on, and she was being treated to her afternoon entertainment close-up.

She almost lifted a hand to check whether she was drooling.

'Well, now that I know you're okay I should probably be off.' She took a long time to get to her feet, and cursed silently when she saw how smoothly he did it.

'How can I repay you?'

She snorted. 'For what? Rushing over here and embarrassing us both?'

'Why would you be embarrassed?'

Good question. 'Because clearly you were fine and I panicked over nothing?'

'You panicked?'

She rolled her eyes. 'It was a hard fall, okay? I was worried.'

She couldn't tell what had changed on his face, but something had. And it made his already too perfect features seem even more appealing. 'So, I'm repaying you for being worried. It's not often that people care.'

'No, it isn't,' she agreed, feeling the words hit a little too close to home. 'But I don't need to be repaid. You're fine. Right?' He nodded. 'So, I'll be seeing you.'

She turned to leave and managed to get a few steps away from the gate before his voice called out, 'Which window?'

She turned back. 'What?'

'From which window did you see me fall?'

'That one.' She nodded to the window on the second level of the house next door, grateful that the chair she'd been sitting on—or the chips she'd been eating while watching him—wasn't visible.

'That's my sister's house.'

It took a moment for her mind to process the new information. 'Your sister?' she repeated. '*You're* Dylan?'

'Yeah,' he said, his forehead creasing. 'Who are you? And why are you staying in my sister's house?'

'I'm Jess. Jessica,' she added quickly. 'I'm staying at the house while Anja and Chet are away.'

His features tightened. 'Away where?'

'Sydney. They wanted to get Anja's new yoga studio up and running before the—' She caught herself before it was too late. She couldn't tell Dylan about the baby. Anja would kill her. And she didn't need to upset one of the few people who cared about her. 'Does she know you're here?'

'No.'

'Oh.'

There was a long stretch of silence before either of them spoke again. And then she asked, 'You've been back for at least a week. Why haven't you come over? Or tried to call her?'

He frowned. 'How do you know how long I've been back for?'

Jess felt her eyes widen, her cheeks heat, before she managed to reply with something other than *I've been watching you*. 'I heard the garbage truck pick up your bin earlier this week.' She held her breath and hoped he'd buy the somewhat lame excuse.

'And how do you know that I haven't tried to call her?'

'She…would have told me.'

He studied her. 'How exactly do you know Anja?'

Something about the way he asked it put her back up. 'I'm her PA.'

'She let her PA stay in her house?' There was barely a pause before he continued. 'She would tell her PA if her brother called her?'

Jess straightened. 'Yes. Your sister and I are also friends. Good friends.' She kept her hand from going to her stomach—to the proof of the bond that she and Anja shared—and forced herself to calm down when an inner voice questioned why she was responding so defensively. 'I didn't realise it was you when I came over.'

'But you knew I lived next door?'

'Yes,' she replied, but it got her thinking about why it hadn't occurred to her that Mr Sexy-Next-Door was actually Anja's brother. 'I knew you lived next door, but Anja didn't tell me *which* next door you lived in.'

'And you never asked?'

You're not exactly a topic of conversation either of us readily bring up. 'It didn't matter.'

'Because my sister doesn't talk about me?'

'Because you weren't here.'

Though both answers were true, it seemed as if Dylan cared more about the option she'd offered. Because when he'd given *his* option his face hadn't tightened the way it had after *she'd* spoken. Hurt hadn't flashed across his face, quickly followed by a blankness she couldn't help but feel was desperate.

'Why *are* you here?' she said after a moment, unable to help herself.

'I live here.' There was a beat of silence. 'This is my home.'

'It hasn't been,' she reminded him, still compelled by reasons she wasn't quite sure of. 'Not for the last two years.'

'No, it has been,' Dylan replied softly. 'But even the best of us run away from home sometimes, don't we?'

Her heart stalled, reminding her of the old car she'd seen just that morning, spluttering down the road in front of Anja's house. Why did it feel as if he was talking about *her*? *To* her? As if he instinctively knew that she'd turned her back on the place she'd once called home? As if he knew that she'd run from the parents who hadn't cared enough to even try to make her believe that they wanted her to stay?

'When are they coming back?' Dylan asked gruffly. Jess shook her head, ignoring the need to push for more answers. To find out why telling her he'd run from home had clearly upset him. It was none of her business.

'The end of the month.' Though Jess had a feeling it would be a lot sooner once she told Anja that Dylan had returned. 'How long *have* you been back?'

'You were right,' he replied. 'About a week.'

So he'd been chopping up wood since the day he'd returned, she thought, and forced away the sudden disappointment that came from knowing she'd no longer be able to watch him. How could she, knowing who he was?

Older brother of her best friend. Uncle to the child she carried.

'Do you know where I've been?'

'The UK?' He nodded. 'Yeah, Anja told me you've been away for…business.'

'Clearly that isn't all she told you,' he said with a self-deprecating smile.

'No.'

The smile dimmed. 'There's a lot you seem to know about me, Jessica, and yet I haven't even heard about you.'

'Does that surprise you?'

'No.' A fleeting shadow of pain darkened his features. 'But I'm back now.'

'So you are.'

'And I'd like to have my return start on the right foot.'

Something pulsed in the air between them, but Jess refused to acknowledge it. 'Yeah, okay. Go for it.'

He smiled at her, and this time it wasn't laden with emotion. It was an easy, natural smile she imagined he'd give when he saw an old friend, or during his favourite movie. But it sent an unnatural frisson through her body.

'You should have lunch with me.'

'No,' she said immediately.

'You have somewhere else to be?'

'No, but—'

'Then have lunch with me.'

'No, thank you,' she said more firmly, hoping none of the panic she felt was evident in her voice. 'You were… busy before I interrupted.'

'After what happened, I think I'm done for the day.'

'I really don't think I should—'

'Please.' His smile widened and she almost felt faint. 'I'd like to get to know the woman staying in my sister's house. The woman who's clearly a good friend of hers.' He paused. 'That's what I meant by having my return start on the right foot. If you and I are on good terms when Anja gets back…'

The seconds ticked by, and then Jess narrowed her eyes. 'You're *schmoozing* me!'

Surprise captured his features, and then he laughed. A loud, genuine laugh that started at those fantastic abs and went all the way up to his perfect hair. It was fascinating to watch. The even angles of his face were animated with joy, those chocolate-whisky eyes she only now noticed he shared with his sister alight with appreciation.

She'd never been much of a beard woman, but Dylan's stubble was dissuading her of that belief. She loved that his skin reminded her of oak—not too light, not too dark. And she *really* loved that he still didn't have a shirt on, so she could appreciate that colour over hard, defined muscle…

'If I told you I was, would that make you want to have lunch with me any less than you already do?' he asked, interrupting her hormone-driven thoughts.

'Probably.' She waited. 'So, are you?'

Now he chuckled. 'No.'

She tilted her head. Watched him. 'You're the CEO of an international engineering company. I'd imagine that requires some measure of intelligence.'

'You're saying I'm not intelligent?'

'Only if you expect me to believe that you're not trying to…charm me into having lunch with you.'

'Well, I *am* taking some time off from work. Perhaps that's why I'm off my game. Why I've made such an unforgivable mistake.'

'You're still doing it!'

He smiled. 'I can't help it.'

'Great. It'll make my refusal so much easier then.'

'No, wait,' he said, grabbing her wrist when she turned. He let go when she turned back. Her skin prickled. 'I'm sorry. It's just…easier to schmooze than to…earnestly ask you to have lunch with me.'

'Why do you want to have lunch with me so badly?'

'You're Anja's friend and…and I'd like to show her that I'm serious about coming back to fix things. That's why I'm here,' he told her softly. 'I want to fix what I broke when I left, and if you and I are on good terms…' He shrugged. 'I wasn't lying about that, Jess.'

As Jess studied him she felt herself soften. She hated that she did, but she couldn't ignore the emotion behind his words. The hope. She also couldn't ignore how much it spoke to her own desire. The deep, dark one that she would never have admitted aloud to anyone.

That some day her parents would show up for her, just like it seemed Dylan had for Anja. That some day they'd want to fix things with her just as badly as Dylan clearly wanted to with his sister.

It was a stupid hope, one her experiences growing up had taught her not to entertain. But still, it made her want to say yes to Dylan. That, and the desire to prevent the child she carried from growing up in the tension, the brokenness that currently existed in Anja's family. The same kind of tension and brokenness that Jess had grown up with.

Jess knew Anja was stubborn, and she wouldn't let the

brother who'd left her after their father had died just come strolling back into her life. Not when that brother had broken her heart by leaving. Not when he'd broken his promise to always be there for her.

'I don't know why you left, Dylan,' Jess said softly, 'or why you didn't come home for two years. That's probably none of my business…though what I'm about to ask you falls under that category, too. But…why haven't you come over to speak with Anja since you got back?'

It was such a long time before he answered that Jess was sure he wouldn't answer her at all. 'I didn't know whether she'd want to see me, and staying away, keeping my mind and body busy with menial tasks…they were all excuses to postpone the inevitably difficult conversation I would have to have with her.'

Surprised by his candour—and more than a little touched—Jess nodded. 'Okay.'

'Okay?'

'Okay,' she repeated. She waited a beat before she said, 'You better have enough food to feed a pregnant woman, Dylan.'

It took Dylan a moment to realise what he'd done. Another to process what he'd said. And even then he wasn't sure what he was doing. Inviting a woman he barely knew into his home? Offering to make her lunch? Sharing his intention of fixing things with Anja? Hoping that she'd be able to give him some insight into his sister?

It was crazy, but his craziness was dipped in desperation. Desperation because his sister hadn't spoken to him— not properly—in almost two years. Desperation because his plan to speak with her when he got home wasn't working.

Because every time he'd wanted to go over to her house to talk with her he'd remembered her face when he'd left.

He'd remembered how broken she'd looked, how her voice had cracked when she'd said goodbye.

How he'd left anyway.

And now, when he'd finally told himself he would go to see her *that night*, it turned out she wasn't even there.

He was disappointed, and perhaps that had been another reason for his invitation to Jess. But then the desperation, the craziness, the disappointment had landed him a meal with a beautiful woman, so was it really that bad?

Yes, an inner voice answered him. *Of course* it was. Because though the beautiful woman knew things about his sister that *he* didn't know—that he wanted to know—she was also pregnant. *Pregnant.* Which meant someone had got her pregnant. His eyes searched her hand for a ring, but they didn't find one.

It sent an absurd surge of hope through him, and he rolled his eyes as he led the way into his house. He bent down when he heard the scurry of paws against the wooden floor and fussed over his Labrador, Daisy, when she came bounding around the corner.

But she quickly lost interest in him and made her way to the woman he'd invited for lunch. Dylan watched as Jess's face lit up and she lowered—carefully, he saw—before rubbing his dog vigorously. It sent another surge through him, but this time it was warmth. A bubble of warmth that floated from his heart and settled in his belly.

A bubble that abruptly popped when he remembered that no wedding ring didn't mean that she was available.

And that a baby meant she *definitely* wasn't available.

'Daisy, back,' he snapped, the words coming out harsher than he'd intended because of his thoughts. The dog gave him a beseeching look but stepped back and sat, and Dylan offered a hand to help Jess up.

'Sorry about that. She gets a little excited around people.'

He sucked in his breath at the sizzle he felt coming

from her hand. Held his breath when the vanilla scent she wore settled in his nose. As soon as she was steady, he broke the contact.

'Don't worry. I love dogs.'

'Do you have any?'

Sadness dulled her eyes. 'No, my parents weren't really fans of pets when I was younger. Or children.' She laughed breathlessly, but he could tell that it was meant to cover up her mistake. She hadn't meant to tell him that.

Well, that makes two of us, he thought, remembering what he'd told her about coming home. And because of it he didn't address her slip. Instead, he approached it from a different angle.

'Why don't you have any now? Doesn't your husband want pets either?'

'No husband.' She shrugged. 'I'm just your typical unwed pregnant woman, I guess.'

She didn't look too bothered by it, which forced him to ignore the hope that stirred inside him again. 'Somehow I doubt that.'

'That I'm unwed and pregnant?'

'That you're typical.'

'You barely know me, Dylan.'

Her eyes met his and it felt as if lightning flashed between them. The seconds ticked by, the current of energy between them grew more intense, but neither of them looked away. Eventually, he said, 'What are you in the mood to eat?'

A moment passed, and then he could see her force herself to relax. 'Do you have peanut butter?'

It was such a strange request that it broke the tension he still felt inside him. 'Yeah, I think so.' He narrowed his eyes. 'You want *peanut butter*? I'm pretty sure there's something more substantial in the fridge.'

'Peanut butter is plenty substantial,' she replied defensively. 'Especially if you serve it with those bananas over there.'

She nodded to the fruit bowl on his kitchen table, and he felt the smile on his face almost before he even knew it was there. 'Peanut butter and banana?'

'Peanut butter and banana,' she confirmed, and smiled. 'I tried to warn you about what you were getting into by inviting a pregnant woman for lunch.'

'Yeah, you did,' he answered, though he struggled for the words because her smile was so...*distracting*. As was her face—the smooth curves of its oval shape, the high cheekbones, those cinnamon eyes, the glossy olive of her skin, those generous lips...

Even her *hair* was distracting. The dark brown strands were clipped back into a messy style that he couldn't decide whether he liked. Mostly because it made him want to tidy it up. *No*, he corrected his thoughts immediately. Because it made him want to muss it up even *more*.

Her clothing was loose, hiding the curve of her stomach. That was why he hadn't noticed she was pregnant at first—though he'd discovered it pretty quickly, so he couldn't blame ignorance for the fact that he'd flirted with her.

But he didn't want to think about what he could blame flirting with her on, so he was glad when she spoke.

'Who looked after Daisy while you were away?'

'Actually, I got her in London and then brought her back with me.'

Daisy wagged her tail when he looked over at her and love filled his heart. She'd saved him from depression, from the loneliness of his grief and anger. From his guilt. And she'd needed him in a way that was more simple than he could ever remember being needed.

His experience of being needed by his mother and sister had always—*always*—been complicated. And he blamed himself. *He'd* been the one who'd chosen to look after their family when his father had abandoned them. When his father had decided that gambling was more important than the woman he'd married. Than his children...

Dylan had been the one to take care of the household when his father's abandonment had meant that they couldn't rely on their mother any more either. So yes, maybe after they'd found out the man had died, Dylan had wanted to leave it all behind. And yes, maybe finding out a few days before his father's funeral that his mother hadn't been the victim she'd pretended to be all those years ago had given him even more incentive to leave.

But he was back now. Because his sister hadn't lied to him, hadn't betrayed him. And it was time that he stopped acting as though she had.

'Daisy's English?' Jess asked, interrupting his thoughts. She snapped a finger and Daisy was at her side in an instant. 'I've never met an English dog before,' she said, cooing at his pet.

'I don't really think they have nationalities.'

'Really? Because Daisy gives off a distinct English vibe. Like she'd invite me for tea and scones every afternoon at three.'

He laughed. 'The English actually have their tea—' He broke off at her smirk, and the laugh turned into a smile. 'You don't care, do you?'

'Not unless I'm going to the UK, which is obviously not happening any time soon.'

'How far along are you?' he asked, and began to prepare their lunch. Since peanut butter and banana didn't seem quite as appealing to him, he decided on a chicken mayo sandwich for himself.

'Just over five months. Um, Dylan?' He glanced at her. 'I know the naked chef is a thing in the UK, but you not having a shirt on… Well, it's really distracting. Do you mind?'

CHAPTER TWO

HIS EYEBROWS ROSE, and then a grin curved his lips. 'I'm *distracting* you?'

'Yeah,' Jess said, and tilted her chin. 'Wouldn't you be distracted if I made your food half-naked? No, don't answer that,' she added quickly, when his grin turned naughty. 'It wasn't the right comparison.'

'Probably not, but I liked it.' He winked, and something flipped in her belly. She was fairly certain it wasn't the baby. 'I'll grab a T-shirt.'

He left the kitchen and finally air flowed easily through her lungs again. She hadn't noticed how hard it had been to breathe around him. But she knew it was a sure sign that she was digging a hole that she might not be able to get out of.

And it wasn't only because of how he made her feel. It was because Jess knew what Anja and Dylan's relationship was like. And because she knew how much he'd hurt her friend by leaving.

Anja hadn't even told Dylan that he was going to be an uncle. Or that his niece or nephew would be brought into the world by a surrogate. She hadn't told him about her miscarriage after years of fertility struggles, or how those struggles and that miscarriage had been the reason she'd decided to use a surrogate.

Or, Jess thought, about the fact that *she* was that surrogate.

Jess couldn't say she agreed with her friend's silence. But then, Jess didn't understand the dynamic between siblings since she didn't have any. Nor did she understand what it was like to be part of a real family unit, where hurt and betrayal resulted from a member of that unit doing something the others didn't approve of.

She could barely call her family a *family*, for heaven's sake, let alone a *unit*.

Anja was the closest thing Jess had to family, which was why she'd offered to be Anja and Chet's surrogate. It was also why she should have been calling Anja, telling her about Dylan's return instead of waiting for him to put a shirt on so that he could make her lunch.

Jess distracted herself by looking around. The open-plan living room and kitchen were filled with light from windows and doors that made up most of the rooms' external structure. From where she stood, she could see a sunroom where she would kill to spend a few hours in the afternoon sun, furnished in muted colours that told her Dylan had incredible style, or had hired someone who did.

The living room was just as stylish, though she wasn't a big fan of the darker finishes he'd chosen. She couldn't deny that it was striking against the cream-coloured walls and solid brick fireplace, but she preferred the warmth of the kitchen. With its light waterfall counter and space around the island, it was the type of room she'd always felt more comfortable in. Understated and tasteful. Despite the fact that she'd grown up in opulence. But more likely because of it.

Before she could go down that path, Dylan walked in wearing a blue T-shirt that did nothing to detract from his sexiness. She almost sighed when her heart did a quick tumble in her chest, and a voice in her head asked her to rethink agreeing to have lunch with him.

'Still hungry?' he asked and, despite the warning, Jess heard herself say, 'Yes, I am.'

She watched him go through the rhythms of making their lunch. Watched as he didn't so much as give her an indulgent smile as he chopped the bananas and plopped them in a bowl, adding a generous dollop of peanut butter as though he'd made the meal countless times before. He finished his sandwich almost as quickly and then offered her something to drink. Before she knew it, she was following him into the sunroom she'd admired earlier.

'You didn't have to go to all this effort,' she said when they sat.

'It wasn't really an effort.' He shrugged and took a big bite of his sandwich.

She followed by spooning banana and peanut butter together, and then lifted it to her mouth. When she'd swallowed, she looked up to see him watching her, a strange expression on his face. She wasn't sure why it made her feel flushed and, though she wanted to, she didn't think she'd be able to blame it on pregnancy hormones. It had her blurting out the first thing that came to mind.

'I quite liked the trees in your backyard before you cut them down.'

'I did, too. But their leaves were clogging the gutters and, with winter coming, I thought I'd do something about it. You know, make sure the gutters work when the rain comes and have wood for the fireplace.'

Dutifully, she said, 'The fireplace is wonderful. Your whole house is.'

His eyes scanned her face and she felt another flush of heat. 'Why don't I believe you, Jess?'

'I don't know,' she replied, and quickly ate another spoonful of peanut butter. She regretted it immediately when she noticed he was still watching her, and tried her best to act casually. When she'd swallowed, she reached for the bottle of water he'd offered her earlier and drank greedily.

'I don't really like the décor,' he continued as though there hadn't been any pause after her answer. 'But I'd already left before it was finished, so I wasn't really involved with the decision-making. Anja was, though, since we used the same guy for both our places, and I prefer hers.'

'I thought you hadn't been back since…since you left,' she finished lamely, though his expression told her he knew she'd meant to say *since your father died*.

'No, I haven't been back, but I saw pictures of both our places. I think Anja purposely gave the designer free rein to get back at me.'

'For what?'

'For leaving.' His eyes stayed on hers. 'Though you'd know more about that than I would.'

'Anja didn't tell me about the décor at all. I think it might have been before my time.'

'I wasn't talking about the décor.'

She forced herself to hold his gaze. 'I'm not sure what you're talking about.'

'About my sister's feelings about me leaving. You mentioned that she told you more than just the fact that I'd left for business.'

'Yes.'

'Care to share?' He gave her a smile that told her he was trying to charm her again.

'No.'

The smile faltered. 'I thought—'

'What?' she interrupted. 'That I'd tell you everything your sister told me?'

He lifted an arm. Rubbed the back of his neck. 'I

thought that since you were her friend, you must know… something.'

'The fact that I'm her friend means that I wouldn't tell you what I know.' Jess set down her bowl and perched on the edge of her chair. 'You didn't ask me over because you wanted the two of us to get along for Anja's sake. You asked me over so that I could tell you something that would help *you* get along with Anja.'

'And if I tell you you're right?'

'Then I'd say that it was lovely meeting you, Dylan, and wish you all the best for your return to Cape Town on my way out.'

He set his lunch down just as she had, and when he met her gaze his expression was a plea she felt hit her right in the chest. 'You must have known that was part of the reason I asked you over.'

She considered it. 'Maybe. But—'

But I wanted to believe that you wanted to get to know me.

She nearly laughed at herself. Clearly she hadn't learnt her lesson yet. People never wanted *her*.

'It seems like you want something from me that I'm not willing to give you. So it's probably best if I just leave.'

'No, Jess, don't.'

'Why not?'

'Because… I'm sorry.' He ran a hand through his hair. 'I've handled this poorly.'

'You're apologising way too much for someone who's only just met me,' she said softly. Coolly.

'So I'll be honest instead,' he replied, his voice tight. 'I wanted to know…what I was coming back to. The extent of the damage I caused by leaving.'

'I think you already do.'

He nodded. 'It would be nice to have some more… context.'

She shook her head and rose to her feet. 'I don't have context to give you. No,' she said when he opened his mouth to protest. 'Your context should come from Anja. Or your mother.'

His face darkened. 'I suppose I'll have to wait for Anja to get back then.'

Jess frowned. 'You don't have to. Your mother lives—'

'Thank you, Jess,' he interrupted, and stood with her. 'It's been lovely meeting you.'

Though Jess didn't understand his reaction, she knew that he was asking her to leave. She would have been offended if she wasn't so…curious. It was clear that Dylan had no intention of asking his mother about what had happened after he'd left. And the look on his face told her that there was a reason for that. A reason even Anja didn't know, or else Jess would know, too.

It was all very interesting, but Jess told herself it was none of her business. Again. She didn't know why she had to remind herself of that so often, so she murmured her thanks to Dylan and walked towards the door.

'Jess—' Dylan said from behind her.

'It's okay.' She opened the door and gave Daisy one last pat. 'You don't have to explain it to me. I get it.' She paused. 'It was lovely meeting you, too, Dylan. I hope your return to Cape Town is everything you hoped it would be.'

She walked out before he could reply.

Dylan stared at the door long after Jess had left, hoping that their interaction wasn't an omen for the rest of his return.

He knew the way things had spiralled between them was his fault. But he'd wanted to know what Jess knew. He told himself it was because it would give him an indication of what Anja knew. Of what his sister thought of him. But, deep down, he knew it was because he didn't want Jess to judge him based on the only thing he'd done in his life that had disappointed his sister.

Because he'd been disappointed, too, and he knew what it felt like. His entire life, his father had disappointed him. It was the best—or, rather, easiest—word to use to describe how Dylan felt about his father. About the man's gambling addiction. About his absence. And perhaps Dylan would have been able to put it all behind him after his father had died if he hadn't found out his mother had known about his father's problems before he or Anja had been born.

He and Anja had spent their entire childhood trying to comfort their mother after their father had left them. They'd no longer been children. Instead, their existence had been dedicated to keeping the woman who'd borne them from spiralling into a deep depression.

What had been the point of all that when his mother had known what she'd been getting into with his father?

When Dylan had found out, he couldn't bring himself to tell Anja. So he'd left, and tried to deal with the anger by himself, away from her. His anger at the secret his mother had kept from them. His anger about the inexplicable grief he felt at losing a man he'd barely known.

He couldn't get past the irony that by wanting to keep Anja from the same disappointment he'd felt in their parents, *he'd* disappointed her. More than that, he thought, remembering that expression on her face when he'd told her he was leaving again. He'd *abandoned* her.

Just like his father had abandoned them.

CHAPTER THREE

JESS WOKE UP to water dripping onto her face.

It took her a moment to realise that water was dripping on to her face, and more time to realise that that wasn't a *good* thing. She sat up and looked at the ceiling, only to see a long, slim strip of water dripping across the length of the room.

Her first thought was that she needed to close the water main, and that she'd figure out where the water was coming from once she had. But when she reached down to put her shoes on, she realised that she didn't actually know where the water main was.

It took her another few minutes to figure out that she needed to ask Dylan for help, and she sighed before slipping on the soft boots she wore as slippers.

The entire floor of the passage to the front door was wet, and Jess's heart beat heavily in her chest as she walked through the water. She locked the door and then rushed to Dylan's house, and waited impatiently for him to answer after she rang the bell.

Seconds later he opened the door, and Jess found herself staring into a bare chest. Again. Why didn't he have a shirt on? she thought, annoyance straightening her spine. Didn't he realise it was *autumn*? She tilted her head up, and only then saw that his hair was mussed from sleep. Which, she discovered, had the same effect on her as his bare chest.

She forced herself to focus on the reason she'd woken him. 'Do you know where the water main to Anja's house is?'

He frowned. 'Yeah, why?'

'No time. I'll explain after you shut it off.'

His eyes swept over her, and for the first time she realised that the only thing she'd done after waking up was put her slippers on. She must look a mess, she thought, wincing internally. But she wouldn't dwell on it now. Which was probably a good thing since a voice in her head reminded her that she'd woken with water on her face, which had probably made her look even worse.

Thankfully, he seemed to take her appearance as a sign of urgency and he walked past her, barely waiting for her to waddle after him before he was at the front of Anja's house, opening a concealed hatch and reaching inside. Then he was at her side again, offering her another view of his naked chest.

'You're going to catch a cold if you don't put a shirt on,' she said, crossing her arms when her comment reminded her that she didn't have much on either. She was more dressed than he was, but her oversized shirt and black pyjama pants were not exactly the items she'd have chosen had she known she was going to see anyone, let alone *him*.

Besides, she wasn't wearing a bra, and she knew her pregnancy boobs weren't going to politely refuse to be noticed, especially in the cold.

'If you keep telling me to put a shirt on, I'm going to think you have a problem with me being shirtless. And then I'd have to ask why you have problem with me being shirtless, and I'm guessing that's not a conversation you want to have.'

As if to prove his point, he ran a hand through his hair. His biceps bulged and her throat went dry.

'I'm only worried about your health,' she managed stiffly.

'Oh, I forgot. Because of your medical background, right?' He grinned and she almost—*almost*—smiled back. Instead, she pressed a hand on his hip and pressed gently, much like she had the day before. And, just like he had the day before, he winced.

She gave him a sweet smile. 'How's your hip feeling?'

'Oh, aren't you hilarious?'

'I'm not the one trying to be a comedian this morning.'

'I wouldn't have had to be anything besides asleep if you hadn't woken me up.' Now he ran a hand over the back of his neck, pushing his chest out ever so slightly. She swallowed. 'What time is it?'

'I…I don't know,' Jess replied as she realised she didn't. She winced. 'I'm sorry for waking you up. I just didn't know what to do…' She waited a beat. 'Thank you. For your help.'

He nodded. 'You have a burst pipe?'

'Your guess is as good as mine. All I know is that I woke up with water dripping onto my face.' She sighed. 'The house is a mess.'

It would be a logistical nightmare for her. Not because she would have to take care of getting it fixed, but because she wasn't only staying at Anja's house to house-sit. No, she had just bought her own place and was staying at Anja's until her new home could be made liveable. It was small, and the deposit had taken most of her savings, but it was her own. A fact that always, always brought her joy.

It reminded her that when she'd cut ties with her parents two years ago she had nothing except her university degree. It could have been enough, especially since her surname meant something in the finance industry she'd been trained for, but she hadn't wanted to rely on that. She wanted something of her *own*. Something that couldn't in any way be attributed to her rich, successful parents whose only concern had been their business.

Not the child they'd mistakenly conceived.

So she'd applied for a job she was wholly overqualified for, doing the day-to-day admin for a yoga studio. She updated and maintained Anja's website, managed bookings, dealt with queries, emails and, for the past year, helped Anja with the admin for opening her studio in Sydney. It had been a dream of Anja's as Chet was Australian and she'd wanted roots there just like Chet had in South Africa.

And the job had turned out to be a dream for Jess— the constant stream of things to do a welcome distraction from the past and the parents she'd walked away from.

For two years Jess hadn't spent any of the money she'd earned on anything besides the essentials. It meant that she was able to afford the small flat she'd bought, twenty minutes away from Chet and Anja's place. But that flat was a mess.

She couldn't begrudge it since its state was why she'd got it at such a good price, but it needed a lot of work before anyone could live there. Since Chet owned a construction company he'd offered to do the work for her, and had refused payment. And then Anja had found out Jess's lease was ending and her landlord was being difficult about letting her stay there on a month-to-month contract and had offered for Jess to stay at their place until her flat was habitable.

She knew they felt indebted to her. Especially since *she'd* refused to consider payment for carrying their child. But really, she saw them as family. As the only family she had. And family did things like that for one another. They cared, and helped, and sacrificed. Not because they wanted anything in return, but because they loved one another.

The concept was foreign to her parents, and that was part of the reason she hadn't spoken to them in two years. But it was okay. She'd found her place.

Except in the literal sense, since her place was currently flooded.

She sighed again. 'I should probably call Anja. Excuse me.'

'There's not much she can do from there.'

'Maybe not, but I still need to tell her before I start sorting it all out.'

'Sure,' he agreed. 'Or, if you give me a moment to put on a shirt, I can have a look and help you sort it out. So when you *do* call Anja you'll be calling her with answers, not just a problem.'

Relief swept through her first, and then came the niggling suspicion. Why was he offering to help her? What would he get from it?

'You're trying to get back on Anja's good side again, aren't you?'

'Isn't that why I do everything?' he replied dryly, making her wonder what he really meant. Dozens of options went through her head but, for the life of her, she couldn't focus on one of them. Realising it meant that she was tired, that she needed help, Jess nodded.

'I'd appreciate the help. Thanks.'

'I'll see you in a minute.'

She watched as he jogged back to his house, taking in the way his jeans rode low on his hips. It gave her the perfect view of a very fine butt, and a muscular back just asking her to run her hands over it.

Jess tried to ignore the way her body responded to the idea, but then she realised that Dylan wearing jeans to bed didn't make sense. If he didn't wear a shirt, he definitely wouldn't wear jeans. Which meant that he must have just thrown on the first thing that had been close by…and that he probably didn't wear any pants to bed either…

The image sent her thoughts down a dangerous road, and suddenly she couldn't stop imagining what Dylan would look like naked. Or what it would feel like to be in that bed with him, turning over during the night to run her hands over that delicious body of his. To snuggle closer and kiss him, to feel the way his body responded to hers. With him naked, there would be no barrier to what would happen next, and she'd be able to—

'Jess?' She jumped and felt her cheeks flush when she saw Dylan in front of her, completely clothed, with a puzzled look on his face. 'Are you okay?'

'Yeah, I'm fine. Ready to go inside?' She didn't wait for his answer and instead walked to the house.

Where had *that* come from? she thought. She wasn't the kind of girl who had fantasies about men she barely knew. Hell, she didn't have fantasies about men at all. She'd never been the type. She hadn't felt the need to date around and see where it would take her. She'd had two steady boyfriends in her life, and both relationships had only lasted about a year.

When her last relationship had ended, Jess had seen no point in trying again. Sure, it might have been because her life had completely changed shortly after the break-up. But she'd worked hard to rebuild it—by herself—for the last two years and she hadn't seen the point in having a man around while she did.

So perhaps the fantasy she'd just had about Dylan was the result of the nothingness she'd had in her life since she'd broken up with her last boyfriend. Or it could have been her over-excited pregnancy hormones. She would put it down to both, and refuse to acknowledge the third option.

That maybe she just *wanted* her best friend's brother.

She was almost relieved when she saw the puddles on the floor when she walked in. It gave her something else to think about. Something else to worry about.

'Wow,' he said from behind her.

'Yeah,' she replied, taking it all in. 'I'm not sure what happened.'

'It looks like it came from the second floor. I'll go take a look.'

While he was upstairs, Jess tried to do some damage control. She used towels to soak up the water on the floor, and wiped all the surfaces that had been affected. Fortunately, it seemed the water had only leaked in her bedroom, the kitchen and onto the passage that led to the front door, missing the carpeted lounge and its expensive furniture.

But she was still out of breath when Dylan returned.

'It looks like a geyser burst. A quick fix, though I'm not sure we can say the same for the ceiling. There's some water damage—' He broke off and frowned at her. 'Are you okay?'

'Yeah, fine.' She waved a hand. 'I'm just not used to not being able to do normal things like dry the floor.'

'Why don't you rest for a bit? I'll finish up here and make the necessary calls.'

'No, you don't have to.'

She stepped onto the towel in front of her to pick up the one just beyond it, but it slipped under her feet and she felt herself falling before she fully realised what was happening. A strong arm went around her waist and drew her up, and then Jess found herself staring into Dylan's eyes.

There was concern there, but she could also see the faint light of anger at her refusal. But seconds passed and neither of them looked away, and soon his eyes changed. The concern, the anger, faded and was slowly replaced by interest.

By attraction.

That was the word for it, she thought. And it was a dangerous thought since something instantly sprang inside her chest at the prospect, at the recognition of what had caused her fantasy about Dylan earlier. She swallowed as the attraction changed to desire, and more seconds passed as she realised that that change was because of whatever he saw in *her* eyes.

Because being reminded about the fantasy she'd had about him earlier had made her body go hot. Had made her tingle, ache. Now she was pressed against the chest she'd spent days admiring, her hands braced against it, and she could feel his heart thudding against her hand. She should move, she told herself.

But she couldn't bring herself to put distance between them. The only movement she wanted to act on was to press herself even closer against him. To feel his muscular body tight against her, and have him feel the softness of her body. Her belly would get in the way, but she could—

The thought stopped her imagination abruptly, and shame took the place of desire. How *could* she be thinking these things when she was *pregnant*? When she was carrying a member of Dylan's family?

There was no way she could entertain these fantasies. She couldn't think about Dylan in any way other than as Anja's brother, the uncle to the child she carried. Getting involved with him had no benefits. It would probably hurt her best friend. It might even hurt the baby.

And though she wasn't the biological mother, while she carried him or her, *she* was responsible for the baby. *The baby* was her most important priority, and she couldn't ignore that just because Dylan made her feel things she'd forgotten she could feel.

Her relationship with Anja was important to her. More important than anything else. She would *not* screw it up.

'Thanks,' she murmured, thoroughly doused of the heat of attraction. 'Why don't you get this cleared up and I'll make the calls? I have the information on my laptop.'

'It's not damaged?' he asked her quietly, taking a step away from her.

'It's in the lounge. The water didn't get there.'

'Okay then.'

With careful steps, Jess made her way to the lounge. There would be no repeat performance of the last ten minutes.

Not now, not ever.

CHAPTER FOUR

BY THE TIME Dylan was done clearing up, the plumber had arrived and confirmed his suspicions: the geyser *had* burst. While they liaised with the insurance company and arranged for it to be replaced and informed them of the other damage, Dylan watched Jess. She'd been acting strangely from the moment he'd answered the door that morning, and he couldn't quite figure out why.

Was it because of the way things had ended between them the day before? Maybe, he thought. But then he remembered the way things had crackled between them when he'd saved her from falling. The way his body had reacted to her body's proximity, and the shame he'd felt when she'd pulled away.

She was pregnant, for crying out loud. There was no circumstance in which that didn't make her off-limits. He needed to remember that, he thought, when his heart stuttered as his eyes rested on her.

But, damn it, there was just *something* about her that pulled him in. That made rational thought not matter, and made hope flair when it shouldn't. And it had nothing to do with her relationship with his sister.

He told himself to pull back, to control himself, and went over to talk with her.

'The insurance is sending out their own evaluators this afternoon,' she said, and he saw the fatigue in her eyes.

'Figured as much when we realised the plumber we called wasn't on their list of approved service providers.'

'I've told them what the plumber identified the problem as, and gave them the details of the geyser. I doubt they'll arrive with it—wouldn't want to waste their money in case it wasn't what we said—but it should be replaced by the end of the day.'

'And the ceiling?'

'They're sending someone out for that and the rest of the damage today, too.'

He nodded. 'I don't think the ceiling will be too much of an effort. Might just be a paint job. The rest will have to dry.'

'It'll probably take a good solid two days,' she replied. 'And the water will probably be off for today. The painting should be done tomorrow, but the fumes might keep me out for at least another day.' She bit her lip. 'It might end up being more than two days.' She rested a hand on her stomach, and the action did something strange to his insides.

'Do you have somewhere to go?' he asked, his thoughts making his words gruff.

'No,' she said softly.

'Where do you live when you're not living here?'

'I just bought a place that isn't ready for me to move in yet. And the lease of the one I rented before is up.' She sighed. 'Anja and Chet are letting me stay here until my flat's ready.'

He processed the information. 'What about the father of the baby?'

She hesitated. 'He isn't an option right now.'

'So he doesn't care where the mother of his child is?'

'That's not—' She broke off. 'He isn't an option. But

this isn't your problem, so don't worry. I'll figure something out.'

'I *will* worry. You have nowhere to go.'

'I'll be fine.'

'Jess—'

'Why are you pushing me?'

'Why won't you accept my help?'

'I *have* accepted your help. With all of this.' She waved her hand around them at the house. 'You've done enough.'

'Not if I leave you to figure things out by yourself,' he argued. 'Letting someone help you isn't going to rob you of anything, you know.'

'Not in my experience.'

He paused. 'What do you mean?'

'Nothing,' she said immediately, shaking her head. 'It doesn't mean anything.'

He studied her. Couldn't bring himself to look away from her. Not when her expression was so captivating. She'd been hurt before, he saw. And realised that hurt had made her lose something of herself.

Though he barely knew her, Dylan found his fists curling and his mind fantasising about being alone with whoever had hurt her. And since she was pregnant and didn't want to turn to the father of her child for help, Dylan was willing to bet he knew who he'd like to hurt.

He forced himself to relax. 'Okay, how about you get some of your clothes and come over to my place for breakfast? You can figure it out there,' he added over the protest he could sense would come from her.

But, instead of protesting, she said, 'That would be great, thanks,' surprising him. He watched as she got up—resisting the urge to help her when her movements looked the slightest bit sluggish—and waited in the passage leading to the front door while she packed.

He used the time to look at his sister's house. Just as

he'd told Jess the day before, he preferred the décor here to that of his own house. Though the architecture was much the same, the bright colours made Anja's house look more homely than his own. When he'd told Anja as much, she'd told him that if he'd been there, maybe he could have made sure his was homely, too.

It had been the first sign of the crack in their relationship, but of course, he'd ignored it. It had been easier to do than facing the fact that he should have been home…

Jess came out then, just in time to stop those thoughts from spiralling. He wordlessly took the small suitcase she had, and turned towards his place. He was almost surprised to see how sullen the sky had become, though he shouldn't have been. It was autumn, and the warmth of the past few days had been more of a fluke than the grey sky.

He opened the door of his house to an excited dog, who became even more excited when she saw Jess behind him. Though he could still see the fatigue in Jess's eyes, she dutifully gave Daisy the attention the dog wanted and then followed him into the kitchen.

It was strange having her in his house again. Which itself was strange, considering that he'd only been living in that house for eight days himself after being away from it for two years. And since the décor had changed while he'd been away, it was almost like living in a new place.

'You can have the guest room,' he told her, leading the way. 'My housekeeper comes in every second day, so the room should be okay to stay in. There's an en suite bathroom, too, so it has everything you need.'

'Thanks. I think I'll take a shower and change.'

'And I'll get breakfast ready.'

'Oh, you really don't have to—'

'I know,' he interrupted her. 'But I'm hungry, too, so it won't be that much of an effort.'

He left before she could argue with him, and started

making their breakfast. Cooking was one of the habits he'd picked up growing up that didn't annoy him. At first it had been for survival. After it had become clear his father wasn't going to come home, his mother had given up on most tasks, including feeding them.

So Dylan had used the money he'd found in his father's safe to buy food, but he'd quickly realised that the money wouldn't last if he didn't learn how to buy sustainable items. And that the items that *had* been sustainable required effort on his behalf. So he'd spent a lot of time watching cooking shows, had flipped through the faded cookbooks in his mother's bookshelf and had taught himself to cook. He'd soon realised that it calmed him, and had roped Anja in, hoping she'd feel the same way.

'You look better,' he said when he saw Jess walk into the kitchen. He plated the muffins his housekeeper had made.

'You mean better than the horror show I was this morning?'

'Not at all. I just meant—' He broke off when he saw her smile, and felt his stomach flip. He ignored it.

'Do you want something to drink?'

'Tea, please.' She settled onto the bar stool at the counter.

'I have more comfortable chairs in the living room.'

'I know. But I won't let this baby rob me of the opportunity to eat while I watch you cook.'

She gave him a cheeky grin, and he laughed. She *did* look better than before. Not only because now she wore a long-sleeved black dress that stretched down to her feet with a belt tied under her breasts accentuating her bump, but because she didn't look quite as tired, as restless, as she had when she'd first got there.

He wondered if that meant he could convince her to stay with him while the work on Anja's house was being done. The thought was as surprising as it was sudden, but when he thought about it he realised it wouldn't be such a bad idea.

Unless he thought about how things sparked between them. And how badly he wanted to kiss her lips, to taste her mouth and feel the fullness of her body against his again...

Which, of course, he wouldn't think about.

He told himself to wait until breakfast was over before he mentioned it, and slid the tea and muffins in front of her. 'Your wish is my command.'

'You're such a good man,' she breathed as she picked up a chocolate muffin.

He bit back a grin. 'Those are the first ones I go for, too.'

'They're delicious. Where did you get them?'

'My housekeeper made them for me.'

'They're *homemade*? You need to ask her for the recipe.'

'You cook?' he asked, and started cutting fruit. He didn't know what was in a pregnant woman's diet, but he figured he'd cover all his bases.

'That's *baking*, Dylan.'

'You bake?'

'No.'

His lips curved. 'So you cook, then?'

'Nope.'

'Then why did you correct me?'

'It seemed like a fun thing to do,' she said with a smile, and then sobered. 'I've been learning how to do both over the last few years. I'm not quite at the level of being able to say that I can cook or bake *well*, but I can feed myself. And these—' she lifted the muffin '—are definitely the kind of food I'd like to learn how to make.'

'What happened a few years ago? That made you want to learn how to cook and bake, I mean.' He set the fruit he'd been cutting up to the side, and began preparing the bacon and eggs.

'I…I moved out of my parents' house.'

He frowned. 'How old are you?'

'Old enough to have been out of my parents' house by then,' she said with a laugh, but it sounded forced. 'We used to have a cook, so there was never really a need for me to learn how to feed myself.'

'You had a cook?'

'Yes.' He glanced over to see the hesitation in her eyes. 'Extravagant, isn't it?'

'I wasn't thinking that.'

'I wouldn't blame you if you did.'

He turned to her and watched as she avoided his eyes. And suddenly he thought that perhaps he'd attributed the hurt he saw in her to someone who hadn't deserved it.

'So you had an…extravagant childhood?'

'I guess you could say that.'

'What would you say?'

'I…was always well provided for.' He could hear the care she'd taken with those words.

'Your parents are wealthy?'

'Yes.'

'So why—' He broke off, knowing that his question would veer into territory she might not be comfortable with. But she finished his sentence for him.

'Why am I working as a PA?' He nodded. 'Well, I wasn't…well cared for. Or cared for at all,' she added softly, and Dylan felt his heart throb. 'So, when I moved out, I stopped talking to them. Which meant I had to take care of myself, hence this job.'

Seconds passed as he digested this new information. 'When you didn't want my help this morning, were you… thinking about them?'

'Only about how they used to throw it in my face whenever I asked them for help.' She paused. 'I remember when I was younger, I started saving for a new laptop. I didn't want to use my dad's old one any more, so I got a job and put away every cent of it so I could buy myself a new one. But my dad's laptop broke before I had enough money to replace it, so I asked them to help me buy a new one.' She lifted a hand, brushed at something on her cheek that he couldn't see. 'I thought that having half of the money for it—that working for it—would make them proud, but—' she cleared her throat '—but it didn't. They helped me buy the laptop, and reminded me of it whenever I acted in a way they didn't approve of.'

He blew out a breath, his heart aching when he saw the fear on Jess's face. Fear he realised came from telling him something so intimate. 'I'm sorry, Jess.'

'Don't be,' she said, avoiding his eyes. 'It's not your fault.'

But still, silence stretched long and awkwardly between them.

Dylan wished he could find something to say to make her feel better. Clearly, she'd had a tough time growing up just like he'd had. So, in fact, he should have known *exactly* what to say to her.

But, instead of helping him to find words of comfort, that fact kept him silent. Because he *did* know how awful it was, and that meant that nothing he could say would make her feel any better. And though he'd only met Jess the day before, something told him she wasn't the kind of person who wanted fake consolation.

He appreciated that. Respected it.

And yet, when he looked at her again, he heard himself saying, 'I guess you and I have more in common than I thought.'

CHAPTER FIVE

'SEEMS LIKE IT,' Jess replied, and wondered why that suddenly mattered. Wondered why she wasn't alarmed by the fact that it did.

Perhaps it was because she couldn't deny how much… better she felt immediately after he said it. It made her feel like less of a fool for bringing up the subject of her parents when she knew she shouldn't have. When she knew that doing so would bring out that side of her that was bitter and resentful.

That *hurt*.

It left a terrible taste in her throat, and Jess drank desperately from her tea to try to take it away. Even though her mind told her the response was irrational. Even though she knew that that taste was imaginary.

Damn her parents for doing this to her, she thought. She squeezed her eyes shut, and then forced herself to open them again. When she did, she saw that Dylan was watching her. Heat rushed to her cheeks, and the air in her lungs grew terribly heavy.

'I'm sorry that they hurt you,' he said.

'It doesn't matter.'

'But they did.'

'And yours hurt you,' she replied primly. 'We survive.'

'Do we?' he asked with a half-smile. 'Do you think we're surviving?'

'You don't?'

'I...don't just want to survive if this is surviving,' he admitted quietly. 'If constantly worrying that I'm repeating the mistakes of my parents—that I'm disappointing the people I love—is surviving.'

'I...feel the same,' she said in surprise. 'About surviving.'

He didn't reply for a moment. 'When I was on the second floor of Anja's house earlier I noticed something strange.' He turned back to the stove and flipped an egg.

Confusion spread through her, but the change in topic and the fact that he wasn't looking at her any more had the breath in her lungs moving easily again. 'Yeah?' she replied, grateful that her voice wasn't nearly as shaky as she'd thought it would be.

She took a deep breath, and then busied herself with adding fruit and yoghurt to a bowl.

'Yeah. A chair,' he said, deadpan, and her hand froze. 'In front of a window.'

She forced herself to move. 'That *is* strange.'

'Overlooking my property.'

'Even stranger.' She set the bowl down in front of her and dug in.

She couldn't admit her guilt if she couldn't speak.

'I thought so,' he continued conversationally. 'Until I realised that that was the window you pointed out to me yesterday. Where you said you saw me fall from.'

'Was it?'

'*And* then I remembered you'd known I'd been here for a week.'

She pretended to think about it. 'I don't remember. Sorry, pregnancy brain.'

'Pity.'

Dylan set two plates—one with bacon, one with the

eggs—on the counter with the rest of the food, and then took a third and began dishing for himself. As he settled on the stool next to her, Jess tried to think of something to say to change the topic of conversation.

Except she couldn't think of anything. All she *could* think about was the fact that he knew. He *knew* she'd been watching him.

She rolled her eyes. Sighed. 'Okay, yes, fine. That's where I was watching you from.'

He lifted his eyebrows and didn't say anything.

Damn it! Why was that so *sexy*?

'I mean, I didn't know it was you. Doesn't that count for something?'

He cocked his head. 'You mean towards the imaginary scoreboard that gives you points for being a pervert?'

'I am *not*—' She cut off her own protest when she saw the amusement in his eyes. 'What would you have done if I was working outside in my bikini?'

'Would it make you feel better if I said I'd watch?'

'Yes.' She sniffed. 'Yes, it would.'

'Then I'd have watched.'

She couldn't resist her own amusement at the expression on his face now. 'With chips?'

'You watched me…with chips?'

'Yesterday it was chips.' She considered her next words. *What the hell?* 'The day before it was popcorn. And the day before that, chocolate.'

'Choc…' he said before realisation dawned. 'How many days have you been watching me?'

'Don't act coy now,' she replied. 'I told you you'd been home for at least a week, so that's how many days I've been watching you.'

There was a beat of silence before his face split into a smile and laughter spilled from his lips. It made him look younger, more carefree, and Jess realised how little of either of those his expression normally held. She thought about his earlier words—about what he'd said about surviving—and for the first time Jess felt sorry for her best friend's brother.

It had been easy to see Dylan as the unfeeling older brother who'd left his grieving mother and sister weeks after they'd buried their father. Easy because she'd only heard Anja's side of things. Because she'd only seen the aftermath of Dylan's departure.

But now, after the time—however short—she'd spent with Dylan, Jess finally considered the other side of the story. That clearly told her that her rash judgement was undeserved. She only had to look at Dylan's face when he wasn't laughing to realise it.

'I'm glad you find it so funny,' she managed, though her thoughts made it sound more serious than she'd intended.

'You don't?' he asked, immediately sobering.

'No, no, I do.' She forced a smile, but could tell he wasn't buying it. 'I'm sorry, I just… I just remembered I spoke with Anja this morning.'

It was the first thing she could think of to say. And when the words changed the air between them, taking away the ease of the minutes before, Jess instantly regretted it.

'What did she say?' he asked quietly.

'That we should do whatever we needed to sort things out.'

'About me, I meant.'

She'd known he had meant that, but had hoped he wouldn't ask. She cleared her throat. 'She has a few things to tie up in Sydney and then she'll be back.'

'When?'

'End of next week, she said.'

He nodded, and a long silence followed his words. She wished she hadn't said anything. Wished she hadn't let her stupid thoughts and emotions interrupt what had been an enjoyable breakfast. She couldn't figure out what to say to make him feel better. Or why she so desperately wanted to.

'You said she wanted to set up another yoga studio there?' She nodded, and more time passed before he said, 'I'll see her when she gets back then.'

'Will you?' Jess asked softly.

He gave her a small smile. 'You're asking because I've been a coward for the past week?'

'I wouldn't say coward—'

'Except I was. I didn't want to face her. Still don't, if I'm honest.' He stared off into the distance, and then his eyes moved to meet hers. 'But I'm going to. I *have* to. It's why I left the UK. Why I'm taking a break from working after doing nothing but work for the last two years.'

'You're a pretty decent guy, Dylan,' she said after a moment.

His lips curved. 'You didn't think that I was?'

'I didn't know you.'

'And you do now?'

'I…' He was right. She *didn't* know him. So how had her opinion changed now after only a few hours with him? 'Well, you helped me this morning. And made me breakfast. You really didn't have to.'

'And you no longer believe I only did it because I wanted you to tell Anja that I had?'

Her mouth opened, and then she shut it again. She'd forgotten about that. *Damn it.*

'Why do I feel like you might have changed your mind about me now?' he asked, and she looked up into his gaze.

'I haven't,' Jess said, though a voice in her head told her that it wasn't entirely true. 'I knew that, remember? And I respect that you want your relationship with your sister back.' Tired now, she slid off the chair as elegantly as she could. 'Do you mind if I rest in your guest room? It won't be for long, and then I'll start arranging where I'll stay while the whole thing next door is going on.'

'Of course you can.'

He stood with her—awkwardly, she thought, even though that word didn't really fit with a man who looked like Dylan.

'I'll see you in a bit,' she said, and then walked back to the room and felt her body sag with relief when she lay on the bed. It had been a tiring morning. Being pregnant had made it worse, but she suspected she would have felt that way even if she hadn't been pregnant.

But the fact that her thoughts and emotions were all over the place she *would* blame on her pregnancy. It was the only logical explanation for the disappointment that still lingered. It was the only way she could explain why Dylan made her feel the way he did. And why meeting him had made her think so much of her own family.

She hadn't been lying when she'd told him she respected that he wanted a relationship with Anja again. But she couldn't quite understand it. Not when she didn't have anything to compare it to. She felt absolutely no desire to repair her relationship with her parents. She didn't think they deserved her in their lives, and she sure as hell didn't think she deserved *them*. And if their actions—or lack thereof—since she'd moved out told her anything, it was that they didn't want to repair their relationship with her either.

Maybe that was why she'd felt so disappointed by what Dylan had told her. Because it had been a reminder of what Jess *didn't* have—a family who would fight for her.

She suddenly hoped Anja would give Dylan a chance. Her friend had gone deathly silent the day before when Jess had first called to tell her about Dylan's arrival. And then she'd politely thanked Jess and put down the phone. When Jess had called that morning, her reaction had been similar, though this time Anja had told her she would try to come home sooner and had asked Jess not to tell Dylan anything about the baby.

It was a fair request. In fact, Jess had fully intended not to say anything to Dylan about the baby. She would let Anja deal with that. After all, it was none of Jess's business.

Except that Jess *wanted* to tell Dylan. It felt wrong not to. Or, more accurately, Jess told herself quickly, she wanted *Anja* to tell Dylan. Sooner, rather than later. Because not all families wanted to fight to stay a family. That was special. But some things—some decisions—could break a family so completely that it couldn't be fixed, even if someone wanted to fight for it.

She didn't think Dylan leaving was that thing, that decision. Especially since she suspected that he'd left for reasons neither she nor Anja knew. Good reasons. But keeping this child a secret from him—keeping the circumstances around the child's conception a secret—might just be...

It exhausted her to think about it and she closed her eyes, pushing the thoughts and emotions away. She wouldn't let Dylan's demons keep her from sleeping.

She certainly wouldn't let her own demons do that either.

CHAPTER SIX

DYLAN LOOKED UP from the book that he was reading when Daisy lifted her head from where it rested on his leg and lumbered off the couch. His heart did something strange in his chest when he saw it was because Jess had walked into his living room, looking just as sleepy and mussed and sexy as she had when he'd opened his door to her that morning.

It didn't seem fair that she could do something strange to his heart when the way she looked was entirely by accident. When the waves of her hair just always seemed to be mussed, when the sleepiness was an unavoidable consequence of waking up.

As for the sexiness... Well, he didn't think she intended to make him think of her that way. Nor did he think she intended to make him picture how she'd look waking up in his bed. How imagining it made his body tighten with a need he didn't understand. With a need he *didn't want*.

'Sleep well?' he asked gruffly.

'Yeah, thanks. Sorry that it was so long.'

'It wasn't.'

'The insurance?'

'The plumbers have come and gone. The ceiling people called to say they'd only be able to make it out tomorrow. You left your phone on the kitchen counter,' he said at her confused look.

She nodded but didn't reply, and the only sound between them was Daisy's attempts to get Jess to rub her belly. He watched as Jess lowered to her haunches and then slowly sat down on the carpet over the wooden floor. With one hand on her own stomach, she gave Daisy what she wanted and the simple image again did strange things to Dylan's heart.

It made absolutely no sense.

How did a woman he barely knew have such a powerful effect on him? A woman who was clearly off-limits? Who was pregnant? Who was his sister's friend?

And yet Jess affected him. She *tempted* him. More than just physically, too. The picture in front of him made him *want*. And what it made him want was even more baffling because he'd never, ever thought about it before.

Family.

Seeing Jess pregnant made him think about having a family. About having his own wife, his own child on the way. It wasn't something he'd ever wanted. His family situation had taught him that some people weren't meant to have children. They weren't meant to be parents.

He wasn't his mother. He wouldn't knowingly bring a child into the world knowing the brokenness of the situation they'd be born into. And he *was* broken. Not as much as his father—his mother, maybe—but he certainly wasn't whole enough to become a father himself.

Which was why considering it made absolutely no sense.

He set his book aside, told himself it was being in the house, being with Jess that was driving him to insanity. 'I'm going for a walk,' he told her, and moved towards the front door.

'Can I come with you?' she asked from behind him and he turned, frowning.

'Why?'

'It's going to rain soon.' She pointedly looked out of the glass doors where the sky was dark, warning of what was about to come. 'I won't have a chance to do it in a while and I feel—' Her eyes went soft, almost apologetic.

'You feel what?'

'Suffocated.'

He lifted his brows. 'By me? Because then you probably shouldn't take a walk with me.'

'It's not you.'

It was the only answer she offered and he sighed. Nodded. She lifted her arms in response and, after a brief moment of hesitation, he strode forward and helped her up. He resented the heat that went through his body at her proximity and stepped away from her as soon as he knew she was steady.

And then he whistled to Daisy and the three of them made their way to one of the most important places of his childhood.

Once, there had been one large house on the property where he and Anja lived. They'd grown up there, and when they'd got older and their mother had moved to be closer to her family, Anja and Dylan had stayed.

'You're lucky,' Jess said from beside him as they walked the pathway to the large forest that stood just behind his property. 'I would have killed to have this in my backyard.'

'I *am* lucky,' he agreed. 'It's because of Anja.'

'What do you mean?'

'We lived here as kids, and she—'

'Wait, what?' He looked over to see confusion on her face. 'You lived here as kids? In…your house?'

'Our houses weren't always on adjacent properties. There used to be one large property, with one large house on it, where we grew up. But we tore the house down when my mother moved to Langebaan and built two separate houses instead.'

She nodded, but didn't respond as they made their way through the forest path he'd taken so many times as a child. The trees were tall and full, the kind that had always made him feel as if he was in a movie of some sort. Daisy immediately sprinted out of sight—as she always did—and she'd find him again as soon as he'd call to her on their way back.

'Why did you say you had this because of Anja?'

'Because she…she wanted me to have it.' His heart ached at the reminder of how generous she'd been. 'When we split the property, she was adamant that I have the pathway. That I have easy access to this place.' His feet faltered just as he passed the tree where his sister had once carved her initials. It was almost as if his feet knew he was talking about her. He forced them forward.

'It was special to you,' Jess said in that understanding way she had. 'To both of you.'

He cleared his throat. 'Yeah. We came here a lot as children. Well, until Anja stopped coming with me because I used to scare her so often.' His lips curled at the memory. 'She told me the place reminded her of a horror movie she'd watched, so how could I resist?'

Jess smiled. 'Naturally.'

'Anyway, after she stopped coming… I used to use this place to think. To…escape.'

'Escape?'

'From the responsibility of looking after my family.' His throat burned with emotion. 'Sounds terrible, doesn't it?'

'How old were you?'

'Fourteen.'

'Then no,' she said. 'It doesn't sound terrible for a fourteen-year-old not to want the responsibility of a family.' She paused. 'Your father left when you were four-teen?'

Of course she knew they'd been abandoned, he thought. She was his sister's best friend. A fact he conveniently seemed to forget.

'Yes.' He paused. 'What did she tell you about it?'

'Not much.' They stopped exactly where he'd stopped all those years ago—at the hilltop overlooking the busy hub of central Cape Town. Where he would dream about a life where his parents weren't such complete disasters. And he hadn't even known then what he knew now about his mother. 'Just that he had an...addiction and he left because of it.'

He nodded and let her words sit between them while he thought about what to say.

'It's beautiful,' Jess breathed after a moment, and he felt her pleasure soothe some of the hurt that always accom-panied thoughts of his past. He could almost forget then that she'd been a part of the reason he'd wanted to come to this place initially. To get away from...*her* and every-thing she made him feel. But now he thought it was...nice that she was there with him.

What was *happening* to him?

'It is, isn't it?' he said instead of pondering the dis-turbing thoughts that had popped into his head. But they were only replaced by more disturbing thoughts—by what they'd been talking about earlier—and he heard himself speak before his mind had fully caught up with the words he was saying.

'I always thought it was strange that Anja wanted to live here.'

'You didn't?'

'No. The house...didn't exactly have the best memo-ries for us. But the place did. *This* place did,' he added, gesturing around them. 'So we told ourselves that we'd

save that and tear down the rest. Build something new.'
He ran a hand through his hair. 'It was round about the
same time Anja met Chet, and she was convinced pretty
early on that they were going to be married. So, instead of
building another big house, we settled for two.' He paused.
'Didn't you ever wonder why they look so similar? We had
the same architect.'

'Actually, I hadn't noticed.'

He noted the tone of her voice. 'Anja didn't tell you
about any of this?'

She shook her head, the expression on her face reflect-
ing the tone. 'She's pretty tight-lipped about some things.'

'Me, you mean,' he offered when it was clear she
wouldn't say it.

'No. Well, not only you,' she said when he gave her a
doubtful look. 'She's told me the major things. But the
details…she didn't really offer them, and I never wanted
to ask.'

'Why not?'

'I…' She faltered. Frowned. 'I guess I didn't want to
push her to talk about something she didn't want to talk
about.'

'Sometimes we need to be pushed to talk about the
things we don't want to talk about.'

'So I should force you to talk about why you left?' she
shot back, eyes troubled, and then she immediately shook
her head. 'No, I'm sorry. I shouldn't have said that.'

'No, you shouldn't have,' he replied. 'Not because
you're wrong—you're not—but you sounded…defensive.'

'No.'

'No?' he repeated. 'No, you didn't sound defensive? Or
no, you're not allowing me to call you out on sounding defensive?' She didn't answer him and he sighed. 'Jess—'

'You're right,' she said with a slight laugh. 'I'm being
defensive because I'm defending my decision not to push

my friend to tell me something just in case it ends up pushing her away. From me.'

Realising the enormity of what she'd just admitted—to him, to herself—Dylan said, 'She probably didn't tell you about the house because you didn't push. Because you knew not to push.'

'I…don't understand.'

'But you do. The fact that you don't ask her about it means you understand,' he told her. 'Anja wanted a clean start. We both did. So, new houses and no talk of the past.' He gestured for Jess to sit down and, after he'd helped her, he settled down himself, their legs dangling over the hill.

'It's easier that way,' she said. 'Except, for some reason, we keep talking about our pasts with one another.'

He didn't reply. Chose not to since all he wanted to say was that it made no sense. Nothing about what was happening between them made sense. All Dylan knew was that he felt as if he'd been caught in an alternate reality where it didn't *have* to make sense. Where all the reasons why sharing with Jess—why getting to know her—was a bad idea ceased to exist.

A voice inside his head screamed that he didn't want this. And yet he found it *easy* to ignore it.

And felt himself sink deeper.

'You told Anja about your parents, didn't you?'

'Yeah, she knows.'

'Good.'

'Good?' she repeated. 'Why's that good?'

'You shouldn't keep it to yourself.'

'I haven't been,' she said wryly. 'I've shared more with you than I ever have with Anja.'

'You…have?'

She gave a soft laugh that went right through him. 'She doesn't know about the laptop thing. Or that they used to hold things like that against me. She only knows that they were…bad parents. That the money made them worse.' She paused. 'Or maybe it's just easier for me to blame the money instead of who they are.'

'There's more.'

'Isn't there always?' she asked with a small smile. 'But you get the picture.' She lifted a shoulder.

He reached out and took her hand, and only really realised he had when she flipped hers over and threaded her fingers through his. He didn't know how long they sat like that, but he *did* know that it felt *good*. That for the first time in a long time he didn't feel alone.

It had warmth spreading through his chest, even though he could acknowledge that it shouldn't have. Even though he could acknowledge that he should pull back, pull his hand from hers, before things could become more complicated. Before the alternate reality became his real one.

Instead, he said, 'I'm surprised you're being so nice to me, knowing what I've done.'

'And what's that?'

'Leaving.' He couldn't bring himself to look at her. 'Hurting Anja.'

'I'll admit, I didn't *want* to be nice to you.' Now he did look at her, and she gave him a small smile. 'I started working for Anja a couple of months after your father died. More than a month after you left.' Jess's free hand lifted, and she began to trace circles on her stomach. 'Of course, I didn't know that then. Anja was always professional with me, though I could sense that something was… off.' The circles grew larger. 'Then one day I found Anja crying and she told me about your father's death, and… how much she missed you.' Her hand stilled. Fell to her lap. 'I think that was the day our professional relationship changed into friendship. And I immediately took Anja's side in it all.'

'You should have. I've been a terrible brother.' Shame,

guilt, anger washed through him. 'You *should* treat me like I'm a bad person.'

'But you're not.'

'I am to Anja.'

'No, Dylan. You just…hurt her. But you're a decent man, just like I told you this morning.' She squeezed his hand and then gently pulled hers out of his. He instantly felt a little emptier. 'And if I base my opinion of you on how you've treated me since we've met instead of what I thought I knew about you *before* we met, it's easy to be nice to you.'

'Even though I told you the way I've treated you might be because I want to get on Anja's good side?'

She laughed. 'Trust me, if you wanted to get on Anja's good side, being nice—or whatever it is you're being to me—would *not* be the way to go.'

'Why not?' Her expression changed, closed. 'Jess—'

'Do you plan on telling Anja why you left?' she said instead of answering his question. She didn't want to talk about it, he thought. Which he should respect. Even if it *was* strange that she'd drawn the line with that.

'Of course,' he replied, though he could hear the hesitation in his own tone. She nodded but didn't respond, and he watched as her hand went to her stomach again.

He frowned and, for the first time in a while, thought about her pregnancy. About the implications of her pregnancy. About how those implications meant he shouldn't have brought her to this place—to *his* place—which would, no doubt, always remind him of her whenever he came now. About how it meant that he shouldn't be talking to her like he hadn't to anyone else before, how he shouldn't allow himself to be comforted by her—to comfort *her*—when there was another man in her life.

Even if that man did appear to be absent for the moment.

'How has it been going?' he asked to keep himself from getting lost in the hope that thought brought. It was more urgent now, more pressing, and his mind had cleared enough for him to know he couldn't allow it to be.

'How has what been going?'

'Your pregnancy?'

'Oh, fine.' She waved a hand. 'I can't complain.'

'Can't? Or won't?'

She laughed softly. 'How is it that you can see through me so easily, Dylan?' The words felt like a punch in the stomach, but she didn't give him a chance to double over. 'I can't *and* won't complain. There are so many women out there who would love to be in my position.'

'Not entirely,' he murmured, and she gave him a confused look. 'I'm sorry, you probably don't want to be reminded of it.'

'I have no idea what you're talking about.'

She was going to make him say it, he thought, and sighed. 'You're pregnant and alone, Jess. You didn't even want to call to ask the father of your child for help this morning. I don't think that's a position many women want to be in.' He waited and then added, 'You don't have to pretend like it doesn't bother you.'

She blinked. And then she threw her head back and laughed. It sounded just as much in place in the forest as the birds he usually heard chirping in the trees. He wasn't sure what confused him more: that he'd thought that, or that she was laughing at her predicament.

'I didn't realise I'd made a joke,' he said stiffly.

'Oh, no, I'm sorry. I didn't mean to—' She broke off, bit her lip. And then she sighed, and the expression on her face changed to what he thought was resignation. 'I'm not pregnant and alone, Dylan. No man has abandoned me.'

'But—'

'I made you think that?' He nodded. 'Sorry. It's only because…it's complicated,' she said slowly. Seconds ticked by, turned into minutes, but neither of them spoke. Eventually Jess looked at him and something inside him flipped at the emotion in her eyes.

'Dylan…this baby…it isn't mine. I'm just…the surrogate.'

CHAPTER SEVEN

JESS HELD HER BREATH, hoping that she hadn't made a mistake. She knew she probably shouldn't have said anything to Dylan. But whatever it was that had her opening up to him—that had her telling him about her parents, that listened to his concerns about his past—had demanded that she tell him the truth. So had the part of her that had softened at his concern that she was going through her pregnancy alone.

It would be fine, she thought now, releasing her breath as she watched him. She wasn't betraying Anja by telling Dylan that she was a surrogate. As long as he didn't know that she was *Anja's* surrogate, it would be fine.

She hoped.

'You're…a surrogate?'

'That's what I said,' she replied lightly, hoping that it would defuse some of the tension between them.

'But…how? I mean, why?' Dylan shook his head and angled his body towards her.

'Well, I have a…friend who struggled to fall pregnant.' It was the best explanation she could offer.

'So you…offered to carry her child for her?'

She tilted her head, felt her heart sink. 'I did. Is that a problem?'

'No…no, it's not.' He lifted his eyes to hers. 'I'm not judging you, Jess.'

'Really? Because it really feels like you are.' And it was such a surprise that her throat felt clogged.

'It's just…a lot to take in.' Emotion crossed his face. 'I've never met…someone like you,' he said, looking away. 'I guess I'm struggling to understand why you'd do this to yourself.'

'Do what to myself?' Jess asked, cautioning herself to pull back when she wanted to snap the words at him. 'I get that you're trying to process this information, which is fine, I suppose, but you don't *have* to understand my choices.' She wanted to get up, storm off, but she knew she wouldn't be able to with her stomach in the way. She glanced down at the distance to the ground from where she was, and clenched her jaw. She couldn't risk it. 'Would you help me up? It looks like it's about to start raining and we should probably get back.'

He nodded and helped her up without a word. She felt even more annoyed when her skin prickled at his touch. When her body became so much more aware at his proximity.

But it gave her steam to storm off, and she walked ahead of him through the trees, leaving the buildings of Cape Town behind them.

It really was a beautiful place, she thought. And now that she knew how personal it was to him, she wondered why he'd let her tag along. Why had he told her things even Anja hadn't told her?

Why had *she* shared things with him? About her parents? She'd told him more about them than she'd ever told Anja. And why did she feel so disappointed by his reaction to finding out the baby she carried wasn't hers?

All of it worried her. And, just like she'd first thought when she'd met Dylan, it convinced her that she couldn't become involved with him. Or come between him and Anja. Anja was as close to family as she had, and she couldn't do anything to damage that. And she should probably stay away from Dylan if she kept that goal in mind.

Besides, she didn't *want* to become involved with Dylan…did she?

Just as she thought it there was a sudden clap of thunder, followed by the sound of rain. Not the steady, calming rainfall that often started rainy days, but a hard, angry downpour that had them both coming to a stop.

'I'm sorry,' Dylan said after a few moments. 'We should have left earlier.'

'Don't apologise,' she breathed, eyes on the rain. They were under the shield of the trees, which seemed to have formed some kind of canopy protecting them from the majority of the water. From where they stood, they could see the rain pouring down in front of them. 'It's all a part of the view.'

'I didn't quite anticipate this one,' he said with a soft laugh. 'Though it *is* something.' Neither of them spoke as the drops around them grew heavier.

'There's a part of me that wants to stay here until the storm is over.'

'Because you don't want to get wet?' Dylan asked, turning towards her.

'Because it's so beautiful. Angry, but beautiful.'

'Yeah, I know that feeling.'

Her eyes met his and she felt a shift in the air between them.

'What makes you think I'm angry?'

'Because of the way I responded to your…news back there.' His face tightened, but he didn't look away.

'It doesn't matter.'

'I think it does.'

His words stirred something in her chest, and she shook

her head. 'It shouldn't. Our lives, our decisions, don't affect one another.' Though those lives, those decisions *did* seem to be intersecting, she thought. 'The smartest thing we can do is to remember that.'

Silence followed her words, and she felt the change in him before she saw it on his face.

'Are you always…smart, Jess?' he asked slowly, taking a step forward. Breaching the gap between them.

In her mind she stepped back, maintaining the distance that would ensure she wouldn't do something that would prove the exact opposite of her words.

In reality, her feet stayed exactly where they were.

'I like to think so,' she replied, her voice husky.

She wondered why, and then got the answer when she suddenly found herself pressed against Dylan's body. She swallowed, and a voice in her head desperately warned her that she couldn't make this mistake.

It warned her to move, to run, and get a room in a hotel as far away as possible from the man who held her in place with only his eyes.

But then the voice was muted by another, louder one in her mind. One that shouted only one thing.

Stay.

'I don't think I'm being very smart now.'

'With me?' Dylan asked, his eyes heating, his arms going around her. 'Should I be offended?'

'Not unless you think I'm wrong?' When he didn't reply, she nodded. 'I didn't think so.'

She kept her eyes on his as she brought her mouth closer, closer still, until finally their lips touched.

Jess felt thunder boom inside her at the contact. Felt it break something, and then, like the rain, that something poured through her body into her blood, rushing through her as she sank into the pleasure of kissing Dylan.

Because the man could *kiss*. There was no hesitation

in the way his lips moved, no uncertainty in the way his tongue stole her breath. Her body trembled as her blood carried a headiness through her that she'd never felt before. As if its purpose had become more than to simply carry oxygen through her body. No, now it felt as if it carried thrills, sensations, *awareness* through her veins, and her hands tightened at Dylan's waist in response, as if they wanted to grip the feeling.

As if they wanted to capture it and never let go.

Dylan groaned as his hands moved over her body. Over the curves of her hips, her rounded belly, her breasts. They ached from his touch when his hands lingered, and then heated when he kneaded, softly, gently, adding more pressure each time so that the ache turned into longing, into desire, into *fire*.

He pressed her back until her feet hit a tree, the force of it sending a puddle of water right on their heads. But neither of them stopped. No, the coolness helped keep the fire at bay. Helped them start the kindling all over again.

Jess ran her hands over his back, over the muscles she'd admired ever since she'd first seen them in his backyard. Over the ridges she'd fantasised about. His shirt was plastered against his body from the water, and she moaned softly at how it saved her the trouble of going under his shirt to feel what she wanted.

Her fingers swept across the hardened planes, her hands moving from his back to his biceps, and then between them to his pecs.

It was so defined, so damn sexy that suddenly it felt as if she'd lost her breath, and she had to pull away so that she could breathe. His chest heaved as much as hers did as he rested his forehead against hers, and when their eyes met his lips curved into a smile that was the perfect illustration of what they'd just done.

Reckless. Spontaneous. Dangerous.

'It's raining,' she said huskily.

'Yeah, I know,' he replied with a soft chuckle. 'We both knew that before…*this* happened.'

'No, Dylan, I mean it's raining here, on us.' Just as she said it, drops splattered hard on both their faces. 'I don't think we can stay here any more.'

'No, we probably shouldn't.'

He took her hand and then whistled for Daisy. Seconds later, the dog came sprinting through the trees, wet and blissfully unaware of what her owner had just got up to. Together they ran for his house—although Jess couldn't quite call what she was doing running. But Dylan didn't seem to mind, and soon they were in the house, completely drenched.

'We should probably get out of these clothes,' she said, and felt her face burn as soon as she said it. 'I don't mean—'

'I know,' he said with a slight smile. Silence beat between them, and then he shook his head. 'But you're right. Besides, I should sort this little bugger out.'

He looked down at Daisy affectionately, and Jess felt something tumble in her chest. Not surprising, she thought, considering that everything inside her felt as if it had come apart.

'Dylan—'

'No, Jess,' he interrupted. 'We don't have to…talk about it.'

'I'd love to *not* talk about it,' she said with a bark of laughter. 'But how can we not? This—what just happened? It's not a good idea.'

'You think I don't know that?' Dylan answered, his expression serious.

'No, I'm sure you do,' she replied quietly, and felt fatigue seep back into her bones. 'So maybe you're right, and it's better that we don't talk about it.' Why did that make her so sad? 'I'm going to have a shower and then I'll call a hotel or something for the next few nights.'

'You can stay here.'

'No, I don't—'

'It won't happen again, Jess,' Dylan promised. 'And you being here is better. You'll be near if they need you next door. And you'll be able to call Anja if she needs to approve anything.'

They were good points, she knew, but still, agreeing felt like it would be the wrong decision. She didn't know how much of that was because her insides were still a mess from their kiss.

So she said, 'I'll think about it,' and walked to the room he'd shown her to that morning. She stripped off the wet clothing and showered quickly, and then dried the water from her hair before plaiting it and pinning the plaits around her head in a crown.

She pulled on thick woollen tights that she'd had the foresight to pack, and an oversized jersey that was just as thick, just as woollen. It made her look like an unshapen mess, but somehow that made her feel better. There was no way she would be tempted into seducing Dylan wearing that. No way he'd be tempted into seducing her either.

And because trying to find other accommodation seemed to require more energy than she had—along with going back out into the rain, getting the keys to her car, driving in the horrendous weather—her choice seemed to be made. She would stay there that night.

She should go out and tell him, she thought, but instead she climbed under the bedcovers, telling herself she would only rest for a moment. That she only needed comfort for a moment.

She'd made a mistake. Kissing Dylan had been a mistake. Because now that she knew what it felt like, she wanted more of it. And that wasn't an option.

She couldn't risk her friendship with Anja for more. It didn't matter that Dylan had been kind to her. That he'd listened to her. That it felt as if he understood her.

The attraction between them couldn't matter, nor the emotional connection. More than just being for Anja's sake, it was for *hers*, too. She didn't think that when Dylan found out whose baby she was carrying he'd understand why she'd kept it from him. Jess already knew that he'd be hurt because Anja hadn't told him about it, and she suspected *she* would be the target of the anger that hurt would turn into since he seemed so desperate to keep things civil with Anja.

It was easier to put some distance between them now, Jess told herself. Prevention was better than cure, and she needed to prevent the inevitable hurt that would come from entertaining anything other than a cordial relationship with Dylan.

Decided, she pulled the blankets closer around her and closed her eyes.

He was restless. Primed for a fight. Had been from the moment Jess had reminded him that their kiss was a bad idea.

The fact that she was right didn't have anything to do with it. No, he was upset because somehow she'd kept her mind when their kiss had made him lose his. When the kiss that *she'd* initiated had crossed the clear—albeit unspoken—boundaries between them, but *she'd* been the one to remind them of those boundaries after it had happened.

And yes, fine, maybe he'd wanted it to happen. Maybe he'd closed the distance between them in the forest because he'd wanted one of them to initiate a kiss. But he was only human. How was he supposed to resist the beauty, the vulnerability of her, wrapped up in that little bubble of anger?

When that bubble had screamed of the passion he'd got to experience only minutes after he'd thought about it?

It all made him feel so edgy that he knew nothing good would come from facing Jess in that state. So, after he took care of Daisy, he peeled off his wet clothes and replaced them with gym clothes, and made his way to his home gym to expel some of the energy.

If it hadn't been raining, he'd go back to his task of chopping wood. It was laborious work, something that kept his mind and body busy. Something that distracted him from the fact that he should have gone to speak with his sister.

Unfortunately, now he could only seem to keep his body busy. No matter how hard he pushed himself during his cardio, his strength training, his thoughts kept looping back over the last few hours. Over his words, hers. Over her reactions, his.

He finished his workout, showered and went back downstairs. All the while, he was trying to figure out what he should say to her. The only thing that he came up with was an apology, but what would he be apologising for? For kissing her back? For enjoying it? For facing the fact that they'd made their lives infinitely more complicated by acknowledging their attraction to one another?

None of it made sense, but he knew he couldn't avoid her for ever, so he told himself to man up and went to find her. He wandered around the house, but she wasn't in the living room or the kitchen, and for one sick moment he worried that she'd left without telling him that she was going. As a last resort, he checked the guestroom and relief flooded through him when he saw the shape of her under the covers.

His eyes swept over her. Her face was flushed from the heat of sleep, her hair in some kind of plait pinned at the top of her head. A woollen-covered arm rested on her belly on top of the covers, rounding off a picture Dylan knew he wouldn't be able to push out of his head with ease.

He shut the door just as quickly as he'd opened it, careful not to make a sound and wake her, and put as much distance between him and the room as he could. Daisy looked up at him from her station in the corner of the kitchen when he walked in and whined when he leaned over the counter, his heart beating so fast he couldn't catch his breath.

What *was* that? he asked himself eventually. What was that burst of emotion in his chest at seeing her? What was the fierce protectiveness that had surged inside him?

Whatever it was, it wasn't welcome. And yet it wasn't unfamiliar. It took him some minutes, but the image of Jess sleeping had him realising why he'd reacted so uncharacteristically to her surrogacy news.

He felt *protective* of her. And he was worried that this pregnancy would somehow hurt her. That he wouldn't be able to keep her from getting hurt.

In some part of his brain he knew that it wasn't his job to protect her. Knew that his need to do so could only mean trouble. But he couldn't figure out why he still wanted to, despite knowing better.

He sucked in a breath. It was going to be a long night.

CHAPTER EIGHT

JESS FOUND DYLAN in front of the fire in his living room.

Rain thrashed against the glass doors, lightning flashed every few moments. Daisy was curled up next to Dylan on the couch, whining ever so softly every time thunder sounded. Jess didn't blame her. It seemed that they were experiencing one of the famous Cape Town storms, and if Jess had been Daisy she'd be curled up next to Dylan, too.

Except she wasn't Daisy, and she'd given herself a stern warning against thoughts like that. Reinforcing her resolve, she walked towards them slowly. Daisy popped her head up when she saw Jess, but Dylan kept staring into the fire. As though there was something he could see there that no one else could. As though it held all the answers to life's mysteries.

'Hey,' she said softly after a few more seconds. Daisy immediately jumped off the couch and rubbed herself against Jess and, obliging the dog, Jess gave her the attention she wanted. But her eyes were still on Dylan. Stayed on him, too, when his gaze met hers and she saw the pain there.

There was a long, long pause before it cleared and then he said, 'Hey.'

'Are you okay?'

'Fine,' he replied. 'You fell asleep.'

'Yeah, I did. Sorry. It's been more of an exciting day than I'm used to. Knocked me out.'

'That's fine.' He paused. 'Did you figure out what you're going to do?'

'I was hoping that your offer was still on the table.'

'Of course,' he told her, though his tone made her uncertain.

'Thanks.' She waited for him to say something more and, when he didn't, she added, 'I can be out tomorrow.'

'Why?'

'You just don't seem like you want me here.'

'No, it's not that.' He leaned forward now and drained the glass she hadn't noticed on the table in front of him. 'It's just been…an exciting day,' he repeated her words.

'That's true.' She fell silent and, rather than contemplate his strange mood, decided to channel her energy into something useful. 'Would you like me to make us something to eat?'

His brows rose. 'I thought you said you couldn't cook?'

'I said I only started to learn a few years ago. That's a lot of meals, Dylan, so I think I can make us a…pot of curry,' she said, improvising.

'You're going to make us…curry?'

'Why not?' She'd made it a couple of times before. She was pretty sure she could do it again. 'It's the perfect meal for this kind of weather.'

'Oh, I'm not arguing about that. I'm just wondering whether— No, you know what? I would love some curry.' He patted Daisy, who'd curled up next to him again when it became clear she wasn't going to get any more attention from Jess, and stood. 'Come on, I'll show you where everything is.'

Jess would have found it hard to describe the next hour. But she *was* sure that no one would mistake it for any kind of cooking show. *Especially* not with Dylan watching her every move with amusement from where he sat at the counter.

'You don't have to watch me, you know,' she said irritably when she couldn't figure out how many cardamom pods to use.

'You might need my help figuring out where everything is,' came his reply. She rolled her eyes and counted out five and then threw them into the pot, where her efforts were looking more like a stew than a curry.

She hoped by the time the chicken started cooking that it would be in better shape, but she was sadly disappointed. She sighed noisily, causing Daisy to look up in concern from her corner, and Dylan to leave his post at the counter to peer into the pot.

'This is your…curry?'

'It tastes better than it looks,' she said defensively, spooning up some of the sauce and offering it to him. His expression was neutral as he tasted it, and then his eyes met hers and suddenly she wasn't thinking about the sauce any more.

She'd seen scenes like this in movies before. Had wondered how feeding someone could ever really be erotic. But clearly it could be, she realised, her eyes still caught in his. Because now she wasn't thinking about Dylan tasting the sauce, but her lips.

Her skin.

Would his expression still be so neutral then? Or would he offer her something to taste in return? Like *his* lips? Like *his* skin? It would be so much better than the food she'd made that evening, and she knew that the slight kick in the sauce would have nothing on what would happen between them…

She swallowed, and her hand faltered. She cleared her throat. 'Well?'

A beat of silence passed before he answered. 'It's not bad.'

'Not…bad?'

'But it isn't curry either.'

She looked down at the pot, and then up at him again. 'Then what is it?'

'I'd say tomato stew.'

'But…but there's curry spice in it. It has a kick.'

'Well, the kick doesn't make it curry.' He narrowed his eyes. 'How many times have you made this?'

Heat immediately seared her cheeks. 'A couple.'

'Okay.' But she could see that he didn't believe her. 'Let's turn this into curry then, shall we?'

The next half an hour was distinctly different from her solo foray into curry-making. Mostly because of the way Dylan took her through the steps. It could have been a cooking show now, she thought. Or, more accurately, a one-on-one appointment with a cooking instructor.

Dylan was patient, and explained the steps to her before encouraging her to do it herself. She forced herself to ignore the thrill that went through her every time he touched her or drew closer to show her an ingredient or check how she was coming along.

But still, the time they spent fixing supper was lovely, and settled some of the tension that had still been lingering between them since that afternoon.

'I have to say this is pretty good.'

They were sitting in the dining room adjacent to the sunroom she'd admired the day before. This room was also enclosed by glass doors, the solid wooden table clear of decoration, with only a beautiful chandelier adorning the space. Simple and tasteful, she thought, and wondered if it was the room that had her thinking that, or whether her perception of the décor had been changed by the man sitting opposite her.

'Yeah, I think we're a pretty decent team,' Dylan replied with a smile. But almost as soon as he said it his smile fell away, and Jess heard herself speaking before the tension could return.

'You're an amazing cook. And unexpectedly patient.'

He laughed, and relief went through her. 'Yeah, well, I learnt patience when I taught Anja.'

She stared at him. 'Anja's a *terrible* cook.'

'Hence the need for patience,' he said with another laugh. 'It didn't take us long to realise cooking wasn't for her, and so she was relegated to sous chef for as long as we lived together.'

The silence that followed told her he was lost in the past. And, for the life of her, Jess couldn't figure out why she wanted to help him find his way back to the present. Or at least find a way to be in the past with him.

'It sounds like you two were quite a team.'

He looked up. Smiled. 'We were. I always told her we were a well-oiled machine.' His hands stilled and Jess kept herself from asking him if he was okay again. 'Did she tell you about that?' he asked suddenly, but continued before she had the chance to reply. 'No, she wouldn't have. You told me she didn't tell you the details.'

'Do you...' she started. Faltered. Cleared her throat. Tried again. 'Do *you* want to tell me?'

His eyes met hers. 'I probably shouldn't.'

'Of course,' she said immediately, insecurity dictating the thudding of her heart.

'But I'd like to,' he continued gruffly, and she nodded, too afraid she wouldn't have a voice if she tried to speak. She waited for him to find his words, eating in silence while he did. And when he started to speak she continued, knowing it would be difficult for him to share if she was watching him.

'Anja must have told you that my father was an...absent father, long before he actually left. He went to work every morning, came back home, showered, ate, and then left for the casino. Every day, like clockwork.'

Jess's eyes strayed to Dylan's face, her hands stilling, and she realised he was too engrossed in his story—in the emotion of it—to notice that she was watching him.

'But my mother was fine with that. She...she was able to handle that because she got to see him each day. Because some days he would return at night and sleep at home. She got to see him, and I think that was the most important for her.' He lifted his fork, ate, but Jess could see the actions were mechanical. 'And then he stopped coming home at all. I was fourteen, like I said. Anja was twelve. Both of us suspected he was gone when the routine stopped. When my mother checked out, we knew it was permanent.'

'That's...terrible, Dylan. I'm sorry.'

'I thought we already agreed we didn't have to apologise to each other for our crappy families?' he said with a wry smile. It quickly sobered. 'I remember thinking how strange it was. That even though my father barely spent time at home, not having him there at all changed... everything. We didn't used to have to worry about the house, about food, about my mother. And then—' he set his fork down, wiped his mouth with a napkin '—we had to worry about everything.' He threw the napkin aside. 'The house staff stopped coming. We had to take care of the things they used to do ourselves.' Jess saw him clench his jaw. 'And we had to take care of my mother.'

Her arms ached to comfort him, but Jess refused the urge. 'I don't understand. There was enough money. Why—?'

'Because my father had been handling all that money. He'd been running the house, paying the staff, making sure everything ran smoothly until the moment he stopped coming home. Then, everything stopped.' Dylan paused.

'Immediately after he left, I used to think the fact that he looked after us for those first fourteen years—that he hadn't used all his money on gambling—meant that he must have loved us. But then I'd remember that he *left* us, knowing that my mother didn't have access to his money, and all of the wishful thinking would disappear.' His words were so bitter, the ache in Jess's arms grew.

'Why did he leave?' Jess asked quietly, voicing the question she'd wanted to ask Anja for two years.

'I think gambling became more important to him.'

'I don't—'

'Or,' he interrupted, 'he lost control. It had been a tenuous control, anyway. Addicts…they can't indulge their addictions. If they don't get help…' He trailed off. Sighed. 'So really it wasn't about us.'

Seconds passed in silence, and again Jess resisted the urge—though it had become more pressing now—to comfort him. She told herself it was only because she understood what it was like to be abandoned. And she knew what it was like for that abandonment to be about the person who was doing the abandoning, and no one else.

Except you still think that your parents' attitude towards you has something to do with you.

Jess forced herself to speak. To distract herself from the annoying voice in her head. 'How could he keep gambling? Didn't the money ever run out?'

'The success of the family business prevented that from happening. My grandfather had made sure that my father would get a percentage of the profits every year, paid out monthly, until he died. He always had money.'

'And what about you? And Anja? And your mother?'

'My father didn't *quite* look out as well for us as his father had for him,' Dylan said with a thin smile. 'We were okay for a while after he left. My father kept cash in a safe for emergencies—that's what he told us, though now I realise it was probably for him, just in case he needed some quick cash to fund his habit—and we used that to keep us going for a while.' He picked up his fork again. 'Anja and I figured it out.'

'What happened when the money ran out?'

'I—' he cleared his throat '—I went to my father's work. I hoped I would find him there, ask him to come back.'

'But he wasn't.'

'No. Turned out his job there wasn't really that important. He was more of a…figurehead for the empire that held his name. My name,' he added. 'When I asked for him, they told me that he hadn't been there in months.'

'What did you do?'

'I asked to speak with someone who could help me.' He gave her a small smile. 'I was brazen for fourteen, but fear had forced it.' The smile faded. 'I was terrified I wouldn't be able to look after my family.'

'Oh, Dylan.' Jess reached over, laid her hand on his arm, before pulling back again.

'It worked out.' The smile was back, hiding some of the vulnerability she saw on his face. 'They sent me to the CEO. Ridge had worked closely with my grandfather, considered him a friend. He knew about my father's problems, but had no idea about what was happening with us. He made sure that we were taken care of until Anja and I got access to the trusts neither of us knew we had. My grandfather had set that up, too, though he died before we were old enough to know him.'

'How long until you got your trust?'

'Seven years.'

'So for seven years you were at this man's mercy?'

'It wasn't like that. Ridge was good to us. He taught me everything I know. Because of him, I could actually run the company my grandfather started when Ridge stepped down.'

'You've done a great job of it.'

'At what cost?'

'What do you mean?'

He shook his head, and Jess opened her mouth to press. But she stopped herself. Thought that maybe he felt as if he'd told her too much. So she didn't push. Instead, she thought about the man who had taught Dylan about his family's company.

When her stomach churned, and her memory stirred, she tried to push the thoughts away. But it was too late. Her mind kept replaying the thought. *A stranger taught Dylan about his company. Your own father wouldn't teach you about his.*

'It's been fine while you've been gone, you know,' she said suddenly. Desperately. 'They've both been fine. Anja and your mom.'

'I know. I've spoken to them. My mom—' His face tightened, his jaw clenched. 'I had her in London with me for Christmas last year.' When he lifted his eyes to hers, a pain she didn't understand shone in them. 'Anja wouldn't come.'

Why didn't she believe that that was the reason for the pain?

'She had her reasons,' Jess said instead of asking him about it. She thought about Anja's reasons for not spending Christmas with Dylan and their mother, and it took a surprising amount of strength for her not to tell him what those reasons were.

They'd done their second embryo transfer in December, and Anja had wanted to be around when they did the tests to find out whether Jess was pregnant.

It had been a stressful experience since the first transfer hadn't taken. Anja had told Jess she hadn't wanted to see her brother on top of it. Then, Jess had believed it was because Anja hadn't wanted to add to her own stress by seeing the brother who'd hurt her so badly. But now Jess wondered if it wasn't because Dylan knew Anja well enough to know that there was something on her mind, and Anja would have been forced to tell him about the baby before she was ready.

Perhaps, if things had been different, Anja *would* have joined her mom and brother for a happy Christmas, and the inevitable drama of Anja's return wouldn't be hanging around their necks like an invisible noose.

But things *weren't* different, and Jess only hoped that the fact that the second transfer had taken—that there was a baby on the way—would make Anja more open to her brother's return.

And why is that so important to you? an inner voice chided her.

'Do you have siblings, Jess?' Dylan asked, interrupting her thoughts.

'No, I don't.' She forced a smile. 'I'm an only child.'

'So you don't really know how long they can hold a grudge.'

'Maybe not,' she allowed. 'But I've had one against my parents for a really long time. Does that count?'

CHAPTER NINE

'Why?'

'I've already told you they're terrible people.' She laughed, but it sounded strangled. He watched her hand go to her stomach, fingers spread over the roundness of it as though she was protecting the child she carried from her words. His heart ached. 'There's really not much more to it.'

'You keep saying that, but we both know it's a lie.' He kept his gaze on her face. 'You said you haven't seen them since you moved out.' She nodded. 'What happened?'

'What do you mean?'

'What happened to make you move out?' he clarified. 'You knew they were terrible people long before you moved out, didn't you?' Her eyes dropped from his, but she nodded again. 'So what happened to make you leave?'

He was suddenly desperate to know. Perhaps because he'd done the same thing two years ago—walked away from his family. But he'd had his reasons. His father's death had caused memories he'd ignored for years to resurface. Emotions he didn't want, didn't understand, had surged inside him.

And then he'd found out his mother had known his father had been an addict before she'd had children. She hadn't even tried to deny it when he'd confronted her. All of it had been too much for him to handle—or to keep from Anja—and so he'd left.

When guilt had nudged him, he'd tried again with his mother. He'd invited her to London, had thought they could work through it. But then, neither of them brought it up. Each day he'd told himself to, but he just…hadn't been able to. Much like he hadn't been able to walk over to Anja's house after he'd first arrived in Cape Town…

There were reasons he'd left, he thought again. So there must have been a reason Jess had left, too. He told himself he only wanted to know because he'd spilled his guts to her. But at the back of his mind he knew that wasn't true.

'What happened that made you leave, Jess?' he asked again, softly this time.

Her face went tight. 'There were…a lot of things. A lifetime of things.'

'Did they…hurt you?'

'It takes effort to hurt someone. I was nowhere near that important to them.'

His eyes took in her expression, her voice, the way her shoulders had suddenly hunched. He put his hand over hers. 'Why would they have you if they didn't think you were important?'

'Because my mother fell pregnant unexpectedly.' She paused. 'I was an…inconvenience. They didn't want me, but they didn't *not* want me either. At least not enough to do something about it.'

He stopped himself from apologising. Told himself to just listen.

'I wasn't a part of their plan. They told me that, over and over again, whenever I did something they didn't approve of. Even when I did,' she added softly. 'Remember I told you about my job as a lifeguard?' He nodded. 'I applied for it at sixteen so that I could buy my new laptop. And they *hated* it. It was at my father's country club, and they told me it made them look poor. And that looking poor wasn't a part of *their plan*. That dropping me off every day reminded them of how much it wasn't a part of *their plan*.' She stopped. 'What they actually meant was that *I* wasn't a part of their plan.'

Dylan wasn't sure what was worse. His situation, where his mother had willingly had them, knowing what they'd be born into, or Jess's, where she was made to feel unwanted for most of her life.

'You know what's funny?' she interrupted his thoughts. 'I think my father actually liked the idea of an heir.' She tilted her head. 'Until I actually appeared and I was nothing like either of them. I actually *cared* about people. Heaven only knows where that came from.'

'I guess you taught yourself more than just how to cook,' he offered quietly.

'Yeah, maybe.' She smiled, and scooped the last piece of her chicken into her mouth. 'That was wonderful, thanks.'

'Dessert?' he offered spontaneously, even though he'd stopped midway through his own dinner because of their conversation. Her gaze lowered to his plate and she gave him a pointed look before shaking her head.

'I've distracted you.'

'I think we distracted each other.' He smiled at her. Made a show of eating his food. She smiled back. And his heart flipped in his chest.

Stop, an inner voice warned, even as another part of him—a stronger part—told him that he'd opened up to her for a reason. Perhaps because there was…*more* there, between them. Perhaps because he *wanted* more.

He swallowed, and began to listen to that inner voice.

'There's not much more to tell you, you know,' she said, studying him. He wondered what she saw. 'When I left university I realised it wasn't my responsibility to point due north for them any more. They were adults. So was

I. And, like mature adults who didn't agree, we went our separate ways and now live separate lives.'

'They haven't tried to get in touch with you since?'

'No.' Sadness tinged her face before it was gone. 'But then, I haven't tried to contact them either. You should really finish your food,' she said, changing the subject 'It's delicious, prepared in the kitchen of one of the most revered chefs in Cape Town.'

She winked but stood, and started clearing her own dishes. Dylan might have thought it rude if it had been any other person at any other time. But he thought he understood why Jess she was doing it. She wanted to get away from him, from his questions. And, since he felt a bit raw himself, he understood.

So he finished his meal silently, and then cleared up his own dishes before joining her in the kitchen to help tidy their supper mess. The way he and Jess worked in tandem reminded him of how he and Anja had once worked. How it had been them against the world. Against their parents.

He thought about how he'd left Anja. Asked himself if that made him any better than his father. His stomach rolled with the fear of it, before it lurched with the knowledge that he *wasn't* like his father. His father hadn't needed them, but Dylan *needed* Anja. He'd discovered that when he'd been away. When he'd been plagued with how much he missed her. With how much he wanted them to be a family again, even just the two of them.

So he'd come back to try to make that happen…

But what if she didn't forgive him? What if he'd hurt her so much that, just like they'd done to their father, Anja turned her back to *him*?

The thought absolutely terrified him. Enough that he realised he couldn't afford to complicate the situation with his feelings for Jess, whatever they were. He couldn't afford to need Jess. To want her.

And so he wouldn't.

'Jess?'

'Yeah?' She was drying her hands and looked at him, and the homeliness of it sent a shot of something deep and unfamiliar through his body.

And strengthened his resolve.

'It won't happen again.'

'What won't?'

'You know, earlier…' It was strange, the heat rising up his neck. He'd faced much worse in his professional life—with his family—and yet here he was, embarrassed by a kiss.

'Oh. Oh,' she said again, her eyes wide. 'Okay.' She nodded. 'There's no hard feelings.' There was a beat of silence before she said, 'No, I didn't mean—'

'I know.' He cut her off with a slight laugh. 'Though it's a hell of a pun.'

'It was, wasn't it?' she said, chagrined. An unspoken attraction slithered over them as their eyes met again, and then she shook her head and stepped back, as if somehow it would kill it. 'Thank you for letting me stay here. I'll be out as soon as everything is fixed next door.'

'You can stay as long as you like.'

He didn't bother clarifying the implication, and she nodded and ducked her head.

But not before he saw a pretty red colour stain her cheeks.

She murmured goodnight, and left the room. Long after she had, Dylan stood in the kitchen, Daisy by his side, staring after Jess.

The next day passed in a blur of busyness.

The ceiling company had told them they would have to plaster certain sections and then repaint the entire ceiling. The good news was that they'd be able to do it all on the same day, so most of Jess's time was spent walking back and forth between Anja's and Dylan's houses, making sure the guys had everything they needed and checking on their progress.

She arranged for cleaners to come in the next day to make sure the house was one hundred per cent before she moved back in, and told herself it wasn't an excuse to spend more time with Dylan. She was *happy* about the busyness. It meant she didn't have to think about the attraction that had sunk its fangs into her the day before and wouldn't let go, no matter how much she wanted them to.

It also meant she didn't have to think about why she'd opened up to Dylan about her family. Sure, she hadn't told him everything, but she'd told him enough to make her uncomfortable. Or did she feel uncomfortable because he seemed to understand what she was telling him? That what he'd shared with her told her that he understood more than she even gave him credit for?

Unable to find answers for those questions, Jess stayed out of Dylan's way as much as she could. She answered queries about when Anja's next class would be, posted another reminder of Anja's absence on the yoga studio's social media. After a brief hesitation, she sent Anja an update on the house, and then thought it might be nice to send a picture of her baby bump as well.

It had only been two weeks since Anja had left, but Jess's belly had grown during that time and perhaps the reminder of her child would help Anja deal with her feelings about *other* members of her family.

She was trying to take the picture herself when Dylan walked in.

'I'm clearly interrupting something?'

'I'm just trying to—' She stopped the automatic answer before she told him the truth, and then gave him a smile. 'I want to take a picture of the bump for the mother and father.'

His eyebrows rose but he only said, 'Can I help you?'

'Yeah, please.'

She handed him the phone and a few seconds later she had it back with the pictures. She sent them to her laptop before shutting it. Things had suddenly become awkward and she didn't want to send the email with Dylan hovering around. It had guilt nudging her, and she realised how little she liked keeping this secret from him. But she couldn't tell him. She *wouldn't*. She had to think about Anja, and not whatever it was that had her thinking about Dylan.

'Why are you taking pictures of your stomach?' Dylan asked into the silence. 'Don't you see the parents? Your friends?'

Careful, she warned herself. 'Yes, but they're away at the moment, so I thought it might be nice to take a picture to send them.'

'How long have they been away?'

'Not too long. And they'll be back soon, too,' she added, anticipating his next question. 'They're good people, Dylan. This isn't the kind of situation that belongs in a documentary.'

She'd meant for it to be a joke, but he didn't laugh. After a while he said, 'I'm not judging your choice, Jess. Honestly, I'm not. I just can't help but wonder what happens to you after you give birth to this child.'

'I move on with my life,' she replied simply, though the question sent discomfort through her. 'It's a part of the agreement, when you do something like this.'

Though it wouldn't be for her, she thought. Not entirely. Because she'd still see the child every day when she went to work. She'd help Anja with the baby while Anja was on maternity leave, and then go back to her normal administrative duties.

That was her plan, at least. She'd taken Anja's PA job because it had seemed like the perfect opportunity to get away from her family, from their legacy. To create *her own* legacy. And while she enjoyed the organisational challenge of being a PA, it wasn't the only thing she was capable of.

She had a degree in finance. A choice that had been made when she'd still had hope her father would hire her after she'd graduated. She would be able to take over the family business one day, and finally be a part of the Steyn family. A real part. A *wanted* part. Except her father had no intention of including her, and that had been the straw that had broken the camel's back.

She told herself to snap out of thoughts of the past, but the present wasn't any better. Dylan's question had reminded her of a thought she'd shoved down a long time ago. That maybe it would be better if she didn't have to see the child she'd carried day after day. She didn't regret her decision, or think that she'd long for the child to be her own. She knew what she'd signed up for.

But she *was* worried about the things she couldn't anticipate. Like the emotion of childbirth. And the hormones that would overcome her once she saw the child who had grown inside her for nine months.

So perhaps making use of that finance degree would be a good move after she gave birth. She'd be able to give herself time to deal with the unanticipated without the emotional stress of seeing the baby every day.

But she wouldn't tell Dylan that. And she couldn't tell Anja that. But she *would* think about it.

'I appreciate your concern, Dylan. I really do.' And she meant it, she thought. 'But I know what I signed up for, and I know what it might mean for me.' She shrugged. 'I'll figure it out.'

He nodded, but his expression told her that he wanted to argue. She wouldn't let him.

'I'm going to take another look at what's happening next door.'

'No, I'll go. You were working before I got here.'

He was gone before she could protest.

CHAPTER TEN

Dylan stayed out of Jess's way for the rest of the day.

Her answers had irked him almost as much as the pull he felt towards her and was desperately trying to ignore. By the time it hit six o'clock, he was fed up with it, and decided they needed to get out of the house. Fortunately, the rain had subsided early that morning, so he made a few calls and went to find Jess.

'Hey,' he said when he found her in the sunroom. 'Not much sun to see any more.'

'You're about fifteen minutes too late. The sun's just set, and you have the perfect view of it from here.'

'I'll have to make time to see it then.'

'You never have?'

He smiled at the surprise in her voice. 'Not recently. But then, I haven't been home long. There'll be plenty of opportunities.'

'I suppose.' She paused. 'Have you come to find me because of my amazing culinary skills?'

'No,' he said, his lips slanting into a smile. 'I think we can both use a break from that tonight.'

'From my cooking? I'll try not to take offence to that.'

'From any cooking, actually,' he said, the smile turning into a grin. It was easier than he thought it would be, covering up the way his heart thudded in his chest. 'I thought we could go out.'

'Go out?' she repeated, straightening.

'Just for supper,' he added quickly. Less easy now, covering up the nerves. 'It wouldn't be a date or anything.'

'Of course not,' she said so stoically he swore she was teasing him. 'Because we're just—' She broke off with a frown. 'I was going to say friends, but I'm not sure that's what we are.'

'It's what we can be. What I'd like to be.'

But that was a lie, he thought, almost as soon as he'd said it. He didn't want to be *just* friends with her.

The realisation dislodged something in his chest he'd been ignoring since he'd met her. Since the night before, when he'd told himself he *had* to ignore it.

'Then we should seal our new friendship with a dinner out, I guess.' She smiled at him, but there was something behind the smile that told him she knew it wouldn't be that simple. 'I'm going to take a shower and then we can go. I'll see you in thirty minutes?'

'Great,' he said, and she nodded and left. A few minutes later he followed her lead, hoping that the pounding of the water against his body in the shower would give him back his ability to think logically.

Because he hadn't been. If he *had*, he wouldn't be taking her out to a restaurant. He wouldn't be entertaining their *friendship* knowing that there was something between them that could easily—*easily*—demand more.

And he couldn't have more. He'd told himself that just the day before. Had thought of all the reasons why he couldn't have more. He *knew* that he needed to focus on fixing things with Anja. On learning to forgive his mother.

Besides, there were too many complications with Jess. Too many reasons not to get attached, and risk being hurt. Too many reasons not to pursue any relationship—even a friendship—with her.

So why was he so excited to spend an evening with her?

He dressed quickly, and tried not to think about it. And then he went downstairs to wait for Jess.

His breath was swept away as soon as he saw her.

She wore a pretty blue dress that was printed with pink, yellow and green flowers over tights and boots. She'd twisted her hair up into that plaited crown again— so intricate-looking and yet so simple. He supposed the description could work for her, too. There was something so intoxicatingly intricate about her beauty, about her demeanour, and yet she wore it so casually, so easily that it seemed simple.

But he knew it wasn't. Nothing about her was.

'You look lovely.'

'Thanks,' she said with a shy smile, revealing yet another layer that wasn't simple. He'd never seen her shy before. Even when she'd been running her hands over his naked chest the first day they'd met. 'So do you, by the way.' She tilted her head. 'Maybe lovely isn't the right word.'

'Why not?'

'I don't know if your manly ego would accept it so easily,' she teased. 'So, I'm going to go with—you look very handsome tonight, Dylan.'

'Thank you,' he replied with a smile. He offered her his arm and she slid her own through it, the scent of her flowery perfume following them. He led her into the garage and opened the car door for her before sliding into his own seat and pulling out onto the driveway.

Then he took the road that would take them to the restaurant he'd only been to once before. Ironically, it had been on a date, and he remembered being so uninterested in the woman who'd accompanied him—he'd made mistakes in the past, too—that he'd spent a decent amount of time noting the details of the restaurant décor.

But he'd so been impressed that he'd thought that one

day he'd take someone he actually liked there to enjoy it with him.

'Where are we going?' Jess asked, interrupting his thoughts.

'It's a place not too far from here, actually.' He took a right, and drove the winding road up the hills that were so abundant in Cape Town.

'Are you going to tell me the name?' she asked, amusement clear in her voice.

'Buon Cibo. It's Italian for good food.'

'You're taking me to an Italian restaurant?'

'Yes.' His eyes slid over to her. 'Is that a problem?'

'No. In fact, I'm going to go out on a limb here and say that it establishes our friendship on a pretty great foundation.'

He chuckled. 'You like Italian food?'

'Love it. When I was younger…' She trailed off, and then cleared her throat and continued. 'When I was younger, my nanny was actually Italian. I'm not a hundred per cent sure where my parents found her, but I was glad they did.'

'Because of the food she made?' he asked, hoping to make her laugh. Felt warmth spread through him when she did.

'Yes. And because she was warm and kind. Things that hadn't really been a part of my parents' MO. Anyway,' she continued after a moment, 'she used to make delicious carbonara pasta. And a delicious lasagne. And— You know what? All of her pastas were delicious.'

He smirked. 'And this was before the baby?'

She stuck her tongue out at him. 'I guess we'll see if Buon Cibo delivers on their promise.'

She stopped speaking just as he pulled in front of the restaurant, and he enjoyed the way her eyes widened. The exterior of Buon Cibo was designed to look exactly like the little cafés in Italy, except it had two large trees on either side of the door that had been decorated with small lanterns. He helped Jess out of the car, and enjoyment turned to pleasure when she saw the interior. When her reaction told him she shared his opinion of the place.

Small round tables were spread throughout the room, suited for two or four people, making it clear the place was meant for intimate dinners. Chandeliers hung from the wooden ceilings, offering light throughout the dim room, accentuated by the flickering of candles on each table.

The wall opposite the entrance was glass, and revealed that the restaurant was directly next to the ocean. Water plunged against the rocks, against the glass, in a stormy and enthralling rhythm that spoke of a passion patrons could be tempted into repeating at the end of their date.

Not that this was a date, his inner voice told him. Nor was he interested in exploring passion with Jess when he knew they would never come back from it.

He was grateful for the distraction when the maître d' showed them to their table, though he didn't know how he felt about the fact that it was right next to the thrashing waves.

'This was not what I pictured when you said we'd be going out for dinner,' Jess said as they waited for the waiter.

'You don't like it?'

'No, I love it. I just wish I'd known how…intimate it was.' Her cheeks went a riveting shade of pink. 'I would have put on something a bit more appropriate.'

'How would you dress in an…*intimate* setting like this, Jess?' His voice had gone husky at her unintentional implication.

'I…no, I didn't mean it like that.'

'I know. But it's more interesting for me to think it,

anyway.' He grinned, hoping that teasing would cool the fire in his body.

'That's not how you're supposed to treat friends, Dylan.'

'I wouldn't know. My friends have never quite looked like you.'

'Stop,' she said softly. A warning, he thought, and instantly pulled back.

'We should ask about their specials, but I'd recommend the lasagne, if you're in the mood for pasta.'

'How could I not be?' she asked brightly. Gratefully, too, he knew, and mentally kicked himself for taking things too far.

'Why don't you tell me about what your life was like in the UK?' she asked once the waiter had taken their drinks order.

So he did.

He told her that the first thing he'd been struck by when he'd arrived was the cosmopolitan nature of London. It had reminded him a lot of Cape Town, and it had made him more homesick than he'd imagined he would be. He told her about the work he'd done. How he'd introduced himself to clients he hadn't yet had the opportunity to meet since taking over from Ridge.

And—though he didn't quite phrase it that way—about his obsession to bid for engineering jobs with clients who would enhance his company's reputation and portfolio. His success with those bids. How it had made him feel as if he was honouring his grandfather, the man who'd looked out for him and Anja even after his death.

How the success had made Dylan feel as if he was making up for his father's failures.

He told her how much he'd missed the warm South African weather. How he'd never quite managed to warm up even when they'd told him it was a summer's day. And, after the briefest moment of hesitation, Dylan told Jess about how much he'd missed home. And how often he'd wanted to come back.

'Why didn't you?'

'It didn't feel like the right time,' he answered. 'I… wasn't ready.'

'And you are now?'

'I don't know.' He gave her a wry smile. 'Maybe I just didn't care about the right or wrong time when I decided to come home.'

'You should tell them that. When you see them, I mean.'

'When I see Anja,' Dylan corrected automatically.

'No.' She frowned. 'When you see Anja *and* your mother.'

He opened his mouth to reply, but the waiter returned with their drinks just then and asked to take their order. Jess ordered bruschetta for her starter and went with the lasagne for her main. He ordered carpaccio and decided to have the carbonara for his main, telling her that she could have some of it if she wanted to taste.

She lifted her eyebrows. 'That's awfully kind of you, Dylan.'

'You sound surprised,' he said with a quirk of his lip.

'I'm not. Just…touched.'

He smiled at her now, and when she smiled back his heart flipped.

Get it together, Dylan.

'What were you doing before you started working for Anja?' he asked, desperate for a change of topic. One that wouldn't veer into the territory of his complicated emotions about his mother.

'Studying. I have a degree in finance.'

'Really?'

'Don't sound so surprised,' she replied, amused.

'I just…wouldn't have suspected that someone with that kind of degree would be working as a PA.'

'That's part of the reason I did it.' She fiddled with the salt shaker on the table. 'It was so different to the path I'd chosen to study, and I needed…different.'

'Why?'

The fiddling became faster. 'I studied finance because my father has an investment company. One of the largest in Cape Town.' Her fingers moved to the pepper. 'He inherited it from his father, and I thought he might want to share it with me some day.'

'But he didn't?'

'Nope.' She gave him a brave smile, but he could see the hurt. 'Apparently—' she blew out a shaky breath '—he'd been mentoring someone else at work.' Now she cleared her throat. 'To take over from him.'

'Someone who wasn't family?'

'Yes.'

'When did you find out?'

Her eyes met his. 'Just over two years ago.'

And, just like that, he got the answer to what had happened two years ago that had led her to move out. 'Did he make you believe that you'd be able to join the company some day?'

She laughed hoarsely. 'Not once.'

'Then why…' His words faded when he realised how terrible his question would sound. But she finished it for him.

'Why did I still want to? Why did I study a degree that would give me the necessary qualifications to be able to?' She dropped her hands to her lap. 'Because I wanted—' She broke off on a sigh. 'I don't know, Dylan.'

'What were you going to say?' he prodded gently. When she shook her head, he said, 'Jess, you don't have to pretend with me. Just tell me the truth.'

He held his breath during the pause after his words, and only released it when she answered him.

'I wanted to be a part of the family.' Anguish was clear in her voice, on her face. 'I thought that if I turned myself into someone that *could* be a part of the family—if I was a part of the business, if I stopped telling them where and why they were going wrong—they'd include me in their unit. It might not have been a conventional family,' she added, 'but my parents were a team. A—'

'A family that didn't include you,' he finished for her. 'Jess, I'm so—'

'Don't you dare apologise—' she interrupted him with a small smile '—I've moved on.' She paused, and Dylan thought she wasn't nearly as convincing as he suspected she wanted to be. 'And it wasn't that they wanted to exclude me entirely. My father *did* tell me I could marry the man he'd been grooming to take over.'

Dylan nearly choked on the wine he'd taken a sip of. 'He wanted you to *marry* the man? He actually said that?'

'Yeah, very seriously, too.' She rolled her eyes. 'He took my refusal just as seriously. It was clear then that what I'd wanted with my parents—what I'd hoped for—wasn't going to happen. So I moved out.'

'And you realised that what your parents did—how they acted—had nothing to do with you?' He had no idea why he'd said it, but when she looked up he knew she needed to hear it.

'It had *something* to do with me.'

'No,' he told her. 'If you believe that, then I need to believe that my father's addiction had something to do with me. That the fact that he didn't fight harder to overcome it—that he left us—had something to do with us. That my mother choosing to have us despite knowing my father had a—'

He broke off, realising what he'd said. Realising that he'd just told Jess something Anja didn't know.

Silence followed his words and, just before he could

start panicking, Dylan met Jess's eyes and something passed between them that had him feeling…calmer. As if they'd reached some unspoken agreement that told him Jess wouldn't tell Anja what he'd just told her.

It was a disconcerting feeling, and he cleared his throat. 'It's not you, Jess. It's not us.'

'Do you believe that?'

'Yes,' he replied honestly. 'Coming to terms with it, on the other hand…'

Her lips curved into a half-smile and she nodded. Again, something passed between them. But this time Dylan could identify it as a kind of understanding he'd never experienced before. Not even with Anja.

He felt it draw him in, though he told himself to fight it. Reminded himself that he wasn't interested in a relationship, in a future—that thinking of either was dangerous.

He struggled with it as the waiter arrived with their starters. They were about halfway through them when he tried to distract himself. 'Do you miss them?'

'My parents?' He nodded, and she lifted her shoulders. 'I had reasons for leaving them. I *have* reasons for not keeping in touch with them. Those reasons are more important than what missing them feels like,' she said quietly. 'But I guess I do miss them.' She paused, tilted her head. 'Or maybe I just miss the parents I wish they were.'

CHAPTER ELEVEN

JESS COULD SEE that Dylan was considering what she'd just said. It was obviously something that hadn't occurred to him before. He wore the exact same expression of surprise as when he'd told her that his mother had known about his father's gambling problem before he or Anja had been born.

Since Anja had never mentioned it—and Jess was sure it was something she *would* have mentioned—Jess knew that Anja didn't know. That it was part of the reason Dylan had left.

And somehow, without words, she'd promised Dylan *she* wouldn't tell Anja either.

She told herself it was because she didn't want to get in the middle of it. Of *them*. It was the only logical explanation. Any other explanation would be anything *but* logical.

It implied that Jess didn't want to tell Anja because *Dylan* didn't want her to. Which, in turn, implied that Jess felt a certain…loyalty to Dylan that trumped the loyalty she felt to Anja. Because if Dylan knew this and Anja didn't, it meant that he'd found out and hadn't told her. And, if that was true, Jess knew it would complicate Anja and Dylan's reunion even more.

So Jess would choose to believe that she'd agreed to keep the information to herself because she didn't want to get involved. And she would choose to believe that the guilt she felt was worth it to save Anja—and possibly the baby she carried—from the pain of a broken family.

'It's hard,' Dylan said suddenly, interrupting her thoughts. 'To face that the people who raised us weren't who we hoped they'd be.'

'Especially when they're gone and we have to face that they'll *never* be who we hoped they would be.'

He gave her a small smile, but they finished their starters in silence. Jess found herself looking at him every few minutes, and wondered if he realised how expressive his face was. Probably not, she thought, or he would have tried to hide the emotions that were clear there.

Compassion thrummed through her veins, followed closely by coldness when she realised that she shouldn't be bonding with Dylan. She shouldn't be learning the nuances of his face, of his voice. She shouldn't be understanding that he'd left because he'd been in pain.

Because leaving had caused *Anja* pain. Anja, her best friend. The only person in her life who actually seemed to deserve Jess's love. Who'd made Jess feel loved. Dylan was not her friend. No, he was the man who'd broken a piece of her best friend's heart. He was her best friend's *brother*.

So what if he seemed to understand her? If it seemed they had a lot in common? He was off-limits. And she couldn't—*wouldn't*—consider the dangerous emotions that were suddenly whirling around inside her.

Instead, she said the only thing that she could: Dylan needed to open up to someone else.

'You need to talk to someone about your father's death.'

'Excuse me?'

'You heard me. You need to talk through your feelings about your father's death, about him leaving. About—' she hesitated '—about your mother.' Left it at that.

'You mean...like a therapist?'

'That's not a bad idea, but it's not what I meant.' She let the words linger. 'I meant a…friend.'

Seconds passed before he said, 'I don't have that many friends.'

'You have Anja,' she told him. 'And your mother. No,' she said over his protest. 'I don't know the details of what happened with your mother, but if it can be salvaged, salvage it.'

'I…don't think that's going to happen.'

'Dylan—'

But the arrival of their main courses interrupted what she was going to say, and the turmoil on Dylan's face prompted her not to continue when the waiter left. Instead, Jess dug into her meal with a gusto she'd only experienced as a pregnant woman.

'Do you want some of mine?' Dylan asked, the turmoil now replaced with faint humour. It made him look softer, more handsome.

No, Jess!

'Yeah, thanks.' She took a forkful of spaghetti, but paused before she brought it over to her mouth. 'What's funny?'

'What do you mean?' he asked with an innocent expression that immediately had her narrowing her eyes.

'Are you *laughing* at my eating habits?'

'No.' But he laughed aloud now, and her eyes narrowed even further. 'I told you I was ordering this so you could taste it.'

'But then you looked at me like you thought I *needed* to taste it.'

'I did *not*.'

'You better not be lying to me.'

He chuckled. 'I'm not. Now, do you want to taste the pasta, or are you going to spend the rest of the night arguing with me?'

'I want to taste the pasta,' she grumbled, but winked at him.

The rest of the evening wasn't as tense as the first part, though the ghost of it hovered over them for the rest of the night. But, since neither of them brought it up, the conversation was light, happy, as though they hadn't spoken about their pasts that night.

It was late when they finished and as they walked out of the restaurant Jess paused to turn back. 'This was a really lovely evening at a really lovely place.'

'I'm glad you liked it,' he replied, standing next to her. 'Jess…'

Something about his voice had her turning towards him, and she sucked in her breath when she saw his expression.

'I know that this is probably the last thing that we should do after everything that's happened—after everything we've said—today,' he whispered, closing the distance between them and lifting a hand to her cheek. 'But I'm going to anyway.'

She opened her mouth to reply, but his lips were on hers before she could. It tasted sweet, a mixture of dessert and coffee. But beneath it Jess could also taste the man. That pure masculine taste that she'd only really experienced once before.

With him.

This time, though, the kiss wasn't as desperately heady as the one they'd shared in the forest. This kiss was soft and deliberate, a gentle sigh that had her heart racing. She felt the heat of his hand on her face as his other hand settled gently on her waist, a slow burn that went from the point of contact straight to her blood, warming her body as leisurely as a bath would.

With bubbles, too, she thought foolishly when he deepened the kiss—still tender, still cautious—and it felt as if there were bubbles in her stomach, on her skin. She gave a soft moan and pressed closer, her own hand sliding up from where it had rested on his chest to cup his cheek. His beard prickled, aroused, and it was strange that the feeling was more jarring through the contact of her hand than against her face.

She was breathing heavily when she pulled back, and she felt a flip in her stomach that had nothing to do with the way Dylan had made her feel. The hand on his face immediately lowered to the movement and, smiling, she looked up at him.

She wasn't sure what she'd expected. But it wasn't the following of his hand to where she'd put hers. It wasn't the reverent look on his face as he felt the slight pressure of the baby moving inside her.

It reminded her that he wouldn't be nearly as touched when he found out whose baby she was carrying. It told her that she was playing both sides. That she was betraying Anja with whatever was happening between her and Dylan. That she had betrayed Dylan by getting involved with him—even though it had been unintentional—when she was connected so deeply to his sister.

Tension crept into her body and settled in the muscles of her shoulders, her neck. She stepped back, away from him, and then walked to the car, waited for him to unlock it so she could get in. She didn't give him a chance to open the door for her this time—didn't give *herself* a chance to deal with the confusion on his face. She only shook her head when he said her name, and told herself to breathe when the tension inside her spread between them.

The ride back home was short, quiet, and Jess was almost relieved when they pulled into the driveway of Dylan's house.

Almost.

Except there was already a car in front of the house

when they got there, and Jess inhaled sharply when she recognised it. She let the breath out in a shudder just as Dylan said, 'Anja's home.'

CHAPTER TWELVE

THERE WAS A sick feeling in Dylan's stomach.

To be fair, he couldn't blame it entirely on returning from dinner with his sister's best friend to find said sister on his doorstep. No, the feeling had started the moment he'd felt the baby Jess was carrying moving against his hand. When he'd seen her face and worried that the wonder and amazement he saw there—that the wonder and amazement *he'd* felt—would turn into heartbreak when she gave that baby away.

The feeling had settled when Jess had walked away from him, breaking the warmth of their kiss and their connection that had grown during their dinner. And when he'd tried to do something about it and he'd got the cold shoulder, the silent treatment on the way home.

But now he was home, and his sister was back, and there would be no more time to think of it.

He pulled the car into the garage and then got out slowly. He heard Jess behind him as he walked to the front of his house where his sister was and, by the time he got there, Anja was standing outside, Chet next to her.

Dylan's eyes first went to their hands—to the tight hold he could see between them. And then he looked at his sister. Really looked. And really saw, for the first time in years. She'd got skinnier. And her face was tougher, its lines creased into a tight expression that told him she wasn't going to take it easy on him. But other than that she looked the same, and the emotion that clogged his throat had him wanting to walk right to her and pull her into his arms.

Instead, he shoved his hands into his pockets. 'It's good to see you, sis.'

'It's a…surprise to see you, Dylan.' Her voice was hoarse and she cleared her throat. 'How long have you been back?'

'Just over a week.'

'And you didn't tell us? Me or Mom?'

'I wanted it to be a surprise,' he said lamely, and belatedly thought that maybe it *was* lame. That maybe his plan to come home and reconcile with his sister was just plain *lame*.

'Well, it's certainly been that.'

Silence spread between them, and then Anja's eyes shifted to behind him and her stormy expression cleared. 'Jess!'

His sister stalked past him as if he wasn't even there and enveloped Jess in a hug. Jealousy beat an uncomfortable rhythm in his blood and all he could do was stand there as Chet walked past him, too, thumped him on the back in greeting and went over to hug Jess.

'Your stomach has grown so much!' Anja said and lowered to her haunches. Jess's eyes fluttered over to him, and something crossed her face that he couldn't quite read.

'Yeah. But it's only been two weeks, An.'

'Much too long for my liking,' Anja murmured to Jess's belly and Dylan's stomach dropped slowly, steadily, his mind still trying to comprehend what his eyes were telling him.

Anja straightened and turned to Dylan. 'Did Jess tell you?'

'Tell me what?'

'You asked me not to,' Jess interrupted, and her eyes went from Anja's to Dylan's. This time he could clearly see the apology on her face.

'So he doesn't know?' Anja asked, but the question wasn't directed at Jess. It was directed at him. Which made absolutely no sense. How was he supposed to know what he didn't know?

'I don't know what you're talking about.'

'Maybe we should take this conversation inside?' Jess interrupted.

'What conversation?' Dylan demanded, his heart thudding from the tension. 'Someone just tell me what you're talking about. Now,' he snapped, when Jess opened her mouth again.

'Relax,' Anja told him. 'This isn't Jess's fault. She's right. I asked her not to tell you.' She shifted closer to Chet and took his hand. 'Jess is carrying our baby, Dylan. Chet and I are going to be parents.'

And immediately Dylan knew why his stomach had dropped earlier. Why he suddenly recognised it as sick anticipation. It didn't matter that it made no sense—how could he have anticipated the news Anja had just told him? How could he have known that Jess was carrying his sister's child? *His* niece or nephew?

But all he knew for sure was that the feeling was there, and it made him feel foolish.

Just like trusting Jess did.

'Why?' he asked hoarsely. 'When?'

'We should go inside,' Jess said again. Dylan nodded, but he didn't look at her. Couldn't. Not even when she said, 'No, actually, you all should go inside. You need to talk about this and...' Her voice faded, though Dylan sensed everyone knew what she was referring to. Him. His return. Why he'd left. 'I don't need to be there.'

'You can be,' Anja said softly. 'You're as much a part of the family as any of us are.'

'No,' Dylan heard himself say. 'She's not. And she's right, this should be between all of us.'

'Dylan—'

'No, Anja, he's right,' Jess said. 'I'll be next door.'

'I thought you said the ceiling wouldn't be done until tomorrow?'

'They finished the painting today. I'll open all the windows and be upstairs. The smell shouldn't be as bad there.'

And then she was gone, leaving Dylan alone with his sister and brother-in-law.

It was silly to cry. Jess knew it, and yet she still felt the tears slip down her cheeks.

She could blame it on the hormones. And they probably deserved some of the blame. But most of it came from the look on Dylan's face after he'd discovered that she was carrying Anja and Chet's baby.

And the vicious reminder that she wasn't a part of their family.

Her breath shuddered out as she opened the windows of Anja's house, the fresh, brisk autumn air relieving the smell of paint in the house. It was better upstairs, as she'd thought it would be, and after she opened the windows her eyes fell on the chair that still sat in front of one of them.

Had it only been a week ago that she'd seen Dylan for the first time? It didn't seem right that she could feel his disappointment in her—his hurt *because* of her—so profoundly when she'd only known him for such a short span of time. And yet there she was, wiping tears from her eyes because of it, and trying to figure out what to do next.

She couldn't stay in Dylan's house any more. She suspected that she'd burnt that bridge, well and truly, though it hadn't been *entirely* her fault. Perhaps if Anja and Dylan's relationship hadn't been so damaged, things wouldn't seem so bad for him. Except that it *was* damaged, and Jess was carrying the reminder of the extent of it.

She knew now that every time Dylan looked at her he'd be reminded. Added to the fact that he'd been acting so strangely about her surrogacy even before he'd known who she was a surrogate for.

So she couldn't stay at Dylan's, and Anja's was out of the question with the smell of paint still lingering in the air. She could find a hotel—there was no way she'd find anything cheap at such short notice—but that would take from her savings. Savings she'd need after she'd given birth and needed to separate herself from Anja and Dylan.

It was clear that would be her only option now. Her friend would put up a fight, Jess knew, but Jess needed space. Away from the baby, and away from their uncle. Though she knew that wasn't the only reason.

She'd become comfortable with her life, just as she had been before she'd started working with Anja. Was it perfect? No, but she hadn't expected it to be. And perhaps that was why she'd lingered, avoiding what she'd needed to do, just as she had with her parents.

But she needed her independence. She saw that now so clearly that she wasn't sure why she hadn't before. She needed to stop relying on people she *thought* were family, and she needed to start relying on herself.

So she would drive to a hotel and spend the night there. And soon she'd move into her own flat. She'd save as much as she could while she still worked for Anja, but she'd start making plans. She *would* survive this. She'd survived worse.

Jess sighed and sank into the couch, her body aching from the strain of being pregnant and the tension of the day. The brisk breeze still drifted through the air and she pulled a throw over herself. She switched on the television, and waited for Anja to tell her their discussion was over.

She would pack up her things and go to a hotel, she thought, even as her eyelids started to close…

Dylan found Jess wrapped in a fleece throw in front of the television. It took him a moment to realise that she was sleeping, and seeing her like that wiped away all the righteous indignation he'd felt from the moment he'd offered to tell her she could come back to his house.

Instead, he settled on the opposite couch, his body and soul weary from the last couple of hours. He could do with a break from the tension between him and his sister. That was the only way he could describe what had transpired between them. He was exhausted, and the space he wanted so that he could figure out how he felt about everything was unavailable as Anja and Chet were sleeping over.

He had plenty of spare rooms—the house had been designed that way because he'd hoped one day to have a big family. To have his and his sister's kids playing around, having sleepovers. He wasn't sure that would happen any more. Which made sense considering that his sister hadn't even told him she was expecting a child.

Could he even call it that? he thought, rubbing a hand over his face. He immediately felt bad about it, and let out a shaky breath. It was all too much for him—Jess, the surrogacy, seeing his sister again.

Finding out his sister had had a miscarriage and how she'd struggled with it afterwards. Finding out Jess had offered to help them have a child when Anja had been so close to giving up. The unselfish reasons Jess had described to him when she'd told him about the surrogacy were so much more profound now. So was his fear for her when she had to give the child away, though heaven only knew why.

She was carrying his niece or nephew and *she hadn't told him*.

Did it matter that Anja had asked her not to? Maybe. But it still felt like a betrayal, that she'd broken his trust. Which was ridiculous, considering that he hadn't even known her long enough to trust her.

Logically, he knew that. But, just like he'd thought before, nothing about the situation with Jess felt logical. It hadn't been logic that had softened, warmed in his chest when she'd shown him her sympathy and told him he needed to talk about his problems. It hadn't been reason that had pushed him into kissing her. There was something more there that had nothing to do with logic, and it terrified him.

And maybe that was why he felt the way he did.

Or maybe it was all a distraction to keep him from thinking about how coldly his sister had greeted him. Or how stilted their interactions had been. They hadn't spoken about anything other than the baby since Anja had told him she was too tiredfor anything else.

He couldn't argue, considering she'd travelled eighteen hours to get home. But he knew it wasn't the travelling that had tired her. It was the first of many difficult conversations they were going to have.

It was going to be a process, he thought. One he couldn't speed up merely because he wanted to. He needed to give Anja time to process. Hell, he needed to give himself time to wade through all his thoughts, all his feelings. About his family, yes. But also about the woman who whimpered so softly in her sleep.

So he stayed in Anja's house for a while longer and, when he was ready, did what he'd offered to do. He closed all the windows and then lifted Jess into his arms and carried her to the house next door.

CHAPTER THIRTEEN

WHEN SHE WOKE UP, Jess wasn't entirely sure where she was.

It took her a while to figure out that she was in a bed. And that that bed was the one she'd slept in for the second time now...in Dylan's house.

So much for getting a hotel room, she thought. And then realised that being there meant someone had *brought* her there the night before.

She didn't want to spend too much time thinking about who.

Because though she knew Chet could easily have carried her the short distance to Dylan's house, he would have more likely woken her. Which left only one option...

Pushing away fanciful thoughts of how sweet, how romantic it must have been, Jess got out of bed and had a shower. She hadn't brought another set of clothes with her, so she pulled on the tights from the night before—ignoring the way her heart sank at the memory of how different things had been when she'd worn them then—and her woollen oversized jersey with boots. It wasn't entirely new, but she hadn't worn this combination before.

Besides, who was she trying to impress? Certainly not the friends who'd seen her with her legs in the air while she'd been impregnated with their child. And *certainly* not the man who'd brushed her off so completely the day before.

With that in mind, she pulled her hair into a bun at the top of her head and began packing. Fifteen minutes later, she walked with her suitcase to the kitchen. She was surprised to find no one there, but she heard the deep rumble of male voices from the dining room. Leaving her suitcase in the kitchen passageway, she made her way there.

It was strange seeing Dylan and Chet there, talking as though there hadn't been a boulder of tension that had descended on them the day before. They stopped when she walked in. Chet smiled at her, but Dylan's face immediately soured before settling into a blank expression. She nearly rolled her eyes.

'I'm not sure how I ended up in bed here last night, but I'm willing to bet it was one of you.'

'Hey, you *are* carrying my child,' Chet replied with a wink, and she felt her mouth curve.

'Though, let's be honest, that wouldn't have kept you from waking me up and telling me to walk back to the house.' Her eyes went to Dylan and she felt the amusement waver. 'Thank you.'

'No need,' he replied smoothly.

She clenched her jaw. 'Well, I think there is, so I'm saying thanks. Also for letting me stay here while everything was happening next door.'

'You're welcome.' His eyebrow quirked. 'Better?'

'Much,' she replied, and then turned her attention to Chet. 'Where's Anja?'

'She went for a run. Said she'd see you when she gets back.'

'Well, she can see me next door. I'm going to head over, make sure everything's okay before the cleaners arrive in an hour.'

'You don't want breakfast first?' Chet asked.

'I'll make myself something at your place.'

'You sure about that?' Dylan interjected now.

'Why wouldn't I be?'

'Just because I've tasted your cooking and…' He let the words drift and annoyance stirred. Which was strange, since she was fairly certain that she would have been amused if it hadn't come from him.

'And yet I've survived for twenty-six years,' she said wryly. 'I'll see you next door, Chet. And…' she hesitated '…I guess I'll see you around, Dylan.'

She pretended that she hadn't seen the questioning look Chet sent her and picked up her bag, giving Daisy a head pat before she left.

It felt strangely as if she was turning over a new page. And perhaps she was, she thought, considering the plans she'd made the night before. Granted, it hadn't worked out for her to sleep at a hotel the previous night, but perhaps that was a blessing in disguise. Now she could keep that money in her savings.

When she got to Anja's place she made herself something to eat, ignoring the way her stomach wished she'd taken up Chet's offer to have breakfast next door. She could have had bacon and eggs instead, and tried to make up for the lack of it by making her single cup of tea for the day.

She was curled up on the couch when Anja walked in.

'Glad to see you're having a good balanced breakfast,' Anja said, flopping down on the couch opposite Jess. Her hair was still wet from her morning shower, the curls piled up on top of her head, much like Jess's.

'Eating for two and all that,' she said, tilting her bowl of oats for Anja to see. 'You can't have had breakfast yet?'

'I haven't, and I'm starving.'

'Why didn't you eat something before you came over?'

'Because it would entail spending more time with my brother?'

Jess's heart thudded at the mention of Dylan. 'Well, you *did* come back to do that…didn't you?'

'I guess. I don't know. I'm just so…*mad.*'

Jess bit back the *why?* on the tip of her tongue and nodded. 'You should tell him that.'

'I don't think it would go down particularly well,' Anja replied dryly.

'Actually, I think it might. He doesn't know why you're mad, Anja, besides the obvious reason. And it's about time you stop carrying it around with you, too.'

Anja narrowed her eyes. 'Since when do you push for family reconciliations?'

She choked out a laugh. 'Since you came back from Sydney as soon as you heard he was back?' A beat of silence passed. 'You can't tell me that you finished everything you wanted to?'

'We finished the last of the work on the studio. I'd hoped to do more…but I wanted to be here. The rest we can do via email or video chat.' Anja sighed. 'I guess you're right.'

'As usual,' Jess teased.

'Ha ha.'

Jess let Anja mull it over and finished her breakfast. She made some coffee for Anja and handed it over. Anja murmured her thanks, adding, 'How do you know? That Dylan doesn't know why I'm mad, I mean?'

She should have worn her hair down, she thought, when she felt the tell-tale heat of a blush start in her cheeks. 'We talked over the last few days.'

'About me?'

'About him, mostly.'

'And?'

Jess struggled to find an answer that didn't make her

feel as if she was betraying Dylan's trust. 'He's come back to make things right. I know,' she said when Anja opened her mouth. 'I know that things are messy and painful between you two. But he's come back, and so did you. For the sake of your child, his niece or nephew, and for *your* sake, you should at least try to talk to him about it.'

Anja rolled her eyes. Then threaded her fingers together. 'Low blow, Steyn.'

'I know,' she said sympathetically. 'But it wouldn't hurt if it wasn't true.'

They sat in silence after those words, and then Anja said, 'He *did* take time off work to be home. He hasn't since—'

'Since he left.'

'Since long before then, actually.' Anja gave her a strange look. 'Are you…is there something going on between you two?'

'What?' There was no stopping the blush now. 'No, of course not. Why would you say that?'

'Because my brother doesn't just share how he feels with people. Hell, I lived with him for almost two decades and I still don't know some of the things he felt then. That's part of the problem.'

'I was just there at the right time, I guess.'

'Maybe.' But Anja looked worried. 'You're not interested in him?'

'No,' she said immediately. *Not any more, anyway.* 'I was civil with him because of you. And this baby.' She didn't have to mention the kisses. 'I know it would be much too complicated, Anja.'

'It would be,' her friend agreed.

'Good thing there's nothing to worry about then, isn't it?' Jess replied, and ignored the sick feeling in her chest at the lie.

Because she *was* worried. She was *very* worried.

* * *

Dylan saw her as soon as he got there, and was about to turn back—coward that he was—when she turned and saw him.

'Oh,' she said softly. 'I'll leave.'

'No, you don't have to,' he replied immediately. Though he was still mad at her, Dylan hated that the easiness between them had been replaced by…by whatever was happening now. A mixture of tension and apology. Of words unspoken and words that had been said. 'I'll leave.'

'No, this is your place.'

She turned, and he could almost see her eyes taking in the magnificent view from the hilltop he'd taken her to a few days ago.

His place of comfort.

Where he'd opened up to Jess.

Where he'd kissed her.

He pushed away the memories when she turned back. 'You shouldn't have to leave just because I'm here.'

'I'm not,' he said in a short tone that proved exactly the opposite of what he'd said. 'I just wanted to be alone.'

'So I'll go.' She walked past him.

The words were out of his mouth before he could help it. 'Why were you here?'

The crackling of leaves and sticks under her feet went quiet. 'I wanted to think.'

'About?'

She gave a small laugh. 'Why don't you take a guess?'

He didn't reply. Couldn't, when what he would guess sounded incredibly self-centred. There was no way she was thinking about him. Even if *she* was part of the reason he'd needed time outside, to think alone.

After a moment he heard the crunching of leaves again, and he whirled around. 'Jess.'

She stopped, turned back to look at him. 'Yeah?'

'Anja and I...we had a conversation this morning.' It had been one of those conversations that had picked his emotions apart and left them out to dry. Naked. Raw. 'She told me you told her to give me a chance.'

She shook her head. 'I told her she needed to start thinking about her child.'

'The child you're carrying.' As if he could forget.

'Yes,' she told him. 'I see your opinion hasn't changed despite the fact that you now know I'm carrying your niece or nephew.'

'I have no opinion on this.'

'You and I both know that's not true.'

'Your agreement with my sister has nothing to do with me.'

He watched her face tighten.

'I'll remember that the next time I have to talk her into having a conversation with you.'

'So you *did* tell her that.'

'For her child's sake.'

'And yet she made it sound like it was for the sake of this family, too.'

'What do you want from me, Dylan?' she asked in an exasperated tone.

'The truth,' he growled.

'Fine. I told her to give you a chance. For the child's sake, for hers, and yes, for you, too.' The admission cost her, he thought, taking in the expression on her face. 'I care about... I care,' she finished, and lifted a hand to brush at her face.

'Why?' he asked, caught by her now. Anger had flushed her cheeks, making the golden brown of her skin almost luminous. 'Why do you care?'

'I'm asking myself that very question right now.'

'And what answer have you come up with?'

His back was turned to the view he'd returned to for

solace, the beauty in front of him now much more appealing. He shouldn't have noticed what a lovely picture she made. Standing in the woods, tall, dark trees around her, dull brown leaves at her feet. She looked like a woodland creature, though he couldn't blame it on the plaid shirt and jeans she wore.

He *did* blame it on the way she carried herself. The ease, the natural rhythm of her. Even when she was standing there, looking at him in annoyance, she looked as if she belonged there. As if her selflessness, her kindness, belonged in a natural setting.

'That I'm crazy.'

'You're not crazy.' If *she* was, then so was he.

But then, maybe that was the answer.

'No? Then how do you explain what's been happening over the last few days? Because you might not have known just how off-limits I was, Dylan, but *I* did. I knew the moment I found out the sexy guy living next door was my best friend's brother, the uncle of the child I carried. I *knew* that I shouldn't have got involved with you.'

She threaded her fingers together, as though she didn't know what to do with her hands. 'And yet, when you brought me here, when you told me all of those things about your family…I felt…I don't know, *attracted* to you.' She said the word with a disgust he struggled not to feel offended by. 'And, you know, because of all that—' she waved a hand at his body, and amusement coloured the insult '—and so I kissed you. And I went on a date with you. And none of that nonsense about us being friends,' she added, 'because we both know that wasn't a friendship date.'

He didn't know what to say. But he'd asked for it, he knew. He'd pushed her, and he couldn't be upset that she was giving him the information he needed. That he wanted.

The only problem was that nothing she was telling him turned off whatever it was that he felt whenever he saw her. It didn't matter how angry—or how raw—he was, his heart ached and his stomach flipped every single time he saw her.

'You know what the worst part is?' she asked. 'That I got in the middle of whatever's going on with you and Anja. I *ran* right in the middle of your family drama while running away from my own.'

'You've helped,' he said softly.

'Have I?' She lifted her brows. 'When you came here, your question was more accusation than gratitude.'

'I'm…sorry about that.' The apology was a surprise. As was the sincerity he felt as he said it. 'The conversation with Anja… It was tough, and I came out here to deal with…everything.' He shrugged, wishing the pain was as easy to shake as the words. 'I'm glad you asked her to talk with me.'

'She wanted to,' she replied after a moment. 'She just needed a shove in the right direction.'

He almost smiled. 'Thank you.'

'Sure.' Silence pulsed between them, and then she said, 'I'm going to leave before we get into another argument that tempts me into shoving more literally.'

He nodded. Told himself what he wanted to ask her wouldn't be worth the turmoil her answer would no doubt bring. And then he asked it anyway. 'Why didn't you tell me, Jess?'

'Anja asked me not to.'

'And it was just that simple for you?' Anger stirred, and then burrowed into him. 'It was just that simple to keep something I should have known from me?'

'Yes,' she replied quickly, and then exhaled sharply. 'That's what you want me to say, isn't it? That it was simple for me to keep this secret from you?'

'I just want the truth.'

'No, you don't, Dylan. You want another reason to be angry with me.'

Disbelief made him splutter his words out. 'You think I *want* to be angry with you?'

'Yes, I do,' she replied. 'Because it would be easier to be angry with *me* than with your mother. With your father. With…' she hesitated '…with yourself.'

'No,' he denied. 'I *trusted* you, Jess. You broke—' his voice went hoarse '—you broke my trust.'

'Because I was being loyal to the only person who's ever been loyal to me?' she demanded. 'Because I was keeping *Anja's* trust?' She shook her head. 'She's like family to me, Dylan. She *is* my family. And you know why that's so important to me.' She paused. 'Whatever you and I shared these past few days—' She broke off and he nearly protested, desperate to hear what she was going to say.

Instead, silence followed her words before she blew out a breath. 'It wasn't easy,' she told him. 'It wasn't simple. But Anja trusted me, too. And—' Jess lifted her shoulders '—being able to trust your family, knowing that they'll be there for you, that they'll do what's right for you, even when it's hard for them? That's what family's supposed to do.'

She stopped speaking then, her eyes studying his face, telling him that she had more to say. He wasn't wrong.

'That's why you're really upset, Dylan. Because your parents broke your trust. They left. Even though your mother was still there,' she continued, 'she wasn't *there*. Not in the way you needed her to be. And I'm sure…what you found out about her made that feel even worse.' Dylan felt the agreement inside him—felt the truth of it—but he didn't speak.

'You're angry at her because of it. And at your father, for all the horrible things he put you through. But you're also angry at yourself. For leaving,' she said when he looked at her, and he wondered how she knew things he hadn't even admitted to himself. 'So if you need to deal with that by being angry with me, go right ahead. But realising it and facing the anger you have is going to help you fix what's wrong with you and Anja.'

She left then, but he didn't follow. He needed time to think, especially since Jess had just added to the list of things he needed to think about, easily summarising feelings he'd struggled to figure out for the longest time in just a few minutes. By the time he made his way back to the house, Dylan knew just how right Jess had been.

And damn if that didn't complicate things.

CHAPTER FOURTEEN

DAYS LATER, ANJA told Jess that she, Chet and Dylan were taking a trip to the coastal town of Langebaan to see their mother. The news was unexpected, as was her insistence that Jess go with them.

'No,' Jess said, feeling ambushed. She was still staying in Anja's house, working, thankfully, which helped her keep her mind off Dylan and the inner voice telling her it was time to move on. She'd avoided Dylan as much as she could, which was possible since Anja mostly went over to his house after work. She stayed there for hours and when she came back looked exhausted and emotional. They were sorting it out, Chet had told Jess one night, since he was her only companion for the time Anja was away. And sorting it out was a process, Anja had told her the following day at work. It hadn't been easy since their issues extended far beyond what either of them had known, but they were working through it. And now the final step was to speak to their mother.

Jess's efforts to avoid Dylan were now in vain since he stood on the other side of Anja's lounge, leaning against the wall with his arms crossed. She suspected he was going for a nonchalant look, but he only succeeded in looking broody and sexy and Jess cursed the pregnancy hormones for making her notice.

'You don't need me there,' she said, looking from Anja to Chet. She studiously avoided Dylan. 'I'm just going to be in the way.'

'No, you won't be,' Anja told her. 'My mom wants to see you again. And, you know, the baby,' she said, which was a real punch in the gut for Jess. How could she say no?

Her eyes flickered to Dylan, and then back at Anja again.

Oh, yes, *that* was how.

'It won't be comfortable for me to sit in the back of your car,' Jess protested, clutching at straws now. 'Either of yours,' she added, looking at Chet.

Both of them had trendy little cars that were incredibly impractical for a pregnant woman—and for a family. Anja was planning to trade in her car before the baby was born, but there was no way she'd be able to do it before this impromptu little trip.

'We've already thought about that,' Anja said, her enthusiasm a stark contrast to the fatigue she'd shown over the last few days. Jess could feel her resistance weakening. 'Dylan will drive up in his car. He's agreed for you to drive with him.'

'Has he now?' she asked, and cocked an eyebrow at Dylan. He gave her a smile that made her want to punch it from his sexy mouth.

'Yeah, and he has more than enough space. Besides, Jess,' Anja continued, her voice softening. 'None of us want to leave you here alone.'

And, with that, her resistance broke all together. 'Fine, but don't think I don't know you were working me.'

'I was *not*,' Anja said in mock insult. 'If I was—and, I repeat, I was not—I would have mentioned how much we consider you to be a part of our family, and that any family trip would be incomplete without you.'

With a laugh, she ducked out of the way of the cushion Jess threw at her.

Though she'd been joking, Anja's words had stayed with Jess in the days before they took the ninety-minute drive to Langebaan, a tiny town on the West Coast of South Africa. It had made Jess realise how much she wanted Anja's words to be true. And that had made her wonder— or panic—about whether she'd offered to be Anja's surrogate because she so desperately wanted to be a part of that family.

Of any family.

At the time, it hadn't even occurred to Jess. She'd only offered because she'd wanted to help, and it had been a real, tangible way for her to do so. She loved Anja—more than the employer she was, or the friend she'd become. She loved Anja… Well, Jess imagined she loved Anja like she would a sister…

Except she'd never had a sister—or any sibling—so how could she possibly know?

Now she worried that she'd become Anja's surrogate because she'd wanted to protect that love. *Her* love. *Her* feelings. Because surely Anja couldn't turn her back on Jess when Jess had carried her child? She couldn't stop caring about Jess, or toss her away like Jess's parents had…

Unless she could.

Because Jess would have served her purpose then, wouldn't she? She would have done what she'd offered to do, and given Anja the child she'd always wanted. What would keep Anja from turning from Jess then? What would keep that bond she thought she shared with her friend from crumbling?

Jess had already learnt that she didn't have much purpose in her life. The degree she'd worked so hard towards was useless. No matter how hard she'd tried, her parents didn't want her. And if she didn't have a purpose—if she was useless—why would Anja want to keep her around?

Jess sucked in her breath. Told herself not to cry.

But the tears came anyway.

'I know this might not be exactly how you would have liked to travel,' Dylan said wryly. 'But we could at least try for some civility.'

He felt Jess shift beside him, but kept his eyes on the road. It was bad enough that he was stuck in such a confined space with her. He wouldn't look at her, too, and have that sexy and sweet look she had going for her distract him even more.

He'd been annoyed when his sister had told him about the plan. Partly because he'd had to put Daisy in a doggy hotel while they were away. Partly because he'd had to leave his house and he'd just grown comfortable living there again.

But mostly it was because he really didn't want to speak to his mother about the past. But as soon as Anja had found out that their mother had known about their father's gambling problem before they'd been born, she'd been determined to find out why their mother had decided to have them.

Though that determination had only come after the shock, the tears, the hurt, he thought. And knew that they were only in store for more of the same.

But they'd been making progress, and for the first time he'd been able to articulate why he'd left. Because he'd felt as if their mother had betrayed them. Broken their trust. Because she'd abandoned them by reacting the way that she had to their father's abandonment, even though she'd *known* what she'd signed up for.

Because he hadn't wanted to add the pain of knowing all that—pain he knew the extent of—to Anja's grief. Because he hadn't been able to deal with his own grief over a man who hadn't deserved it.

He hadn't mentioned his fear that maybe *he'd* abandoned Anja just like their parents had. Didn't want to in case Anja didn't feel that way, and he'd put it in her mind. No, he'd rather keep that to himself. And, even without disclosing it, Dylan felt…hopeful. Hopeful that maybe their family could move past the hurt, the abandonment, the betrayal.

And perhaps that was why he'd agreed to take the trip. For the sake of closure. And as for taking Jess along… what was he supposed to do? Say no? That would have for sure sounded his sister's alarms, and he knew that she already had her suspicions about his relationship with Jess. He suspected the only reason she hadn't asked him about it was because she'd had the conversation with Jess, and she'd chosen to trust her friend's word on it.

Good thing, too, or the progress he and Anja had made might have been wiped away.

'I'm sorry,' Jess replied, interrupting his thoughts. 'I didn't realise civility required words.'

'Well, we have over an hour left of this trip, so if you're happy with being quiet for the rest—'

'I am,' she said quickly, and he frowned.

They weren't on the best terms, he knew, but this withdrawn, sullen person wasn't the Jess he'd got to know. She wasn't even the one he'd fought with that night that felt like so long ago, or the one he'd had the terse but somehow productive conversation with in the woods.

'Are you okay?' he asked.

'I thought we were going to be quiet?'

'And if I thought that you wanted to be quiet because you were annoyed with me, I would have been. Except that isn't the case.'

'You're an expert in my emotions now?'

'No, but I'm a good businessman and that requires being able to read people.' He glanced over, and then looked back at the road. 'It helps that I *do* know you.'

'I think you're overestimating your knowledge,' she said, but he could sense her resistance was waning.

'Or underestimating it,' he replied quietly. 'What's wrong?'

He saw her shake her head and then bite her lip. He didn't push, didn't say anything else since he understood her hesitation. Understood that he was responsible for it. They'd been put in a hell of a situation, he knew, but his behaviour hadn't helped.

He'd overreacted. Or he'd just reacted, he thought, to his trust being broken while he was still trying to deal with his mother breaking his trust. While he was still trying to deal with all the other things Jess had pointed out to him.

So he needed to apologise for taking it all out on her. And perhaps now was the time that he did.

'Look, if it's about what happened with us—'

'It's not.'

'No?'

'No.'

There was a beat of silence while he processed that, but then he said, 'Well, I wanted to apologise anyway. I reacted too harshly about the baby. It wasn't entirely…your fault.'

'Entirely,' she repeated, and he felt her gaze on him.

He sighed. 'I felt betrayed, Jess. I told you that.'

'And I told you why I couldn't tell you.'

'Yeah, and I understand that. But—' his grip tightened on the steering wheel '—but I wish you'd told me. Warned me.'

She didn't reply immediately. 'I…I couldn't just tell you. Firstly, I barely knew you. And when I started to get to know you,' she said as he opened his mouth to protest, 'Anja had already asked me not to say anything to you about it. So I didn't.' She cleared her throat. 'But I am sorry for my part in…in hurting you.'

He nodded, but couldn't bring himself to say anything. He appreciated her apology. Her loyalty to his sister. But… Well, he'd wanted Jess's loyalty, too. To him.

And that was the real problem.

'If it makes you feel any better,' she said quietly, 'it wasn't simple for me. I *wanted* to tell you. It felt…wrong not to. But—' she lifted her hands '—I couldn't betray Anja's trust. So I settled on telling you the baby wasn't mine and hoped that it would help you, I don't know, understand.'

Dylan felt some of the pieces that had broken inside him come together again. 'I…appreciate that. Thank you.' He paused. 'And I'm sorry, too. For reacting the way that I did. I shouldn't have…been so blunt. I didn't mean what I said about you not being a part of the family.'

She nodded, and the words were the last they said for another few kilometres.

'It wasn't just about you, you know,' he heard himself say into the silence. 'It was difficult for me to hear it because—' He broke off. Told himself to get it over with. 'When I found out my mother knew my father was an addict before she had us, it felt like a betrayal.'

'When did you find out?' she asked softly.

'A few days before his funeral.' He took a deep breath. 'They'd put all my father's stuff in a box at work after it was clear he wasn't coming back. Gave it to me when I first started. I put it in a storeroom and never looked through it until I got the news that he'd died.' Dylan paused, took another breath. 'When I did, I found meticulous records of his expenses dating back long enough for me to see how he'd paid off the house. How he'd set money aside for the staff, for us. And how he'd used everything else to fund his habit.'

'That must have been hard.'

'What was worse was that it proved my father had his problem long before we were born. Before my parents had even married. And when I confronted my mom about it—' he lifted a shoulder '—it didn't go well.'

'Oh, Dylan,' she said on an exhale. In those two words Dylan heard everything that Jess wanted to say. That she understood his reaction now. That she was sorry it had happened. It soothed something deep inside him.

'Does Anja…?'

'Yes,' he replied when she trailed off. 'I told her about it a few days ago. Hence this little family trip.'

'Are you okay with that?'

He took a moment to think about her question. About how she'd known to ask it. 'I'm not thrilled. Things were… awkward when I saw my mother at Christmas, and we didn't even end up speaking about it.'

'Maybe things were awkward *because* you didn't speak about it.'

'Maybe,' he murmured.

'So this trip might be exactly what you need to move through it.'

He let the words settle in his mind. Felt the hope of it fight back against the burn of betrayal. Maybe things *would* get better after this trip. Maybe, after finally being honest with one another, they would become a family. A real one, without the weight of betrayal and hurt and resentment hanging over them.

But hearing Jess's opinion spoke to his biggest regret. And now all he could think about was how things could have been sorted out so much sooner if he'd just come home.

Or if he'd never left.

'Things seem to be better between you and Anja now,' she said into the silence.

'Better, but not the same.' He ran a hand over his beard. 'It's going to take some time.'

'Of course it will. But progress is progress.'

'Except—' He stopped himself before he could say what he'd been thinking.

'Except?'

'It's nothing.'

'Oh, so you're going to keep quiet *now*?' she asked dryly, and he felt his lips lift.

'Annoying, isn't it?'

She grunted, and his smile widened into a full grin. And perhaps it was that that had him saying, 'I can't believe she didn't tell me about the baby. About any of her fertility issues.'

'It was…hard for her to talk about.'

'But we're *family*. And we were close before…' He let the words linger. They were another reminder of the mistakes he'd made.

'She thought she was a failure,' Jess said. 'I don't think she wanted to tell you and have you believe that of her, too.'

'*What?* Why would she feel that way? Why would *I* believe that?'

'Because she wasn't thinking logically. She was only thinking about how she couldn't do the one thing that she was supposed to be able to do as a woman.' Jess shrugged. 'I was there, Dylan. She was so hard on herself.'

The words made pain splinter through him. 'I wish I was here. I wish I could have helped her through it.'

'I know.'

'I shouldn't have left, Jess.'

It ripped from him, the admission.

He was suddenly incredibly grateful that a business crisis had delayed Chet and Anja's departure and they weren't travelling behind him and Jess. Dylan had agreed to go ahead with Jess so that they wouldn't have to tell their mother they would be late. It meant that he could take a few minutes to regroup, to recover from whatever had made him tell Jess the thing he worried about most.

He took the next exit, which led to a pit stop that he only realised was familiar after they stopped next to the small café. They'd stopped there on family trips, he remembered, when they'd taken the short journey to visit his mother's family. He didn't dwell on why the familiarity of it was suddenly comforting, or why he held out his hand when he got out of the car, waiting for Jess to take it.

All he knew was that he felt better when she did. More so when they stopped in front of the little pond next to the café, birds frolicking in the water, making the most of the sunny autumn day.

They stood in silence for a long time while he figured out why he'd stopped. But Jess spoke first.

'Do you know why you left, Dylan?'

'Yes.'

'Why?'

So he told her all the reasons he'd figured out himself over the past weeks. And when he was done she squeezed his hand.

'It's normal to turn away from the things you can't deal with,' Jess said. 'We all do it.'

'Anja didn't. She stayed here and faced it. The memories of it. The grief of it.' He watched as a duck dipped itself under the water and shook it off.

'Anja had Chet, Dylan. She had me. She had a support system. One outside of the family that had caused her pain.' He looked down at her. 'It makes a difference.'

'Why are you being so understanding?'

'Why are you determined to torture yourself like this?'

'I'm not—' He broke off, and shook his head. 'It's not

torture. It's the truth. I *abandoned* her. Just like our parents did.'

'You didn't abandon her. You took some time to figure out how you were feeling about your parents. About your childhood that was cut short. Did you do it in the right way?' she asked. 'Maybe not. Maybe you should have told Anja about what you'd found out. Maybe you should have shared how you were struggling with your grief and the anger. But that doesn't mean you abandoned her.'

'But my mother—'

'Was a flawed woman. And your father was a flawed man. So are you. We're all flawed,' she said with a smile. 'We all make mistakes. But we move on from them. We learn from them. And you being back tells me you *have* learnt from it.'

She faced him when he didn't reply, and narrowed her eyes. 'You're not only scared about that though, are you?' And only when she asked did he realise that he wasn't. 'What is it, Dylan?'

'I—' He stopped himself, but only for a moment. It was too late to play coy, and he was so tired of keeping it all to himself. 'Why did his death affect me so much? Why am I so unhappy and angry about it when I only really knew him for fourteen years?' He ran a hand over his head. 'Even *saying* that is generous.'

Her hand fell from his, and then lifted to cup his cheek. 'Maybe it's because you're still stuck in the hope that he could have been different.'

CHAPTER FIFTEEN

'WHICH IS FINE,' Jess told Dylan, dropping her hand. 'There's nothing wrong with wishing you had something you didn't.' It felt as if she was talking to herself. 'But you have to let go of the unrealistic expectations if you want to move on. If you want to move forward.'

'You're right,' he said after a moment.

'Don't sound so surprised.'

His lips lifted, taking some of the torture out of his eyes. 'I'm not. It's just…we have a lot in common, don't we?'

'I wasn't talking about me, Dylan.'

'Maybe not, but, despite what you might think, I've learnt how to read you. Enough,' he said before she could protest, 'that I know you were thinking about yourself, too, just now.' He turned to face her and took a step closer. 'Enough to know that something's wrong with you. Has been since before we even took this trip.'

She wanted to tell him that something *was* wrong. She wanted to share her fears with him just as he'd shared his with her. But it wouldn't help. She knew because when he'd told her that he hadn't meant it when he'd said she wasn't a part of their family she hadn't believed him.

'We should probably get back on the road.'

He stared at her for a few seconds, and then gave her

a curt nod. She almost sighed, but was afraid the sound would break whatever control had convinced Dylan that he shouldn't press. They were on the road a few minutes later, and Jess settled on looking out at the rolling hills, interspersed with long stretches of green fields and cattle, that they passed.

It was a pleasant trip, driving along the West Coast. Soon they would take the road that led to the coastal town of Langebaan, home to one of the most popular casinos in the Western Cape. The realisation made her think about Dylan's father, and whether his parents had met here, in this town. Whether it had been the start of his father's addiction.

Jess hoped that what she'd been able to offer Dylan at the pond had given him comfort. That it would be enough to help him work through what he was going through. And that once he had he would be able to turn to Anja when Jess was no longer there.

Because the more she thought about it, the more she realised that she had to leave. If she didn't have a purpose, what use would she be? She only had to look at her parents to know that. She only had to remember that they'd abandoned her long before she'd abandoned them. They'd done it from the moment she was born, no matter how hard she'd tried to prove herself.

Her father had rejected her even though she'd tried to make herself useful in the company. Her mother... Well, her mother had never really paid any attention to her. They'd never let her forget that her presence in their life hadn't been something they'd wanted.

And it turned out that being unwanted, feeling rejected—abandoned—were all pretty close together on the 'make Jess feel crappy' spectrum.

She hated that feeling. And she was still dealing with the remnants of it from her parents. She didn't need it from her friends, too. So she'd do what she'd done with her parents after she'd realised they wouldn't change and welcome her into their team. She would pull away, put distance between them, so that when the day came and she left, they wouldn't be so surprised.

Because *she* would leave, she thought. She would leave them before they left her.

'You've been quiet today,' Anja said from behind her.

Jess forced herself to give her friend an easy smile— even more so when she saw that Dylan was behind Anja— and went back to looking at the waves of the ocean in the distance.

Mia Nel's cottage was small but it was situated in the perfect position. Just outside the small town of Langebaan, where it was close enough to get whatever she needed within an hour, and far enough that there weren't many tourists around.

The beach was basically her backyard and for that alone, Jess told herself, the trip was worth it.

'It's been a long day,' Jess said as Anja and Dylan settled into the comfortable outdoor chairs on the small outdoor patio.

'It has been, but that's never stopped you from talking before,' Anja teased.

'Maybe it's this baby I'm carrying,' Jess teased back. 'Crazy genes can do that to you.'

'Oh, don't you dare blame my baby for your sullenness!' Anja's eyes twinkled, and then she grew serious. 'Are you sure you're okay though?'

'I'm fine.'

She felt Dylan's gaze on her, but she ignored it and kept her own gaze on the sea in front of her. It was a fair question. Jess knew that she'd been quiet since they'd arrived. She'd been sociable, of course. Had calmly accepted the love Mia had overwhelmed her with the moment they'd met.

But she'd kept herself from becoming too invested in the emotion. Because she knew it wasn't for her. It was for the baby she carried, and she couldn't forget it or avoid it. Ever since Anja had returned, the idea that Jess's time was running out had only grown.

She shook off the weight that settled on her shoulders at the thought of it. It was for the best. *Reject them before they can reject you*, a voice whispered into her mind.

She closed her eyes for a moment before asking Anja, 'So, what are the final accommodation arrangements for the trip?'

It did its job at distracting Anja, and Jess felt the air loosen in her lungs in relief. Though she couldn't deny it was also because she and Dylan would be spending the night in Mia's spare rooms, while Anja and Chet stayed in a cottage they'd rented a few doors down.

She didn't want to be alone with Dylan now. Not with his piercing gaze. Not with the knowing looks.

She felt as if he was looking straight through her. No, it felt as if he was looking straight *into* her. Into the part of her that was cowering like the little girl she'd been when she'd first realised her parents didn't care for her like other parents cared for their children.

It was annoying, being dragged back into the past. Which was why, as soon as the conversation lulled between the three of them, Jess excused herself for the night. She still had to face her demons, but if she wasn't near Anja and Dylan she wouldn't be tempted to belong.

She hoped.

'She's acting weird, isn't she?' Anja asked Dylan as soon as Jess left for the night.

'Yep.'

'Did she say anything to you on the way over?'

Do words of wisdom about my own emotional problems count?

'No. I asked, but she pretty much gave me the same answer she gave you when you asked.'

'It's so *strange*,' Anja said with a shake of her head. 'Jess isn't like this.' There was a beat of silence before she said, 'Do you know if something happened?'

He debated with himself about whether he should tell Anja. The truth had been working out pretty well for them. His relationship with Anja was slowly improving because of it. And he knew once they had a conversation with their mother they would finally get some closure.

Honesty had brought him a lot of what he'd wanted since he got back. Honesty and Jess. He sighed.

'It could be the fact that we...that I...'

Probably should have figured out what you were going to say before you started talking, dummy.

'It could be because of me.'

'Because of you?' Anja repeated in that slow way she had that told him she was trying to hide her real feelings.

'Yes. While you were gone, Jess and I...' He ran a hand over his head, again unsure of how to describe what had happened between him and Jess over those days before Anja had returned. 'We got close.'

'Got close?'

'Are you going to keep repeating what I say?'

'Yeah, I am. If that's what it takes to keep me from knocking your head against the table.'

And there it was, he thought, and braced for the on-slaught.

'Are you telling me, Dylan Theo Nel, that you are *seeing* my best friend? The woman carrying my child?'

'We're not seeing each other. Nothing that official.'

'Nothing...' He thought he saw the colour drain from

her face. 'Please don't tell me that "got close"—' she lifted her hands in air quotes '—is a metaphor for some kind of hanky-panky—' She broke off. 'I think I'm going to puke.'

'Oh, stop being so dramatic,' he said, though he'd expected the reaction. 'Nothing happened.' Not in the way she thought, at least. 'But we did have…something.'

'She told me I had nothing to worry about.'

'Because there was nothing to worry about when you asked her. We both knew something between us would be complicated, so neither of us wanted to pursue it.'

Again, not entirely the truth, but only because he was just realising what the truth was as he said it. *He* wanted to pursue it. He had wanted to pursue it from the moment he'd met her. From that first kiss. And still he wanted to. The realisation stumped him.

A long silence passed before Anja spoke again. 'When you say there was nothing to worry about when I asked, does that mean there is now?'

'Depends on whether you're worried about me and Jess being together.' As soon as he said it, he realised how much he wanted Anja to be okay with it. And suddenly the conversation took on a whole new importance. 'Are you?'

'Am I—? Hold on.' Anja lifted a hand. 'I'm trying to process everything you've just said in the last few minutes. It's going to take some time.'

Since he needed some time himself, he didn't say anything. Instead, he tested how he felt about this latest development.

Of course, he'd known there was something between him and Jess. What he *hadn't* known was how invested he was in that something.

It didn't make sense, he thought. At least not on paper. They'd only known each other for a few weeks. And only two days of that time had been spent on something resembling dating. The rest of the time they'd either been arguing or talking about things so difficult for them that dating had been the last thing on their minds.

But the facts couldn't explain why his heart thudded that much harder when she was around. Why he couldn't keep his eyes from straying to her. Why he wanted to see her reaction to jokes that were made, or stories that were told. Why he still thought about their kisses, and how much he wanted to repeat them.

It didn't explain why he felt so comfortable that he *could* talk to her about things. Or why he sensed that she was unhappy about something. No, the facts couldn't explain any of that. And it was finally occurring to him why that was.

He was falling for his sister's best friend. The woman carrying his niece or nephew. The woman he'd only just met.

And none of the reasons he'd told himself why that was a bad idea seemed to matter any more.

His lips curved.

'Okay, I'm done thinking,' Anja said, and Dylan hid his smile. He didn't want her to think that he was mocking her. 'I'm not going to say that I'm happy about this development. It's messy. And complicated. And, I don't know, it feels incestuous.'

Dylan frowned at what he once again thought was an exaggeration, but kept the opinion to himself.

'But clearly whatever's going on between you and Jess…means something. To both of you.'

'Not sure I'd go that far,' he muttered.

'No,' Anja said immediately. 'Me not totally freaking out about this does not mean I'm going to counsel you on Jess's feelings.' She frowned, and then sighed. 'Except to say that Jess was…hurt by her parents. It takes a long time for her to trust, and if you've done something stupid— which, knowing you, you probably have—it'll take longer

for her to get there. But now that you've mentioned it—'
she slid a hand through her hair '—I did notice *something*
between you. Coming from both sides.'

'Really?' he asked, and was only slightly disgusted by
the optimism he heard in his voice.

Anja's face broke into a smile. 'Yes, you dork. Now,
back to what I was saying. It's complicated, and it's messy,
but…but if it's what you two want, then I'll support it. Just
don't, you know, do it, until my baby is out of the way.'

'Firstly, what is wrong with you? And secondly…
thanks, An.'

'Don't thank me yet,' she said and stood. 'I'm going to
be pretty miserable about this for the foreseeable future.'

'Completely understandable.'

She narrowed her eyes, and then sighed. 'Don't complicate things if it's not worth it, okay?'

'Okay.'

'And don't…don't hurt my friend.'

'I won't.'

Anja left with those words, and Dylan sat back with
a smile, watching the waves crash into the boulders and
then pull away. It hadn't been the easiest conversation to
have but, once again, Dylan felt that his honesty had paid
off. Not only because he'd told his sister the truth about
things that had happened between him and Jess, but because it had clarified a lot for him.

First, it *was* worth it.

Second, he would do his best not to hurt Jess.

And third, he was going to convince Jess of both those
points, no matter how long it took.

CHAPTER SIXTEEN

'So,' Jess said the next afternoon, 'I just had a chat with Anja. And it was…surprising, to say the least.'

She and Dylan were at the restaurant where they'd all just had lunch. She'd spent the morning walking through town—if it could be called walking, considering the number of times she'd rested—while Dylan, Anja and Chet had spent the morning with Mia. She hadn't minded entertaining herself. Understood that the reason they were there was so that those conversations could happen.

But that afternoon they'd all had lunch together. Afterwards, Mia had an appointment with a friend, and Anja and Chet had decided to drive to the next town to buy some things for the baby. Which left her and Dylan alone.

Handy, considering she had a bone to pick with him.

'You told her that we kissed?'

'What? No, of course not.'

'Then why did she follow me to the bathroom to tell me that she's okay with us being together?'

'She did that?' His lips twitched, but he shook his head. 'I'm sorry, I didn't realise she would speak to you about it.'

'*It*? What is *it*?'

'I…might have told Anja that there was *something* between us. Not that we'd kissed or anything,' he said quickly. 'But that there was…something.'

She opened her mouth, and then shut it again. Figured it would be better to keep the first words that wanted to come out of her mouth to herself rather than hurl them at him. But the entire exchange had made her feel sick, and she drank from the bottle of water she'd ordered with her meal before she spoke.

'So, let me get this straight. You told my best friend—the mother of the child I'm carrying—that there was *something* between us.'

'Yes.'

'Why?'

'Because there *is* something between us.'

'No, there isn't.' He gave her a look, and she gritted her teeth. 'Maybe there *was*, but we both know that there can't be.'

'Why not?'

'Because…' She trailed off, realising now that her main reason had been Anja, and that no longer seemed to be a problem. 'Because I'm carrying your niece or nephew and you don't agree with that choice,' she finished triumphantly.

'What?' he said, his face twisted. 'That's not true.'

'Isn't it?' she asked mildly. 'Because I distinctly remember your objections to me being a surrogate for someone else.'

'That was before I knew it was Anja's baby.'

'So your concerns aren't valid any more because this baby is your sister's?'

He ran a hand over his head, and she recognised the action as something he did when he was thinking. 'No,' he said finally. 'They still are. But I guess at least I know I'll be there for you now. We all will be. So, you know, you won't have to go through whatever you go through alone.'

It took her a while to figure out how she felt about his words. About the fact that he assumed he would be there for her. That they all would be there for her. It was as if he knew exactly what her biggest fear was, and was speaking directly to it.

It melted her damn heart.

But it couldn't, she told herself. Because it wasn't real. She wasn't only deluding herself into believing that it was.

'So that made you comfortable enough to tell Anja about us?'

'Well,' he said, leaning forward, 'we both noticed you haven't been yourself the last few days. She asked me about it yesterday and I told her that…it might have been because of me.'

She stared at him, and then she laughed. 'You are *so* full of yourself.'

His eyebrows lifted. 'You're saying I'm wrong?'

'I'm pretty sure I told you that you were in the car on our way here.'

'So I don't have anything to do with the way you've been acting lately? Nothing?' he repeated, as though, somehow, repeating it would change her mind.

It didn't, but it *did* point out that while he wasn't entirely the reason for her pulling away, he was certainly a part of it.

'There's too much going on for me to simplify it like that,' she replied softly. 'And you telling Anja makes it… worse.'

'Why?'

'Because now she has another reason—' She stopped herself from saying the words. From saying that Anja knowing about whatever had happened between her and Dylan would just give her another reason to abandon Jess when it was all over.

She'd been surprised when Anja had spoken to her earlier, and her first thought—her first fear, she knew, remembering how her throat had closed—had been that.

And even though her friend had told her she was fine

with it, could Jess believe her? And if she could, how would she work? Would she date Dylan and be forced to see how little she meant to their family day after day?

'Jess,' Dylan said, his expression telling her that he'd been trying to get her attention for some time. 'What's going on with you?'

'Nothing.'

'It's *not* nothing,' he said, and slammed a hand on the table. She resisted a wince, and met his eyes evenly.

'You don't have to believe me. But I'm not going to tell you. No matter how hard you slam your hand against the table.'

'I'm sorry,' he said, but his jaw was still clenched. 'You're just so damn *stubborn*. It's frustrating.'

His brows were knitted together, the anger clear in the planes of his face. And all she could think about was how cute he was when he was angry. She sighed at the flutter in her stomach.

'Don't feel like you have to entertain me for the afternoon. I wouldn't want to frustrate you more than I already have.'

'Jessica.' It was said on a soft exhale of air, and again she watched Dylan rub a hand over his face. 'I don't know what I'm going to do with you.'

'You don't have to do anything with me.'

'Except that I want to.' His hand fell down to the table. 'Hell if I know why, but I want…you.'

Her heart thudded, and she gripped the napkin that had been beside her hand tightly in her fist. 'Is that why you told Anja? Because you *want* me?'

'I told Anja because I wanted to be honest with her. You encouraged me, remember?' She nodded, unable to speak. 'So I decided to go for it. To put everything on the line. And it's been working. Really well. We've finally made…progress. Real progress. In our relationship, *and* with Mom. So when she asked me, I thought I'd be—' he shrugged '—honest.'

She couldn't argue with his logic. Not when she could see how freeing it had been for him. 'I'm glad it's been working for you. I just wish you'd come to speak with me before you told her. Or, at the very least, warned me that you *had* told her.'

'I am sorry for that. But I meant what I said earlier. I didn't think she'd actually talk to you.' He shook his head. 'I should have known that she would, though. You're best friends.'

She didn't reply. Not when he made it sound so simple— so *special*—and she didn't know if it was.

'There's somewhere I want to take you.'

'What?'

'You said I didn't have to spend the afternoon with you, but as soon as I found out we'd be alone I knew I wanted to. So you don't have much of a choice.' He grinned at her, and called the waitress to get the bill.

'Are you kidnapping me?'

'Do I have to?' he said wryly, and she couldn't help the curve of her lips.

'It probably wouldn't look good for you, kidnapping a pregnant woman.'

'I could do it,' he said sombrely. 'For the greater good.'

She snorted. 'What greater good? Keeping your afternoon plans?'

'Exactly. Now, are you going to come with me, or do I have to resort to Plan B?'

'And you called *me* frustrating,' she replied, rolling her eyes, and got up with Dylan as soon as he paid the bill.

He chatted as they walked and, since that wasn't the kind of word she'd thought she'd ever associate with Dylan, it made her think that he was nervous. The thought was just as unwelcome as when she'd thought him angry and cute, but this time she didn't push it away.

Instead, she chose to indulge herself.

She was walking along the beach with a handsome man. A man who'd said he *wanted* her. The thrill she'd forced away before went through her spine now, and she relished it. It wouldn't be long before reality set in again. Before she was forced to face it and the fact that Dylan would tire of her eventually. He would figure out that *wanting* was temporary, and needing soon replaced it.

And no one had needed Jess in a long time.

So, for now, she would enjoy it.

Jess looked up when Dylan stopped walking, and for the first time noticed that they'd reached the pier.

'Are we going to be…watching the boats go by?' she asked when the seconds passed and he didn't say anything. It was the only thing she could think of, since there was no one around except a large boat at the edge of the pier and others in the distance.

'No,' he replied. Were those nerves she heard in his voice? 'We're going to watch for whales.'

'Really?' She perked up. 'That's awesome. Can you see them from here?'

'No,' he said again, and now she *definitely* heard the nerves. 'But we can see them from the boat.'

He nodded in the direction of the boat she'd noticed earlier, and she frowned. 'You mean we're going to…sit on that boat and watch the whales? I guess that would work, but—'

'No, Jess. We're going whale-watching in that boat. With it doing what it's supposed to do. You know, sail.' He lifted a hand, and then dropped it again. 'I hired the boat for the afternoon.'

CHAPTER SEVENTEEN

'YOU HIRED...?' JESS's voice faltered. And then she said, 'You hired a boat for this afternoon. For...a day trip? With a couple of people?'

Her reaction was making his spur-of-the-moment decision seem like a bad one. And he hadn't thought it was. At first. But from the moment they'd left the restaurant, he'd been thinking exactly that. She was *not* dissuading him of that notion.

'No, for the two of us. I wanted you to be comfortable, and I thought that it might give you a break from thinking about...whatever's going on with you.'

He held his breath as she considered his words.

'I have one question for you,' she said after what felt like for ever, turning to him. The wind fluttered through her hair, making the wavy strands of it stir. He felt the movement mirrored in his chest.

'What?'

'Are you going to take your shirt off?'

It took him a moment to realise she was teasing him, and the only reason he did was the saucy grin she gave him that had different parts of his body stirring.

'Only if you plan on watching me,' he said in a growl.

She pretended to think about it. 'Well, there *is* an art

to it.' Paused. 'And I *have* become somewhat of an expert on watching you without your shirt on—'

He cut her off with a kiss. Quick and hard. And pulled away before he could be tempted into savouring the taste of her lips—or the surprise on her face. Instead, he took her hand and led her to the boat.

He helped her on board, and then handed her a safety vest before putting on his own. When he was done, he nodded to the captain and they were off.

He'd been teasing her when he'd told her she should watch him. Which was ironic now, considering that he couldn't keep *his* eyes off *her*. She was captivating. She grabbed his arm whenever she saw something—or thought she saw something—her face alight with excitement. And clasped her hands together when that something turned out to be a whale.

They were lucky enough to spot a seal at one point, too, and the absolute glee in her expression made every reservation he'd had about taking her on a boat trip worthwhile.

'I can't believe I've never been on one of these before,' she said as the captain turned the boat around. She accepted the water he'd got from the bar, and drank from it thirstily before continuing. 'It feels like it should be a compulsory experience for everyone at least once in their lifetime.'

'I'm glad you enjoyed it,' he said with a smile, and sat back, enjoying his own drink.

'Oh, don't be so smug. There was very little chance I wouldn't have enjoyed it.'

'There was enough of a chance. What if you got seasick? A high possibility, considering you're pregnant.'

Her hand immediately went to her belly. 'I didn't really suffer from motion sickness before, and I'm happy to say carrying this little guy or girl hasn't changed that.'

'How has it been?' he heard himself ask.

'The pregnancy?' He couldn't pretend he hadn't asked. He nodded. 'Good, for the most part. I was exhausted the first trimester. Still am, though it hasn't been quite as debilitating since.'

'Do you enjoy being pregnant? You don't have to answer that if you don't want to,' he said quickly when she frowned.

'No, it's not that. I just haven't really thought about it.'

The hand on her belly started to move, and he watched as she drew little circles, over and over, around her stomach. It wasn't the first time he'd seen her do it, but it *was* the first time a small, unknown part of him had stirred.

'It hasn't been a bad experience so far,' she said. 'I know it can be, so I'm one of the lucky ones who doesn't puke at every opportunity. So, I guess physically I don't mind it.'

'You don't mind that your body won't ever be the same again?'

She gave him a look. 'Is that really the question you're going with?'

He felt heat creep onto his face. 'I didn't mean it like that.' And then he wondered what 'like that' meant, and the heat become fiercer. 'I just… I don't know. Forget it.'

She laughed and, mingled with the sound of the water crashing against the boat, it sounded magical. 'Oh, I know what you meant. It was just too good an opportunity to miss.' She tilted her head, and then looked out at the sea. 'It's not that I don't mind it. I just keep thinking that it'll be worth it.'

'Even though it isn't your child?'

She looked at him, and it almost made him regret asking. But she answered him.

'Yes, I think so.' There seemed to be a long time between her answer and the next words she said. 'Anja was… devastated after the miscarriage.' She lifted a hand. Let it drop. 'That doesn't even seem like the right word to use.

It's too…neat. Tidy. It doesn't describe how she sobbed every day for two weeks. Her entire body wrenched from it.' He saw her fingers curl, tighten. And couldn't blame her when he looked down and saw his fingers had done the same.

'Giving her the chance to have the child she wanted so badly without going through the fear of that again…' She lifted her shoulders. 'Yeah, I guess it is worth it. Even though it isn't my own.'

'You really love her, don't you?'

'I do.' Her eyes filled and she looked away from him. Even when he took her hand and squeezed.

The rest of the trip was quiet, and Dylan worried that Jess had pulled back into herself again. By the time they reached the pier again, he knew that he was right. But he didn't say anything about it as he helped her off the boat, and said his thanks to the captain.

'We should get back to your mom's place,' Jess said softly when they reached the edge of the pier.

'Sure,' he said easily. 'I know a shortcut. It cuts across the beach though.'

'I don't mind,' she replied after a second, and shifted, looking down at her shoes longingly.

He smiled. 'Need help?'

She gave him an embarrassed grin. 'Would you mind?'

'Sure.'

He bent down and helped her out of her shoes. While he was there, he took off his own and soon they were walking down the beach.

The sky was a soft orange-yellow colour, an indication of the time of day. It had been a nice day, he thought. One of the few they'd get before winter came in full force. Even now he could feel the chill of the cool autumn air, and looked at Jess, wondering if she was getting cold.

But her face was turned up to the sun, her eyes closed,

and his feet stopped. Hell, his entire world stopped. She looked like an angel. The light made her bronze skin glow, highlighted the brown of her hair. For the first time he saw the almost blonde strands in between the dark brown, and the discovery had him reaching out to her, taking her hand before he knew what he was doing.

She opened her eyes and turned to look at him, and the easy expression on her face turned guarded. 'What? What is it?'

'You're beautiful, Jess.'

Her face went red, and he kept her hand in his, not allowing her to turn from him. She wouldn't push him away this time.

'Don't do this, please.'

'Do what?' he asked her softly, tugging at her hand so that she came closer to him. 'Are you asking me not to tell you how beautiful you are? Because I'm not going to stop doing that, Jess. Not when you're the most beautiful woman I've ever seen.'

'Yes, that,' she said exasperatedly. 'You're making it harder.'

'What are you talking about?' But she only shook her head.

It angered him. And anger had him taking her hand and putting it around his waist. He reached his other hand around her waist, and now she had no choice but to look at him.

'You're driving me crazy, Jess. You have been from the moment we got into that car to come here. You give me cryptic answers to simple questions, and there's *pain* in your eyes, damn it.' He tightened his hold on her, afraid of what letting go might mean. 'Do you know what it does to me, to see you in pain?' He barely waited for the slight shake of her head. 'It *kills* me. I don't know how it happened, but I care about you and I can't seem to escape how much I want it to be the same for you.'

'You don't mean it, Dylan.' Vulnerability crept onto her face, and for the first time he saw more than pain. He saw *fear*.

'How can you tell me I don't mean what I feel?'

'Because you *can't*,' she whispered. 'How can you feel that way about me when my parents, who've known me my entire life, don't?'

He felt her arm drop from his waist, but she didn't move away from him. Because of it, he could see the sheen of tears in her eyes.

Because of it, he could brush them away from her cheeks when they fell.

'It's only a matter of time before you, and Anja, and Chet realise there's something about me that's…that's *un-lovable*. You'll realise that I'm no longer useful once this baby is born and I'll have to pick up the pieces of my heart when I'm no longer in your lives.'

Her breath shuddered from her lungs, and she rested her head on his chest. It completely undid him. The simple action. The complicated emotions. He held on to her tightly. As though somehow he could squeeze those insecurities—those absolutely ludicrous insecurities—out of her.

But her words had cleared up a lot for him. She was afraid the people she loved most in the world would abandon her. And it made sense, too, since the people who were *supposed* to love her most in the world had.

And she was scared about her surrogacy. For once, he thought, she'd had a natural reaction to her unusual situation. And now he knew where *his* hesitation had come from, too. From a fear that she would be hurt. That giving the baby she carried to someone else would damage her in a way she wouldn't be able to recover from.

But *her* fear was much less selfish than that. She was

scared Anja wouldn't want her any more. And in that moment Dylan suddenly realised how much Jess loved his family. His thoughts went back to everything she'd said about carrying the baby, about doing it for Anja, and he realised that she already *was* a part of his family. She just hadn't realised it yet.

But, most importantly, her words had made him realise how wrong she was. Because she *was* lovable.

Because *he* loved her.

CHAPTER EIGHTEEN

IT WAS INCREDIBLE, the things Dylan could get her to reveal. She looked up into those eyes that saw everything, into the arresting features of his face, and knew she didn't have a chance against the onslaught of emotions.

If she added how full her heart felt because of the way his arms held her close to him, as though he would never let her go, she was helpless.

And hopelessly in love.

'I'm sorry, I shouldn't—'

'No,' he said, cutting her off. 'You should have. We might not know what we are yet, Jess, but you can tell me anything. And I'll be there to listen.'

A lump sat in her throat. 'You don't—'

'I do, and you're going to stop doubting it.' He pulled back from the embrace, both her hands in his now. 'I know you've been hurt. And abandoned. You shouldn't have been, Jess. You didn't deserve it.' His eyes were hot, serious, and she almost, almost believed him. 'You didn't deserve it, Jess. I'm saying it again because I need you to hear me. To believe me.'

Was her face that obvious to read? 'I do.'

'No, you don't. And that's fine for now. Because we believe what our experiences teach us, and your experiences haven't shown you that you can believe me.' He paused. 'Or they have, but you haven't seen it.'

'What do you mean?'

'How long have you been friends with Anja?'

'You know the answer to that,' she said softly. 'Two years.'

'Has she done anything in the last two years to make you believe that she wouldn't be there for you once the baby's here?'

She shook her head.

'Then why do you think that she won't be?'

She couldn't answer him when the lump in her throat doubled. It was accompanied by tears burning in her eyes. It took all of a few seconds for them to roll down her cheeks and, for the second time, Dylan brushed them away.

He had a tender look on his face, and she hated what it did to her heart. No, that wasn't true. She didn't hate it at all. But she *was* afraid of it. Because she'd never felt this way before, about anyone, and she didn't know if she could trust him...

'What's it going to take for you to believe me?'

'Kiss me,' she heard herself say. Surprised herself with the words. But then she wanted it more than she'd thought possible. 'I want you to kiss me and make me believe that—'

His lips were on hers before she got a chance to finish her sentence, and she sank into the kiss. Sank into the moment.

For her, the moment was goodbye. It was setting aside the hope he'd stirred in her, and placing the love she'd only just discovered she had for him in a box somewhere inside her, to visit, to cherish whenever she felt strong enough.

But goodbye had never felt so good in her life. It had never come with a strong man holding her in her arms, with his hands caressing her body. It had never caused her spine to tingle, and her breasts to ache. She pressed closer to him, wanting to give him all that she had inside. Wanting to tell him how much he meant to her. Wanting to make sure that one day, when she was no longer there, he'd remember this kiss on the beach.

That he'd remember the passion, the tenderness. That he'd remember how her hands felt on his body, sliding up, underneath his shirt, kneading, skimming. That he'd remember the moan he gave when she scraped her nails lightly over his back, and the one that came from her when he nipped at her lip in response.

They drew away from each other, breath shuddering from their lungs, and then Dylan lifted his hand and set it on her cheek, his gaze intense as it met hers.

'I'm not going anywhere, Jess. And I'm going to prove it to you.' His thumb grazed across her cheek. 'You can believe me.'

'Why?' she asked, her heart hurting. 'Why is it so important that I believe you?'

'Because I love you.'

He stopped her reply with another kiss, and this time she was swept away in it. She didn't think about what he'd just told her, only felt it, and allowed the sweetness of his kiss to convince her to believe it.

And it did.

The time when they kissed, when their tongues tangled with one another in a sweetly intense duel, Jess believed that Dylan loved her. That he wouldn't leave. She could see herself as a part of his world, as a part of his family. She would give birth to Anja's child, and she'd still be a part of their lives.

Her own life wouldn't change all that much. She'd get a new job and find her own place, but she'd still see the people who'd changed her life so much. And there would be a baby she'd share a special bond with, who would enrich her life further.

Fantasy, she thought, but gave herself a few more minutes of it before pulling back.

'Dylan,' she said hoarsely.

'Hmm?' He smiled when he looked at her, but it faded. 'What?'

'We can't—'

'No,' he said, taking a step back. She immediately felt colder, and only then noticed the sun had lowered and it was dusk. 'Don't say that we can't. Say that you don't. Because that would be the only reason why we can't.'

She opened her mouth, tried to say what she needed him to believe. But she couldn't. Because she'd been hurt in her life by rejection, by abandonment, she wouldn't hurt someone else in the same way. Especially when it wasn't true.

'You feel the same way.' The darkness that had been on his face lifted.

'I didn't say that.'

'Because you're scared.'

He saw right through her, she thought, and resented it so very much. 'How far is your mother's place from here?'

'Jess—'

'How far?' she asked tersely.

'A couple hundred metres.'

'So let's get to it.'

She walked in the direction she remembered he'd been leading them in, and sighed in relief when he fell into step beside her silently. She didn't want to talk any more. Not to him, not to Anja. All she wanted was to go home and—

She cut her own thoughts off when she realised she'd thought about Dylan's house when she'd pictured home. That she'd thought about *him*. It had her feet stopping. Had her grabbing his hand, pulling it and forcing him to stop with her.

'I love you, too, Dylan,' she said hoarsely. 'But it doesn't change anything. It can't,' she said when she saw him open his mouth. 'It can't change anything because I'm…I'm not strong enough to deal with whatever might happen if this doesn't work out.'

'It'll work out.'

'You don't know that,' she said, and shook her head. 'No, it's just better for us to…'

Her voice faded as she realised she didn't know what would be better. Or, she thought, what would be worse. For her to fall into this web of hope they'd spun around them, only to find out she'd been fooling herself—she'd been fooling her heart—in the process? Or to ignore it, and constantly be tempted by the hope—the *love*—that Dylan was telling her to believe in?

She had to figure it out, and she couldn't do it with Dylan by her side.

'I'm not going anywhere,' Dylan said softly, and for the briefest moment Jess thought that she'd spoken out loud.

'You say that now.'

'So, I won't say it any more,' he replied simply. 'I'll show you.'

He leaned forward, kissed her forehead, and then continued walking back to his mother's cottage. After a moment Jess followed, her head and her heart a mess.

Since Dylan had never told a woman outside of his family that he loved her, he wasn't quite sure what should happen afterwards. But having her avoid being alone with him… Well, it was safe to say that that hadn't even made his list of possible consequences.

Especially since she'd told him she loved him, too.

And yet, as soon as they reached the cottage that night, Jess excused herself for the evening. And then she made sure that there weren't any more opportunities for them to be alone for the rest of the trip.

It was fairly crafty—it clearly required a lot of manoeuvring—and, if Dylan was honest with himself, she impressed him with her efforts. She woke up before he did, disappeared for a walk on the beach and only returned when everyone had arrived for breakfast. If she woke up later than he did, she would only appear after his mother had already got up and would dive into the breakfast preparations, using it as an excuse not to speak with him.

She went to bed before he did. Stuck to his mother's side at every spare moment. When Anja arrived, she'd switch between the two. And Anja was the perfect deterrent, he thought, remembering how she only needed to send him a look when he tried to get Jess alone and he would abandon his efforts.

If he hadn't understood it—expected it, even, knowing what he did about Jess now—he would have been more offended. But he *did* understand. He understood that she was scared. Terrified, he corrected himself, thinking about her expression on the beach. And the only way she would get over that fear was if he showed her that she had nothing to be scared of.

Which he could focus on now, he thought, since his trip to Langebaan had been somewhat successful.

Their conversations with their mother had been... hard. Hard and painful and, at times, ugly. His mother had greeted him with the nerves, the hesitation he'd come to expect from her. That had always been her personality, though he couldn't deny that there had been a part of him hoping she'd come out of her shell after their father's death.

But it seemed his death hadn't changed that much for his mother. When Anja had asked her why she'd chosen to have them, knowing what their father was, she'd broken down. Had defended him at first and, when he and

Anja had refused to accept that, had admitted it had been selfish.

But the more they talked—and it had been strange going between tense, difficult discussions and meals with Jess where everyone pretended nothing was wrong—the more Dylan realised it had been more about *hope* than selfishness. He'd heard it loud and clear in the way his mother had described the joy of feeling them grow, move inside her. Of sharing that with their father.

She'd told them her pregnancies had been the only time he'd been the kind of man she'd always wanted him to be. And Dylan had finally realised that he and Anja had been his mother's hope that he would *stay* that man. That each day after they'd been born she'd hoped for that man to pitch up again. And each day, when that man hadn't—when it became clear he'd left for good—she'd mourned.

She'd broken down in front of them. Had told them how sorry she was for failing them by loving their father. By abandoning them. Hearing the words, the apology, had loosened something inside Dylan. Perhaps because for the first time he believed that she wanted to make up for it. And that maybe she would finally become the woman—the mother—Dylan had always hoped she would be.

It didn't magically allow him to forgive her. And it hadn't done much to change his opinion of his father. But it *had* made him think that things weren't as black and white as he'd thought. Perhaps if he'd still been alive, Dylan could have had the same conversation with his father. Maybe that would have given Dylan a glimpse into the psyche of the man he'd resented all his life. Maybe it would have helped Dylan to understand him.

Now, Dylan realised that his grief was part dealing with his father's abandonment, half wishing that he hadn't died so that Dylan could have tried to understand him sooner.

The guilt that came from that—the regret—had merged with his anger and that had made Dylan *grieve*.

He knew it would take him time to work through it all, but Dylan was choosing to move forward. Moving forward meant working on forgiving his parents for not being who he'd wished they had been. For abandoning them. It meant working on accepting who his mother was, and learning to move on from who his father had been. It meant appreciating the closeness he and Anja had started forging again, and making sure that she knew he would never jeopardise their relationship as he had in the past.

And, most of all, moving forward meant making sure Jess knew he was serious about showing her he loved her.

'This must be torture for you,' he said mildly into the silence in the car. Jess might have been able to avoid him in Langebaan, but on their way home it was just the two of them. He almost enjoyed the sound of her shifting in her seat.

'I don't know what you're talking about.'

'Of course you do,' he replied. 'You hate being alone with me.'

'That's not true.'

'Really? Because I clearly recall you honing the skill of avoiding it over the last few days.'

'I did—' She broke off when he gave her a look, and then sighed. 'I don't hate being alone with you. I just know that being alone with you is…tempting.'

He felt his lips curve. *'Tempting?'*

'Yes, tempting.' His head turned in time to see her roll her eyes. 'You know you are.'

'And I'm not even shirtless,' he said with a smirk, and chuckled when she slapped at his hand on the gear knob. He let the silence that fell on them sit, felt her get restless as it did. He didn't mean for it to make her uncomfortable enough to talk to him, but he couldn't deny he didn't appreciate it when she spoke.

'I don't get it. I don't get *you*.'

'What are you talking about?'

'Why are you…why is this…why don't you sound annoyed with me?'

'Oh, I'm annoyed with you,' he replied easily. 'I'm pretty annoyed, actually.'

'I know I shouldn't have avoided you, but it was easier than—'

'And that's why I'm annoyed,' he interrupted. 'Not because you avoided *me*, but because you're avoiding your feelings for me. That you see them as complicated.'

'And you don't?'

'No.'

'You really don't think our admission of love for one another is going to complicate our lives when we get back?'

His heart did a flip. 'No. Because it won't.'

Seconds passed, and Dylan felt himself grow anxious, the easiness of the silence before gone.

'You know I'm moving out of Anja's place soon, right?' she said finally, and he softly exhaled the air he didn't realise he'd been holding in his lungs.

'When?'

'Chet told me he'll be finishing work on my flat the end of next week.'

'Okay.'

Minutes passed this time. 'And I'm not going to work for Anja after the baby is born.'

'You're…' His hand tightened on the wheel. 'Does Anja know?'

'Not yet. I'll tell her, though.'

'When?'

'At the right time.'

'I don't think there's going to be a right time for that conversation,' he muttered.

But she replied seriously, 'Probably not. But I can't work for her any more. Especially not after I give birth.'

'Is that your plan, Jess?' he asked quietly. 'You're going to push away the people who love you?'

'I'm going to *protect* myself.'

'No, you're pushing us away.' Dylan told himself to stay calm. 'I know what it's like to be abandoned. And I know the fear that it'll happen again can make you want to abandon the people you care about before they can abandon you.' He only then realised how true his words were.

'I'm not abandoning anyone,' she said. 'I'm trying to make sure this whole process is…easier on all of us.'

He didn't reply immediately. Instead, he took his time thinking about what he wanted to tell her. 'Do you know what this trip made me realise?'

'What?'

'That that fear of abandonment will stay with you until you let the people who love you show you it won't happen.' He let out a shaky breath. 'After my father died, I didn't give my mother a chance to tell me why she'd done what she'd done. And, now that she has, it's helped me to understand and…it'll help me to forgive.'

'Are you telling me to…give my parents a chance?'

'That's entirely up to you. But no. What I meant was that you have to give people chances. You have to give *us* a chance.' He reached over, took her hand. 'We're your family, Jess. Give us a chance to show you that we won't let you down.'

CHAPTER NINETEEN

'BUT YOU'RE NOT my family,' Jess told him with a clenched jaw. 'That's the whole point of this. I'm *not* a part of your family,' she said again, her voice cracking. 'I'm not even a part of my *own* family.'

It still hurt. She *hated* that it still hurt. And that perhaps it always would.

'Then maybe it *would* help to give your parents a chance.'

Surprise had a laugh spilling from her lips. Not because his suggestion was funny, but because it was *ludicrous*. 'I *have* given my parents a chance. I've given them *countless* chances.' She paused. Let the hurt pass through her now. 'They haven't tried to find me in two years, Dylan. They've made what they think about my chances pretty clear.'

'You haven't tried to get in touch with them either,' he reminded her.

'Because I shouldn't have had to. *I'm* the child. I'm *their* child. If they don't care enough about me to find out where I am, why should I care about them?'

'And you're happy with that?'

'I have to be.'

'Jess—'

'Enough, Dylan,' she interrupted. 'Nothing you say is

going to convince me that I need to speak with my parents. I know where I stand with them. Even though they haven't heard from me in two years—even though they don't know where I am—they've never tried to find me.'

'You don't know that.'

'I do,' she said, exhausted now. 'And that's the point. I *know* they haven't looked for me. Their only child. I've made it easier for them by leaving. I've made it easier for *myself*. Now I don't have to constantly feel unloved and unwanted. Now I can just move on and—'

'And let *us* love and want you.'

'No.'

'Yes,' he disagreed. 'Look—' he sighed '—maybe I shouldn't have suggested you see your parents. But I just… I just wanted to help take away that pain in your voice.'

'I…appreciate it. But—'

'I'm not done yet,' he interjected. 'You might have had a painful experience with your own family, but you have a new one. A better one. *Our* family.' He reached over and set his hand on hers, where they rested in her lap. 'You're a part of our family, whether you like it or not, Jess. I've had conversations with Anja that have told me you were long before you agreed to carry her child. You are now. And you will be after you give birth, too.'

Tears burned in her eyes and of course there was no way she was able to hold them back. He looked over at her and a few seconds later he pulled the car to the side of the road and drew her into his arms.

She heard her sobs before her mind registered that she was crying. And, once it did, nothing could stop them from wrenching through her. He murmured comfortingly to her, pressed kisses into her hair, and she stayed in his arms as long as she could. Even when the sobs passed, she stayed. And wished she could stay for ever.

But she couldn't, and minutes later she withdrew from

his arms. She accepted the tissues he offered her—heaven only knew where'd he got them—and tried to compose herself.

'Sorry,' she said hoarsely.

'Don't apologise.'

'It's pregnancy.'

He smiled. 'Sure.'

'And…well, you know.'

His smile widened. 'I do.'

But, after a few more moments, Jess said, 'Thank you for this.' She waved a hand between them. 'And for all you've said. But—' she inhaled, and then blew out the air shakily '—I'm not ready to…be *in* this. Not until—'

'You're sure I mean what I've said?'

'No,' she said, and then sighed when he shot her a look. 'Okay, maybe. But we both have a lot to deal with when we get back. I have my new place, I need to find a new job, and there's—' she lifted her hands '—the baby. And you just got back after being away for two years. I'm sure you'll have a lot to do at work here, and with your family…'

She faded when she realised it all sounded like excuses. And when she saw the way he was studying her.

She wondered if he could see that her admission of love for him had broken something inside her. That it had healed something, too. That his admission of love had made her want, need, hope for things she hadn't dared give herself permission to want, need or hope for before. That all of it had fear and panic beating inside her in an uncomfortable rhythm and she needed time to deal with it.

'I can give you time, Jess,' Dylan said, and Jess wondered if she'd said aloud what she'd been thinking. Or maybe he could just see through her, like she suspected.

'I can give you all the time you need,' he continued, and something flickered in his eyes that made her heart throb. 'Just…don't push me away. Don't push any of us away. Let us figure it all out. Together.'

Feeling a little helpless, she nodded, and after another few moments Dylan pulled his car back onto the road. For the rest of the trip, Jess couldn't help but think about what had happened over the last few weeks. And each time she did, she wondered one thing:

What if I believe him?

'Do you think Anja will ever get over the fact that I got another job?'

They were at Dylan's house. A fire was crackling in front of them, rain slamming against the windows around them. Daisy was on the carpet in front of the fire, sulking because neither of them had left her enough space to lie on the couch with them.

It was officially winter, and the weather had given them little reprieve. But Jess didn't mind it so much since she'd spent a lot of it in front of a fireplace, doing exactly what she was doing now.

Dylan, Anja and Chet had helped her with her move. Most of her things had been in storage, and it had been fairly easy to move in. But since she was pregnant, headed into her third trimester then, she hadn't been able to do nearly as much as she'd wanted to. So they'd been her hands, and after a few days she was living in her own home.

Since she was still working for Anja, things had gone on the same for them. Most days she'd spent the evening at Dylan's place after he got home from work. He'd cook for her—or them, as Anja and Chet often joined them for dinner—and the evening would end with a cup of hot chocolate in front of the fire.

Then she'd go home, and do it all over again the next day. It wasn't a routine Jess had thought possible after they'd returned from Langebaan, but somehow she and Dylan had managed to develop a…relationship that had allowed for it.

Even if that relationship did have a lot more sexual and emotional tension than either of them would have liked.

'Speaking from experiencing how long she can hold a grudge, I think it'll probably take some time.' Dylan was stretched out on the couch next to hers, looking incredibly sexy. She wished she hadn't noticed, just as she had countless times in the last three months. And, just as it had countless times in the last three months, a voice in her head warned her that their current relationship wasn't enough for her.

'It's only been a week, Jess,' Dylan continued, interrupting her worrying thoughts. 'And it's definitely going to take more than a week. Though you should probably leverage the baby now as much as you can.'

'I don't understand why she's not upset with you,' Jess grumbled, forcing herself to play along. 'You're the one who convinced me to interview at your company. Hell, you're probably the reason I got the job.'

'That's not true,' he replied. 'I only recommended you to them. I wasn't involved in your hiring.'

'But what did you think was going to happen when you recommended me?' she asked. 'You're the CEO. If they didn't hire me—'

'I'd have fired them all?' he said in a tone that clearly told her he thought the idea was ridiculous.

She smiled. 'Exactly.'

But Jess knew it wasn't true. She'd been hired into a junior position—something that would have been appropriate for someone straight out of university. Which was fair, she thought, considering her experience meant that she *was* basically just out of university.

But none of the people she'd met had given her the indication that they'd been coerced to see her. And based on the professional, kind and fair way she'd been treated, she didn't think her interviewers believed hiring her would influence the way their CEO treated them.

So while she knew Dylan's recommendation held weight, she liked to think her organisational knowledge and the financial experience she'd gained assisting Anja with the new studio had been the push she'd needed to get the job. Though the fact that they'd agreed for her to start after she'd given birth was *definitely* Dylan.

'Well, it doesn't really matter now anyway since you've already accepted and signed the contract,' he told her. 'And as for Anja not being upset with me… I actually think she prefers you working in the company. It means she knows you'll be taken care of.'

'But she's still mad at me,' Jess complained, and tried to push herself up. When that failed, she tried to get comfortable with the pillow behind her. It was really a bit pathetic, but she couldn't do much since she'd ballooned in her final trimester. Now, even the simplest things were hard.

'Here, let me help.'

She wanted to protest, but she couldn't because, damn it, she needed his help. She tried to hold her breath against his manly scent, against the way it always made her body feel achy and needy. But just like her body had ballooned in the last three months, so had her feelings for him. And while she still wasn't ready to face what that meant, it had heightened her physical attraction to him to the point where she couldn't deny that she wanted more.

'Thanks,' she said when he was done, and leaned back against the pillows again. She'd hoped changing position would help with the strange feeling she had in her back, and for a brief moment she thought that it had. But as soon as she was comfortable again, it reappeared. Almost like a band stretching across the breadth of her back, tightening. It was a little painful.

'I should definitely leverage it,' she said with a huff. 'Being this pregnant is *not* fun.'

He smirked. 'I can't imagine it is. But at least you carry it well.' He sat back down, and she laughed when she saw that Daisy had claimed part of the couch after Dylan had got up.

'You have to say that,' she said once she'd sobered. 'You l—' She cut herself off with a frown. Was she really just going to say because he *loved* her? That went against all the rules she'd given herself about speaking about their feelings for one another. 'Because you love the little thing making me so uncomfortable,' she said instead.

'Well, he or she is family,' Dylan replied with a thin smile.

She knew that smile. It was the one he'd give her whenever he restrained himself from speaking about his feelings for her. He'd agreed to give her time, she thought, but he hadn't agreed to keep himself from talking about how he felt about her. She knew that the only reason he did was because he wanted her to feel comfortable.

And didn't that just make resisting him so much harder?

The band tightened around her back again, and she closed her eyes. Hissed out a breath.

'Hey, are you okay?'

When she opened her eyes again, Dylan was at her side, concern etched into every angle of his face. 'Yeah, I'm okay.'

She gestured for him to help her sit up straight and when he did she took a few moments to breathe.

'Jess, I think we should go to the hospital.'

'No,' she said immediately. 'It's just some…discomfort.'

'No, it's more than that.'

'Braxton-Hicks contractions then. I've been having them all day.'

'All day?' Dylan said with alarm. 'We've been together since this morning. Why didn't you say anything?'

'Because I'm *fine*.'

As she said it, Jess felt something shift and soon after warmth puddled between her legs. She sucked in her breath. 'Dylan.'

'Yeah?'

'Please tell me that you dropped some kind of liquid on me.'

'No, wh—?'

He broke off when he looked down and saw her stained pants. Jess would have felt embarrassed by it if her heart hadn't started pounding, nearly cutting off her breath.

'Jess, honey, I think your water just broke.'

'No,' she breathed. 'No, it's too early. I think you just spilled something on me.'

'I don't have anything in my hands.'

She hated how gentle his voice sounded. 'Then I peed myself,' she snapped. 'It's three weeks too early for my water to break.'

'So let's get you to the hospital and sort it all out. They can tell you whether you peed once you're there.'

'No.' Now she was pleading. And ignoring how strange it was that they were talking about *pee*. 'Dylan, please, it's not time.'

'You're worried.' It wasn't a question. He brushed the hair from her face and left his hand on her cheek. 'There's nothing to be worried about.'

'Not worried,' she rasped. 'Scared. Terrified. I don't know... I don't know if I can do this.'

'I know. I know you're scared. But you're strong. And you *can* do this. I haven't had more faith in anything than that.' He leaned forward and kissed her forehead.

And in that moment, as ill-timed as it was, Jess could

no longer deny that she wanted to be with him. She loved him. And he loved *her*.

'Stay with me,' she told him as the band tightened around her back again. 'Please.'

'I will.'

And he did.

Dylan didn't know he could be so tired. And *he* hadn't been the one to give birth!

He imagined that Jess was feeling a million times worse than he was, except that she was still awake, smiling faintly at Anja and Chet as they cooed at their newborn son.

A nephew, he thought, a grin curving his lips. There was a little boy in his family. Sure, right now he looked all rumpled and new, but one day he would be kicking ball with his uncle who lived right next door. He'd be going on hikes, doing outdoor sports. Dylan figured his imagination would have conjured up much of the same images had his sister had a daughter but, either way, thinking about it was pretty great.

And made all of the turmoil of the last few months worth it.

His eyes settled on Jess again, and he felt his heart swell. She was amazing. It wasn't the first time he'd thought it, and he knew it wouldn't be the last. But witnessing her today…

She'd been amazing.

As soon as they'd got to the hospital she'd turned into the quintessential woman, prepared to do exactly what nature intended of her. She'd screamed in pain—and internally he'd screamed, too, since she'd insisted on holding his hand throughout the process—but as soon as the contraction was over she would go quiet, and softly apologise for acting exactly as anyone else in her position would have.

Six hours later—*six*—Jessie Dylan White had been born. Named after his godparents, Dylan had been told, and he'd had to pretend to drink water when he'd heard to keep them from seeing how emotional he'd felt. Jessie was a good size, good weight and perfectly healthy. And he'd been welcomed into a family who loved him.

He was a lucky kid, Dylan thought. He had great parents, a grandmother who would do her best not to repeat the mistakes of the past, an uncle who was already willing to give him anything he wanted, and a godmother who was a warrior.

He'd seen Jess's face when Anja had told her the name of their son. Had seen the annoyance Anja had felt for Jess fade away after they'd embraced. He'd known that the annoyance was temporary, and only because Anja had yet to see how important it was for Jess to believe that she was loved not because she'd provided something but just because she was worth it.

He'd spent the last three months proving exactly that to Jess. He'd told her he'd give her time and he had, even when it had pained him to do so. But he'd run from pain before. He'd run from the people he loved. He wouldn't now. Because Jess needed to believe that he'd always be there for her.

So he had been. And it was worth all the anguish when he could see on Jess's face that she finally believed it.

Jess turned her head and met his eyes, and her lips curved into a soft smile. His heart galloped in his chest and he smiled back at her, wondering at how much she'd changed him. Before he'd met her, he never would have enjoyed feeling his heart pound for someone.

Now, he relished it.

The nurse came in then, ushering them out by telling them that Jess needed her rest. He stood when Anja set the sleeping Jessie back into his crib, smiled when she kissed his forehead and moved to follow them out of the room.

'Dylan,' Jess said before he could leave.

'Yeah?'

'You showed up for me.' Tears shone in her eyes. 'I…I believe you.'

'What do you believe?'

'That you love me,' she said with a smile. 'That you'll stay.'

His heart filled. 'I do. I will.'

'You made me believe you.'

'I know.'

'And you waited until I was ready to tell you I believed you.'

'I did.'

'I love you.'

It took him a moment before he could speak. 'I love you, too.'

'And this time I believe that it *will* change everything. Because I believe in you. And I'm going to—' she took a breath, blew it out '—I'm going to wade through the deep, dark waters of commitment for you.' She gave a small laugh. 'I'm really high on pain meds. Can you tell?'

He chuckled, and met the nurse's eye. 'May I?' he asked. With a wink, she gave him a nod and walked out.

And in two short steps Dylan was next to the woman he loved, pressing his lips to hers.

EPILOGUE

'IT'S BEEN TOO long since we've been here,' Jess said, stretching out on the reclined beach chair on what had once been Dylan's mother's back porch. 'Too long, I think.'

'Well, we've had a lot on our plates,' Dylan replied, scooping her into his arms and plopping her down on the day bed just next to where she'd been stretching out before.

She cuddled back against him when he joined her, before realising that she should have been offended by his ungentlemanly behaviour. But by then she was already enjoying where she was too much. In the sun at a beach cottage with the most handsome man she'd ever met.

Who *just happened* to be her husband.

'I guess, but it just seems like a waste. Like we missed opportunities to use this place as a holiday home.'

'We've had plenty of other, just as enjoyable, holidays,' he said, nuzzling her neck. Gooseflesh shot out on her body as it always did when he did that, and she smiled lazily.

'*Very* enjoyable.'

'I like your dirty mind, Mrs Nel.'

'It's something of a talent, I think.'

She smiled and settled back into Dylan's arms, thinking about how much had happened since they'd last been in

Langebaan. It had been three years. *Three years.* At first, there hadn't been a reason to return. Dylan's mother had moved to Cape Town once Jessie had been born, wanting to be closer to her family. Wanting to show them that she was different now. And, since Dylan owned the cottage, he'd had it renovated into a larger home since he'd believed their family would expand in the coming years.

He'd wanted it to be a holiday home for them. A place they could come to for some R&R. The renovations had taken a year to complete, and then they'd had their wedding and a brief working stint in Dubai and it had never been a good time to return.

Until now, she thought. She couldn't have planned it any better.

'Dylan?'

'Hmm?'

'I think we should go see my parents.'

Dylan shifted against her and when she looked at him she saw concern in his eyes. 'Why?'

'Well, it's been five years and… I don't know.' She sighed. 'I keep thinking back to what you told me after we left this place three years ago. But I wasn't ready to see them then. I didn't have anything, and I was afraid—' she turned onto her back, let her fingers flutter up to play with his hair '—I was afraid that going back would break me because I had nothing. But now…' She smiled at him, pushed up for a kiss. 'Now, I have everything. And it seems like the right time.'

Jess didn't want to carry around the weight of the negativity she felt towards her parents any more. They were always in her thoughts, the hurt she'd once feared always lurking in the recesses of her mind. She wasn't the same person she'd been when she'd left them—that hurt no longer had the same power over her—and that alone gave her the courage to speak with them. To finally get some closure, and accept whichever form it came in.

Good or bad.

And though she didn't think that they deserved the chance—especially after they hadn't responded to the wedding invitation she'd sent them—Jess now knew that *she* deserved it. She deserved to know whether they regretted their decisions. She deserved to leave them behind if they didn't.

She had a family now, and she wasn't so completely desperate for their love any more. She could move on if she had to. She *had* moved on. But she wanted the opportunity to tell them that she was happily married, successful in her career, and that…

'I'm also pregnant,' she said in a rush, 'and it feels like it's a good time to move on from the past and clear up all the what-ifs.'

She held her breath as she watched the stunned expression on his face.

'You're *pregnant*?'

'Yeah. And it's our baby,' she joked. It was a lame joke, she knew, but she was desperate to break the tension that had suddenly fallen between them.

'I've only known for a few days, and I know we haven't thought about it in some time, so I didn't want to tell you immediately, and we were coming here, and I thought that it would be the perfect time to tell you.' She paused, but he still didn't speak, so she continued, 'I guess I shouldn't have just blurted it out. I should have done something cute and filmed it and put it online.'

She barely paused to take a breath. 'And I shouldn't have sprung it on you after telling you I wanted to see my parents. But I was thinking about our child, and how we'd feel if some day they didn't speak to us. Of course, it's not the same, but—'

He cut her off with a kiss, deep and filled with so much passion and emotion that she felt raw. When he pulled back, he leaned his forehead against hers.

'You're pregnant.'

'Yeah,' she replied, her breath ragged.

'I…I'm going to be a father.'

'Yes.'

'We're pregnant,' he said again, and this time he laughed and gave her another kiss. And when he sobered he said, 'I have no idea how to be a father.'

'I have no idea how to be a mother. But we've figured out a lot together, my love. I think it's going to be okay.'

'Me, too,' he said with a smile.

'So…you're not mad?'

'Why would I be mad?'

'Because…we haven't spoken about it.'

'Recently,' he added. 'But we spoke about it after Jessie was born. And again, after we got married. Life's been so busy since then…' He shook his head. 'I don't know how to be a father, Jess. And heaven knows I had the worst example in the world. But I'll be there for this baby. Our baby.'

He set a hand on her abdomen, and the heat of it—the sweetness of it—seared through her body. His eyes met hers and what she saw there made her heart fill. 'Our baby, Jess. Yours and mine. We'll figure it out together. And if you need to talk to your parents to help you figure it out, we can.'

She smiled at him. 'I never thought this day would come for me. Where I'm a part of a family that's not broken, about to have my own child. You made that possible for me.'

'I could tell you the exact same thing.'

'Yeah, you could.'
He chuckled and pressed his lips against hers.
This time neither of them pulled away.

* * * * *

A BACHELOR,
A BOSS
AND A BABY

RACHEL LEE

Chapter One

Blaine Harrigan might have been the most delighted man in all of Conard County when he heard that a new planning manager had been hired. For years now the position had been vacant, the comprehensive plan was at least ten years old and he'd been dealing with all the county engineering while aware that they needed to update the plan. And he needed someone between him and the planning boards, which were made up of city council and county commission members. A little conflict of interest didn't make his job any easier, especially with an out-of-date plan that they overrode readily *because* it was so old.

When he heard they'd hired Diane Finch, he'd read over her résumé and given a huge sigh of relief. She looked competent and had great recommendations from her previous job in Des Moines. Better, she sounded more than capable of standing up with him to the so-called planning boards that had started looking more to their personal interests than what was best for the county and city.

Well, maybe she wouldn't stand up with him at first, not with her job so new, and not until she learned the lay of the land. But a professional planner? She probably wouldn't be keen to play along with ideas that could make her look bad or adversely affect her career.

What's more, she had to be aware that the county and city couldn't get useful grants without an updated plan and a planner to write the proposals and oversee performance.

He'd probably have to wait awhile for the ally to emerge regardless. That was all right with him. He'd been poking his finger into the dike to stop the rash of self-serving plans for over five years now.

More than once he'd considered looking for another job, but his Irish blood wouldn't let him run from a fight. Besides, he'd grown fond of Conard County, different in so many ways from Galway, where he'd grown up. Life had brought him here, and while he'd always be homesick for the beauties of Galway, he found different beauty here in the mountains and rolling prairie. He'd also found a place he was willing to defend and maybe sink some permanent roots.

With that random assortment of thoughts rolling

around in his head, he strolled through the basement hallways in the courthouse, heading to the rooms that belonged to the planner. Diane Finch, according to the grapevine, had arrived early this morning, and for some reason the court clerks and the many city and county employees who filled the offices down here had been looking rather amused and whispering quite a bit.

He wanted to know what was going on. Was she a golden-scaled dragon or something?

Painting a smile on his face, he knocked briefly on the closed door and entered, ready to meet the woman he hoped would work with him. The sound that came through the door should have warned him, but since it shouldn't be there, he'd assumed it was drifting down from the floor above.

He froze in astonishment as he stepped in. The unlikeliest of sights greeted him.

A lovely young woman with golden-blond hair, wearing what appeared to be a gray slacks suit, stood at a bare desk with a baby on it. She appeared to be busy trying to put a fresh diaper on the squalling, struggling bundle of pink bottom and pulled-up yellow cloth. The golden eyes that rose in surprise to look at him also appeared almost frantic.

Questions could come later, he decided in an instant. Swiftly closing the door behind him, he asked, "Need a little help there?" His brogue, so carefully erased, somehow pushed its way through.

"You've got kids?" she asked almost plaintively.

"I helped raise me five brothers and sisters. You're new at this?"

"Very," she admitted.

Without any hesitation, he rounded her desk and nudged her aside a bit. "I'm used to cloth diapers," he remarked, holding the baby safely with a big hand placed gently on her tummy. The little bottom didn't look irritated, so he just went about grabbing a wipe from an open container beside a disposable diaper at the corner of the desk. He cleaned the tot quickly before opening the fresh diaper with one hand and placing it on the little girl. Despite the child's wildly waving arms and legs, it only took a few seconds, then he had her diapered and dry. Pulling down her onesie, he fastened the snaps easily.

Instead of quieting, the baby continued to cry.

"She been fed?" he asked.

"Just."

"Ah." Without another word he picked the child up and placed her on his shoulder, not caring he was probably going to need a fresh shirt after this. "Hush, little treasure," he murmured, gently patting and rubbing her back with practiced ease while pacing the small office. After he took about a dozen steps back and forth, the babe's fist found its way to her mouth and she quieted. Moments after that a small burp escaped her.

"There we go," Blaine said, "but it's probably not the last. You mind?"

She sank into the chair behind the desk and gave

him a crooked smile. "Not at all. I'm so totally new to this I'm learning everything the hard way."

"No prior practice, then?"

She shook her head. "Daphne is my cousin's child. She's in the hospital and I'm fostering. I thought it would be easy."

Blaine allowed a quiet chuckle to escape him. "It's not hard. You probably need to worry a whole lot less. Unless the tot is sick, what it most needs is love, food and a clean nappy. Simple. And it will all go a lot easier when you relax."

She looked askance.

"She feels your nervousness, so she gets uneasy. By the way, I take it you're Diane Finch?"

She nodded. "And you're…?"

"County engineer. Blaine Harrigan. Do the bosses know you've got company?"

"You mean Daphne? No. I was hoping I could find decent day care when I arrived in town. That *certainly* isn't as easy as I thought. I'm also learning I have a lot of qualms about leaving her with someone I don't know." She sighed and drummed her fingers briefly on the arms of her chair. "This is going to cost me my job, isn't it?"

"Bringing the baby to work? I suppose it could. I also suppose I could help you batter the bosses down. It's only temporary, after all."

She sighed and closed her eyes. "That's a nice offer, Mr. Harrigan, but I'm very much afraid this isn't going to be temporary. At least not the part where I foster Daphne. I should get some kind of day care sorted out, though."

"Then we'll start with that," he said. Now he had a sleeping child on his shoulder and he was reluctant to put her down in the car seat in the corner. He also wanted to know what had happened to bring Diane Finch to the point of taking care of her cousin's baby indefinitely when she was obviously so unprepared for the task.

She was a beautiful woman, all right. He couldn't help but notice the way that satiny blouse caressed her breasts when she moved and her jacket fell open. Nice shape, adorable face and what appeared to be natural blond hair. Attractive like a flower to a bee. *Not the time to be thinking such things, boyo*, he told himself.

But now he was also seriously intrigued. "So, how did you come to be a foster mother?"

Her face closed a bit. "My cousin is seriously ill. She can't care for Daphne and probably won't be able to for a long time. That left me or putting her in the foster care system. Maybe for adoption, although my cousin…" She broke off. "Anyway, it's me and Daphne for as long as she needs me."

That raised more questions than it answered, but he let it go. She didn't know him from Adam, and this was very personal ground. There were few secrets in Conard County because most people knew each other, but Diane was new and she was probably going to face a lot of prying. He well remembered how he'd been questioned. A new face always drew attention. He didn't need to add to it.

But he had to admit to feeling some admiration for a woman who'd foster her cousin's baby while starting a new job. Not many would want the combination, he was certain. And Diane, by all appearances, was very new to this baby thing. He wondered if she'd find it presumptuous if he offered to help. Probably. Talk about sticking his nose in the tent.

Bemused, Diane watched the tall, muscular man holding tiny Daphne on his shoulder with such ease and calm. Daphne had come to her care only four days ago, when she'd been almost packed and ready to hit the road. Her cousin MaryJo, with whom she'd never been very close, had been committed indefinitely to a mental hospital with paranoid schizophrenia. Diane had been too busy the last couple of weeks to do more than to peek in on MaryJo and her new baby, and hear how sick she had become. The three-month-old Daphne had barely entered her consciousness until the social worker had told her that Daphne would have to go into long-term foster care because MaryJo couldn't possibly be a safe caretaker.

The instant she heard the words *foster care*, Daphne had loomed large on her radar, far larger than her poor cousin. Diane simply could not let that darling baby go to strangers, and the social worker also pointed out that MaryJo was too mentally ill to legally put the child up for adoption.

Adoption?

There wasn't even a father to turn to. Whoever he'd been, he was apparently long gone.

Adoption? No.

The last days had turned into a whirlwind of packing, signing papers, gaining permission to take the child to her new job, getting baby supplies and a travel bed—oh, yeah, and a car seat—then Daphne had been delivered into her care.

Diane had never doubted that this was right thing to do, but it had all landed on her like a train wreck, and she was still figuring out how to handle everything. Most especially how to care for the baby. She didn't have siblings, and she'd never watched anyone else's kids because she'd been too busy with an after-school job at a local law office. What did she know about kids?

Only that she couldn't let Daphne wind up in the foster care system. And part of her problem, as she'd discovered since she'd arrived in town two days ago, was that she didn't want to leave the baby in anyone else's hands, either. Most day care around here was in-home. The one early-learning center didn't have an opening. Her reluctance to trust someone else with the baby's care was likely to become a big issue.

So here she was, her first day on the job, with a baby. Yeah, she expected trouble, but she didn't know what else to do. She couldn't have begun to explain why she cared so much about a baby she'd only had for a few days, or why she was feeling so reluctant to put her in a stranger's care while she worked.

Yet a stranger had just diapered Daphne with practiced ease and was now pacing slowly with the sleeping girl on his shoulder. Daphne was still tiny at three months, but Blaine Harrigan made her look minuscule.

He was dressed casually in a short-sleeved khaki work shirt and jeans. The last place she had worked, a polo shirt and slacks was as informal as it got. Apparently things were different here. He certainly looked like a man ready to work hard, a sharp contrast to the way he handled Daphne: easily, gently, yet confidently. She envied that confidence. She wished she could siphon off a gallon of it and put it in her veins.

Well, she'd get there eventually. She'd learned everything else she'd needed to in life. Usually. God, she hoped she wasn't kidding herself and running headlong into a big failure.

"Are you looking forward to this job?" he asked her.

For the first time, she realized that his voice seemed to resonate from deep within his chest, below baritone but maybe not quite bass? An interesting, slightly rough sound. "I think so, yes. I know I was before life got out of hand."

He smiled faintly. "This little one, you mean? Ah, she won't be any trouble now. I was wondering, you worked in a larger city before. Why come to a small town?"

"The challenge," she said. "An outdated comprehensive plan that needs to be rewritten, and that covers an entire county. I'll have a lot of input. I've always wanted that."

He hesitated as if he wanted to say something, but then resumed his gentle pacing, rubbing Daphne's back all the while. "Did you visit first?"

"Of course. I came out for the interview. I'm surprised I didn't meet you then." And she was. They'd have to work closely together. She began to wonder how this place functioned.

"I was on vacation. I didn't hear a thing about you until I got back."

Okay, that was strange, she thought. Given his position, he should have had some say in her hiring. For the first time, she felt uneasiness about the job itself. Was there something going on here? But she couldn't ask Harrigan, because he worked here, too. Until she had a read on everyone involved, asking questions could be dangerous. Wisdom dictated that she keep everything on a professional level.

Although that was already a limit she had broken, considering her infant cousin was riding on the shoulder of the county engineer. Very professional. Under other circumstances, she might have been amused. Starting a new job, not so much.

Then, for the first time, she really saw his face. Looked at it and took it in, and felt her stomach flutter. Dark, nearly black hair with blue eyes so bright the color was arresting. The rest of that face was great, too, squarish, a good chin, with fair, unblemished skin. His last name suggested he was Irish, as did a few hints in his pronunciation. He couldn't have left the isle very long ago, she thought. Western sun and wind hadn't kissed him for long.

Fortunately, Daphne made a small sound, drawing Diane's attention before she stared at Blaine too long. Somebody should have warned her that a man holding an infant was more irresistible than one standing solo. She never would have dreamed. She watched as he pulled a visitor's chair back from her desk and slowly lowered himself into it. The chair was springy, and he rocked gently.

Then she felt embarrassed. "Would you like me to take her back?"

He smiled over the baby's head. "It's been a while since I held a baby. I'm liking it."

She felt her mouth frame a smile in return. She had to admit that this early into her new role as a mother, she was glad of a brief break. She'd had no idea that her patience wasn't infinite, that she'd be losing a lot of sleep and that she could get frazzled by a baby's persistent crying.

The new character insights didn't exactly make her feel proud. Now she not only needed to deal with a job and the baby, but she needed to deal with herself, as well.

"So what brought you here, Blaine? I'm assuming you didn't grow up here." An assumption based on those faint traces of an accent.

"No, I grew up in Ireland, I did. Galway. I'm liking it quite a bit here, but missing my family."

"You said a big family?"

"I'm one of six. The eldest."

"That's a big family," she agreed.

He leaned back a little farther and crossed his legs loosely. Tight denim left no doubt that his lower half was built as well as his top half. Diane swallowed and dragged her gaze away.

After a bit, he spoke again. "You look tired. Not sleeping well?"

Finally she felt a bubble of real amusement, for the first time in days. She'd begun to wonder if she still had a sense of humor. "What do *you* think?" An attempted joke that might have sounded like a challenge, but his demeanor didn't change. God, was she going to have to watch her tongue now, as well? Somehow she needed to get more sleep.

He nodded. "Babies are hard at first. It does get better, though. Just snatch your sleep whenever you can. So has anyone primed you for how things run around here?"

She sat up a little, fatigue forgotten. "What do I need to know?"

"Only that members of the city council and the county commission make up the county planning board. Two hats, you might say."

She wanted to drop her head into her hands. In an

instant she began to envision a skein of tangled relationships all knotted up with ego and personal aims. No real control on them at all, except for when they might get angry at one another. Why had they even wanted a planning manager?

Oh, yeah. They needed an updated comprehensive plan in order to apply for government grants. She was the path to get there. To be fair, however, her job always became political at some point. Money carried a lot of weight, and developers had enough of it to be persuasive.

She had hoped, however, that she might be little less boxed in here. Small population, for one thing, and no rapid growth for a while. Most of what was needed was bringing the plan up-to-date on new regulations from the state and federal government. Environmental regulations had increased dramatically... and there was seldom a way around them. She had that on her side, at least. Also, she needed to create a plan that would display a good future for the county and city, a good environment for the people as well as one that encouraged careful growth.

Still, it was bound to be tough, and even tougher when the cabal running matters was very small.

She kept her face smooth, however. She didn't know Blaine Harrigan and didn't dare express anything untoward. Now that she was here with her cousin's baby in her care, she couldn't afford to lose her job. To protect herself, she had to stay here at least a year, so she wouldn't put a problem smack at the top of her résumé. Wonderful. She couldn't afford a catastrophe.

"You get used to it," he rumbled, gently patting Daphne's back. "When are you supposed to meet with the gentlemen and lady?"

"Tomorrow evening. I hope by then I can find childcare. Do you know of anyone good?" she asked hopefully. If she had to choose someone, she'd rather they came with a recommendation.

A quiet laugh escaped him. The baby stirred a little and settled quickly. "I'm not in the way of having a family. But I have friends I can ask. I'll call around today." He rose slowly, taking care not to jar the baby. "I need to be off. I've got a meeting at ten a few miles out of town about a road repair. Might require some work on the culvert. I'd invite you but for the wee bit, here."

"Oh." A truncated pointless response, but she was holding her breath anyway as he slowly bent and placed Daphne in her car seat. To her relief, the child didn't wake.

"I'll see you later," Blaine said as he straightened. He winked at her. "We'll be together a lot. In fact, you and me might need to become a damn army of two." A nod, then he let himself out.

An army of two? Diane bit her lip wondering what he meant. Had it been some kind of warning? Then she wondered at the ease with which he'd taken over with Daphne. Too bad he wasn't looking for childcare work.

Resting her chin on her hand, she looked down at the baby and wondered how all this had happened. Well, the job, at least, was her fault. It might turn out to be a very good job, too, despite what she'd heard from Blaine.

But Daphne? While she was having trouble facing it herself, it remained that Daphne's presence in her life was probably going to be long term. As in permanent.

MaryJo had been growing sicker for years, but it had been a slow process. A lot of it had been brushed away as quirks. Then, last year, MaryJo's parents had died in a flash flood in Texas, and that seemed to have pushed MaryJo past her tipping point.

First had come the social workers, then had come a pregnancy during which she couldn't take any meds, and the next thing Diane had known, her cousin had a full-blown psychotic break. After the baby was born, the meds didn't help much.

MaryJo heard voices that told her to do terrible things. She even hallucinated. In short, MaryJo had vanished into an alternate universe, and nobody believed it was safe to leave Daphne in her care, or even nearby. To this day, Diane was ashamed of how little time she'd spared for thinking of her cousin on the far side of the state. She'd gotten the wrap-up from a social worker after MaryJo was hospitalized.

Then, a little less than three months after Daphne's birth, the baby had come to live with Diane.

Inevitably, though, Diane looked down at the

sleeping child and smiled. Except when Daphne was fussing and inconsolable, Diane always felt happy looking at her. Something about a baby.

Then she turned back to her desk and opened the folder containing all the notes for her new job that someone had left.

Around noon, a quiet knock sounded on her office door. She glanced at the still sleeping Daphne and decided she'd better answer it rather than call out. Rising, she rounded her desk and opened the door to find two women of about her own age, early thirties, standing there with big smiles. One had silky chestnut hair to her shoulders and wore a Western shirt with a denim skirt and cowboy boots. The other was a redhead who wore a flaming red slacks suit that she carried off with panache.

"I'm Aubrey," said chestnut hair. "And this is my friend Candy. We're in the clerk's office. We heard you brought your baby, and everybody is dying to see her, so we thought we'd skip down here first and prepare you. And maybe you'd like to go to lunch with us?"

At once startled and charmed, Diane returned the smile. "You can peek, ladies, but she's sleeping for the first time since 1:00 a.m. I'd rather nothing wake her."

"Of course not," said Aubrey, keeping her voice low. "I've been through it. Sleep before everything."

Deciding it was okay, Diane stepped back and

opened the door wider. Both women crept in quietly and looked down on the angelic baby who only a few hours ago had been wearing horns and carrying a pitchfork. The mental image suddenly made Diane want to laugh.

"Ooh, how sweet," breathed Candy. "She's so pretty. And that's saying something about such a young one."

Aubrey elbowed her gently. "Wait till you have your own. But yeah, she's gorgeous, all right. We'll tell everyone to give you space, but now we can report back so they won't be so curious. I didn't know you were bringing a family. I thought you were single. Well, we all did."

Diane flushed, realizing that the questioning had begun. She wondered how long before it turned into a cross examination.

"I am single. This is my cousin's baby. I'm taking care of her because my cousin is seriously ill."

"That's a shame," said Aubrey. "About your cousin, I mean. Well, I guess you don't want to carry the baby across the way to the diner, but would you like us to bring you back lunch? And if you like coffee, don't get it out of the machine in the hallway. It's terrible. But walk half a block and you'll get it world-class."

"That's good to know, because I do love coffee and tea. Especially a latte, but..."

"Oh, we're part of the modern world," said Candy. "The diner makes lattes. I do wish we'd get a decent Chinese or Mexican restaurant, though. Maude's great, but basic." She hesitated, then asked, "Do you want a salad or a sandwich? I can recommend the Cobb salad."

"Or the steak sandwich," Aubrey chimed in quietly. "That usually makes two meals for me. You wouldn't have to cook tonight."

"I love Cobb salads," Diane said, but she couldn't help thinking about a steak sandwich. Full of calories, but over two meals… "Let me get my purse. I think I'll have the sandwich, after all."

Candy quickly waved her hand. "Consider this a welcome-to-town present. It's just a little thing. While we're out, does the baby need anything?"

Yesterday's trip to the market had pretty much taken care of that. "I'm stocked," she said with confidence.

The women both smiled and began to make their quiet way to the door. Then Aubrey looked back. "Do you need day care?"

Diane's heart leaped. "Yes. But…"

"You don't know who to trust," Aubrey finished. "How could you, being new in town? My brother's wife works at the early-learning center. I'll see if she can find you a space. Be back in a short while?"

With waves, the women left. Diane checked on the baby once again then settled at her desk, wishing for coffee and an answer to cosmic questions. She'd been so career focused until this, but now she had another life to worry about.

Forgetting the folder she needed to read, she sat and stared at the nearby baby. Daphne had already changed everything, and Diane suspected the changes had only just begun.

She just wished she had some experience to guide her.

Blaine stood on the road in question, surveying the situation. The road was elevated a few feet above the surrounding ranch land, which helped keep it dry and, in the case of blowing snow, relatively snow-free much of the winter.

But there was no question that the recent heavy rain and runoff had caused the road to dip dangerously, right over a culvert meant to equalize water buildup between the grazing land on either side and to prevent ponding as much as possible. But the recent rains had been anything but usual for this area, and problems had begun to turn up.

Climbing down to a lower position, Blaine scanned the figures the surveyor had gathered, then eyed the situation for himself. The question was whether they could save the culvert and road simply by clearing the asphalt, building up a layer of solid earth and gravel, then repaving over it.

Neither option would be cheap for the penny-pinching county commission, but the right option had to be chosen regardless of cost. A road cave-in could cause worse problems. And no matter what his decision, a lot of people were going to be bothered by a necessary detour.

His colleague Doug Ashbur, from the roads department, was inspecting the other end of the culvert. He called along it to Blaine the instant he saw him.

"Abandon hope," Doug called, his voice echoing. "I don't know about your end, but the metal's rusting out down here, and the concrete casement is cracking."

"Grand." The view from his end wasn't any better. He saw more than rusting steel and cracking concrete. He also saw a definite dip in culvert beneath the sinking road. The entire thing was trying to collapse.

He stepped back a few yards, being wiser than to enter that culvert in its current condition. Past engineers and road builders had tried their best, but the simple fact was that with the typical hypercold winter temperatures and the eventual thaws, that concrete was bound to crack. Even a minuscule crack would worsen with temperature changes, the ice expanding when water filled the small cracks, enlarging them, until this. The galvanized steel pipe under the concrete had been someone's attempt years ago to prevent a catastrophic failure.

It had worked so far, but now it was a question of how long they had.

He eyed the ground above the culvert, beneath the road, and saw evidence that the ground was extruding from the smooth slope that must have once been there. So the concrete was no longer adequately bearing the weight of the road, the steel pipe was collapsing and the ground between the culvert and road had evidently washed away from the weeks of rain that must have penetrated through cracks in the old asphalt. An accident waiting to happen.

He called to Doug. "We'd better redirect traffic and close this road. See you up top." He climbed the bank, using his hands when necessary, then went to his truck, where he pulled off his thick leather work gloves and stood staring at the dip.

It didn't look like much now. There was also no way to be sure when it would become a big deal. It was far too weakened to be driving trucks and cars over, but it might last months. Even through the winter. And that was counting on luck a bit too much for his taste.

Up here he could feel the ceaseless breeze that never stopped in open places. While it was early autumn, the air was still warm and smelled a bit like summer. A very different summer than in Galway: warmer, drier, dustier. Sometimes he missed the cooler, wetter clime of home, but mostly he liked it here. Different, but with its own beauty, like when he turned to look at the mountains that loomed so close to the west. Any morning now he'd wake up to see the sugary coating of a first snowfall.

Doug joined him. "I'll order up equipment, Blaine. It might be a few days before I can get it all together. You know how it goes."

He most certainly did. This county didn't have any resources to waste, and his too many bosses all had their eyes on things beyond the event horizon, like finally getting that oft-promised ski resort built and finding other ways to make this county more attractive and create jobs. Oh, and wealth. He was sure that had to fit in somewhere.

The ranchers around here weren't much interested in the big schemes. They just wanted to survive another year. But that meant they needed decent enough roads to carry cattle to the stockyard at the train station, roads over which to get to town and see their kids get to school…oh, a million reasons why folks these days couldn't just be cut off from the rest of the world for months at a time.

Like it or not, expensive or not, the county was going to have to fix this culvert.

"I believe we've got enough in the budget," he said to Doug. "This clearly can't wait."

"I agree. But we've got a dozen others that aren't much better."

"At least they're not already collapsing. Let's get the signs up. You have some barricades?"

Doug laughed. "Never travel without them. Okay, I'll work on pulling together the equipment and crew." He paused, looking back at the dip in the road. "How you want to do this? Another culvert?"

"We talked about other solutions, you remember. The problem is that if we don't use culverts, the erosion just expands to eat the road." As dry as this place was in general, he was often surprised how much of a headache water gave him. Usually in the spring, however. The last rains had been record-breaking for September.

While he put out some orange cones and staked some detour signs at the crossroad, his thoughts wandered back to Diane. He wondered how she was going to like dealing with the good ol' boys of Co-nard County. He wondered if they'd give her a hard time about the baby.

Mostly he wondered why she was haunting his thoughts and why he kept thinking she was a tidy armful. And why his body stirred in response.

Well, he assured himself, that would wear off. It had to. Anyway, he'd hardly talked to her. Chances were he wouldn't continue to feel the sexual draw when he learned what she was really like.

Wasn't that always the way?

Chapter Two

Diane went to her little rented house that night with a briefcase full of files that had been left on her desk and a baby who'd eaten enough today to satisfy a horse…well, relatively speaking. It seemed as if she needed to be fed about every two or three hours, even though the social worker had said that should begin to slow down. Not yet, obviously, and it might continue through the night.

Oh, yeah, get the girl a pediatrician. Maybe she ought to start keeping a list so she didn't forget something. The move and taking charge of an infant had left her a bit scatterbrained.

At the last moment, before settling into a small house she hadn't yet been able to turn into a home, she thought to check her diaper stash even though she'd bought quite a few yesterday. Who would have thought such a bitty thing could fill so many diapers?

She counted and decided she had enough for a couple of days. Plenty of formula, too. And since Candy and Aubrey had brought her a huge lunch from the café, she didn't need to cook.

Good heavens, she thought. The baby was sleeping contentedly, she could dine without cooking and she had time to kick off her shoes and collapse on the recliner that had been delivered just yesterday. Beaten and creaky, it held a lot of memories of her father, a veteran who had largely retreated to a distant land inside his own head. Memories of her father, as rare as the good ones had been, were something she didn't want to lose entirely.

She wandered down the hall to the bedroom she hadn't had time to unpack yet and opened a suitcase to pull out her favorite old jeans and a checked shirt as softened by age as the jeans. Her grungies, her comfies, whatever anyone wanted to call them. That night she had nothing to do except care for Daphne and herself...for the first time since she'd accepted this job. She supposed she ought to feel slothful for not unpacking just a little, but frankly, she was worn out. She could live out of a suitcase for another day.

When she emerged from her bedroom, slightly freshened for the evening, she heard Daphne stirring, making little sounds that might soon turn into a full-throated cry. Diaper. Feeding. Blaine had been right about one thing: it was actually very simple. Demanding but simple.

In a very short time, she had become practiced at pulling out a bottle and filling it with room-temperature formula from a can. The woman who had turned Daphne over to Diane had told her she didn't need to warm the baby bottles as long as the formula was at room temperature. However, it had been chilly outside, so she put the bottle in a pan of warm water from the sink and gave it a few minutes to lose any chill.

She tested the warmth of the formula on the inside of her wrist, then went to rescue her increasingly noisy charge. A finger in the diaper told her that could wait, so she gathered the child to her and let her drink from the bottle.

Sitting in her recliner without putting her feet up, she became fascinated with watching Daphne eat. Her little eyes, beginning to get darker and resemble her mother's, watched her back. Intense. Content.

Amazing. After just a few days she could feel her heart reaching out to this child, taking her in, wrapping her in swiftly growing love. If MaryJo got well, it was going to hurt to have to give this baby up. Hurt like hell.

But the social worker's assessment had been brutal: MaryJo would never be well enough to care for her own child. If she improved, like so many with her illness, she probably couldn't be trusted to stay on her meds. And if she didn't keep taking her medication…

Diane shook her head a little and began to hum softly. Daphne continued to watch her, then with a surprisingly strong thrust of arms and legs, she turned her head from the bottle.

"Enough of that, huh?" Diane asked. "A little gas bubble, maybe? You eat more than that."

Daphne scrunched up her face, so Diane quickly put the girl over her shoulder and began to pat and rub her back. She felt a bit embarrassed that Blaine had done it for her earlier, clearly thinking she didn't know to do such a thing. But she'd forgotten in the midst of her overwhelming day.

She wouldn't forget now. Rising from the chair, she paced and patted, continuing to hum quietly. When the little burp emerged, she offered more formula.

"Easy peasy," Diane said. Twenty minutes later, she had the child changed—she decided she was going to need a changing table soon—dressed in a fresh onesie and apparently content enough to yawn.

"Success." The best evening yet. She paced with the little girl on her shoulder some more, drawing out another tiny burp, then moved her to the cradle of her arm. Daphne waved one fist around then shoved it toward her mouth. In an eye blink, she fell asleep.

A very successful evening. Diane was smiling happily as she settled Daphne into her small travel bed. She needed to get a crib soon, too. But first there'd be another round of hungry baby around eleven.

One of her girlfriends had told her before she left her old job that she was lucky, missing the first three months of caring for the baby. "By four months," Lucy had said, "I was beginning to wonder if the little brat would ever sleep through the night. You remember. I was in a fog of sleep deprivation all the time."

Diane didn't really remember, because she hadn't seen a whole lot of Lucy after she birthed her first child. "Too busy" had been Lucy's response to every invitation. She probably had been, too.

For that matter, she felt a bit guilty about how little she'd seen of MaryJo in the past five years. The kind of closeness some claimed with cousins had never existed between them, and there was little enough to pull them together when they no longer lived in the same town.

MaryJo's parents had divorced a long time ago. She'd never seen her dad again. Then her mother had dived into a bottle and never emerged. The most amazing thing was that those two had been together when they got caught in a flash flood in Texas. As if they might have been reaching out to one another again? No one would ever know now.

It was hardly to be wondered that MaryJo was troubled, but the social worker assured her that the causes of schizophrenia involved so many factors nobody could pin all of them down. Bottom line, she really didn't need to worry about Daphne getting it.

Diane hoped that was so. She couldn't imagine that darling child growing up to be so ill.

She was just about to move to the recliner and close her eyes for a little while before heating up the remains of her lunch when someone knocked at the door.

Her heart accelerated. She'd come from a much larger city where knocks on the door at this time of night were a bit threatening. Too late for regular deliveries, and friends always called first. Plus, she really didn't know anyone here, so it couldn't possibly be a friendly call, could it?

On the other hand, as an official now, her address was had become public record, so finding her wouldn't be hard if someone wanted to rant about something. Lovely idea.

But she shook herself, telling herself not to be ridiculous, and went to answer it.

She should have guessed. Blaine Harrigan stood there, wearing a light jacket now and holding a potted red gerbera daisy. "To brighten a windowsill," he said with a smile. "I take it your new boss is happily sleeping?"

Just seeing him drew a bright smile from her and a rush of warmth. Man, she didn't even know this guy. It was too soon to be happy to see him, wasn't it?

Heck, she didn't care. It was nice to see him, to feel as if she might have made her first friend here.

She stepped back, inviting him in. "Thank you for the daisy. I just love it. What a kind thought." She looked at the bright flower with a sudden feeling of comfort, as if she weren't a total stranger here anymore. "I was thinking about making some tea. Would you like some?"

"I never turn down a cuppa," he answered. He handed her the flower, and she motioned him to follow her to the small kitchen and dining area. She placed the daisy on the sill over the sink then turned to find him standing in the doorway, evidently awaiting an invitation to sit or go.

"Have a seat," she said, pointing to the ridiculously small table with two chairs. This place had come partially furnished, a relief to her because she hadn't wanted to ship her things from Iowa. None of it had been worth shipping. Her life revolved around her work, and decorating had mostly involved plastic storage containers and repurposed boxes. Hey, it had served her needs.

But now…well, what was here could do with a few additions for the baby.

"So you're enjoying a little peace and quiet," he said as she filled the kettle and put it on the gas stove.

"Until around eleven," she agreed. "I'm sorry you caught me in such a mess earlier. I'm new at this, but I'm not stupid. I don't know why I didn't think of burping Daphne. I do it all the time!"

He laughed quietly. "No excuses needed. You're tired, probably overwhelmed. I mean, a new job and

a new baby all at once? And more to come, I believe. I'll bet the little one starts creeping and crawl-
ing soon."

"She's already trying," Diane admitted. "When
I put her down on a blanket. But I've only had four
days with her. A lot to learn." She hesitated. "You
said you were from Ireland, right?"

He nodded.

"Then my tea is probably going to appall you."

He leaned forward a little on his chair. "Tea bags?
I've learned to admire their advantages. Easy and
quick, especially for a single guy who only wants
one cup. Now, if I really want to brew a pot, I can
do it, but usually I'm on the run."

"I wouldn't even know where to begin. I make a
pot with tea bags."

"I'll show you when we have some time. Anyway,
I'm going to buzz into yer meetin' with the commissioners tomorrow."

"The culvert?" she asked, turning to pull out two
mugs and a box of tea bags and put them on the table.

"It has to be replaced quickly. The road is sinking,
the concrete is cracking and the steel drainage pipe
is buckling. Me and Doug from the road department
closed off the road today. I don't want some poor
rancher to start driving over it and find his bonnet—
sorry, hood—six feet in the ground."

Diane nodded. "Not good. Do you like milk and
sugar?"

"I'll go for straight. Thanks. Yeah, the budget has

been way too tight for too long. Been patching and mending as best we can, but there's only so long we can push things off."

"I know. Infrastructure is one of my pet peeves. Nothing works if you haven't got it."

"Ah, some common sense!"

She couldn't repress a giggle at that. She wasn't totally unfamiliar with the difficulties he mentioned. No place ran like a smoothly oiled machine, no budget was ever sufficient and personalities always got in the way. "Did you expect something else from an urban planner?"

His grin broadened. "I've known all types in my life."

She was still smiling as she poured boiling water into the mugs over the waiting tea bags. Soon the rich aroma of black tea began to waft through the kitchen. "So why did you leave Ireland?" she asked. "I've always wanted to go there."

"Now that's a story," he answered. Once again his deep voice took on the rhythms of the American West, leaving behind the hints of Galway. And they were just hints, poking out from time to time. He'd clearly been in the States for a while. "Like many places in the world, Ireland was booming just before the economic crash. Unlike many places in the world, we didn't recover quickly. We had too much boom. We were bringing in workers from all over the world, building fast, growing, and then…" He shrugged.

"Whatever. Life was getting harder, finding work

was getting harder and I had a bit of the wanderlust in me. I hopped through a few jobs, then stopped here."

"Why?"

He shrugged. "Because I like it. It's different. Galway's beautiful with mountains and plenty of seashore, and the town itself has a lot of charm in parts. But I have to say, I wasn't prepared for the sheer size of your country. I was astonished and spellbound. And then I saw the mountains here. They dwarf anything I'd ever known before, plus there's a whole lot of wide-open space, space almost beyond imagining. It would be hard to tear me away."

She nodded and set her tea bag on the saucer in the middle of the table. Lifting her cup, she closed her eyes for a few seconds just to inhale the fragrant steam. The questions buzzing her head were dangerous, so she diverted. She didn't dare ask about people she would be working with. "All tea comes from a single Asian plant, from Yunnan in China. It grows elsewhere now, and there are probably varieties, but most of the flavor we love has to do with how the tea is aged." She opened her eyes.

"Where did that come from?" he asked.

"Trying to avoid asking you about the members of the commissions and boards I'm going to be dealing with."

He cracked a laugh, a deep sound that rumbled as if it rose from the depths. "I shouldn't say much. A bunch of eejits, but not always. They're politicians.

You can count on them to look out for themselves. Take the culvert I told you about. That's going to need to be replaced as swiftly as possible. I'll have to let them know what I'm going to do, even though I believe I have the money in the roads budget. They like to be informed. Oh, keep that in mind, Diane. They want to know everything. Some of them will raise Cain because there are probably ten things that they might consider more important. Finally they'll settle down and give me the go-ahead simply because they don't want a dozen of the largest ranchers around here to be having to detour by miles all winter. But the argument will reassure them that they're the ones in control."

She understood him perfectly. That was a game she'd played before. She also knew how to win... usually.

"But that's just a handful of people," he said. "The rest of the folks around here are the kind of people I'm happy to spend time with. At least those I've met. I think you'll enjoy most everything here, unless you like to live in high style. The closest thing we have to a nightclub is a roadhouse, where I'd advise you to never go alone. Then there's Mahoney's Bar, which is as close as I've ever found to my local pub." He paused. "Now, you might like that somewhat. Busy, friendly place."

She was smiling again, enjoying his description. Relaxation had begun to fill her anew as she thought that she probably hadn't made a mistake in accepting this job.

Daphne's sudden entrance into her life had given Diane more qualms about coming to Conard County than she'd initially had by far. When it was just her, it was all a big adventure. With Daphne it had become intimidating. She had begun to start thinking about all kinds of things, from day care to eventual schooling. Was this the best place to give her little cousin all the opportunities she should have? And what about the quality of medical care?

Thoughts that had never plagued her before plagued her now. "Becoming an unexpected mother is a bit shocking," she said, musing and only half-aware she was speaking. "A whole new set of worries I never had in the past, and bam, at the worst time possible, in the middle of a move and starting a new job."

"Yeah, most people get a little more warning, like about nine months."

Again he made her laugh. There was a sparkle in his amazing blue eyes and only humor around his mouth. A good-looking man. She realized she was experiencing an adolescent urge to just drink him in with her eyes. At once she raised her cup and turned her attention to her tea, hoping to find safety there. She had too much on her plate, and anyway, as far as she could determine, romantic relationships with colleagues could be fraught with danger and a lot of potential discomfort.

"Thanks so much for the tea," he said, rising. He crossed to the sink and rinsed his cup before setting it on the counter. "I'll see you in the morning, Diane. I'm sure you need some downtime after everything."

She rose, too, and followed him to the door. "How much trouble do you think they're going to give me over Daphne? Aubrey said she'll ask her sister-in-law to find room for her at the day care center."

He paused with his hand on the doorknob and gave her another smile. "I told you we were going to be an army. I meant it. First one gives you a hard time is going to hear from me. You're entitled to time to settle everything. Good night."

"Thank you again for the flower," she called after him.

He gave a quick wave, then strode away into the night. He moved easily, evidently fit and apparently accustomed to walking. He passed from the pool of light under one streetlamp to the next until he vanished around a corner.

Only then did she close and lock her door. Back in the kitchen, she smiled again as she looked at the bright red daisy on her windowsill. A thoughtful gesture. He couldn't possibly have guessed how much she loved gerbera daisies. They always reminded her of a drawing, so perfect it hardly seemed possible that they were real.

Then, trying to divert her thoughts from Blaine without much success, she put the remains of her steak sandwich and salad on a plate, opened a bottle of diet root beer and headed for her recliner.

Settled in comfortably, she waited for the next feeding and wondered if she could find that novel she'd been reading before her whole life had been packed into boxes and the trunk of her car. Having so little furniture of her own that was worth keeping had made the move easy and cheap. But now there were boxes stuffed into every corner, awaiting her attention. Boxes that had been labeled by the movers she had hired. She wondered how well they had done their jobs.

Well, she could wait to find out. The important thing was that she had her dad's easy chair.

And Daphne. That baby was becoming incredibly important to her.

Poor MaryJo. Diane couldn't begin to imagine the hell her cousin must be enduring. She just hoped the doctors could help.

Then she started eating, taking her time. Even cold the sandwich tasted delicious. She wiggled her toes and felt tension start to leave her legs.

Man, she had been wound up today, although she hadn't really been aware of it. For a little while when Daphne had refused to stop crying, yeah, then she'd been frantic.

But Blaine had come along, handling it all for her and assuring her it wasn't all that difficult a thing to take care of a baby. Then Aubrey and Candy and their warm welcome.

She just hoped tomorrow would go as well. With a full tummy, she put her empty plate and bottle onto the box beside her chair and allowed herself to doze. Behind her eyelids danced the memory of a man offering her a red gerbera daisy.

Chapter Three

For her first meeting with her new bosses as an employee, Diane chose a three-piece black outfit with slacks, a matching sleeveless shirt and a modified trapeze top that moved slightly when she walked but had the effect of minimizing her curves, such as they might be. Drawing attention to her gender had never yet proved to be an asset at work.

Daphne seemed to be in a sunny mood, eating her breakfast while looking around as if taking the whole world in. Tucked safely in her car seat, she waved her little arms and legs freely, causing Diane just a bit of trouble as she tried to strap the girl safely into the back seat of her car. Diane didn't mind the wiggling, however. She just wished she could share the child's happy mood. Right then she felt as if she might be going to her execution.

Aubrey and Candy had come to her office because they'd heard about Daphne. That probably meant everyone else with an interest had heard by now. What would she do if they refused to let her bring the child with her until she could find suitable care for her?

Her stomach had begun to feel like lead. The oat cereal she'd eaten felt like it wanted to stage a revolution. She paused to check the diaper bag once more, making sure she had enough for the day. And if she didn't, well, there was lunch hour and a trip to the pharmacy on Main Street or the grocery at the edge of town. She wasn't in the wilderness, for heaven's sake.

Mentally bucking herself up, she drove down streets beneath big old trees that were just beginning to brighten with autumn color. She had a designated parking space behind the courthouse, and she slid into it. After she turned off the engine, she sat for several minutes, trying to center herself.

She was startled by a gentle rapping on the window beside her. Turning her head, she saw a pleasant-looking man in a sweatshirt and jeans. She rolled her window down a crack.

"Hey," he said. "I'm Wyatt Carter, the judge around here. You're the new urban planner, aren't you? Is everything okay? You didn't move for so long, I had to wonder."

Diane felt her cheeks heat a bit. "I'm fine. New-job nerves."

He nodded. "I get that. Come on, I'll walk you in and we'll stare everyone down."

That made her smile at last. "Do I really need protection?"

He tilted his head as if thinking, then shook his head. "Actually, not at all. That's what I have a gavel for."

Which was how she came to be walking down the corridor in the courthouse basement with the judge carrying her diaper bag while she carried Daphne in her all-purpose car seat in one hand and her brief-case in the other.

Quite a start to the day, she thought as she entered her office. Wyatt—he'd already insisted she drop the formality—placed the diaper bag on her desk. "I'm just two floors up, and we're having a full day in the court. If you need anything from me, one of the clerks can bring me a message. But honestly, I think everyone down here will help you without hesitation. Have a great day and remind the council members I still own the gavel."

Well, he'd certainly helped her get over some of her nerves, she thought. Was this town a Disney creation? Everyone she'd met so far had been amazingly nice. She placed Daphne in a corner out of the way after checking her diaper, then gave her a small, not too noisy rattle to use. Clutched in one little fist, it waved in every direction, then wound up pressed to the girl's mouth. Everything seemed to wind up there. She made a mental note to check around her house very carefully before putting the baby down on a blanket on the floor.

Or maybe she should get a playpen. Man, the list was adding up. Playpen, changing table, crib. Then more clothes, because her onesies would stop fitting soon.

Seated at her desk, she pulled the files out of her briefcase, feeling only one pang of guilt that she hadn't spent any time on them last night. Not that they needed intense attention. One was the comprehensive plan from so long ago, and she'd read that before applying. It read like comprehensive plans everywhere except for being outdated.

Then there was a series of folders that amounted to the local wish list, she guessed. Airport runway expansion. Updating the parks. Help to attract new business. Some funding for repairing the high school, which had apparently met with… She caught her breath. A bomb? Really? She wouldn't have expected that here. Probably some kid who'd thought he was being funny. Or brilliant.

The one that most caught her attention was a plan to widen one of the roads up into the mountains to turn it into a scenic drive that would end at an historic mining town that, of course, needed work to make it safe. But that was the kind of thing she loved—preserving historical sites, making them into attractions that would ensure their longevity.

Some of these projects would likely have to be handled by bond issues, but some could well qualify for grants from various sources. And that would be her job. That and updating the comprehensive plan to comply with new regulations.

Leaning back in her chair, listening to the quiet sounds of the rattle, which would probably elicit tears by falling on the floor soon, and listening to the baby noises Daphne was making, she closed her eyes and remembered why she had taken this job in the first place.

Conard County wasn't all built up like the other places she'd worked, most recently Des Moines. When she'd come out for the interview and looked around the area, all she could see was possibility. Of course, she couldn't make it all happen, and she wasn't sure it would be good for the community if she did, but some of it could be brought to life here. The potential, the virtually clean slate…yeah, a lot could be done here, and with those mountains so nearby, that merely expanded the things they could accomplish.

The scenic road was one great idea. She'd also read how repeated attempts to build a ski resort had fallen through, the last time because of some serious landslides.

She didn't understand why it couldn't be done. Those mountains weren't going anywhere, but they needed funding for an independent geological survey. That last failure had occurred because of record-breaking rain. Surely that could be planned around. Earthquake activity seemed to be minor. She'd suggest the survey as one of her projects.

Oh, she'd been bubbling with ideas since her interview, but she had to be careful to avoid the "new broom" effect. There was bound to be resistance to any change around here, so she'd better find her way among the people who'd be affected. Maybe a town hall or charette, a survey of what folks besides the commissioners wanted around here. Community input was essential.

She glanced over and saw that Daphne had fallen asleep, the rattle still clutched in tiny hands. Toys suitable for an infant, she thought, adding that to her growing mental list. She wondered what other unthought-of things lay around the corner.

She returned to the files, trying to organize them in a useful way for the work ahead of her. Sources for grants would be her first move, and for that she needed projects that might garner private funding. Turning to the computer on her desk, she opened a new digital file and began to transfer information. Why in the world were these files still paper, anyway? Had they been around that long?

Much as she didn't feel like working, she actually made some headway in her organization and was starting to feel fairly good about her morning when the door opened.

Looking up, she saw Blaine poking his head through a five-inch opening. "We're up. The mayor,

the council chairman and the chief commissioner
have decided they want to meet with you *now*."

Diane's stomach turned over, then became queasy.
Anxiety because it was barely noon and the public
meeting was supposed to be at six. "Now?" she said
pointlessly.

"Well, I got you ten minutes. Better make sure
the tot is comfy and you have a bottle. Don't panic,
it's not the lion's den and I'll be there."

"I'm not panicking," she lied bravely. "What happened?"

"People talk. And some other people want to get
the jump on their, um, colleagues. In short, they
want the first whack and want information before
the others get it."

She understood that all too well. When it came to
personal power, adults could act like toddlers. "This
isn't a good start," she remarked.

"Is any? I'll be back for you and Daphne in ten.
Or would you rather I ask someone to watch her just
for now?"

"Thanks, but I might as well put all the cards on
the table right now." If it was to be a fight, she was
ready for it, she believed. Planners like her weren't
a dime a dozen.

Blaine walked down the hall, his thumbs hooked
on his jeans pockets. This was indeed not a good
start. The eejits had hired this woman while he was

away and could offer no input, and now they were going to have a turf war over her?

He had to give her marks for taking the tot right into it with her. Apparently, Diane Finch like to have the air as clear as possible. Well, so did he.

But not the damn fools they were about to meet. Oh, no. The muddier the better for them.

Then he brushed aside the thoughts as unproductive. He'd managed to work with these people for over five years now, and going all crackers on them in defense of Diane wasn't going to help anyone. He still had a culvert to take care of, and he and the roads department would be getting the blame if the commissioners stalled it.

As for Diane, she probably wanted to keep this job for a while. To withstand the inevitable storms that were coming, she needed to be firm and able to stand for herself. The politicians weren't all bad, after all. But they all had their moments.

Like any other human, he decided humorously. Show him a perfect person and he'd be sure he was looking at the Blessed Mother herself. Anyway, if it became necessary, he knew a few ways to step in to make them back off her.

Inside the chamber on the second floor of the courthouse, just beneath the courtrooms and judges' chambers on the third floor, only one commissioner had arrived. Madge Corker, a graying woman of near sixty, sat in her usual chair and eyed him with a smile.

"So we have a baby with us now, Blaine?"

"If ya won't mind, I'll be letting the planner explain it herself."

"Don't go Irish on me," she said lightly. "Usually I like to listen to that accent, but when you carry it too far, I have trouble understanding. I think we need to understand today."

"No doubt," he answered, plopping himself in a seat in the front row. "I've a culvert I need to talk about. I was planning that for tonight."

A sound of amusement escaped Madge. "You were always good at diversion."

"No diversion except around that culvert. Detours."

Another sound of amusement escaped her, then two men entered, wearing pressed Western shirts and jeans. The local dress-up. If you took an iron to it, you didn't need the three-piece and tie.

Neither of them looked remotely amused. Of course not. Men had a thing about babies at work. Women in the clerk's office were still trying to get a private closet for nursing.

Jeff Holdrum, the first to enter, was a portly man, just portly enough to look well-to-do and to sport a small spot of egg yolk on the front of his shirt. Minor Allcoke was a weedy man who looked as if he'd been starving all his life. Except Blaine had more than once watched him eat as if he were a three-hundred-pound rugby player.

As the two new arrivals took their place at the council table on its dais, Blaine felt some apprehension.

"This is all looking rather official," he said. "Where are the others?"

"That's tonight. Where's Ms. Finch? She's supposed to be here."

"I gave her ten minutes." He glanced at his watch. Then, just to annoy them, he switched to an upper-crust British accent, which he seldom used. "Only seven have passed. To avoid being rude, you understand."

For a second, he enjoyed watching them look a bit embarrassed. What was it about speaking the queen's English in the queen's accent that seemed to make Americans feel a bit…scolded? He wasn't sure.

Jeff Holdrum cleared his throat. "This is just about getting to know her."

"Right-o. I thought you already interviewed her."

"Some…things have changed."

"Hell, life has a way o' doing that, don't you know." Then he folded his arms and waited. He just hoped Diane didn't begin on her back foot. Weakness didn't stand up well against these folks. Given Madge was a woman, he hoped she was here to protect Diane, but he'd also seen enough women go after other women to know better than to hope.

He felt the unmistakable change of room pressure as the door at the back opened. Three sets of eyes left him and looked to the rear. He was tempted not to look at all, but then he changed his mind.

Diane was walking up the center aisle with the baby carrier all decked out in fresh yellow in one hand, the denim diaper bag over her shoulder and a briefcase in hand. He eyed her with admiration. Not only was she lovely, she'd also been serious about putting all her cards on the table. No mistaking it. Her stride was almost defiant.

"Hello," she said. "I'm sorry if I kept you waiting." She placed the carrier on the floor and next to it the diaper bag and briefcase. Then she walked up confidently to the dais and offered her hand. "We've met before, of course," she said. "At my interview. It's nice to see you again."

She even managed to address them all by name, a feat since she had only met them once nearly two months ago.

"What can I do for you?" she asked. "I've been looking into grant resources for various projects on your list, but it would be helpful if the projects could be prioritized for me. It would also help with writing the new comprehensive plan."

Straight to business. Blaine settled back to enjoy watching Diane take charge of this entire questionable meeting.

After a moment, Madge spoke. "We'd need everyone together for that. This is a special meeting."

"I gathered." Diane smiled and took a seat close to the child and her two bags. "I'm all ears."

Madge seemed reluctant, so it was Holdrum who put his foot in the potential quicksand. "We weren't aware you had a child. I believe that was one of the questions asked on your application, about your general family situation."

"It was," Diane answered pleasantly. "But if you look at my application, you'll find I didn't answer because the question is illegal. I thought it was just a holdover that hadn't been corrected so I ignored it. Regardless, I don't see why that would be a problem. Haven't you all worked when you had children?"

Allcoke cleared his throat. "Are you just babysitting, then? For how long?"

"I'm fostering for my cousin, who is seriously ill. I will have Daphne indefinitely. Again, why would that be a problem? And why do you need to know?"

The three commissioners traded looks. "It might interfere with your work," Holdrum said, nearly swallowing his words.

"Really? I'm seeking day care for her, but even so, making an issue out of the fact that I have a child to care for strikes me as illegal. So was the question on the application which I ignored, but I wasn't inclined to make an issue at that time."

Bravo, Blaine thought. She'd just cornered them. Maybe not the best way to get off on the right foot, but no question who was holding the reins right now.

Madge at last spoke. "Apparently we're sounding like an inquisition. That isn't our intent, but tonight these questions will arise again, and we need to know if there's some way we can forestall them or at least knock them down. Trust me, I'm on your side. Fostering a child is not an easy thing to do."

No, thought Blaine. It wasn't. It was also another thing for these folks to gnash their teeth over if they chose.

Daphne chose that moment to make her presence known with a loud cry and waving arms and legs.

"Allow me," Blaine said, moving swiftly. He opened the straps holding the child safely in place and lifted her to his shoulder. "There's a good girl," he said, patting her bottom. "Feeding time?"

Diane opened the flap on the diaper bag and pulled out a bottle, removing the cover from the nipple. Blaine shifted the child to the crook of his arm and started feeding her. "Nothing like a babe to remind you of the important things," he remarked as Daphne began to suckle quietly. He gave a stern eyeball to the three people on the dais.

Just then the back door opened again, and Wyatt Carter strode in, his black judicial robe flapping around his denim-clad legs.

"Can we help you, Judge?" Allcoke asked.

"No. I'm taking a recess because I heard about this little impromptu meeting. I'm sure you don't need me to remind you that meeting without a quorum and without public notice isn't exactly... copacetic. Then I heard all this was about a baby."

He walked over to take a look at Daphne tucked so securely into Blaine's arm. "Almost as cute as my daughter, although I guess I'm prejudiced." Then he faced the commissioners again.

"You really don't want to mess with this," he said. "I can give you chapter and verse if you like, but this woman is entitled to have a child, and she's entitled since she just moved here to take a little time to find proper care for the baby. Until then, her private office will do, and I don't see how the child's presence there will disturb anyone."

Holdrum raised his hands. Allcoke looked a little red. Madge smiled almost secretly.

"We were trying to forestall any problems at the public meeting tonight," Holdrum said.

"Oh, I can make time to come tonight if you think you'll need my legal opinion. And Blaine here doesn't seem at all disturbed by holding an infant and feeding her, something I'm quite sure he volunteered to do. In fact, if I know our county engineer after these past five years, I'd place odds on him liking to have the child around."

"Amen," said Blaine. "Wasn't about to let these gob—commissioners ride roughshod over Ms. Finch, who, by the way, was doing a grand job of standing her ground."

Wyatt Carter turned to look at Diane. "I'm sorry if I got in your way, Ms. Finch. I'm quite sure you're capable of handling this matter by yourself. My wife's like that. But in my opinion, you shouldn't even have to face this." He smiled. "I guess I was premature."

Diane shook her head. "I'll stand my ground, but it's nice to have support, Judge."

"Wyatt," he corrected again. Then he turned to the commissioners. "I've held fire on this subject, but I'm aware that a number of the clerks would like to have a room set aside for nursing their children. Which just goes to show there's nothing wrong in this county with women bringing their infants to work. If you want something to argue about tonight, I suggest the nursing room would be a good topic. And remember, I hold the gavel."

Then he strode out, black robes streaming behind him.

"Wow," whispered Diane.

Blaine was pretty sure that only he heard her. He rocked the baby gently, enjoying watching her drain her bottle.

For a few minutes the commissioners remained silent. Only Madge didn't look seriously annoyed.

"Is there something else I can do for you?" Diane asked pleasantly. "It'll soon be time to change a diaper, then I'd like to get back to work on all the projects you're considering. Some will be more easily accomplished than others, but I need to be familiar with them all to write the plan and start seeking grants."

Allcoke cleared his throat. "You want a list of priorities?"

"If you can give me one. It might come down to my judgment about how quickly we can gain grant money for some of them. For example, if I can get money in six months for that scenic road, I'm sure you'd like me to do that rather than wait on a grant process that could take years."

Now heads were nodding with her.

"We'd like your assessment, Ms. Finch," Madge said. "That would be a great help to us."

"Just call me Diane, please," she said. "Very well. I'll view the proposals and ideas from the perspective of earliest funding. It might take me a few days."

Holdrum waved a hand. "Take as long as you need," he said glumly. "After all, we haven't had anyone working on this in entirely too long."

"Would you like a presentation tonight, a general outline of what I'm planning to do?"

"That would be nice," Holdrum agreed. He sighed. "I wish I'd never allowed myself to be pushed into this, Ms. Finch. I'm sorry."

"Victory," Blaine said when they returned to her office and closed the door. At once, Diane set about changing Daphne's diaper, then burping her gently with a receiving blanket thrown over her shoulder.

"The big guns certainly arrived," she said. "I never expected that."

"Well, the whole damn place has been buzzing today because everyone heard about this so-called meeting. Hardly surprising that Wyatt showed up. I'm not prepared to instruct those people on what's legal and what isn't. Not my place, and I happen to like my job. But Wyatt…well, all he did was back up what you were saying. You're allowed to have a kid. The law favors you. When *he* said so, they could hardly argue."

Diane paced the small confines of her office, loving Daphne's baby scents, loving the warmth on her shoulder. The little girl made some cooing noises, then drifted into contented sleep.

"What do you think that was all about?" she asked. "It seemed strange."

"'Twas indeed. At first I thought it was intelligence gathering, but then I had another idea when they asked the question about the application you supplied."

She stiffened a little, then forced herself to relax so as not to disturb Daphne. "As in I lied on it?"

"Perhaps. No way to be certain. But I'd sure like to know what eejit was behind it."

"Me, too."

Daphne expelled one of her adorable gas bubbles, and Diane used the edge of the receiving blanket to wipe a little milk from her mouth. "This one makes a lot of washing. I'm glad my rental has a washer and dryer. I'd go nuts trying to keep up with all this if I had to use a public laundry. Is there even one around here?"

He shook his head. "Haven't seen one. The apartment complex has laundries for its tenants, but I guess most folks around here have their own machines, however old. I hear the appliance repair guy does a booming business."

"I can easily imagine that." She continued to pace, a glance at the clock telling her it was nearly lunch hour. Well, she'd brought along a peanut butter sandwich for herself and some cucumber spears. No need to go out with the baby, something she tried to avoid because she didn't think she was ready to deal with even something as small as a cold.

Her knowledge of small children seemed ridiculously limited for a thirty-two-year-old woman. Embarrassingly paltry. For the first time in her life, she thought about getting a how-to book. *Mothering for Dummies* or something.

She glanced at Blaine and saw that he was watching her carry Daphne with a small smile on his face. "Are you missing babies or something?" she asked baldly.

He blinked, as if startled by her blunt question, then laughed. "I suppose I am. Seems like we always had one in the house needing attention."

"Most boys would have resented that." She paused. "Most girls, too, I guess."

"Me mam worked hard. Everyone pitched in what they could."

Six kids? She could well believe it. Glancing down at her shoulder, she realized Daphne had drifted off to sleep again, her little fist pressed against her mouth.

"I need to get her a playpen," she remarked. "I'm

not sure where to go, but I have no baby furniture at all." Then she switched tack abruptly. "How did the judge get involved in that meeting? And why?"

"Wyatt's a good sort," Blaine answered. "I know he's been stewing for a few months about the nursing room and trying to find a way to insert himself."

"He didn't have any trouble inserting himself a short while ago," she retorted, a tremor of amusement in her voice.

"Well, he's not the sort to be running around shoving his opinion on everyone. The commissioners gave him an excuse. I'm surprised he didn't show up with a flaming sword."

"Or gavel," she answered. She shook her head a bit. "I could have handled it."

"Sure, and weren't you doing just that? He made it clear, I thought, that you could deal with any adversaries, but he seemed to be having a problem with their little illicit meeting."

She nodded her head. "He did bring that up. Rather forcibly. But still mildly." The judge had a presence to him, she thought. As Blaine did. She doubted very many messed with either of them.

"Well, I need to be getting out there to meet with a man who wants to do some work on his storefront. I don't know if you've gotten around to reading all that stuff yet, but we *do* have historical preservation ordinances. Gotta make sure he doesn't get too carried away."

"Thanks for everything, Blaine."

"No thanks needed. I had a culvert to talk about, and somehow we never got around to it. Not that it matters, since the meeting never happened."

She wondered if he were giving her some advice in that last statement. It wouldn't surprise her. Getting those commissioners into trouble wouldn't be a very good way to start out, and even the judge had merely warned them.

The door closed behind Blaine, and she decided that she might as well get some work done before Daphne woke up again. She seemed more active during the day now that the confusion level had died down a bit. Diane could only suppose that was good. A baby couldn't possibly sleep all the time, but it would be awfully nice if she weren't awake a lot at night.

After she'd settled Daphne into the carrier, she sat at her desk again and studied the heap of folders. She needed to get that mess—it was a mess, looking like a long-accreting wish list that might be only marginally useful—onto a computer, where she could organize everything by likelihood of a grant and likelihood of ever completing it, then nail down the folks involved about what they really wanted.

Because somehow at least some of this had to be incorporated into the plan when she was getting that straight with all the newer state and federal environmental regulations.

Blaine was going to talk to a guy about his historical facade? The county engineer? Didn't they have someone to handle that?

Remembering the list she'd seen in one of her drawers, she pulled it out and began to scan names. The date at the top said it was recent, but nowhere did she see anyone in charge of following the historic district rules. Or many rules, come to that. She wondered if that would now fall to her, as it apparently had to Blaine.

One of the downsides to a small rural area, she supposed. Well, she'd wanted more authority and responsibility. It appeared she was about to get it.

Then she looked at the stack of papers again. Damn, she needed an assistant to help get all this stuff into some kind of order. To get it on a computer where she could edit and rearrange easily.

Because she wasn't just taking over for someone who'd kept everything up-to-date. Nope, she was on an archaeological expedition.

Chapter Four

The meeting with the full city council and commission went off without a hitch, and Diane even got permission to hire an assistant and was offered an adjoining office. She suspected that Judge Wyatt Carter's appearance earlier had put them all on their best behavior. Not a peep about Daphne, either.

By Friday evening, she'd finished unpacking as much as she could, and took inventory of what she still needed. A chest of drawers would be very useful. A changing table. A playpen that could double as a crib unless she found one she really liked. Some more baby clothes, because at the rate she was going, she'd wear out the washer and dryer on small loads.

Daphne hadn't come to her with very much, and she hadn't had a whole lot of time to take care of shopping for her. The social worker had helped her over the first few steps—the car seat, the diaper bag, the set of bottles and formula—but then she'd been on her own, and there hadn't been much she could do until now.

Nor did she have any idea where to shop or even if she could find what was needed in this town. At that moment, Daphne was wiggling and proving that a receiving blanket wasn't big enough to create boundaries for her.

At least the floor was wood. That could be lightly mopped and kept clean. If this place had been carpeted, she wouldn't have dared put the baby down on it, at least not until after one heck of a steam cleaning.

Leaning back in her recliner without lifting the footrest, she watched Daphne with fascination. This little life was absorbing more and more of her attention, something she hadn't expected. All day long, even while she was working and Daphne was sleeping, thoughts of the baby danced around in the back of her mind. It was, she thought with amusement, exactly like the early days of a love affair.

Daphne was creeping—at least Diane thought that's what it was. She'd wiggled from side to side, pushing with her legs. The blanket wasn't exactly helping her, but it wasn't hindering her much, either. So much effort to move a few inches.

Then Daphne reared up, pushing downward with her arms, and startled herself by rolling over. She'd been doing that all along, at least since Diane had received her, but this time she proved not to be at all pleased by the change of view.

She let out a loud cry and her face turned red as she waved her arms.

"I guess you need to learn to turn over again when you want to," Diane said with a laugh. Rising, she gently rolled Daphne. At once the incipient temper tantrum calmed. The girl evidently had places she wanted to go. She resumed creeping, only to stop a minute later, close her eyes and fall asleep.

Such a peaceful scene. Amazing how beautiful a sleeping child could be.

The buzz of her cell phone, resting on the box she was using as an end table, surprised her. She reached for it mostly out of habit. She hadn't been here long enough to create friendships, and her friends from the past usually called on Sunday afternoon when no one was too busy to talk.

She answered, expecting a sales call of some kind.

"Hi," said Blaine Harrigan. "You were speaking of baby furniture. Freitag's is open late tonight, it being Friday and all. Would you and the tot like to look around? Plus," he added, a hint of amusement in his tone, "I'm blessed with a chariot big enough to transport any items you might decide to bring home."

Diane, who'd just been settling in for a relaxing evening with Daphne and a book, felt a leap of pleasure. An evening with Blaine was bound to be better than a book, and Daphne might actually enjoy the stimulation. For all she didn't want to expose the baby to some illness, the child *did* need to see and experience something besides an office and a living room.

And lately all kinds of things had been dancing through her mind, things like a mobile for the baby to watch, little toys she could grab and gnaw on...

"Oh, yes, I'd love that!" Her answer was enthusiastic, but she honestly didn't know whether her enthusiasm was more for shopping or for being out with Blaine.

She guessed it didn't matter, though. She not only had a new job and a new baby, but she also had a new life to build. Friends made any locale a far more enjoyable place to live.

Although, she thought as she picked Daphne up in order to change her and dress her more warmly for the outing, the baby would probably limit her social life for a while.

That was okay, she thought as she snuggled the warm little body close. This mother thing was okay, more okay than she'd expected.

Blaine had been so busy with the culvert and a number of other issues that seemed to spring up like weeds that he'd hardly seen Diane since the day of the meeting.

But that didn't mean she'd been out of mind while she was out of sight. No, she rather haunted him like a wraith at the edge of his mind.

No, not a wraith, he corrected himself. Damn, the Irish in him was getting the better of his thoughts. A wraith wasn't a good thing. In fact, the idea of a wraith could make a chill run down his spine, and he didn't hold himself to be especially superstitious.

But Diane had been haunting his thoughts, popping up unexpectedly at odd moments, accompanied by an impulse to go see her. It had been years since a woman had reached him that way, an occasion he didn't like to remember because he'd been young and callow and had made an utter arse of himself. Anyone with a hair of sense would have realized she wasn't interested, that she was merely patting him on the head like a puppy.

He'd survived that and put it in the past, but he hoped he was wiser now. He was certainly older. But there was no escaping the way Diane appealed to him. Easy enough to handle, he assured himself. And right now all he was doing was helping a new coworker settle in.

He dumped all the maps from the back seat of his SUV into the cargo area to make it ready for Daphne's car seat. It was going to be just like old times, putting a car seat in a car.

The coming autumn was putting a bit of nip in the evening air, so he closed the car door before going to get Diane.

She opened the door immediately, and the smile she gave him suggested that she might have been dealing with a bit of cabin fever. Well, she'd hardly had a chance to do anything except work and care for the babe. She was hunting for an assistant, but every time he popped his head into her office, she'd been buried in files, tapping at her computer or changing a diaper. Not much of a life for such a fine young woman who didn't have any help at home.

The baby was already in her car seat and covered by a light receiving blanket. Blaine took her and peeked under the blanket. "Sure and she's growing."

Diane laughed. "Her clothes certainly say so."

The drive to Freitag's Mercantile wasn't a long one. "Well, nothing in this town is much of a drive from anywhere else," Blaine said. "Freitag's goes back to the earliest days of this town. I hope you're liking creaky wood floors and crammed space. I'm thinking we should carry Daphne in without the seat."

"That crowded, huh?"

"Loaded with all sorts of good stuff. I think the owner's trying to prevent people from driving to bigger cities."

Diane laughed. "A noble goal. Business stays at home, then jobs stay at home."

"I'm in the way of thinking some of the sales-people in there have had those jobs since Freitag's opened."

A laugh spilled from Diane again, this time freer and more comfortable than the first.

She climbed out without his assistance and opened the rear door, disturbing Daphne as she removed her from her seat. "Come on, sweetheart, we've got all kinds of new things to look at."

Indeed, thought Blaine as he took charge of the diaper bag.

Woman and child walking into the store. An iconic image, he thought, despite the modern clothes. Damn, he was turning sappy, a questionable thing for an engineer. Logic. Science.

And a woman and a baby.

Laughing at himself, he walked into Freitag's behind her. Daphne was awake, bright little eyes hopping around, one fist against her mouth. He wondered how long it would be before all the unaccustomed stimulus overwhelmed her.

The baby merchandise was all stashed in a large alcove at the rear of the store. It wasn't the biggest selection, but it was adequate for whatever Diane might consider to be her immediate needs.

Rubbing Daphne's back, Diane began to wander around looking at everything. "Changing table," she remarked.

"Useful," he agreed. "Mam used an old chest of drawers. After six babies it didn't look very grand."

Diane laughed again, quietly. Daphne apparently liked the sound, because she began to coo. Diane shifted the girl into the cradle of her left arm.

"Here, let me hold her," Blaine said. "It'll be easier for you to look around."

Diane turned to him without reluctance and passed Daphne to him. He understood what a compliment that was. He had already noted how closely attached she was becoming to the child, and many mothers were reluctant to put a child so young in a virtual stranger's arms.

Once Diane made up her mind what she was going to do, Blaine went to find a clerk to help organize it all. Soon the back of his SUV was loaded with boxes containing a crib, a changing table and a playpen. Diane hesitated over the high chair, then decided it could wait a bit.

After that it was several bags of infant clothes, some washcloths and other necessities. A whole layette, basically, something Daphne hadn't come with.

Watching Diane give herself over wholeheartedly to providing her small cousin's needs, he smiled. The little one had no idea how fortunate she was. Diane was throwing her heart and soul into this.

The last purchase was a musical mobile, with colorful soft shapes hanging from it. Then Diane passed over her credit card and didn't even wince when she saw the total.

"Let me move all the boxes inside," Blaine suggested as they reached her house once again. "I can come over tomorrow and help with the assembly. You'll be happier once things are set up to your liking."

Diane made an amused sound. "Next I guess I'll need to shop for my own furniture. Not much came with the place. Anyway, with Daphne creeping now,

I need ways to keep her confined so I can go cook a dinner or something. I can't watch her every minute."

"That's what we have ears for."

He felt her look at him as he pulled up in front of the house. "Meaning?"

"You'll discover as she gets older especially that your ears are better nannies than your eyes."

"Right now," Diane answered, "my ears are telling me that she's getting cranky and hungry and probably needs a diaper change."

For certain, the noises from the back were sounding less like the coos she'd been making at the store and more like *Will someone please pay attention?*

"You take charge of the baby," Blaine said as he switched off the ignition. "I'll bring in the purchases. Just wave me through to where you want them."

"That's an awful lot to carry," she said as she opened her door and put one foot to the ground. "I'll help as soon as I settle Daphne."

"Not to worry. I've a strong back and I've carried more than that in my life. Loads of brick, in fact, when I was studying engineering."

"That's a story I want to hear," she said.

"And leave the car seat. I'll get that, too."

For the first time he passed the nearly vacant front room and kitchen. There were two small bedrooms in the back, and Diane told him to take everything to the one on the right. As he carried in the boxes and bags, it seemed to him that this small bedroom was about to become very crowded. Well, he supposed she'd want the playpen up front, but still, it would be a squeeze to fit the crib, the changing table and the small chest she'd bought. And the room didn't have a closet!

He was used to that at home. That was why armoires had been created, but even if he'd had one, it wouldn't fit here. He paused, using his skills to envision the best layout so Diane wouldn't be tripping over herself trying to move in here.

A glance in the other bedroom, the one she occupied, suggested it wasn't much bigger.

Well, space wasn't a problem he could solve in this rental house.

Diane had changed Daphne's nappy on the living room floor atop a blanket, and now she was feeding the babe, who at last appeared content. And alert. That girl seemed like she didn't want to miss a thing. From time to time, she released the nipple and made little vocalizations that almost sounded as if she were talking. Then she'd go back to her bottle, her eyes fixed on Diane.

"So," he said as he looked around, "how long are you planning to live as a minimalist?"

Diane shook her head a little, but she wasn't frowning. "Most of what I had before came from a secondhand shop, and I don't mean an upscale one. I also relied on boxes to be tables. I never intended to stay forever in Des Moines, so I furnished as little as possible, and hardly any of it was worth bringing with me. Saves a lot on moving costs. This chair is the only piece of furniture I actually brought with me."

He dropped onto the floor and sat cross-legged, elbows on his knees. "Might make entertaining a few friends difficult." He was glad that she chuckled quietly.

"It might," she admitted. "I realize I have to get at least a few things." She paused. "I can't stop thinking about how the judge charged into that meeting the other morning."

Blaine tilted his head. "I can't say I expected it. However, Wyatt Carter is a straight arrow, and it probably chapped him a bit to hear about some of the commissioners meeting without public notice. I think I mentioned that to you. And then there's the whole thing about a nursing room for the mothers who work in the courthouse. That's been hemmed and hawed about for a year. Maybe more," he said after a moment. "Be that as it may, you wouldn't think the politicians would find it all that difficult. A small room, a chair or two. Oh, and a lightbulb."

She giggled softly. "You make it sound so easy, but it turns the patriarchy upside down."

"Now how could that be?" he said. "None of the patriarchy would exist without a mother who nursed them."

"Maybe that's what gets to them."

"Hmm." He rubbed his chin. "Well, whatever made them stubborn, I know it was irritating more than the clerks. Wyatt was getting irritated by the way it was dragging on, but it was wholly under the purview of the powers that be. Namely commissioners and councilmen who sometimes can be too stubborn for no discernible reason. And why it should all fall to them anyway, beats me. Seriously? The janitor could have just made them the room, and who would have argued about it then?"

Diane was now grinning. Daphne appeared to be done with her bottle, so Diane laid her tummy down across her knees and rubbed gently while the child reached for invisible objects, stretching her arms and opening and closing her tiny hands. The soft coos and trills had returned. Soon they'd be followed by sleepiness.

"You want me to put that playpen together for you tonight?" Blaine asked.

"I don't think there's a rush. But thank you. In fact, thank you for everything you've done tonight."

He waved his hand, indicating it was of no importance.

"How is the culvert going?" she asked as she placed Daphne on her receiving blanket to inch her way around until sleep found her. A small soft toy was there for her to grab, but Blaine, without answering her question, stretched out near the blanket's edge and dangled a key ring, causing it to make a quiet ringing sound.

At once Daphne arched her back to look.

"I won't let her grab them," Blaine said. "I hate to think of how much grime they have on them."

"I'm not worried," Diane answered. She'd had Daphne long enough now to realize that sterility was an impossible ideal. The girl would put anything in her mouth, including a dead fly a few days ago. She was still healthy.

And she was fascinated by the keys. With great effort and focus, she pushed herself toward them.

All of a sudden Blaine stood up. "I have a better idea."

Diane watched him stride toward the back of the house and returned her attention to Daphne. A better idea?

A few minutes later, she had her answer as Blaine set up the playpen, an easy task since basically it just needed to be folded open and locked. Then he clamped the mobile on and started it playing.

Daphne was scooped up with her blanket and settled in the playpen on her back, where she became instantly fascinated by the mobile and its slowly turning brightly colored shapes of stars, fishes and cats. An eclectic assortment, Diane thought with amusement.

Then Blaine disappeared again and returned with one of the paper bags she'd brought home. This one contained not clothing but toys. Cute little toys she hadn't been able to resist, items for Daphne to gnaw on, grasp and eventually throw, she guessed.

Satisfied at last, Blaine returned to his cross-legged position on the floor. "Now," he said, "you can run to the loo or take a shower without having to straitjacket her in her car seat."

Diane laughed. "How did you know what I was doing?"

"I told you, I was the eldest of six. I had to practice all kinds of devious methods to get a moment or two to myself."

She looked at him there, sitting on her floor with his arm draped over one upraised knee, and began to feel like a very bad hostess. "You've helped me so much and I haven't even offered you coffee or tea."

He shook his head, one corner of his mouth lifting. "I don't recall asking for anything. Besides, I'm enjoying myself. I miss my family. This is kind of making up for it."

A tingle of unease settled in her stomach, but she couldn't have said why. "Are you thinking about moving back home?"

"In the foreseeable future? Nah. The youngest is grown-up, me mam has found a new man and there's not much need for me at home. My visiting is enough. Besides, I believe I told you I like it here."

So he wasn't leaving. Why that should matter to her...well, she didn't want to think about that. She'd known the man less than a week. Bad enough that she thought about him at odd moments and felt her feminine side weakening with desire. Nothing worse, she reminded herself, than getting involved with a coworker.

"What about you?" he asked. "You told me your cousin is sick, but is there no one else?"

Diane focused her gaze on Daphne, who seemed to have fallen asleep despite all the new distractions. Or maybe because of them. A trip to the store that had kept her wide-awake with fascination, and now the new toys and mobile. She reminded herself that she needed to keep the girl stimulated. Dang, she had missed the mother genes, evidently. Come to the game unprepared. Daphne wasn't a doll who could be tucked into a corner. She needed a whole lot to keep her thriving.

"Diane? Bad question?"

She sighed. "I don't want to advertise this."

"I'm not given to gossip, if that's what you're meaning. I may listen, but I seldom repeat unless it's something casual and harmless."

She hesitated a little longer, then decided life would probably be easier if she had a confidant. Lately life had been overwhelming her, and even with her old girlfriends she'd felt it wisest to just put a bright face on everything. She hadn't even told them what was wrong with MaryJo.

"I'll be honest, Blaine. There are some things in society that are considered…" How could she even explain it? "Shameful?" She tried that on, then left it. "It's unfair, but that's the way people react."

He nodded slowly. "And that would be?"

"My cousin is a paranoid schizophrenic, and she

was hospitalized because she doesn't respond to drug therapy."

"She's out of her blazing mind, then."

Diane compressed her lips, feeling a spark of anger but unable to deny what he said. "You could put it that way."

He shook his head and stood up. "I don't mean that in a bad sense. Sometimes I'm too blunt for my own good." He paced a couple of steps then came back. "You have a teapot? And a box of loose tea?"

"Teapot yes, loose tea, no."

"Then I suggest we repair to the kitchen where there are two chairs and have a bit of tea, the inevitable cure for everything in my homeland."

"Britain, too, I guess," she said, smiling wanly.

"We don't mention them. Too many bad memories still in the air." But he spoke pleasantly, not at all critically.

She checked Daphne again, but the child was happily sleeping, so she followed Blaine into the kitchen.

"Tell me where to find everything?" he asked.

So she pointed out what little she had, then settled down to let him make the tea as he chose.

"Your cousin is that ill, then. Not much hope, I expect?"

"They weren't offering any."

"No other family?"

Another question she hated to answer. "Her father disappeared before she was born, and her mother was an alcoholic."

"Was?" He set the kettle on to boil and opened the box of tea bags. From the overhead cupboard, he pulled down her Japanese teapot with the wicker handle. "I like these," he said, indicating the pot. "Was?" he repeated.

"MaryJo's parents—well, that's a strange story. They split when MaryJo was little. She never saw her father again. Her mother became an alcoholic, which didn't help anything. Anyway, a couple of years ago, the two of them got together briefly in Texas. No one knows why they met up and probably never will, but while they were there, the two of them drowned in a flash flood."

"Good God," he said. "That must have been devastating for your cousin. And how strange they got together!" He shook his head a bit as he moved around the kitchen. "Will I ever understand people?"

"I don't know. It's sad, but my family had little contact with hers. I'm not sure why. I guess the situation turned them off. Anyway, my parents moved a lot and seldom went back to Gillette—my dad was in the oil business and…any ties just evaporated. I sent MaryJo Christmas cards. Does that make me awful?"

He leaned back against the counter, waiting for the kettle to boil. "No. Families are created by blood. Not by choice. Sometimes they don't work out. With as little contact as you had with your cousin, she's a stranger, isn't she?"

"Unfortunately. Or maybe fortunately. I don't know." Diane looked down, feeling a wave of guilt accompanied by some grief. The fact that she didn't know MaryJo didn't make her feel a whole lot better.

"So that left you to take care of the daffodil," he said. He arranged tea bags in the pot, the tags hanging out, and poured boiling water into it. Along with a couple of cups, he set it on the table then sat across from her.

"You're awfully alone," he remarked. "At least in terms of people who might help you with the babe."

"I knew that would be the case when I took this on." She put her chin in her hand, just looking at him because he was so easy on the eyes, and realized that her ears were tuned toward the living room, listening for Daphne sounds. "You called her daffodil?"

"Better than Daffy."

That drew a tired laugh from her. "True that."

"But back to you," he said. "Taking on a baby is huge. It's not like you were eagerly awaiting a bundle of joy and taking parenting classes or whatever. It must have been sudden."

"It was. But I couldn't do anything else, Blaine. When that social worker started talking about putting Daphne in foster care, it was like everything inside me shriveled. And there wasn't even a chance she could be adopted into a good home, because my cousin isn't well enough to give her up, so that would involve all kinds of court hearings that might drag on for years. The only thing I was sure of was that I couldn't let Daphne be handed over to strangers.

They might have been nice strangers, but…at least I know the kind of person I am."

"A kindhearted one," he said decisively. He poured tea into their cups then lifted his for a sip. "Ah," he said.

"The tea bags worked?"

"They did. Like I said, I'm not some kind of connoisseur. I'm a man on my own, and when I'm in a hurry, I'm not picky."

She watched him. He closed his eyes, savoring the tea, the lines of his face relaxing somewhat. All the while she watched, she felt as if her entire being were being pulled toward him.

Gah! she thought and tore her gaze away. A handsome Irishman was *not* going to turn her into a puddle. She couldn't allow it. Too much settling in to do on the job. Too much she needed to learn about being a good mother for Daphne.

"How's the culvert project?" she asked for the second time, seeking safe ground.

"Ah, well." He set his cup down and refilled it from the pot. "The plans are being drawn up. I'm working with the roads department to see if we can come up with something more durable, but given the climate hereabouts, I doubt it. We'll try anyway, because the detour already has a half dozen ranchers climbing our backs. It adds quite a few miles for them to get to town. Be that as it may, chances are we'll use the concrete culverts we already have at the lot, sink another galvanized steel pipe in for extra reinforcement and once again wait for nature to do its work."

Diane felt a bubble of amusement. "Isn't that always the way with roads?"

"Aye, but I can hope. I mean, I keep thinking of the Appian Way, two thousand years of foot and cart traffic. And there are roads in Mexico and Peru that are centuries old."

"Dream big, do you?"

He unleashed a laugh that seem to rise from the depths of his being. "Guilty."

He'd been likable from the start, but in that instant she knew she liked him above average. A glance at the clock told her Daphne would probably give her an hour before waking again, and Blaine seemed in no hurry to leave.

Not that she wanted him to. His company was pleasant, calming in a way. But exciting, too. It was that exciting part that worried her.

"I told you my mother, otherwise known as Mam, got herself a new man."

Diane's interest pricked immediately. "I don't remember. Is that a problem?"

"Not for her, I gather. I only go home once a year." He leaned forward, resting his elbows on the table. "What concerns me is the very strong feeling I get that he'd rather I not show up at all. Now, there's no reason for him to be jealous of me. I'm hardly there. But I find myself wondering what is it he doesn't want me to know or find out."

Diane drew a sharp breath. "Oh, Blaine, really? But what about your other brothers and sisters? Surely they'd have noticed if something was wrong?"

He shook his head. "They're scattered all over the EU now. You go where the jobs are. So Mam is essentially on her own in Galway."

Diane resisted an urge to reach out for his hand. "Friends? She must have friends."

"She certainly used to. Neighbors have moved away over the years, but there was always church. My mother was one of those who had a string of rosary beads in her hand most of the time, went to Mass every single morning, did a lot with parish events."

Diane nodded slowly. "And now?"

"Not so much. I asked her last time I was there, what about church? Daily Mass? She said she went when she felt like it. That doesn't sound like her. I asked the others to check it out, but they're not seeing any more than I am. Mam's lost interest in the church. She wouldn't be the only Irish person to do that since the scandals, but her faith was something different. At least I thought it was."

Diane bit her lip. "Could she be ill?"

"She doesn't appear to be. And I might be overreacting since I'm so far away. Natural, maybe, that when a new man appears in your mother's life you get a little uneasy."

Diane could understand his worry. The situation

would generate concern. "Have you tried talking to her about it?"

He tilted his head. "I believe we all have. She insists she's quite happy. I'm probably worrying entirely too much. She hasn't married the bloke, and the family silver is still in the drawer where she's always kept it. It's likely everything is fine and there's no reason for any of us to wonder about it. Perhaps we're all just having trouble seeing a stranger where Da used to be."

She nodded, thinking it over. Of course, she knew nothing at all about the real situation, so what did she have to offer? A word of sympathy? Then something he had said struck her. "You have family silver?"

A grin slashed across his face. "Sounds all important like, doesn't it? Like we must be descended from landed gents or something. But it's just a few small tarnished pieces, come down through generations and no one knows from where. Maybe an ancestor who worked in one of the grand English houses as a maid and lifted a piece from time to time."

"Oh, I like that story."

He laughed. "Believe me, it's the likeliest way a Harrigan could have come by some silver." He rose. "I've got to be on my way, Ms. Finch. There's a darts game waiting for me at the pub…er, bar, and I mustn't be late. Shall I come by in the morning to help with the rest of the furniture?"

It had taken Blaine a while to settle into Conard County. As friendly as the place was, like in many small communities, you needed to be around for a while to be accepted as a local—or rather, *almost* a local. He fancied he might just be arriving at that exalted place.

He hoped he was helping ease Diane's way into all this. Remarkable woman, he thought, not for the first time. Not so much for deciding to take on this position and moving here to the middle of everything— or the middle of nowhere, depending on your measure. No, what impressed him was that she'd so readily taken on her cousin's child, and at the most inconvenient time imaginable, just as she was starting a new job and having to move away from everyone she knew.

Of course, it probably helped her admirability factor that she displayed such an attractive bundle of curves.

That was a thought he quashed quickly, steering away from it with long practice. If he wanted a woman, it would be best to look far enough away that no one here would know about it, unless he was prepared to ignore the constant interest from the local denizens.

He'd experienced his share of that in Galway. 'twas a big enough city, but within it were smaller communities who'd lived together for generations. Hard to keep any secret there, and hard to ignore all the unwanted advice.

There was still some feuding left over from the days when the place had been ruled by the tribes.

Wealthy, powerful and…aw, to hell with it. To this day people traded on their relationship with one tribe or another.

A certain drawer with silver in it might even go back to all that.

But as he climbed out of his vehicle and strode toward Mahoney's, he pushed away thoughts of home. Darts tonight, after a pleasant evening spent with a pleasant young woman and her darling babe… Could a man ask for much more?

Oh, yeah, he thought as he pulled the door open and the sound of voices and music poured out along with the familiar scent of stale beer and even some smoke. A man could ask for a whole lot more.

He just hadn't been in the asking mood for a very long time.

Not since Ailis. Nor did he want to be thinking of that woman right now.

He'd barely crossed the threshold before a green bottle of chilled ale was thrust into his hand, and Dan Casey, a local deputy, was urging him toward the group gathered at tables around the dartboard. He was greeted with waves of the hand and voices asking where the hell he'd been. Most of the men he played darts with were county employees, whether sheriff's deputies or road workers or firemen. It made for some interesting conversation to go with a couple of late-night beers. They usually shut the place down around one in the morning.

Like back at home. Here he truly felt the comfort

of long familiarity, as if he were at his local pub in Galway.

With one difference. He had his own very expensive set of tungsten-tipped darts. He'd never been able to afford them before, but now he could. When he pulled the black leather case out of his hip pocket, he heard Jake Madison say, "Ooh, look out now. The man's come fully armed."

Loud laughter ran around the room, and Blaine returned it with a grin. "Been sharpening my points, you gobboxes. We're ready to go."

Except that Diane kept drifting through his thoughts, her and the baby, and his concentration failed him from time to time.

He wasn't going home the winner tonight. Nor did he care.

Chapter Five

Saturday morning.

Rising early because he'd promised to put together some baby furniture today, Blaine stopped by the diner to rustle up a couple of breakfasts that included cinnamon rolls, a box of buttered toast just in case and a couple of tall lattes. He liked a coffee from time to time himself, and he suspected Diane did, as well. Something about the way she made tea persuaded him that the drip coffeemaker on her counter probably wasn't there for show.

Maude's daughter Mavis, a clone of her mother, put the takeout in a bag for him and sent him on his way.

This morning, the nip of early autumn had at last

arrived. He enjoyed the crisp air and freely admitted
he didn't always miss the grayer, wetter and cooler
climate in which he'd grown up. Oh, he missed going
on out the fishing boat sometimes, and spending a
hard day bringing in a catch they could sell. His two
brothers had leased out their da's boat to a family
they'd grown up with. The Quinns. Hard, dangerous
work was fishing, and the seas the more dangerous
for being so far north in strong currents. The Quinn
boys were working their butts off, but according to
his brother Liam, they were only a couple of years
from paying the boat off. Good on 'em.

In some ways life had been harder back when his
family depended on fishing, but better, too. There'd
even occasionally been enough extra money for all
the kids to go to the flicks. What grand times those
had been.

He was halfway to Diane's little house when his
cell rang. Dang, he hoped it wasn't something urgent,
but a quick glance told him it was Diane. All right,
then. He'd be there in three minutes, so no point
pulling over to answer. He wondered if she wanted
to postpone for some reason.

He was smiling as he knocked on Diane's door.
When it opened his jaw dropped a bit. Her hair was
going every which way, her robe was belted crook-
edly and in the crook of her arm was a rigid, screaming, red-faced Daphne.

"What happened?" he asked.

"I don't know."

Forget an invitation. He moved inside, causing her to step back. "I'll just put the breakfast and coffee on the table, shall I? Then you tell me what that child is doing."

"Screaming," she said as she followed him into the kitchen. "I don't know, Blaine. She woke me up shortly after six, and I haven't been able to figure out anything to calm her. Diaper change didn't help, she didn't want to eat when I offered the bottle, I'm not sure if she feels warm or if that's just the screaming. I'm worried."

He turned. "I gather." If he hadn't seen it in her face, he'd have recognized it in her voice. Tight with apprehension. Edged with exhaustion. Then he reached out and took Daphne from her. The girl's stiffness shook him a bit, too, but it wasn't the first time he'd seen an infant resemble a post. Any serious discomfort could do that, but it didn't always mean anything bad.

A series of questions needed answering. "How was her stool? Unusual in any way?"

Apparently such discussions were new to her, because her eyes widened and her jaw dropped a shade. If Daphne hadn't been so distressed, he might have laughed. "You've got three forms of communication with an infant, Diane—what exactly is coming out of either end and are they screaming like bloody hell. Let's start with the bottom. We already know about the screaming."

"Her diaper seemed normal. But this morning it's

like she's been constipated, maybe? Straining? But I can't be sure, Blaine! I've only had her for a little more than a week. Maybe she has screaming spells periodically."

He nodded, shifting Daphne from the crook of his arm to his shoulder, where he patted her. Her screaming was loud enough to make him wonder how much hearing he'd lose. Of course, he'd been screamed at like this before. "No vomit?"

"Nothing."

He held Daphne away from him for a few seconds, studying her. Her little feet sawed the air, and her fists waved. "She sure does look angry. Mostly miserable."

He hesitated as he pulled the baby close to his shoulder again. He was about to scare Diane to death, he supposed, but no way around it. "Get dressed and put something warm on her. We'll go to the emergency room." He braced, half expecting an explosion of anguish. Of course, his mam had always been good at going over the top. Diane surprised him.

"You think it's that bad?" Diane asked, her voice cracking.

Using his free arm, he pulled her close to his side and kept his voice as soothing as he could make it. "I don't know what's going on, so we'd be best to check it out. You said she's been crying for hours. That's not usual unless she's been colicky, and in the space of a week, I'd think you would have seen that at least once before. But I'm not a doctor, and I believe that visiting one might make all three of us feel better." At least that was his hope. But this sure didn't sound like colicky crying to him. He'd had two brothers with it.

Diane nodded, fright giving way to the need for action. "Yes, of course. God, I've never felt so helpless in my life!"

Blaine watched her turn to go get swaddling for the baby and asked, "After you dress, would you mind grabbing the two coffees I brought? I don't have any idea how long this will take."

And a coffee might be just the thing for both of them. He rocked Daphne, trying to ease her misery and completely failing. This must be why Diane had called him a little while ago. Inexperienced with a baby crying like this? She must indeed have felt helpless.

'Twas a fact—little could make a human feel as helpless as a crying babe that couldn't be soothed. Or wear one out as fast.

Strapping Daphne into her car seat was a battle. The girl was rigid as a board and fought every attempt to bend her even a little.

"The hospital is close?" Diane asked, a tremor in her voice.

"A few minutes by car. The babe won't have to endure the seat for long."

At last they got her secured, then Diane slid into the front seat beside Blaine and they took off through the quiet Saturday morning at speeds that should have gotten them a ticket. Although, thought Blaine, if any cop stopped them, one listen to Daphne's distressed crying would probably get them an escort to the hospital.

He didn't want to let Diane know, but he was worried, too. He'd helped his mam raise two colicky babies, and that uproar had a way of beginning in the evening, not in the wee hours, although he supposed it was possible. But to go this long without having seen it once? Not likely. His experience with colic had taught him it usually occurred several times a week. Could a child develop colic at three months? For that he had no idea.

Anything was possible, he supposed, but he had just run smack into the limits of his knowledge of babies. Plus, Daphne's crying didn't hold the fussy sounds of a colicky kid. It sounded pained, and that was sufficient cause for worry on a Saturday morning when the only place to go was the emergency room.

Sufficient cause to feel huge relief when he at last pulled up beside the emergency room entrance at Memorial Hospital.

"You just go ahead and take her in," he told Diane. "I'll park and come find you."

Diane lifted the shrieking Daphne out of her car seat and held her close as she hurried through the emergency room doors. Unprepared. Inexperienced. *What that hell am I doing being someone's mother?*

The mental self-kicking at least eased the fear

that lurked in every corner of her mind. This baby depended on her, and she was helpless. *Helpless.* Oh, God, she should never have taken this on. An experienced foster mother would know what to do.

But she didn't regret accepting Daphne. She looked down into that scrunched-up, reddened face and all she could feel was love and a need to get her help. Stiff as a board. Oh, God, the child was stiff as a board. That had to mean awful pain, right?

All of a sudden, she was in the middle of a swirl of people in blue scrubs. Apparently Daphne's screaming sounded like a problem to them, as well.

"How long as this been going on?" a woman asked.

"Since shortly after six. She won't eat."

"No vomiting?"

"No."

At the center of the whirlwind, she was ushered into a cubicle.

"The doctor will be here shortly," said the pleasant woman. "In the meantime I'm going to have someone come in to take your information." Then she paused and laid her hand on Diane's shoulder. "Relax. She sounds far too strong to be in imminent danger, okay? Dr. Dave will get her feeling better just as soon as he can. And if you need me, my name is Mary."

Mary was quickly replaced by a young woman pushing a cart with a computer on it. The questions began to come, but before the admission was complete, Mary returned and took Daphne from her arms.

Diane had the worst urge to cry out, *Don't take her from me.*

But that would help nothing. Steeling herself, she let go of the baby, feeling as if her skin had been ripped away.

Mary placed her on the bed with the sides up and began to unwrap her. "Screaming like this will drive you nuts," she said cheerfully. "I know, I have a couple of my own. I wasn't sure if both of us would survive the colic." She flashed a smile at Diane.

"You think it's colic?"

"First off, I'm not the doctor, so I can't say anything. But the baby…" She looked at Diane again.

"Daphne."

"Daphne's going to get the best care. I'm just going to take her temperature."

Then came the rest of the questions from the woman with the cart. The insurance part shut down the instant Diane said she was working for the county government. No ID required. They didn't even ask if Daphne was her legal daughter. She'd deal with that later. Right now, helping the baby was all that mattered.

With Daphne stripped down to her tiny undershirt, her diaper gone, Mary used the thermometer with practiced ease.

"No fever," she announced. "That's good." She wrapped the babe tightly in a blanket. "It makes infants feel more secure to be tightly wrapped. It's not going to help much right now, obviously, but a tip for another time."

"Thank you." Diane leaned back in the uncomfortable plastic chair, fatigue trying to overwhelm her even as she felt as if she were dangling over a cliff edge in fear. Daphne was still screaming and stiffening as if trying to push something away.

No, that wasn't normal, she thought. It couldn't be. She should have come here a couple of hours ago when she had begun to realize she couldn't make the baby feel any better.

Failure. The word popped up in her head. It wasn't exactly unfamiliar. She'd grown up with it. Then there had been Max. He'd been quick to fling that word around, too. She failed at everything, from cooking to cleaning.

And now she was failing Daphne. A shudder ran through her, and her eyes felt as if they were burning holes in her head.

Minutes dragged. Blaine arrived, standing to one side behind her, his hand welcome on her shoulder.

Then a man swept into the room, stethoscope hanging around his neck. "Hey, Mary, what are we looking at?"

"Screaming for about four hours, stiffening and pushing, no vomiting, no fever, and despite all that pushing, she hasn't moved any stool."

"All right."

Diane watched anxiously as the doctor pulled the

blanket away and began to press gently on Daphne's tummy. "Some rigidity," he remarked. Mary typed it in on the computer near the head of the bed.

Then he pulled his stethoscope off his shoulder and put the earpieces in his ears. He clasped the diaphragm between his gloved hands for a minute, probably warming it up, then pressed it to Daphne's tummy, listening. He moved the diaphragm around, pausing to listen again and again.

"Bowel sounds are sluggish. Something's slowing up the works."

Diane bit her lip, trying to imagine what that might mean. The exam continued, occasional words being passed to Mary for the chart. At no point did Daphne's crying ease. It was a wonder she didn't become silent out of sheer exhaustion.

Then the doctor pulled the ear stems free and leaned over Daphne, running his hands gently over her, from the top of her tummy down to her groin.

"Ah," he said, straightening. "Mom, you want to come see this?"

Diane leaped to her feet. What had he seen? She hadn't noticed anything in all these hours, and she'd changed Daphne half a dozen times hoping to find the answer in a diaper.

"Here," the doctor said, pointing. "You see this small bump?"

Daphne peered. It wasn't obvious, but she was sure of one thing. "I've never seen that before."

"Probably not, or you'd have heard this scream-ing before. I believe it's a hernia."

She looked up quickly at the doctor, her heart jumping, her stomach fluttering unhappily. "Is that dangerous?"

"Depends, but it's an easy fix. I'm going to get an ultrasound to confirm my suspicion."

But Diane wasn't happy to let it go at that. "Why does it depend?"

The doctor smiled over the squalling baby at her. "If it goes on too long, depending on how large a her-nia it is, it could incarcerate the bowel. That would be a problem. This doesn't appear to be that bad—the bowel sounds were normal, if sluggish. I'm bet-ting this problem is just showing up. But we'll see. In the meantime..."

He pressed on that small bump in Daphne's abdo-men until it was flat. "Gently," he said.

It was as if someone had flipped a switch. Daphne stopped shrieking, instead snuffling and making hic-cuping sounds as she began to settle.

"There you go," the doctor said. "You can hold her, but don't feed her. The ultrasound tech shouldn't be long, but...what I just did is pretty much diagnos-tic. A small incision, some stitches and this girl is going to be just fine."

"But what did you just do?"

"I pushed her intestine back through the hernia. It won't last, unfortunately, but for a little while she can rest."

Diane sank back into the chair, feeling as if someone had let all the air out of her. The child was going to be okay. One little press and Daphne had become quieter. A couple of stitches inside and she'd be better. Right?

"We'll talk about the surgery after I look at the ultrasound," the doctor said. "I'll see you again shortly."

Diane wanted only one thing—to hold her little girl again. But she sagged in the chair as if someone had cut her strings. It fell to Blaine to wrap the baby up in a blanket and place her in Diane's arms.

She looked at him, wishing she could fall into the pools of his blue eyes. They brought good things to mind, like sunny summer skies, so at odds with the moment. "It's going to be all right."

"That's what it sounds like." The corners of his eyes creased as he smiled. "Although I wouldn't be surprised if she starts screaming again before all this is done. A hernia."

"I'm not even sure what that is."

"He'll tell us, I'm sure, but it's my understanding it can be an opening in the intestinal wall. That's why he could push her intestine back in."

Diane tried to absorb that while rocking gently and looking down into Daphne's face. The girl had fallen into exhausted slumber, a relief of huge proportions for both her and her daughter.

Her daughter. She realized that was the first time

she had thought of Daphne that way without any qualifiers. Her daughter.

There was a scrape, and she looked around to see that Blaine had pulled another chair into the cubicle. He put it beside hers and sat, reaching over to place his hand on her arm. "How are you managing, Diane?"

"Relieved. Worried." She gave a small, tired laugh. "Is it possible to feel both at the same time? Because I think I do."

"Wouldn't surprise me. Poor little tot, poor little mam. You're both wiped, I'm thinking."

"You can skip the diminutive with me," she told him. "Just because I'm a woman…"

He quickly held up a hand, looking as serious as a judge. "I didn't mean any such thing. Sometimes my tongue slips into old ways."

She nodded and let it go. More important things to worry about, anyway. Daphne needed surgery. The doctor might make it sound minor, but Diane wasn't inclined to think any surgery could be perfectly minor, especially not if it involved anesthesia. Such a tiny person in her arms, utterly vulnerable.

She couldn't sit any longer. Holding Daphne close to her breast, she rose and began to pace the tiny cubicle. She felt as if ants of anxiety crawled all over her. The doctor made it sound so simple, but she was sure nothing involved with surgery was that simple. No way. All kinds of things could go wrong, and she was sure that before they went ahead with an operation, she was going to be handed something to sign, something that warned her of every potential peril involved in what they were about to do.

But what else could she do? She couldn't allow Daphne to keep suffering these bouts of pain, and there was no guarantee that they would remain harmless over time. *Incarcerate* was a word used by the doctor, and her mind threw up all kinds of terrifying possibilities. Whatever it took, she had to try her utmost to get her daughter cured, and creating imagined problems wouldn't help.

She paused her pacing, looking down once again into that small, sweet face, relaxed and sleeping at last. The tyke had to be exhausted, but Diane wasn't doing much better. Helpless. God, she had just faced the worst sense of helplessness in her life. Somehow, she sensed that this little girl was going to give her that feeling more than once over the years ahead.

"It's normal to be nervous," Blaine remarked in his deep, slightly gravelly voice. "Mam nearly lost it when my brother Liam fell off his bike and was coldcocked. Kid was definitely alive, but by the time the docs reassured her, I think we'd held a full wake and were moving onto a memorial."

He was trying to make her laugh, she realized. Lighten her fears. She tried a smile but was sure it didn't reach her eyes. "I'm sorry I'm not handling this better, Blaine. It's minor, right?"

He sprang from his chair to surround her and the baby with his large, powerful arms. "It's not minor.

It'll probably be fixed all right, and things will get better, but it's not minor. Don't you apologize. I'm fairly certain no mother wants to be facing any kind of surgery for her babe."

"But he made it sound so…so…"

"Routine? Maybe it is for him. He's got his hands inside people all the time. For you it's not routine."

His words drew her up, releasing her tension enough for a small bubble of humor to burst out. "His hands inside people all the time?"

"Sure, and what else does a physician do? One end or the other, or with a scalpel, they're inside someone. That may be okay for him, but not so easy on the rest of us."

A small, amused sound escaped her. "You're priceless, Blaine."

"I'm quite sure not many would agree with you."

Another thought struck her. Apparently her mind was slipping back into gear as fear faded a little. "You don't have to hang around here. This could take all day. I feel guilty for taking so much of your time."

"I'll be hearing none of that. Wasn't planning to be anywhere else today except putting some furniture together for Daphne."

At last she was able to settle on the chair again, Daphne snugly in her arms, filling a hole inside her she'd never felt before. "I'm sure you have a life. You've spent a lot of time this week looking after me and Daphne."

"I have a life." He repeated the words as if thinking about them, his face falling into unusually charming lines. "I guess I do. Let me see. It's the weekend, so the county is going to have to wait unless there's a true emergency. So what would I be doing? I might take my horse out for a ride. Or I might settle at my home desk and work on a floor plan for a dream house that I'll probably never like well enough to build."

"Really? Why not?"

"Because I never learned to dream realistically." He flashed a smile. "By the time a house would have everything I could possibly want in it, I'd need to be a very wealthy man, and civil engineers generally don't command that kind of pay. So it's just a dream. But I like it. Right now I'm also thinking about buying a run-down ranch and fixing it up. For my horse, of course. What about you? What do you do with your free time?"

"What free time?" she asked drily. "I think that vanished with Daphne."

"Only for a few months. You'll find it again."

Just then Daphne stirred and made a little sound. Her lips puckered and the tip of her tongue appeared. "She's getting hungry."

"Then I guess she'll be squalling again soon, because the doc said not to feed her. Don't you have a dodie for her?"

"Dodie?"

"Ah…" Blaine hesitated. "Pacifier."

"Oh! It's one of those things I haven't gotten yet. She doesn't seem to look for one."

"Maybe not. It's a soothing thing for babies, but not everyone approves."

"What's to disapprove?"

He shrugged. "People with children can argue about a great many things. Seems like there are a million ways to do things. Don't get overwhelmed by advice. My mother used dodies. Said it saved her mind."

"I can imagine, with that many kids."

"We didn't make life easy for her." He winked. "Nor did we get much easier. Scamps to the last of us. I'm convinced she had a personal relationship with the Blessed Mother because she referred to her all the time. As in, 'Blessed Mother, what were you t'inking, Blaine?'"

A silent laugh escaped Diane as she realized just how glad she was to have him with her. He was keeping her from plunging all the way into the fear that had been gnawing at her since she realized Daphne's crying wasn't mere irritability. Little by little he was pulling her up, steadying her.

Considering how much lay ahead of her still, she was extremely glad he hadn't opted to take off and come back later. At some point she was going to have to turn her precious little bundle over to strangers who would operate on her. She couldn't feel comfortable about that. Just couldn't.

Before she could chase the rabbit of worry any farther, a pretty young woman wheeled in a machine nearly bigger than she was. "Hi, I'm Cassie from ultrasound. I'm just going to take a look at the baby, all right? Her name is Daphne, isn't it?"

"Yes."

The tech nodded, scanning a screen. "Suspected hernia, lower right quadrant. Does that sound correct to you?"

"Yes." Diane felt her nerves tightening up again. Why so many questions?

"Please bring Daphne over here and place her on the bed," Cassie said. "And please unwrap her."

Diane rose, realizing that the boulder was rolling downhill again, that she wasn't going to be able to do anything about any of this except let others care for Daphne.

Her hands shook a little as she began to unwrap the blankets. Daphne woke and made a few irritable cries.

"She's going to be even more angry with me, Mom," Cassie said. "I keep the gel on a warming pad, but I can't make it too warm. She's not going to be happy about this. You just stand on the far side of the bed and hold her hand and left leg. I'd like to minimize wiggling so I can get a clearer view. Dad, you can help, too, if you like."

Part of Diane noted that Blaine had been identified as Daphne's dad and that he didn't object, merely came over to help if he could.

Barely realizing she was doing it, Diane began to coo to Daphne, talking quietly, reassuringly as she sometimes did when she was feeding the girl.

Daphne's eyes darted around then found her face. She leaned in as close as she dared, trying not to get into the tech's way.

Of course, that didn't help much when the cool gel hit Daph's skin, along with the probe.

"Easy there, girl," Cassie said gently, her attention on a screen that was showing a whole bunch of stuff that didn't make any sense to Diane. "Ah," Cassie said on a breath. "I think we've got it. Let me just do a little more…"

Daphne definitely didn't like this. Her cries became angrier, and both Blaine and Diane tried to keep her from squirming too much.

"There we go," said Candy. She pulled a disposable cloth out of a dispenser and wiped away all the gel. "She'll calm in a minute. Even adults don't always like this. You can wrap her up again if you want. The doctor won't be long."

A minute later she trundled out with her machine and Diane heard her say, "Mr. Madden, are you back again? What's that leg up to now?"

Diane reached around for the blanket, but Blaine grabbed it first and wrapped Daphne up snugly. He held her for a minute, looking down into her tiny face, then turned her over to Diane.

"Hard to hand her over," he said gruffly.

"I know. I don't want to let go of her. But I guess I'm going to have to." Then she lifted her gaze from her daughter to him. "I can't begin to tell you how grateful I am. I know she's going to be in good hands, but it helps not to be alone."

"I'm glad to be here," he responded. "But I wish that doc would hurry. Tenterhooks were never designed to be comfortable. My God, these people act as if they have all day."

None of that was very flattering, but Diane could understand his feeling, because she shared it. The intellectual realization that Daphne wasn't the only patient they were dealing with didn't help at all. Selfishly, she wanted her daughter to have everyone's full attention.

Daphne was starting to squirm, her face reddening. "Oh, no," she whispered. "Not again. Hurting like that…" She might scream. She might drown this ER with a volume Diane couldn't match.

Blaine took Daphne and put her on his shoulder, patting her back rather firmly.

"What are you doing?" she asked.

"Damned if I know. Maybe a change of position will keep things from getting worse. Hell, maybe I should dangle her by her ankles so all the pressure goes in the other direction."

"I heard that." Into the room walked the doctor. "Sorry for the wait. Let me call up those sonogram results and show you what I can. Daphne will be going to surgery in about thirty minutes, as soon as the surgeon is done with his current patient. You need to relax, Mom. This isn't life-threatening, even though it's miserable for her."

"You're sure about that?" Diane said almost defiantly. She was beginning to feel as if she was caught in a nightmare without end. She tried to tell herself she was being ridiculous, but the feeling persisted. She wanted a speed that a hospital couldn't possibly provide to someone who wasn't dying then and there.

Blaine slipped his free arm around her shoulders. He gave her a gentle squeeze.

"Okay," said the doctor, pulling up an image. "Without a practiced eye, it's hard to see, but about two inches of her intestinal wall haven't grown together. That's actually not a terribly unusual thing, although we more often see it in boys. Anyway, nothing abnormal, and I'm glad to tell you we can take care of this immediately. There's absolutely no reason to wait. She'll be going home with you late this afternoon once she recovers from the anesthesia."

Hope leaped in Diane's heart. "Today?"

The doctor smiled. "Today. Really. Now, what's going to happen next is we're going to have to start an IV. That's usually the first thing we do when someone is to be admitted, but I didn't want to do that until we were certain what we were dealing with and when we'd deal with it. Of course, if I'd seen any sign of dehydration…" He shrugged. "We're going to put it in her forehead."

Diane froze. She felt Blaine stiffen beside her.

"What do you mean?" Diane demanded.

"The best way to give a child this small an IV is to place it in a scalp vein." He leaned over and touched

Daphne high on her forehead. "About here." Daphne made an irritated sound and tried to suck her fist.

"Why there?" The idea horrified Diane.

"Because it's the best, easiest and safest place for a child this young. I promise you, you don't want us trying to find a vein in a waving arm or leg, especially not through the layer of baby fat. We can do this in a minute. Anywhere else and we're going to have to restrain her and look hard. Looking for a good IV site is sometimes…"

"Painful," Blaine finished. "Watched it with my mother when she had trouble birthing Leanna. I swear, the woman doesn't have any veins."

The doctor smiled faintly. "I've run into folks like that. Anyway, Mom, trust me. This won't bother Daphne, and it's only for a few hours, anyway. But I'm going to ask you to leave her with the nurses, because you're not going to want to watch it."

Diane didn't need a diagram. Ten minutes later she'd been banished to a waiting room with Blaine, and her heart and arms felt empty.

"He sounds so…cavalier."

Blaine shook his head. "He's not. He's just used to this in a way we aren't. For him it's all in a day's work. At least he was sensitive about explaining where the IV has to go and why."

Blaine took her hand and held it snugly. A miracle of a man, she thought. Anyone else would probably have fled from this situation. Not even remotely was it his problem.

"I'm so glad I met you," she told him honestly. "I'd have been so lost without you, and you're so…so stalwart. A lot of guys would have headed for the hills."

"Stalwart, huh?" he said with a devilish smile. "I'm liking that. Also, just so you know, I'm not one to run for the hills. Mam tried to raise me with some sense, but I get all stubborn-like sometimes. Just so ya know," he repeated. Then his grin faded a bit. "I'm not unique, Diane. I learned that a long time ago."

"Who would have told you that?" It was a question that didn't expect an answer. Of course no one would have said such a thing to him. But to her dismay, he *did* answer.

"Apart from getting knocked upside the head for being so full of myself, you mean?" His smile faded even more. "No joke. Her name was Ailis."

"Ailish?" She tried to repeat it but wasn't sure she said it correctly.

"Call her Alice. My first big nosedive into a heap called love."

She felt her heart squeeze for him. That amused her briefly, but her thoughts darted right back to Daphne. This shouldn't take long, she assured herself. The doctor had made it sound like a quick nip and tuck. Trying to distract herself, she said absently, "Sometimes you don't sound like you come from Ireland. Is that on purpose?"

"Some of it. I need to be understood, and a good, thick Galway accent might get in the way. But most of us grew up speaking English, Diane. Even if not the queen's own English."

"No Gaelic?"

"Irish Gaelic is something we have to make a special effort to learn. Some is being taught in school now, but what's the point in a country where everyone speaks English?"

She nodded, taking it in. "It seems a shame."

"Seven hundred years of a shame," he replied.

Mary appeared in the door of the small waiting room. "We're taking Daphne to surgery now," she said. "I'll come get you as soon as she's in recovery."

Diane leaped to her feet. "How long?"

Mary smiled. "I can't say exactly. This shouldn't be time-consuming. Why don't you go to the cafeteria and get a light meal? You'll hardly have time to eat it."

"That sounded reassuring," Diane remarked as she watched Mary disappear. She reached out blindly and found Blaine's hand. "They keep calling me Mom."

"Well, you are the gal's mom. It hardly needs the adjective *foster*, if you ask me." He turned toward her. "From what you said, you may be the only mother the child ever has. Now let's go check out the cafeteria. You need something in your stomach, and I know I do. Hell, I even left the coffees in the car. I wasn't worrying much, was I?"

"But you seemed so calm," she objected as they strode toward the cafeteria.

"Rule," he said. "Only one person allowed to panic at a time."

"I like that rule," she agreed, her heart lightening a bit. Daphne was heading into surgery. The doctor had said it was minor. In theory she should get her baby back with nothing but a small scar and a couple of stitches, and then Daphne would never have this pain again. That was a good thing, however rough these hours had been, including the ones looming ahead of her.

The cafeteria wasn't terribly busy. A few people, looking as if they had someone in the hospital, sat at some of the small tables. A few people in scrubs occupied others. It wasn't a large cafeteria, but the selection was good. Evidently they had passed breakfast at some point and were now on to lunch. Sandwiches dominated the offerings.

Diane selected a ham and swiss on rye with a small salad. Blaine chose roast beef on a hard roll—two of them, actually. Apparently he had a large appetite. They had no trouble finding a table to themselves, and Blaine left her for a few minutes to return with coffee.

"The tea was out of an urn. I can't vouch for it," he said as he put a paper cup in front of her. "Of course, I can't vouch for the coffee, either."

"All I'm going to say is thank you." She closed her eyes for a few minutes, head tilted forward, as she tried to release the tension in her neck. God, it was going to take more than a hot bath to wash away this tightness. Time had truly developed leaden feet, and the first thing she did when she opened her eyes was seek a clock.

Time seemed to be as much a secret in a hospital cafeteria as the average department store. She thought about pulling out her cell phone, then decided against it. She had no idea how long this would take, so why count minutes?

"Eat," Blaine prodded kindly. "You won't be much help to the daffodil if you need a bed beside her."

Obediently she picked up her sandwich. Blaine was already halfway through his first. "Why do you call her daffodil?"

"It's better than Daffy?"

She'd forgotten she'd asked that question before, but against all reason, that dragged a laugh out of her. "I guess so." At last she bit into her sandwich, enjoying the crunch of fresh lettuce and the beautifully melding flavors of ham and cheese. Dang, she hadn't even realized how hungry she was, but as her mouth tasted sustenance, her stomach grumbled to remind her she hadn't eaten since dinner last night.

Then she remembered something. "Who was Alice?"

He stopped with his second sandwich halfway to his mouth. "Now why would you be wanting to know about her?"

She flushed faintly. "Curiosity, I guess. You mentioned her."

"I did." He took another bite of sandwich.

"I gather she made you feel bad."

"I believe I explained it was my dive into the questionable nightmare called love."

She couldn't help it. A little giggle escaped her. "A flattering description of romance."

"Did I say it was a romance? Blessed Mary, it was no such thing. It didn't get that far."

"Oh." She chewed and thought. "Then what was it?"

He sighed, took a long draft of his coffee or tea and put down the second half of his sandwich. "I'm not in the way of discussing such things."

"You struck out, then."

"Ack." He regarded her, his blue eyes intense but a hint of amusement around his mouth nonetheless. "Ailis can only be explained by my callow youth. And only my callow youth could have caused me to be such a nuisance. She hardly saw me, and when she did she slapped me back into my place. 'Blaine Harrigan,' she said, 'I've got better things to do with me time than be annoyed by the likes of you.' Quite clear, I thought, but I'd been enough of a fool that my friends had a great time teasing me."

He spoke lightly about it, but she wasn't sure she could accept that. After all, he'd mentioned in the first place, bringing it up when denying he was in any way unique. This Ailis or Alice must have cut him hard.

"She could have been kinder."

He shook his head, and now the smile was unmistakable. "I told you I'm stubborn. I should have taken the hints."

But the few minutes of calm and normalcy began to desert her. She needed to get back to the other side of the hospital; she needed to know what was happening with Daphne. Some word. Any word.

Blaine evidently sensed it when she dropped her sandwich and stirred.

"Let's go," he said, rising. "Shall I bring that coffee for you?"

"Please."

Damn, she was yo-yoing, something she wasn't at all used to. She'd lived a reasonably calm life, focused around her job and a few friends to have a good time with on weekends. The only person who'd ever brought her close to this kind of up-and-downing was Max, and he didn't hold a candle to Daphne.

Right alongside her worry for the girl, an amazement was beginning to grow. One week and she'd given her heart to Daphne, apparently. Man, she'd thought it would take longer than that.

But maybe there was something special about infants. Maybe they just naturally brought out maternal instincts. Although, she thought wryly, until recently she hadn't thought she had any.

Evidently, she did now.

Chapter Six

An eternity seemed to have passed before Mary came to find them. "She's out of surgery," the nurse told them cheerfully. "We'll give her some time to wake up and then you can see her, all right?"

Blaine looked at Diane and thought the woman looked like she'd been through the wringer. She'd hung on to her emotions really well, but the worry and stress had just about used up her reserves.

Hardly surprising. His own mother had looked like a scarecrow by the time Liam had wakened from his concussion. Nothing like the investment of a mother, he thought.

About five minutes later, they received what probably qualified as one of the most important visits of the day. A doctor walked in, not the one they'd seen in the emergency room, and sat in a chair facing them.

"Daphne's parents, right?"

Blaine didn't answer but Diane merely nodded.

"I'm Dr. Howe. I performed the surgery on your daughter. It was uncomplicated and she's just fine. The nurse is going to give you some treatment orders you'll need to follow for a week, but she's young and healthy and Daphne will be perfectly well in no time at all. We gave her some antibiotics through the IV to prevent any possible infection, but you're going to have to stay up with it at home." He looked to each of them, awaiting a nod.

Only then did he smile. "For what it's worth, I wish it were this easy to fix everything. Your little girl won't have any problems, and maybe best of all, she won't remember this."

"But I will," Diane murmured, barely aware she spoke aloud.

"Yes, you will," the doctor answered. "Dad? I think Mom needs a little nap when she gets home, don't you?"

"Absolutely."

"We'll be releasing Daphne shortly. She's waking, and she didn't need much anesthesia at all. She'll be kicking and cooing by the time you get her."

What a lovely picture he painted, Diane thought. Then without warning, Blaine wrapped her in his arms and held her close, her head on his shoulder.

"You can relax now," he said quietly. "I've even been told I'm a grand babysitter."

Somehow she didn't doubt that at all.

Blaine took over because it seemed right to him. Diane had been through a wringer, however good the outcome. He hadn't, simply because he hadn't made the same kind of emotional investment in the baby yet. Plus, he hadn't been wakened to screeching that had to have been terrifying to someone who'd never heard it before.

Diane dozed on his shoulder and he held her comfortably, hoping it would both rejuvenate her and make the time pass more rapidly. Whatever these medical people meant by "shortly" took quite a bit longer than that. The clock on the waiting room wall seemed to be keeping good time, and it told him that this had probably lasted as long as it had felt. Midafternoon was creeping up on them and the baby still hadn't been released.

But at last it happened and they were taking her home. The nurse, Mary, had advised them that Daphne might not be hungry or thirsty for a while. The IV would have met her needs for liquid and sugar, plus she'd probably be tired enough after all this to just want to sleep.

Blaine eyed the small white bandage on her forehead where the needle had evidently been inserted and murmured, "Poor girl," as he placed her in the playpen, the easiest place for her to move about if she wanted. Plus, Diane could keep an eye on her from the comfort of her recliner.

Diane looked pooped enough to need that nap that had been suggested, but she seemed fixated on Daphne, as if she were afraid the girl might stop breathing. Not knowing what else to do, Blaine brought her one of the sticky buns he'd bought hours ago and handed her the small plate.

"I just had a sandwich," she reminded him.

"Half of one, as I recall, and not as recently as you think. It's been a busy long day. Calories, woman. Calories."

"What time is it, anyway?"

"The afternoon is mostly gone."

Diane stiffened. "It seemed like a long time, but that long?"

"Daffodil here was getting the best care," he reminded her. "They didn't want you popping out the door with her only to come running back in because she was bleeding or something. The recovery room probably took longer than either of us noticed."

All of a sudden he wished he could look another direction. She'd slept with his arm around her for longer than she knew, and the experience had provoked him with simmering heat. It had also distracted him from noting just how long they'd waited. He wished he could drag his gaze away from her for fear of what it might reveal. If eyes could speak, his were probably shouting. Wrong time. Maybe never. *Get a grip, Blaine.*

* * *

She looked at him, into his deep blue eyes, trying to pull her scattered and scattering thoughts together. "How…"

"Well, you may not remember, but you dozed on my shoulder for a long while." He made it sound light, simple. Not as sexual as she'd found it, despite all that was going on. In fact, some of her reactions to being held by him had felt crass to her. Maybe just a form of denial?

She lifted a hand to her mouth. "Oh, Blaine, I'm so sorry."

He waved away her apology. "No need. I'm not complaining. I was glad to see you get a little sleep, though I doubt it was restful. You still look like you could use more of it, too, so nap if you like."

She shook her head, suddenly feeling very, very sad. "I'm taking over your life. I never meant to do that."

"I haven't resisted, either, and I'm perfectly capable of saying no. I seem to remember inserting myself last night and this morning. Besides, what's a little help with a sick baby and some furniture assembly? Any neighbor would help with either. Now relax."

"How can I when I feel guilty?"

"Guilty?" He dropped to the floor, sitting cross-legged.

"I need to get you a decent chair," she remarked, but she'd averted her gaze.

"Forget the chair. I've sat on harder ground and with six kids we often didn't have enough chairs. So what's making you feel guilty?"

"Everything," she said extravagantly, waving her hand. The strange sadness that had crept up on her was probably making her as stupid as the fatigue she was feeling.

"That's a whole lot," he said when she didn't continue.

"Well, look at me. I came out here to take a new job, just figuring that somehow everything was going to fall into place. I know damn all about caring for an infant, I still haven't found a good day care for her, partly because I've been too busy to really look, so that's hanging out at the courthouse. Then she gets sick and I don't even know what to do about it. I'm a big failure, and I can't imagine what I would have done if you hadn't showed up this morning."

"Ah." He leaned back, bracing himself on his hands. "Let me reiterate. You quite naturally accepted a job you wanted, right?"

"I shouldn't have."

"I think you're getting the sequence a bit out of step here. You accepted the job."

She nodded, getting the feeling that he was about to make her feel even more inadequate, and after today, she was quite certain she deserved it.

"Anybody would have accepted a job they wanted. What else got me all the way out here so far from me home that I can't even talk right?"

Damn, he was going to make her laugh. She didn't want to laugh. She'd made a whole bunch of screw-ups in just a week. She kept her eyes closed for fear that if she looked at Blaine right now she'd probably jump into his arms for comfort. Comfort from what? Everything had turned out all right with Daphne, hadn't it?

"I see the corner of your mouth twitching. It's not sacrilege to laugh. As events happened, you must have quit your old job when you accepted the new, unless you're more of a scamp that I would believe. Like anyone else, you were getting ready to come out here for this one when, all unexpectedly, your cousin's baby needed you. Instead of simply saying no and leaving the child to be a ward of the state, you took on an unexpected responsibility."

She couldn't exactly argue that, although it wasn't looking so very smart right now. She wasn't even a good caretaker for Daphne. That much had become abundantly clear this morning.

"Now you have your hands full while starting a new job in a way you were utterly unprepared for. I think I told you, most people have nine months to get ready. How many days did you have?"

She sighed, clenching her hands, and admitting it. "Only a week, because I was leaving, and then she was in my care for only a couple of days before I got here—which made it even more stupid."

"Not stupid. You needed to keep this job, now more than ever because you had an extra person to care for. Thus, here you are. Since I see a living, breathing baby in the playpen over there, just what exactly did you mess up?"

She bit her lip, fighting back that inexplicable sorrow that kept trying to wash over her. At last she looked at Blaine. "I don't have day care, for one thing. The board isn't going to tolerate this forever. And I didn't know what I should do this morning! If you hadn't come over…"

"If I hadn't barged my way in, you'd eventually have reached the same conclusion—Daphne needed a doctor, and the only place to get one on Saturday morning is an emergency room."

"You can't be sure…"

"I can be quite sure," he said firmly, "that you're not the unkind, uncaring sort of person who would have let that child cry for much longer."

She sat up straighter, looking at her daughter. *Her daughter.* The realization settled in her heart for the second time that day. She was now Daphne's mother. For real. And she knew next to nothing about what this child needed.

"I'm scared," she said quietly.

"About what?"

"She's my daughter. Blaine, it just hit me today."

He scooted closer and rested his hand on her knee. The touch was comforting, warm. "What did?"

"That this isn't some temporary thing. I mean…I know my cousin will probably never be well enough to care for Daphne. That's why they hunted me up.

She'd already spent a month in the care of social services, and they hoped I'd take her rather than an unrelated foster family."

"Which you did."

She shook her head a little. "I don't think... Something about today made me truly realize that this isn't temporary. That she's mine now. My *daughter*."

He tilted his head to one side and squeezed her knee gently. "This is somehow more terrifying? I seem to have come into the middle of the conversation."

"It's more terrifying," she said truthfully. "This isn't some temporary thing I'm dealing with for a few months or a year. I think I was deluding myself at first, believing that MaryJo would get better. Only from what the social worker said, MaryJo is never going to get well enough to care for a child. Why did that not penetrate before?"

"I'm not sure what you mean by penetrate. You already told me how sick your cousin is, and that she'd never be a mother to this child."

"I know. It was all laid out. I knew. I just didn't *know*, if that makes any sense."

"Ah," he said in his deep rumble of a voice. "It was real to the head but not yet to the heart?"

She nodded slowly and raised a hand to massage the tension growing in her neck. "I think that's probably a good way to put it. But it sounds stupid. All day today I've been thinking how inadequate I am to this, how I should have thought more clearly rather than acting instinctively about Daphne. What kind of mother will I be? I never even babysat!"

He raised his knee, resting his arm on it. She wished the movement hadn't taken his hand away, because it had been so comforting. She didn't even bother to try to talk herself out of the feeling. Today was a mess of feelings and fears.

"While today may have seemed to prove me a total liar," he said, "the truth still is that caring for a baby is easy."

"Like I'm going to believe that now?" Indeed, her mind was running around like a skittering mouse, imagining or trying to imagine a million other bad things that could happen to Daphne. The world suddenly seemed full of threats, and that baby was utterly dependent on her to deal with them.

"It's easy," Blaine repeated firmly. "Think about it, woman. You've been caring for her for over a week now and she doesn't look any worse for the wear."

"Until this morning."

He snorted and uttered a word that she was quite sure didn't qualify as polite even in his home country. "Listen to me, Diane. I mostly raised four of the six me mam had, and if I couldn't break 'em, you can't, either. What happened today was *not* the result of anything you did or didn't do. Gad, babies are only half-baked, ya know. It's not unusual to find some little thing that hasn't finished growing. Most of 'em take care of themselves, but every now and then this happens. Me younger sister, Bridey, was born tongue-tied."

The surprised Diane right out of her preoccupation with imagined horrors. "What's that?"

He curved up one corner of his mouth. "Given how much the gal talks, it might have been better to leave her that way. Naw, it just meant that her tongue was still attached to the bottom of her mouth. After a little cut it's all better. It's the same for the daffodil over there."

Diane desperately hoped he was right. She looked over at Daphne. "Shouldn't she be waking by now? She certainly must need a diaper change."

He rose in one fluid movement then lifted the sleepy baby into Daphne's arms. "You take care of that, Mama. I'm in the way of heading over to the diner to get us a dinner."

"You don't have to stay," she said impulsively, although she was very glad of his company.

His eyes creased at the corners as he smiled, then he winked. "I figured that out. I'll be back."

She looked down at the drowsy bundle in her arms and hoped he meant that.

Blaine left the car behind and walked the three blocks to the diner. The evening air was cool and pleasant, the twilight just beginning to deepen. Kids played outside, waiting to be called to dinner, their voices cheery on the gentle breeze.

He figured after the day's stress, Diane would

probably be glad of some one-on-one time with Daphne. Quiet time to regain her footing. A chance to follow the postoperative directions for wound care without someone breathing over her shoulder. Tonight wouldn't be difficult, anyway. They'd placed a waterproof bandage over the incision and had given Diane a few more and some antibacterial swabs to use if the bandage got loose.

Other than that, they seemed to think the kid would pretty much be good to go by tomorrow. No special treatment required. Return for follow up with the surgeon on Monday.

In all, neither of them could have asked for a better outcome. And now that he was by himself, Blaine was fully willing to admit that most of the confidence he'd displayed this morning had come from the need to keep Diane calmer. She was frantic with worry. He hadn't been doing much better. He'd held a lot of babies over the years, and he could tell when there was serious pain involved. That cry was a class unto itself.

But now that Daphne was on the road to recovery, he started thinking more about Diane. There'd been a refrain wandering through the things she'd been saying, and it was becoming clearer to him.

He wondered what the hell had savaged her self-confidence. The woman had an advanced degree in urban planning. From what he'd heard in casual conversation with the commissioners since he'd learned of her hiring, she could have easily chosen a job in a much bigger city, or with a huge developer. Instead she had chosen to come here because she wanted to try out her ideas and run the show.

Understandable. Courageous, even, because if she messed up, there'd be no one else to blame. It would all fall on her.

But how often, today alone, had he heard her self-doubt? He was quite sure he'd heard her talk about failing more than once.

Someone must have done that to her, because her accomplishments hadn't included failures he'd heard about. Not from the commissioners who'd hired her, not from her résumé, not from her letters of reference. Perhaps she was only confident when it came to her work, and not outside it.

Not that he could imagine any reason for that. She was a beautiful woman who could stir a man just by breathing. Or at least could stir him. He'd have to be careful he didn't let that show, because Diane had quite enough on her plate right now.

The walk to the diner wasn't a long one, but he walked slowly. Usually he was accustomed to striding swiftly, but tonight he wanted to give Diane that little bit of time. Maybe she'd want him to leave as soon as he brought dinner. He couldn't blame her.

Today had been stressful for hours, sitting in that hospital waiting for her child to be returned, wondering what was going on, the fear before the diagnosis… all of it added up to a rough day.

Especially for a woman who had just invited a child fully into her heart.

That struck him—her explanation how today the reality had come home. This was no longer a temporary gig, but a permanent one, and the responsibility seemed to be overwhelming her.

Well, if she'd let him, he'd be glad to help a bit with that. While he'd sometimes resented it when he was younger, now he was glad that so much had been expected of him in the way of taking care of young'uns.

Like any youngster, he'd wished for more time to spend with his mates. But when he'd picked up Daphne for the first time on Monday, he'd realized how very much he had missed caring for his siblings.

Just goes to show, he thought. You never knew what you had until it was gone.

Then he was facing the diner and could delay no longer. He had a hankering for a piece of Maude's fine apple pie, but that wouldn't suffice. Diane needed a decent meal.

He stood outside the door, reading the menu taped to the window, trying to find something different but nutritious. The default steak sandwich that everyone around here loved so much might be too heavy after the day she'd had. He could still remember his mother preferring light meals after an upsetting day.

Diane could be different, but he didn't want to find out the hard way. Eventually he settled on some homemade chicken soup and a stack of Texas toast. If that didn't do, he'd come back for something else.

As he'd been standing there, people coming and going had greeted him. It was a nice feeling to be known by so many, and he hoped Diane would soon enjoy it. In the meantime, he headed inside to place his order and discovered everyone already knew what had happened to Daphne.

Who the hell at the hospital had talked, he wondered, but with amusement. It could have been a janitor. They might not be covered by HIPAA rules. What did he know? Hard to keep a secret in this town, anyway.

Maude gave him a bucket of soup big enough for an army, added a huge stack of toast and threw in several pieces of pie.

"You know the way to my heart, woman."

She sniffed. "It's the way to every man's heart."

But he caught a glimmer of humor in her usually harsh expression. He wondered if the heart attack a few months back had softened her up some. Gad, if that were true, nobody in this town would be sure she was Maude.

Amused, he stepped outside with two plastic bags of goodies and resolved to make a nice pot of tea when he got back to the house.

He passed others out to enjoy the pleasant evening. Five years here and he was still getting used to the different seasons. It was his Galway upbringing. He liked to say that his home had two seasons:

wet and chilly or wetter and chillier. Which wasn't fair to the old country, because they had some glorious days when the sun broke through the familiar overcast and painted the land in shades of gold and green. At times, when the north wind blew, they even saw a bit of snow.

Still, it was a good joke.

When he reached Diane's little house, he let himself in quietly, unsure whether she and the baby might have fallen asleep.

Indeed they had. Diane was curled in her battered old recliner with Daphne snuggled in her arm and a blanket over them.

All was well in the Finch world. Smiling, he went to the kitchen and started the kettle. He needed some tea, but the soup would be easy to heat later.

Then he settled at the kitchen table and waited, much as he would have liked to just sit and watch mother and child sleep. So peaceful after a day that had been anything but.

Eventually he heard fussy sounds emanating from the living room. Daphne was returning to the world and probably wanted food and a diaper change. He should leave that to Diane, he decided. He absolutely didn't want her to think he was taking over, and he might have given her that sense more than once.

But he was definitely bothered by her feeling like a failure. He'd like to explore the reasons for that if the time ever came. Right now, even after today, they were still just acquaintances. Blaine was of a type to just walk into the middle of a relationship of any kind, and hadn't his mam warned him about that? Often as it was, he didn't suffer much trouble for it, but he wound up with a lot of friends. There still always remained a possibility that he'd be told to scat, the way Ailis had. He'd learned to take his knocks over time, but he sincerely hoped Diane wouldn't send him on his way. He was growing fond of that woman.

A few minutes later, she came to the kitchen with Daphne freshly changed into a new jumper and sucking on her fist as her bright eyes looked around.

"Hey," Diane said. "I need to open a can of formula. Would you mind?"

Clearly she didn't want to let go of the babe after today. He had no problem with that. "Where do I find it?"

She pointed. "In that pantry. The clean nursing bottles are on the shelf beside it."

And there they were, all sparkly clean and carefully capped. "Should I warm it for her?" He'd always warmed bottles when he was taking care of a newborn sibling, but he'd gathered that didn't always happen.

"Poor thing has been taking it at whatever temperature it comes," Diane answered. "No way to heat it at the office. Tonight, though, let's spoil her. It should heat well enough if you set it in a pan of hot water from the tap."

It certainly would. He'd done it before. Plus, it wasn't that cold in this house. Though some folks would think it too early in the season to be turning on the heat, Diane must not agree. He'd heard the hot air turn on several times.

Diane remained at the kitchen table while she nursed Daphne. She'd agreed a cup of tea sounded good, as did the chicken soup.

"A gallon, I swear," Blaine told her. "I sure hope you like it. Maude really loaded me up."

"I love it." But all her attention was on Daphne, as it should be. Totally absorbed in her new daughter. A grand thing, a mother's love.

The soup hadn't cooled much, but he put some in a pan anyway to warm it slowly. The Texas toast would be on the soggy side, but it always tasted good, anyway. Then he waved some pie under her nose. "A feast awaits."

At last, for the first time that day, she truly smiled. Good, she was getting past the shock of it all. It might hit her again later, but when all was said and done, as emergencies went, this one had been benign.

Not everything could be fixed so easily.

He placed a cup of tea and a plate with a wedge of thick toast on it in front of her. He figured if she wanted to, she could hold that bottle with one hand and eat with the other. A necessary maternal skill since the powers that be hadn't granted a mother a third arm.

When Daphne had finished about half of her bottle, now trying to hold it with her tiny hands although she couldn't yet, Diane propped it with the blanket and took a few sips of her tea.

"Delicious," she announced.

"Steeped longer," he answered. "No secret. Our daffodil looks content with the world."

Diane nodded. "Strangely enough, as far as she's concerned, nothing happened."

"Great advantage of an infant's memory."

She laughed softly. "I wish mine worked like that sometimes." She looked up from the baby at him. "Did you get your culvert problem sorted out?"

She'd already asked him twice, but he allowed it to pass because of the fatiguing, upsetting day. "Well, we've made a start on it. We're going to have to dig out the paving, pull out the deteriorating culvert and start all over again, basically."

She nodded. "Nothing to save?"

"Not now. Between a dozen winters and the heavy rains we had last month, it's pretty much collapsed."

"And that historic storefront you looked at?"

"Well, we had a word or two. Seems the owner and I have a different idea of preservation."

That grabbed her attention. "Now you're talking to my hobbyhorse. Does this town have an historic overlay district?"

"You might say it does. Partially. And that's where we got to disagreeing. Evidently his building isn't on the overlay from when it was made years ago and, in my opinion, it seriously ought to be. We'll need you to take a look, but I extracted his solemn promise on the grounds that if he moves ahead without prior approval, he might have to undo everything."

"Nobody wants that," she said. Daphne had stopped sucking on her bottle and was looking drowsy again. In a movement that felt more natural every day, she placed the child on her shoulder and began to gently pat her back.

"So historic districts are your thing?" he asked.

"Most definitely. Part of what I was told when I interviewed was that the city council wanted more of the town to fall under the protections than it currently does. I wasn't certain at the time what they meant, but it's a job I'd love to take on. It doesn't have to be onerous on the property owners, but evidently there's an appearance some in this town want to preserve."

"I'd call it early-twentieth-century Wild West," he remarked drily. "But I can only say that mostly from movies. Most of this place doesn't resemble that, but it comes from that era. I get the feeling people who came here and settled this town were trying to bring their old homes with them."

"It's entirely likely. I noticed the church with the steeple. New England. Same with the courthouse square, right down to the statue."

He smiled faintly. "The statue of a soldier representing a war no one can identify for certain. This area wasn't settled during the Civil War, as I understand it. That came later." He paused. "Meaning no offense here, but this place might do well to honor some of its Native heritage. I'm sure they were here before the late arrivals."

"I'm sure, and I'm not offended. The city fathers might have a different opinion."

"Don't they always?"

She shifted Daphne from her shoulder to her arm, and the little girl barely stirred. "Time for a diaper change and some sleep, I think."

"Do you want me to take off?"

Her eyes widened. "Why would I want that? Man, Blaine, we haven't even eaten the supper you brought. I just need a minute to put her down."

Apparently, he'd wended the thickets safely enough today, he thought, rising to check on the soup and hunt up some dishes. Selfishly, he wished she weren't so preoccupied with Daphne. He'd kind of like for her to be preoccupied with him in that way.

Not likely and probably not wise. Ah, hell. A randy Irishman, a woman who was in the way of being his boss, if not exactly, and a baby that needed all the attention available.

He ought to be used to that by now. Years of experience and all that.

Besides, and perhaps most important, there was something precious and nearly sacred about a woman with an infant in her arms. Bury the attraction. It had no place here and now.

Chapter Seven

By the following weekend, Diane had begun to feel more settled in every way. She had a routine going with Daphne that seemed to suit them both, and Aubrey's sister-in-law had found a space for Daphne in the infant section of her early-learning school. Daphne seemed to be thriving there so far, and where she hadn't previously been a frequent smiler, she seemed to be smiling most of her waking moments now. When Diane when to pick her up at the end of a workday, she was always greeted with a happy shriek and a huge smile. Surely she wasn't imagining that those arms had begun to reach for *her*?

Added to that was the new pediatrician's approval of Daphne's overall condition. The surgery was healing nicely and rapidly, her weight was good for her length—that had made Diane giggle a bit—and all was good. She had begun to roll herself from side to side, she could lift and hold her head up longer now when she was on her tummy and…

Diane drew a deep breath as she realized just how fast Daphne was making strides in her development. Now that she worried less about her ability to take care of the girl, maybe she should expend a little energy on enjoying her milestones.

And start taking some photos.

Her cell phone rang as she was putting Daph into her car seat at the end of the workday on Friday. It was Blaine. She'd hardly seen him all week. He'd been out and about, and she'd been practicing a form of archaeology on the old development plan, the most recent—it was ancient—historical overlay and speaking with her new bosses about their vision for Conard City and the county.

She spoke to them individually, in a way that wouldn't violate public meeting rules, just to find out if they had some sort of vision they wanted her to pursue.

Of course they did. In their varied ways, they wanted entirely more than was possible. Well, that was better than wanting to keep everything the same. But a number of years ago, a ski resort had made an attempt to build up on the mountain, and part of their plan had been to refurbish the town, to give it a more "Western" look.

Which had left them with the Victorian additions

of brick sidewalks on some of the streets and some pretty fancy lampposts that might have looked good in London nearly two centuries ago. Attractive but touristy.

Properties that were registered as historic had to meet a whole bunch of preservation require-ments. What Diane wanted to know was how far they wanted to go with that historic overlay, because right now the old one had been overridden quite a bit.

Her head was all awhirl with the thoughts she'd gathered, and when she at last had Daphne belted into her car seat, she had to call Blaine back.

"Sorry I missed you," she said. "I was putting Daphne in the car. How was your week, and am I wading into some kind of trouble you've heard about?" Because the feedback she was getting wasn't tremendously helpful.

He laughed. "I'm sure you've dealt with self-interested government members before. We'll talk if you have some time this evening. I never got around to putting the crib together after that struggle with the changing table…"

She laughed as she closed the back door and opened the driver's door. "We should have known we were headed for trouble when the box was labeled *Please do not upside down box.*"

"Somebody certainly needed a better translator," he agreed.

She slipped into the driver's seat and poked her key into the ignition. "And you build things all the time. Okay, I'd love for you to come over. I've got to go, because I'm about to drive."

"Fair enough. Dinner from Maude's, or do you want pizza from the place on the edge of town?"

"Pizza actually sounds good."

"I hope it is."

She laughed again and said goodbye. Life here was becoming familiar—she'd dared to take Daphne out to lunch with some of the women from the clerk's office, and all in all, after a little more than two weeks here, she was beginning to feel comfortable.

Except for her job. It was so obvious that the council and commission members who constituted the planning board hadn't bothered to reach an agreement of any kind. This was going to be fun.

She had time when she got home to change Daphne into a fresh diaper and clothes. Ordinarily she bathed her in the evening, but tonight she decided to leave it for morning. The house felt a little chilly to her, and she wandered down the hall with Daphne in her arms to look at the thermostat. Sixty-eight, so the heat was working. Maybe she was the one who was chilled.

Once she'd prepared Daphne's bottle, she settled into what had become her favorite chore—feeding her daughter.

She still hadn't done anything about finding another chair for the living room, she thought as she cuddled Daphne close and smiled into her alert, bright eyes. She was in no condition to invite anyone over, like her new friends at the courthouse and the judge's wife, Amber. Regardless, Blaine ought to have a better seat than the floor, especially with all he'd done for her.

Putting that changing table together had been quite an experience. At one point she'd turned the directions upside down to see if they made more sense. The diagrams, which should have crossed any language barrier at all, had some big blanks.

She'd learned something, though. Blaine had a massive vocabulary of cusswords in what sounded like two languages.

"Pardon me," he'd said at one point, "but cursin' lubricates the brain cells."

She had laughed and still wanted to laugh as she remembered it. For all his cussing, he'd never once expressed frustration in any physical way, but he sure gave his language a workout. It had been quite a show.

He'd managed to put the entire changing table, drawers and all, together in a remarkably short time, considering that the directions were so useless he'd practically had to figure out how to build it himself.

"I should have used the county shop and made you one myself," he said at one point.

"Tsk, using county property for a personal project?" she'd teased. "I think we'd both be in hot water."

"As if this lot care," he muttered in response.

But that had been last weekend, and now that

she'd had a week to get to know her bosses better, her opinion hadn't improved a whole lot. They were politicians, most of them not really very good at it, and all of them more interested in their day jobs. In short, she thought all of them owned businesses and most of their attention was on ways to improve that. Too much, maybe. She didn't know yet.

Blaine arrived just as she was gently pacing with Daphne, encouraging her to expel any gas. The child seemed far more interested in waving her hand and staring at it than burping.

"My, she's growing active," Blaine said as he paused to drop a kiss on the fuzzy little head before going to the kitchen with the pizza box. "I forgot to ask what toppings you like, so I took a wild guess. Lots of veggies and some pepperoni. Okay?"

"Sounds great." And it did. Already the aroma was making her mouth water. "Thank you."

"My pleasure. So how's the tot been doing this week? I've hardly seen you."

"She's in the learning center now, and she seems happy with it. As for me, I've been picking the brains of the members of the planning board."

"Ah." He turned with a smile and reached for Daphne. "May I? So do you need brain bleach after talking with that crew?"

"Not quite," she managed to laugh. "Let's get to that in a minute."

She passed Daphne to him, enjoying the way he held her daughter. She didn't know why, but it still surprised her that a guy would be interested in a baby that wasn't his own. It was usually women who went gaga over infants. Holding Daphne on his shoulder, he rocked gently from side to side. She was still waving her arm, but she didn't seem disturbed by the change of venue.

"The doc said she's doing well?"

"In every respect," she answered, feeling proud for no discernible reason. She hadn't created the child—all she had done was be her caretaker for a few weeks.

"Well, then, clearly you've been managing motherhood just fine, despite your concerns. Grab some of that pizza before it gets cold."

"I probably need to change Daph. Seems to go along with eating."

"Ain't that the truth," he remarked. "I'll do it. Just eat something, lady. I'll be right back."

She had to admit it was nice to have him take over and allow her to eat a relaxed meal. Sometimes when Daphne slept, she managed to uncoil a bit, but this was all still new enough that her brain had a habit of throwing up things to be concerned about. Would she ever stop listening for every little sound, or wondering when the baby was too quiet if she was still breathing?

Babies are hardy, the pediatrician had said today, echoing what Blaine had told her at their first meeting. After two weeks in her inexperienced hands,

Daph seemed to have proved that, even though Diane couldn't quite seem to believe it.

"She's sleeping," Blaine said as he returned to the kitchen. He'd learned his way around during the great changing table affair and pulled a plate from the cupboard. Two tall foam cups sat on the table, and he pushed one to her. "I hope you like diet soda, because that's what I brought. If not I can make some tea."

"It sounds good, actually." She smiled and took one of the cups, ripping the paper off a straw and poking it through the lid. Tingling cola soon hit her tongue. "Oh, yum. I don't have this very often. And the pizza is great. Thank you."

"Great, she says after one bite." He winked. "I've found pizza to be very much a matter of taste, having eaten it everywhere it seems to have spread. I even hear that people from New York and Chicago can disagree about it quite vehemently."

"I'm not so picky. And this is just fine, as far as I'm concerned."

He nodded and helped himself to a slice. "What was your experience of our planning board?"

She looked up and hesitated.

"Go on," he said. "I don't squeal."

"I'm not sure yet what they really want," she admitted. "Bigger and better, but bigger and better what? For example, they seem to be keen on historic preservation, but when we got to discussing the overlay, they got really fuzzy. I can't decide if they're not sure or don't want to offend some people."

"Probably both," he answered after he swallowed. "Big ideas are easy to come by. Implementing them, not so much. I guess that's your job."

"To an extent, yes, but I also serve many masters."

He laughed a bit at that. "I hear you."

"You've been awfully busy this week, too, haven't you?"

"Getting ready for winter. We have some other culverts that don't look as if they could withstand the weight of a plow, so they'll be replaced. Then there's a road that's in the plan to be paved, but the ranchers don't want it because it'll increase the traffic and they're worried about livestock."

She finished another bite of pizza before asking, "Are they right about the traffic?"

"They may be. This was in the original master plan to be widened and paved, and it would certainly make a grand link between two other roads that are heavily traveled. It's needed from that perspective. I've been considering it, however, and while I think it would be useful in a lot of ways, I'm sure it might cause problems in others. I'll show you next week when you can find time, and you can add your thoughts, if you don't mind."

"I probably should take a look at that and a lot of other things before I get into writing a new comprehensive plan. The other things being what the board members want."

"They want the moon and some green cheese, too."

That made her laugh. It also snapped her thoughts to him in a way that had nothing to do with Daphne or work. God, he was good-looking, she thought. He wore all that perfectly carved masculinity with a kind of comfort that said he wasn't even aware of it.

Brilliant blue eyes with black hair would always be arresting, but the rest of him begged the same attention. Broad shoulders, strong arms, large hands that appeared roughened from work. When he stood to hold Daphne, he displayed a flat belly, narrow hips and thighs that could have used a little more room in those jeans. And when he turned around... Man, she'd never have believed that she could admire a guy's rump.

While she'd noticed men occasionally since leaving college, she hadn't devoted a lot of attention to them, because all too many of the ones she met worked with her.

And now here she was again. Crap.

"You ever marry?" she asked Blaine, then wondered what had possessed her. It was none of her business, for one thing, and it tracked too closely with her edgy, almost squirmy awareness of his masculinity. Some areas of conversation ought to be avoided.

"No," he answered, then reached for a second slice. "Haven't managed to fit it in. Or maybe I just haven't felt drawn to the right woman. Can't say I've been lacking."

She quickly stuffed another mouthful of pizza in to silence the inevitable following question. *Don't ask.*

But a smile caught at the edges of a mouth she seriously would have liked to kiss—and wasn't that unusual for her?—and he answered as if he had read her mind.

"Lacking what, you'll be asking."

She pursed her lips as she swallowed. "I never said that."

He chuckled. "As night follows day. I told you about my experience with Ailis. I'm not the sort to be once burned and twice shy, as the saying goes, and I did dip my toes in the water. As it happens, I never met anyone else who made me want to take another deep dip of that kind. Which is not to say I've been a saint. I do believe Patrick was the last true saint on the isle."

A giggle spilled out of her. "Blaine, you're something else." A quiver ran through her as he smiled back at her. The way that expression reached his eyes just melted her.

"Well, to be honest about it, we grew a fair share of saints in the old days. The very old days. The rest of us weren't quite convinced, it seems." He winked. "Now me mam, she was always one for appealing to the Blessed Mother. I told you that. But it didn't keep her from wearing Saint Brigid's medal, I can tell you."

She liked the picture he was painting of his family. For all he said they'd spread out all over Europe, she got a strong sense from the way he talked that they were still very close. She'd missed that, as she'd missed a whole lot, it seemed.

"What about you?" he asked. "Family other than your cousin? Boyfriends? Exes?"

She looked down, losing her appetite. How in the world did you tell a man like this that you'd pretty much disowned your own parents? "My dad died when I was seventeen. Heart attack. I haven't seen my mother in years."

He didn't say anything immediately, for which she was grateful. It always sounded so bad when she said it, and it seldom helped when she explained that after her relationship with Max had turned so bad, she'd gone for counseling. It was the counselor who'd helped her to understand how her parents had poisoned her and set her up for Max's abusiveness. Or that her own mother and father had never stopped tearing her down.

"That must have been bad," he finally said. "I've seen families that were…toxic. Is that what happened?"

"You could say so. I don't know. I'll never know why I wasn't good enough for them."

She pushed her plate aside, and reached for her beverage. Her mouth had gone completely dry. "This isn't a therapy session," she said flatly. "Sorry."

"No need. It helps me understand why you're so constantly afraid of failing Daffodil, though."

Her heart skipped and she looked at him. "What do you mean?"

"Things you say. It's not like this is just something new you need to master..."

"Well, it is," she argued. "And I tend to master new things."

"Clearly, or you wouldn't have come so far in your career. No, it's the way you often seem to think you must be wrong or *will* be wrong with Daphne. Well, you've had her over two weeks and she's still with us, so you can't be failing."

Her discomfort was growing, but it was no longer from sexual awareness. This man seemed to be penetrating her mind, looking inside into places she tried not to disturb. How had she revealed so much? What was more, she still had plenty of reason to fear failing with Daph. There were a whole lot of years and a whole lot of opportunities to make serious mistakes ahead of her.

Having this child had made her aware of things she hadn't thought about it a long time, things she'd thought she had ditched after her counseling. Funny how some things only hid themselves away and never disappeared.

"You had a boyfriend?" he asked. "I get the feeling he wasn't all that."

"He wasn't. Oh, at first I thought he was." She couldn't sit still any longer, so she stood up and began to clear away the remains of her dinner. "Then came the point when I realized I was in danger of marrying my parents."

"Wow," he said almost under his breath.

"Well, when you're raised by someone who hates you and makes you feel like a constant problem, you think you're much better off with someone who only makes you feel like you don't matter. I was endlessly criticized until I realized it felt like I'd never grown up and left home. So I left him."

"Good for you."

"Maybe." She stood at the sink with a plate in her hand, suddenly tempted to just smash it. But she never did things like that. Never.

All of a sudden, powerful arms wrapped around her from behind, hugging her close to a hard chest.

"Sorry I pried," he said in that voice so deep she could feel its rumble against her back. "I had no idea."

"How could you?" she answered, her own voice thin. Now she wanted to cry. Just a little kindness and she nearly tipped into tears. All these years, all the effort she'd spent to turn herself into a successful career woman and bury all the old scars, and here she was bleeding over her own kitchen sink.

This man had stripped her bare, and he hadn't even intended to. Was she that fragile?

She gripped the edge of the sink, and words burst forth, powered by old pain. "Do you know what it's like to look into your mother's eyes and realize she hates you? That she hates everything about you, from the way you look to the way you act?"

"Good God," he murmured. "Obviously I have no idea. But why would the woman hate you?"

"I don't know." She bit her lip until it hurt, trying to hold back unwanted tears. A festering wound had just ripped open, and while she'd thought it had healed long ago, apparently it hadn't. "I just don't know. I tried to be good, but I was never good enough. She could barely stand to be nice to me in front of other people."

"And your da? Did he do nothing?"

"Not really. He was often a cipher, as if he just wanted to stay out of the way, then he died when I was seventeen. But there was no mistaking it, Blaine. I'm not making it up. I felt the weight of my mother's disapproval constantly, and I heard the unending criticisms. If there was anything right about me, I never heard it."

He squeezed her, holding her a little tighter. "And you eventually cut them off. She's never tried to reach you?"

"Not once." She unleashed a shaky sigh. "God, I sound so self-pitying. In truth, it was a relief to cut those ties. To never again feel obligated to call, only to hear the impatience in my mother's voice because I was keeping her from something else. I kept hoping. I didn't want to believe it, and then I had to."

"Therapy?"

"Yeah. After Max. I realized my folks hadn't been wrong—there was something about me that wasn't right. Why else would I fall in with a guy who treated me like dirt? Then she asked me if he treated me differently than I'd been treated at home. It was like this big, black fog dissipated. All of a sudden I could see so clearly."

Blaine continued to hold her from behind, awaiting any sign she wanted to be set free and keeping one ear cocked for sounds from Daphne. He hoped the girl didn't wake just yet, because much as he wouldn't mind holding her and making faces and sounds to draw a smile from her tiny face, he knew Diane needed this time.

Whatever pieces of herself she was assembling and reassembling after confiding in him, she deserved the time to do it.

And he needed some time to be just plain appalled and furious on her behalf. He was no spring chicken, and in the closely knit community back in Galway, he'd seen a share of terrible parents. They inflicted different kinds of ills on their children. Some had to be pried out of the pub at closing time. Some had carried physical discipline to the point of outright abuse. Sad fact was, not everyone was cut out to be a parent, and not everyone wanted a child even if they had one.

The question he'd never been able to answer was, if they didn't want kids, why did they keep them? If Diane's parents felt she was a major problem, why not give her up? As far as he knew, there was no law against saying you couldn't be a parent. Usually that was better than the mistreatment that could come from resentment and hate.

No wonder Diane had bouts of uncertainty and wondered if she was properly caring for Daphne. She had no experience even from her own childhood. And apparently she'd been raised to believe she couldn't do anything right.

Well, that was evidently a freaking lie. Her résumé was brilliant—she probably could have had her pick of jobs, but she had wanted to come here to have more control, to try out her own ideas. A worthy goal, one he believed she'd succeed at, unless she crippled herself with doubt.

He was half tempted to find out where her mother was hiding and go give her a piece of his mind. Not that it would do an ounce of good for Diane. But sometimes the man in him wished it could find satisfaction with a good, solid punch.

God, she felt so good in his arms. As if she had been fitted to him specially. But she stirred a little, and as much as he didn't want to, he started to drop his arms.

She astonished him, turning around to lean into him. "Thank you," she said.

She was thanking him? For what? A hug that he'd probably enjoyed more than she had?

"Sorry for venting like that," she added.

"I wasn't minding. Just wishing I might be able to do something useful."

She sighed and closed her eyes, saying, "Blaine, a hug was the most useful thing in the world. It's not like the past can be changed."

"If someone figures out a way to change the past, we'll all be in trouble."

He felt her move until her cheek rested on his shoulder. "Sure about that?" she asked.

"Well, if everyone created a past that they liked, we'd be in a world of trouble, don't you think? Nothing would mesh with anything else. Pure chaos."

"I hadn't thought of that." Then she stirred again, and something like a small sound of humor escaped her. "You're good for me. You make me laugh."

"That'll be a good thing, most times."

But the moment had passed, and he felt her move again. She needed him to step back and she didn't want to push him. At least that's how he read it. He dropped his arms and took a step away. Then it occurred to him that he might have read her wrong, and that she might therefore read his movement wrong.

Life didn't need to be terrible, did it?

Should he say something? He didn't know, and he wasn't a man accustomed to holding his tongue.

"I still haven't gotten another chair for the living room," she remarked, taking an unexpected direction. "I hate seeing you sit on the floor."

"I don't mind it a bit. But tell me about that grand old recliner chair you have. It didn't come with the house, did it?"

She shook her head, smiling faintly. "It was my

father's. Don't ask me why, but I'm truly attached to it. Given my feelings about my parents, that seems odd."

"Maybe not so odd. Maybe you have some good memories of it and just don't recall them consciously."

"It's possible. I grew up feeling like I was some kind of problem for him, but he never hated me the way my mother did. Maybe he couldn't stand up to her. I'll never know."

She wrapped her arms around herself as if chilled, and shook her head as if she wanted to brush something away. "The last time I went home was for my father's funeral. His chair was out at the curb. That's how fast my mother wanted to be rid of him. Anyway, I called someone to pick it up, and I've carried it around ever since. Don't ask me why I can't let go of it."

"Maybe," he said carefully, "you realize he was as much your mother's victim as you were."

Her head snapped up a bit. After a minute or so, she murmured, "You might be right."

Then she glanced at him from the corner of one golden eye, a humorless smile curving the edge of her mouth. "Two women, sisters. MaryJo's mom, who was an alcoholic until she died and had a daughter so mentally ill she may never escape the hospital. And then my mother. I don't know if she drank much, especially after I left, but she was certainly pickling herself in some very ugly emotions. I wish I knew why. What did their parents do to *them*?"

He leaned back against the counter and folded his arms. "Would it help to know?"

"Maybe we're just full of bad genetic material."

"Hey!" He didn't like that, and he wasn't going to stand here silently and allow her to lump herself into a heap with some disturbed people. She was clearly fine, clearly talented, clearly kind. What else but kindness could have caused her to take on the baby?

She looked at him again. "Is it cold in here?"

He switched his attention immediately and realized she was right. "Maybe. I'll go find the thermostat. If the heater isn't keeping up, I'll check it for you."

She shook her head a little. "You shouldn't have to do that. I have a landlord who's supposed to handle that stuff."

"Sure, and how fast do ya think he'll get here? You and the girl can't spend the night cold."

The thermostat wasn't difficult to find in the short hallway that led to the small house's two bedrooms. It wasn't the newest device, but it was good enough to tell him the temperature was below where it was set and he didn't hear a heater running.

"I'm going to the basement," he called. "You stay with the daffodil, make sure she's warm."

The basement stairs were both narrow and steep, and creaky besides. He had to tip his head to avoid banging it on a rafter. At least there was a lightbulb that worked, though it cast little illumination when he pulled the string. Oh, look, there was an electric torch on the edge of the stairs. He wouldn't have bet that it would work.

But much to his surprise, it did. The beam was yellow, indicating the need for some new batteries, but it would probably be fine for relighting a pilot light, assuming that was the problem.

Unfortunately, that was not the problem. Age and dust had clogged the combustion air intake. The gas valve was turned to the open position, but he quickly realized, after several attempts to light the pilot, that the safety feature was shutting everything down. No air, no pilot, no gas.

He sat back on his heels, gauging the situation. He couldn't fix this tonight. Even the landlord, whoever he was, couldn't fix this tonight. This was going to call for someone licensed to do the job. He didn't want to risk a slipup by getting out of his own lane into someone else's. Being an engineer didn't mean he knew how to do everything. A simple fix to this, yeah. A teardown and rebuild, nah.

That left Diane and Daphne. No way could he leave them here. His own place wasn't large and it was mostly designed to suit him, but he could fit all of them in there for a night or two.

He gave it one more try, using a piece of metal to tap on the air pipe, but it didn't open up, and frankly if it had at this point, he wouldn't trust it.

Some major repairs were needed.

He climbed the stairs again, making a note to tell Diane not to even try to descend them, at least when she was alone here. It would be easy to take a serious fall. He made a second note to get new batteries for the torch, because it likely didn't have much more life in it.

He found Diane waiting near the top of the stair.

"No dice," he said. "It needs some new parts. Your landlord is going to have to hire a heating specialist. Code and all that. You should call him now so he can get started on finding someone. In the meantime I'll gather up things for you and Daphne."

She had just started down the hall, probably to use the phone, but she stopped and looked back at him. "What have you been planning, Blaine Harrigan?"

He almost blinked. How was it she suddenly sounded like his mother? Well, not exactly, but she sounded Irish for sure. Then he saw a devil light in her eye and realized she was teasing.

"For that, woman, I'm going to take you to me own place so the two of you can keep warm until this heater gets fixed. Now go call that landlord of yours."

Chapter Eight

Daphne, holding true to form, had no problem settling down for the night in the playpen that Blaine had brought along for her. It occupied most of the floor in his tiny living room, but Diane noticed he had an advantage: a sofa and a recliner-rocker that she instantly loved. She smiled up at him from its well-padded embrace.

"Let me guess. This is your favorite chair."

Blaine laughed. "Depends on what I'm doing. If I need to stay awake, that is definitely *not* my favorite chair."

He rented a place in a newish-looking apartment complex outside town that didn't seem very full. The apartment itself was…an apartment. A small kitchen with a bar between it and the living room, trying to make a small area seem more spacious. Three doors opened off the living room, two bedrooms and a bath. Not an inch wasted for a hallway.

It was cozy, though, and over time Blaine had added some personal touches other than the furniture. A very happy-looking and bushy golden pothos hung in the corner near the wide window, the only window here. She watched as he pulled the curtains against the night. Navy blue. His furniture was dark green. An interesting color combination from a man, she thought. She liked it, though.

"I've only got the one bed," he remarked, "but you're welcome to it. Fresh sheets this morning. I can sleep on the sofa."

"And I can sleep right here in your rocker. In fact, you may have to pull me out of it if you want it back."

He laughed. "We'll argue about that another time. I'm thinking about a hot drink, and we barely made a dent on that pizza. I'm going to heat a slice or two in the microwave. Would you like one?"

"The drink sounds good, but I don't feel especially hungry. Thanks."

Since the kitchen was only two steps away, around an open bar with cabinets overhead, he didn't exactly go away. She watched him put a kettle on the stove and ignite the flame beneath it.

"I'm going to scald the pot first," he remarked.

"Why?"

"Because once the pot is warm, the tea I make won't get cold so fast."

"Duh."

He laughed. "Even with heat on in here, it's feeling a tad cold. You want me to turn it up?"

"I'm fine and Daph is wearing her blanket sleeper." She turned her attention to the playpen and wondered if she was overdoing the pink-and-white thing. Daph had some yellow and pale green onesies and shirts with tights, but right now she looked like a heap of pink and white inside her sleeper blanket and with her little knit cap on her soft, fuzzy head.

"I wonder when she starts growing hair," she murmured.

"Everyone's different, I think. Should I search it online?"

It was Diane's turn to laugh. "It's all such a mystery to me. I love the soft little blond fuzz on her head. Someone at the learning center said it was just baby fuzz and not even real hair."

"I don't know about that. None of my brothers or sisters lost whatever they had when they were born. All but one, Saphia, had a pretty thick head of it. She had peach fuzz for the longest time. Daphne, on the other hand, has some very fine blond hair. A bit more than fuzz, I think."

Diane nodded, once again fixated on her daughter. Amazing how that little bundle of smiles and tears had become so central to her existence in such a short time. "The scar from her surgery is healing very well."

"I noticed. I'm betting it won't even show in a few months."

The teakettle whistled, and Blaine poured some of the boiling water into a pretty teapot that looked as if it might be very old. "Is that teapot an antique?"

"Me gran's. Mam insisted on sending it back with me after my last visit."

"Any special reason?"

"When I was young, before I became a grand pain in the arse, I used to sit and play cards with Gran and we drank a whole lot of tea together. Fond memories of that pot. And fonder memories of taking me Gran to the cleaners, as they say."

"What?" The word emerged on a surprised laugh.

"Gran taught me to play blackjack. I beat her, probably because I was a youthful cheat and could count cards."

Diane couldn't help grinning. "You must have been a scamp."

"So Mam said. Anyway, it's not really cheating to count cards, although I hear they'd like you to believe so in Las Vegas. Numbers were always easy for me. They float around in my head the way words do for others, I suppose."

He emptied the water from the pot, scooped in some loose tea, then refilled it with water. "Not long now."

Wistfulness filled Diane. "So you had your grandmother around when you were a child?"

He looked up from placing the cover on the teapot and topping it with a knitted cozy. "Aye, I was lucky. I take it you weren't?"

She shook her head. "I was just thinking how nice it must have been to play cards with your grandmother."

"'Twas all that. She passed when I was eight."

"And now you have her teapot."

"That I do."

After a bit, some timer seemed to go off in his head. He lifted the cozy from the pot, pulled two pretty cups close and began to pour the tea through a strainer into them.

"Ooh, I've never seen anyone do that except on TV."

"I'm guessing public TV," he joked. "Well, ya can use your teeth to strain it, but I've never been fond of that."

She giggled. "I'm sure I wouldn't, either."

A short while later he'd placed a saucer and cup of milky tea on the small table beside her, then took a post on the end of the couch that was catty-corner to her with his own cup and a hot slice of pizza on a paper plate. In the middle of the open floor in her playpen, Daphne slept blissfully.

Calm, comfortable and oh so right. A dream, she reminded herself. One she had once longed for. One she thought she had found briefly with Max, but that had been her own delusion. Living an image that had never been there at all. Not for real.

But this was real. She owned no part of it—she

was just passing through, a guest in Blaine's life—but for the moment, she could dream.

Then a crazy thought passed through her mind. She could do more than dream. She could actually reach for it. It might come to nothing, especially since she and Blaine were coworkers...

"Blaine?"

He looked at her.

"Is there some kind of prohibition in this city or county against government workers..." As it struck her what she was about to ask, she fell silent and wished she had a huge eraser for the words that had slipped past her lips.

"Prohibition?" he repeated. "Depends on what you mean. Against relationships?" He paused, then spoke carefully. "Our fire chief is married to our arson investigator."

"Oh."

"And our sheriff is married to the county librarian. I don't think it's encouraged, but I'm not aware of any rule against it." He took a very large bite of his pizza, as if to make it impossible to talk.

Diane quickly picked up her tea, noting for the first time that it was served in a dainty, flowered teacup, and took a couple of sips. "This cup is beautiful," she said, trying to escape the awkwardness she had generated.

"That crockery was me gran's, too," he said, sounding as if he hadn't quite swallowed that last huge bite. "Remarkable woman." Then his voice cleared as he finished swallowing. "And she'd have swatted me for talking with my mouth full. Anyway, a grand woman by my estimation. She taught me a few things."

Grateful for the subject change, she managed a smile. "Like?"

"Like, if you want something, go fer it or you'll never be getting it."

Her breath stopped in her throat. He hadn't changed the subject at all, and he knew exactly where she'd been headed. Or at least thinking about heading. God, the man was a devil, reading her thoughts as if they were on a marquee above her head. Except that she was probably more transparent than she wanted to believe.

He rose from the couch. "I think I'll have a bit more of that pizza. How's your tea? Want me to warm it?"

Feeling safe again, she passed him her cup and saucer and focused on the baby sleeping in the playpen. Daphne was all that mattered. Her daughter. She didn't need any additional complications.

Except that Blaine Harrigan was turning into a complication she wanted very much to add to her life. "You said you were having trouble with the historic overlay?" Safe subject.

"Some. And I told you I want to take you out this week to see the road we're supposed to pave. It's in the plan, so the planner ought to take a look at it before we start. The best we can do now that it's getting cold is oil and gravel. You know anyone who likes oil and gravel road surface?"

"When it hardens…"

"Ah, but getting there." He placed another cup of tea beside her. "It's crap, is what it is. For three or four months, the road department gets a constant stream of calls about the gravel dinging paint and glass. The plows won't be able to touch it until it's really hardened in, and given the time of year, how likely is that? I ask you, who in their right mind decided that needed to be done *now*?"

She stared at him in some amazement, or maybe it was amusement. She'd never imagined him on a rant like that.

He put his fresh cup of tea on the table between them and the paper plate full of steaming pizza on his lap.

"Someone ordered it?" That rather surprised her. "Who?"

"One of your board members. Ask me why. I don't know, but there's something in it for him as sure as I'm sitting here. Thirty-five may be young, but I've been around a bit, and things like this don't get ordered out of the blue for no reason. But since it's in the plan…" He shrugged. "Not much of an argument I can make except it would be better to wait until next summer."

She hesitated. "But I could make a better argument?"

"I don't know." He leaned a bit toward her. "But

you can sure take a look at the plan overlays. I'd like to know if there's something...special about a piece of land out there. Something that isn't part of a ranch, or that's been sold recently. Or has been put on the market."

"The clerk's office would be a good place to start."

He nodded. "I've got the parcel number. It must be a fairly large piece because of subdivision."

He was right about that. Subdividing parcels to sizes below thirty-five or forty acres could get awfully expensive, so unless there was a big profit to be made, it didn't happen. She wondered what the hell was going on out there.

"But it's Friday night," he said suddenly. "Let's leave work for Monday. If your landlord gets the heat fixed tomorrow, I'll help you put that crib together for Daph."

She smiled. "It almost seems superfluous. She's sleeping well enough in the playpen."

"She's also small right now and easy to lift. In a few months, I venture you'll be glad to be lifting her out of a crib."

He had a point. Then, without consciously making the decision, she went to sit beside him on the sofa. "Mind?" she asked.

Did he mind? All she did was sit beside him, not even close enough to touch, and he felt as if skyrockets were going off inside his head. Ridiculous, since they'd been close before while dealing with Daphne, but this was different. She had elected to be close to him, without the baby as a reason.

"Of course I don't mind," he said roughly. His thoughts danced back to their earlier conversation about prohibitions against relationships. She had brought it up. Was she thinking about it?

He wasn't stupid. He knew that some women found him attractive. They always had. He also knew that it rarely lasted. Even good-looking Irish guys came with flaws. For that matter, so did most women.

"You know," he remarked, trying to keep the moment safe unless she wanted it to become something more, "I used to think that somewhere out there was a perfect woman I'd find one day."

"Not Ailis?"

"Her perfection lasted a couple of weeks. Hormone surges wear off, especially when they're not reciprocated."

He was pleased to hear her chuckle quietly. "They do," she agreed.

"But over time I figured something out. I'm not a total eejit."

She glanced at him with a faint smile. "Not even a bit of a one."

"Of course I am. Everyone has a bit of eejit in them."

She turned a little in her seat and looked at him more directly. "This thing you figured out?"

"Oh, yeah. Sounds so obvious when I say it, but most things do. My blinding insight was that nobody's perfect. Nobody at all. Pointless to be thinking that someone had to be perfect. Truth is, someone only has to be perfect for *me*. And me for her."

Her golden eyes searched his face. "Perfect how?"

"Like two puzzle pieces. They won't be the same shape, they'll stick out in different places and have divots in others, but they fit together. In other words, I needed to be looking for someone whose quirks fit mine. A complementary relationship."

"No success, I take it?"

"I haven't been looking hard, to tell ya the truth." He thought about it for all of two seconds, then reached for her hand. When she didn't pull it away, he dared to lift it to rest it on his chest. "Gettin' older, I guess. What seemed so important fifteen years ago isn't dominating my decision making anymore. You?"

She surprised him by leaning into his shoulder. "Me neither. I am so glad to be done with my teens and early twenties. Now there's time for other things in my life. It's not essential to have a date for Friday night anymore. That used to seem so important, long ago. In fact it feels like another time, another life."

He nodded slowly, trying to tamp down his more primitive urges. Here he was talking about not being as randy as he once had been, but feeling as randy as he ever had. Dangerous. Folly. He needed to keep this intellectual. Sure, and hadn't he been trying to do that since this woman had entered his life? "I remember. Then it became more important to have friends. Which is not to say I don't like sex."

Was he mistaken, or did her color heighten a bit? "Same here."

"It's what pulls us together, sometimes," he said, trying for a philosophical stance he was far from feeling. "It's also not enough by itself."

She opened her mouth to say something, but at that moment, Daphne started waking with a quiet but irritated cry. "It's that time," she murmured. "Almost eleven, right?"

He craned his neck a bit so he could see the numbers on the microwave clock. "You'd be right about that." Babies had wonderful timing. He'd known that for years. He almost laughed, but was afraid that he might be misunderstood after the conversation they'd been having. Intellectual, all right, but dancing around the edges of dangerous territory.

Although he might enjoy getting dangerous with this woman…as long as she was willing.

Diane was diapering like a pro now. Blaine disposed of the soiled diaper while the bottle of formula heated a bit in a pan of warm water. Daph had decided to be fussy. Diane paced with the child in the crook of her arm and bounced her gently, all the while talking softly to her.

It wasn't working.

"She must be famished," he remarked. Without waiting for permission, he popped the cover off the fresh bottle and shook a couple of drops on his wrist. "It's ready."

Diane accepted the bottle with thanks and soon Daphne was working on it with great intensity, a little frown between her brows. He tried to remember if he'd ever seen his sisters or brothers frown at this age, but he couldn't remember.

Diane, however, still hadn't completely recovered from last week's excitement. "I hope nothing's wrong," she murmured.

"She's probably just a bit out of sorts. They *do* have moods, Di."

Her head jerked up to look at him, and then a laugh escaped her. That apparently annoyed Daphne, because she pulled her mouth from the nipple and let out a cry. It wasn't a problem, however, because as soon as the bottle was offered again, she took it. Trying to hold it with her own two little hands.

"Before you know it," Blaine remarked, "she'll be feeding herself, running around in short tight skirts and even shorter shorts and wondering what she ever needed you for."

Diane flashed a grin. "I wasn't thinking that far down the road."

"No, but I saw enough of 'em grow up to have a notion how fast it happens. Kind of amazing, actually. You're living on your own clock, doing a hell of a lot of things with your life and every time you pause to look, you realize they're taller, smarter and more smart-mouthed…"

"Oh, stop," she said, humor making her voice tremble. "That's a long way away."

"Just keep tellin' yersel' that."

When Daphne was finished with her bottle, Blaine offered to take over. "I didn't realize how much I'd missed this," he remarked as he lifted her against his shoulder and took his turn at pacing with her.

"She certainly looks wide-awake now," Diane remarked. "It's a whole different view from back here."

"Usually is."

His old mates back home, and maybe even some of his buddies here, might have found it a bit odd for him to be going all soft over an infant and wanting to hug her like this. Ah, well. Sometimes he thought men could be absolute eejits about the things that mattered. Besides, he'd seen enough tough nuts crack when they had a kid of their own. Funny how that worked.

He decided to talk about something safe for now, something that would give him the opportunity to settle his urges. "If that heater gets fixed—or even if it doesn't, actually—want to take a scenic drive into the mountains tomorrow? I mentioned that old gold-mining town and the scenic road they want to build. Regardless of whether they do a damn thing about it, it's still a grand drive, and the daffodil will probably sleep through the whole thing, giving you a break."

"Sounds wonderful." She smiled. "I'd like to see it."

"Can't go walking around the ghost town. Too

many tunnels under it, and some are collapsing. If they want to make that a tourist destination, some work is going to be required to make it safe. But it would be a draw, I admit. It already is for the brave of heart. Anyway, don't look at it as part of the job. Just enjoy it. It's a beautiful drive this time of year."

At last Daphne settled and seemed ready to go back to sleep. She waved her arms and legs a few sleepy times, as if trying to hang on to wakefulness, but it didn't work. Almost as soon as she returned to the playpen, she drifted off into sleep.

Blaine and Diane wound up back on the couch watching her. After a bit, Blaine laughed quietly. "They tend to be the center of attention. Listen, I put fresh sheets on the bed when I got up this morning. It's yours. You have to be getting tired."

He saw it then, that hesitation, as if she didn't want to leave the daffodil that far away. Typical mom stuff. It probably killed her to leave the girl in day care. He guessed Diane was being subsumed by her new maternal role. Normal enough, but it wouldn't leave room for much else.

Aw, to hell with it, he thought. Nothing quite like the wrong time. "You must be knackered. If you don't want to use my bed, let me get you some blankets."

And what the devil had he been hoping would happen, anyway? The pull he felt toward this woman didn't mean she felt the same, even though he'd sometimes sensed it. Hell, she'd even asked about relationships between employees, so she was thinking about him at least a little.

He wasn't ordinarily shy about taking a stab at it, to see if there was any reason to continue, but this time he felt incredibly awkward. First off, he had to work with her, and a mistake of this kind could create problems all the way down the long corridor of time for both of them. Second, there was Daphne. He'd become remarkably fond of the tyke, and he didn't want to be obliged to stay away.

He opened the hall closet and began to pull out a blanket and pillow for Diane so she could be comfy on the couch. Then he changed his mind. Enough with all the dithering. She could speak for herself. Him holding one-sided arguments inside his head wasn't likely to settle anything.

He shoved the blanket and pillow back, then strode down the hall. Diane hovered over the playpen, at once beautiful and almost sylphlike. Looking at her now, it was hard to imagine the mountains of determination that had brought her to this point: a successful urban planner, a mother to her cousin's child. She might look fragile at this moment, but this woman was made of steel.

When she realized he was just standing there, she looked up from the baby. "Blaine?"

"Will ya come ta bed wi' me?" His accent had burst out of its confines, and he didn't care.

She could have had any reaction at that point and he wasn't sure any of them would have surprised him, from throwing him out of his own place to announcing she was moving to the motel.

But she chose none of those answers. Instead she glanced down once more at Daphne, then rounded the playpen until she stood right in front of him. "I think that's the most romantic proposal I've ever had."

"I doubt it. It wasn't romantic at all. It was the words that popped out of me addled brains. And you're the one addling them."

Her smile seemed to hold a cat's contentment. "I like the sound of that."

He was still dealing with his surprise that she hadn't told him where to stuff it, his coming on to her like that. "I need to work on it."

Her smile deepened. "Just one promise, Blaine."

"And that?"

"If we mess up everything tonight, we act like it never happened. I don't want to lose your friendship."

And with that she set off all the fireworks in his head until he felt like Marco Polo making the biggest discovery of all: gunpowder. "I can promise that."

Hell, he'd managed to carry on as if Ailis hadn't told him where to leave his head, and in front of his best lads, too. Yeah, he could promise that, but damned if he was going to allow it to happen. No muck-ups tonight.

He'd had enough experience with women to feel safe in promising that.

"The main thing," he muttered, "is to listen."

"What?" The word sounded as if it had been surprised out of her, but he was past talking. Hell, he'd been past talking for hours now. He'd done his best to keep that ball rolling, to prevent anything risky from happening…but here he was, walking right into it and feeling the heat growing between them like an explosion about to go off.

Only one dim bulb was on in the room, just enough to prevent a catastrophe in the middle of the night.

But despite the lack of light, his gaze drank her in, every detail, from the gentle mounds of her breasts that were just hinted at beneath her flannel shirt to the delicate curve of her neck.

The day he'd first seen her, frazzled as she'd seemed, he'd tried hard not to notice the way the silky folds of her blouse draped over her, suggesting without shouting.

Every move she had made in that outfit, from her blouse to her slacks to the stray blond hair that had teased her cheek, had reached out to him like an invitation.

He'd buried his reaction almost before he knew he was having it. He had perhaps let thoughts of this day trail across his mind from time to time, but had firmly squashed them. He didn't need an announcement to understand that she must be nearly overwhelmed between a new job and a new baby. She didn't need additional complications.

Yet here she was, her golden eyes dimmed in the

poor light, clearly longing for him yet getting more nervous as he stood here like a dolt letting the moment wash over him in its myriad sights, sounds and feelings.

"I've wanted you," he said as quietly as he could, the sounds emerging from the depths of his chest, "from the moment I saw you."

Her smile returned, looking less nervous. "While I was frazzled with a baby? You had to take over the diapering. What man finds that sexy?"

"A man who isn't put off by babies but has just been confronted by one of the most beautiful women he's ever seen."

"Beautiful?" She almost gasped the word. "None of your blarney, Blaine Harrigan."

"I never kissed the stone." But her teasing mood relieved his unusual paralysis. Could it be that he was worried about whether he would love her well enough? Only one way to find out.

He'd have liked to pick her right up off her feet and carry her to his bed, but this bloody doorway wasn't wide enough. For an instant he thought of that ranch he'd considered buying, and most of all a sprawling homestead with more room than any house he'd ever been in. But that all slipped away as he took her small hand in his bigger one and gently urged her toward the bedroom.

Her shyness and nerves seemed to have dissipated. Once inside his room, she came into his embrace as naturally as if she'd always been there. His own muscular size, built through years of manual labor that around here was as much a part of his job as the desk work, made him acutely aware of how fragile this woman was. Not weak, but fragile. A being requiring gentleness from him in every way. Gentleness he wanted to provide.

Bending his head, he sought her mouth for a kiss. Hard to believe they had come to this without any sexual exploration. Blame Daphne for that, he thought with mild amusement.

But amusement quickly vanished, along with most rational thought, as she opened her mouth to him, inviting him into the warm, moist depths of her very being. Excitement slashed through him, sharp desires that reached his every cell. His tongue was his surrogate, but thrusting in and out of her, tracing the pearls of her teeth, tasting the faint remnants of tea, didn't feel less than total penetration. It felt like the first small step to completion.

Joy joined passion, elevating him until thought very nearly vanished, giving way to feeling. Her arms slid around him, then clamped tightly, her nails digging into this back as if she were hanging on for dear life. Never had he felt so *needed*.

One of her hands slid upward, capturing the back of his neck, turning him into her prisoner. The other slid down and around until she was working at his belt buckle.

She didn't want any fooling around. She was in a mad rush, too.

With effort, he lifted his head. Her eyes fluttered open, looking sleepy. "Blaine?"

"Do we need to be hurrying?" Fast, slow, he didn't care for himself.

"Hell, yes," she said, then clamped her mouth to his once again.

Well, then...

She pulled away and surprised him by beginning to shed her own clothing. He could take a hint, and he stripped his quickly.

Then there was the breathtaking moment, absolutely breathtaking, when all the barriers were gone. The chilly air made her nipples pucker, large nipples with the pinkest of areolae. Her waist tapered down to a woman's hips, not a boy's, with all the curves he so admired, curves that would cradle him, not fight him.

Gorgeous. Farther down he found her long, lithe legs, yet like so much of her, curved, too. No protruding knees, no sign of the underlying bones, absolutely perfect.

The air in the room seemed to be thinning out as he filled his eyes with her naked beauty. Had he created her out of the stuff of dreams, she could not have pleased him more. In response, the electric ribbons of desire that ran through him became more like a primitive drumbeat. His staff was erect, and it twitched in time to his need.

He hoped he pleased her half as much as she pleased him.

He needn't have wondered. "You're perfect, Blaine."

No, not perfect, he thought. The scars of brawls, of minor accidents, of careless moves with a tool... they marked him all over.

She stepped closer and touched a crescent scar on his upper thigh. "What's this?"

The moment almost slipped away, interrupting passion with one of his least favorite memories from childhood, but she deserved an answer. That was one too big to ignore. "Me and some of the lads were riding our bicycles down a hill out a way in the country. We liked it because we could go fast. Too fast."

"Oh, no!" She looked at him, concern on her face.

"As you can see, I'm fine."

"But it was close, wasn't it?" Then she deprived him of reason and thought by cupping him in her hand. He sucked air between his teeth. "Am I hurting you?"

"You're a witch," he growled, and before she could do more, he grabbed her, twisted her and threw her on the bed on her back. "So we want games, do we?"

A small laugh escaped her. "What kind of games do we have in mind, Mr. Harrigan?"

He was sure liking this playful side of her. He straddled her, leaving everything exposed to the gods and her. Then he grabbed her wrists and forced them to the top of her head, where he held them easily with one hand.

"I could make you my prisoner," he rumbled. "An offering on the altar of my desires." He began to caress her from neck to privates, noting how silky she felt everywhere. At once she began to squirm in response, and little gasping breaths started to escape her. "Too much to handle?" he asked, teasing.

"Try me," she gasped back. "Just try me."

"Oh, I intend to." Caressing her with his hand while she wriggled delighted him. Amazingly responsive, and he was enjoying the way she felt beneath his touch.

Electricity seemed to fill the air, feeding his wants and desires as if he were plugged into a power source. Anticipation gripped him with yearning, and an unexpected fear that she might change her mind.

But with a strong pull, she broke his hold on her wrists and her hands landed on his chest, as light as butterflies, but maddening as she slowly began to trace him. A lazy smile curved her mouth as she closed her eyes and gave herself up to the world of sensation.

"I want you," she whispered. "I'm aching with it. Every part of me is alive to you…"

He could say the same, and began to feel a subtle shudder growing in his arms and legs as strength gave way to a stronger need.

Her hands cupped him again, dragging a deep groan from him, then she stroked his erection, nearly driving him to the edge of insanity.

"Witch," he muttered. Ah, by the saints, he couldn't forget…

Rolling onto one elbow, which brought his hips

into electric contact with her, he pawed in the night-stand drawer, hoping the condom wasn't too old...

She grabbed it from him, struggling to rip it open, then with a pleased smile began to roll it onto him. Nobody, ever, had done that for him, and he never would have dreamed that it could be about the sexi-est thing a woman could do.

"Damn," he said without apology, then lowered himself, seeking her welcoming cavern, until he felt the instant where they met and she gave him en-trance.

Slowly, savoring his plunge toward ecstasy, ignor-ing the way her hands gripped his hips and pulled on him, he savored every single split second of their union.

Then at last he was deep within her. Filling her. Claiming her. Uniting them in bliss.

Diane hadn't had long to be surprised by her own boldness. She'd never felt this way before, but some-thing about Blaine drew it out of her, a woman filled with power and her own desires who refused to be denied. If he had turned away...

But he hadn't. He had answered her desire with his own, which was clearly every bit as strong.

There was something very special about Blaine wanting her, but she couldn't sort through that now. Soon she was awash in passion, anticipation and an edgy sort of fear that none of this would really happen, that something was going to tear these moments out of her grasp.

It seemed so impossible…

But as his touches ignited bonfires all throughout her body, she stopped fearing and started experiencing, filled with joy and wonder and a hunger unlike any she had ever known.

Then…then he was deep within her, filling a place too empty for too long, stretching her in ways that made fresh thrills run through her, and a satisfaction that was almost enough by itself.

But not enough, as he soon proved, moving within her, lifting her from reality in a world populated by sensations beyond description, sensations that blinded her, drove her, hung her on a precipice she feared she might not be able to fall over.

But finally, finally, with one deep thrust, he tossed her over that edge into free fall among the stars. She heard his groan as he shuddered, but it merely added to the almost painful sensation of falling into heaven.

Chapter Nine

Blaine fell asleep with Diane wrapped in his arms. He'd murmured sweet things to her, caressing her hair and side gently, telling her how wonderful she was, but then the inevitable happened.

Amused, feeling absolutely wonderful and not at all abandoned, she woke from her own doze and rose and quickly pulled on her undies, socks and flannel shirt. The digital clock beside the bed said it was nearly five, and Daph had yet to miss her five o'clock feeding.

The apartment was a little chilly, but not too much so. She began warming Daphne's bottle in a pan beside the sink and listened to the wind whip up outside. A change in weather coming?

Having recently come from Des Moines, she figured she had enough cold weather gear for herself, but the baby? She'd need to go shopping again.

A trickle of amusement filled her. Nobody had warned her how expensive a baby could be. Especially starting from scratch. Bed, playpen, changing table, mobile, toys, blankets, new clothes as she grew and now winter wear. Oh, and don't forget the mountain of disposable diapers and the formula.

She now seriously understood the point of a baby shower.

There was still some tea in the teapot, probably really strong by now, but she used the strainer and poured some into a coffee mug, not willing to risk Blaine's grandmother's china in a microwave.

Just as she pushed the buttons to heat it, she felt powerful arms slip around behind her.

"The bed was empty and getting cold," Blaine murmured in her ear.

A shiver of pleasure trickled through her. "It's almost five. Daphne's witching hour."

"I figured." He kissed her earlobe, then the nape of her neck, and released her, causing more delightful shivers. She hated to feel his arms slip away. "If it's tea you're wanting, I'll make fresh. That's past the point of drinking. It'd peel paint off a car."

She turned to face him, feeling the smile that danced around her mouth. "Fresh tea, then?"

"Coming up."

The tea was ready and steaming in delicate cups

before Daph stirred. Diane started to move toward the playpen, but Blaine forestalled her.

"Let me? I've been missing the babes. Missing family, come to that. Careful or I'll adopt ya both."

She didn't think that sounded so awful, but it was a luxury to be able to settle on the couch and sip her tea while Blaine tended to her daughter. She curled her legs under her, a favorite position she hadn't indulged often since Daphne's arrival, and pulled the afghan over the back of the couch onto her bare legs. Warm and cozy.

She loved looking at Blaine. So strong and good-looking, with that startling Irish combination of nearly black hair and brilliant blue eyes. But as much as she loved that, she loved seeing the way he cradled her daughter, murmuring to her, his attention completely fixed on her as he called her daffodil. Occasionally he even hummed.

And Daphne's gaze was as fixed on him, never wavering.

As Daph was nearing the bottom of her bottle, Blaine looked up. "I was thinkin'."

"Yes?"

"I was thinkin' I'd like to date you. Normal-type dating. Not just me running over to see what you might need, but taking you out to dinner or a film. I'd suggest dancing, but the roadhouses can get rough. Or you could come with me to my darts game and meet the lads."

She didn't know what to say. He wanted to *date*

her? That meant a lot more than the friendship that had been growing between them, never mind the time they had just spent in bed. That could be dismissed. Maybe. Butterflies began fluttering in her stomach.

"And in case you're worryin'," he continued, "Daph can come with us if you want. We'll just choose things that will be okay for her. Drives in the mountains before snowfall. There's even a ranch I've been mulling buying, and I wouldn't mind your opinion."

She was still trying to absorb all of this. Did this mean something more than friendship? Stupid question. He'd been then one to call them dates. She seized on the thing that seemed totally out of place. "Why would you want my opinion on a ranch? And why in the world are you even thinking about buying one?"

"Because it'd be a big spread of land, unlike anything I could get back home. When I was young and running on the streets and hills of Galway, I loved Western films. I kinda outgrew that, but I never lost my desire for owning a big piece of land and having horses. This place offers so many opportunities. It's a big country."

She nodded, thinking about it. "Years ago, back when I was in college, I went with some girlfriends on a camping trip. We wound up in the seriously misnamed Sunshine Campground."

"Why misnamed?" Daphne must had enough,

because he put the bottle aside and lifted her to his shoulder.

"Because the entire five days we were there, it never stopped raining."

He laughed. "Misnamed indeed."

"While we were there, anyway. The point is, we met a couple from Sweden. They'd planned to drive the country from one end to the other with plenty of time to stop and take in the sights, but they were only halfway across and running out of time. I remember how they kept repeating their astonishment that this country is so big."

"It certainly is, and I like it. If I got a ranch, I could bring me nieces and nephews for visits. They'd be agog at the space, and even more agog at being able to ride horses."

"I bet they would. I haven't ridden in years."

"Did you like it?"

"Loved it." She smiled feeling oddly wistful. "It was actually a course in college. My family never would have paid for regular riding lessons."

"Would you like to do it again? I happen to have a horse I stable with Gideon Ironheart. I'm sure you could ride her, or Gideon would gladly let you choose another mount."

She looked at him. "What in the world are you driving at, Blaine Harrigan?"

His smile spread. "I told you, I want to date you. I think we might have something going here, and there's only one way to find out. As for you looking at the ranch, I couldn't tell you the number of times I heard me mam complain about how men just couldn't see the most obvious things. I don't think she was talking about timber and framing."

Diane laughed. "Probably not."

"Anyway, no rush."

Dating. It sounded so formal. She remembered the first time she went out with Max. He'd had a couple of tickets to some show and said one was a spare. He'd asked her to come but carefully pointed out, *This is not a date*.

She should have walked away right then, but she'd taken it to mean they were just going as friends. Little had she guessed that he'd meant friends with benefits, which had evolved to something more and left her feeling emotionally slashed.

But she and Blaine had arrived at an entirely different place. They'd already had sex. Now he wanted to *date*? He must be trying to say something, but she wasn't sure what.

"What's wrong?" he asked.

She looked up from her lap and realized he'd stopped walking with Daph and was simply watching her while the baby slept against his shoulder.

"I don't know. I mean…dating seems like an afterthought now. Maybe?"

"Wasn't intended to." He sighed a bit, then walked to the back of the apartment. From the sounds she could tell he was changing Daph. When he returned, he placed her daughter in the playpen, and she was still feeling confused about what he was trying to get to here.

He sat beside her on the sofa and took her hand. "I never thought I was good at this sort of thing. Yeah, I dated a few women, and it never worked out and I always figured it was me. Ailis gave me a good idea of that. So you ask a woman out to dinner or to a film, she says yes and never calls you again and never returns your calls. Or…she just turns you down before you get the invite out of your mouth. Common enough, I s'pose."

"Likely," she agreed. "There's certainly nothing wrong with you that I can see."

"Sure and I'm God's gift, can't ya tell?"

That drew a small laugh from her. "Maybe not quite."

"Definitely not quite. Any road… Matters between us have been flowing backward."

That startled her. She twisted so she could see him better. "In what way?"

"Well…I walk into your life by way of the daffodil, and I'm busy falling for the child, and fixing up your nursery, handy lad that I am, so baby came first. Then…we worked together a bit here and there, but hardly so's you'd notice, and we still don't really get to know each other, and then the next step—we have sex. Not that I'm complaining, but aren't things supposed to happen in the reverse order? Me datin' you, us deciding a trip to bed would be grand, then me falling for your daughter?"

He had a point, but the way he framed it made a bubble of amusement rise inside her. She should have been nervous that he was looking for a way out of the rapidly growing intimacy between them, but he was instead looking for a more customary version of events.

"So we did it backward?"

He smiled, tilting his head a little. "I'm quite sure if you read one of them self-help books, you'd find we got it all wrong. Now me, I'm in the way of thinking that I'm very fond of you—and your daughter—but shouldn't we have some of the fun of getting to know one another over a bowling ball or a pint or a game of darts? Or if none of those interest you, over dinner or a drive in the country?"

She liked the idea. Part of her had somehow developed a deep craving for this man, and it wasn't just that she found him so sexually attractive. When she heard his voice in the hallway outside her office, she always looked up hopefully. Sometimes he poked his head in to say hello and she felt he'd made her day…which surely was over-the-top.

No question but she liked him. His question, however, seemed to be was there something more in this for both of them, and he was suggesting a way to find out. Slowly. Carefully. Taking their time. Having fun together.

Her gaze trailed to Daph, sound asleep in her playpen, and she had to agree that in a way Blaine was right. They'd come together quickly and strongly over her child, but there was so much more that was needed if they were to be more than a flash in the pan. It seemed he wanted a whole lot more than that.

He spoke again, tightening his hold on her hand just a bit. "I'm in the way of believing in love at first sight."

She drew a sharp breath and fixed her gaze to his face.

"But believing it, which I do, and trusting in it are two different things. I'd like to think that given time we'd build a future, not just the present."

"Wow," she whispered. In his words she heard a hope that almost felt like it could swamp her. On the other hand, she wanted it. She hoped this could grow, because the taste of it she'd had so far had made her remarkably happy.

"Anyway," he said, "just think about it. If it doesn't appeal to you, that's fine. Your choice."

Her choice? All of sudden she was frightened. So much had changed in her life so quickly—how could she possibly make a decision of any kind? She'd barely gotten used to being a mother, and she was still feeling her way into her job. She'd only fallen into all this with Blaine because he'd been helpful.

So much as it troubled her, she said quietly, "I need time, Blaine. I'm not ready to date. Too much has been changing too rapidly."

His smile shadowed a bit but didn't disappear. "I understand." He leaned back against the couch, still holding her hand. "I'd have fixed that heater for you later this morning," he said, changing the subject. "But it'd be better to have someone with a license do it. I think I said that. I'd hate to make some kind of mistake."

The silence in the room seemed to grow, consuming what had been a beautiful night.

It was all her fault. Tiny fingers of panic squirmed into her heart. Had she just made the biggest mistake of her life?

Then, making her feel even worse, he carried on as if nothing at all had happened. He made breakfast for them as the sun started rising and suggested they take that drive while the light was best.

"With any luck," he added, "we'll get back and find out you have heat and can move home again."

Yup, she thought miserably, she'd blown it.

Chapter Ten

A month later, Daphne was sitting up on her own and creeping around the playpen and floor like a pro. The baby laughed a lot and seemed quite happy with life.

Diane felt less so. She had friends now, women she could gather with on a Saturday afternoon, babies everywhere. She especially liked Ashley McLaren, Marisa Tremaine and Julie Archer, but the gals she'd met her first day, from the clerk's office, were also a lot of fun.

Little by little she was getting the information she needed from the members of the planning board, and by way of them from the city and county officials.

Talk about grandiose ideas. She wasn't sure most of the residents around here would be thrilled with the kind of growth these people envisioned, but that was the point of inviting those who would have an interest to a public meeting. Lots of ideas were bound to get shot down.

She was busy, Daphne was healthy and she should be thrilled with the way things were going.

Except for Blaine. He was still friendly, still popped in to talk to her at least once a day, and every weekend he stopped in to lavish love on his "little daffodil." During those times, they talked quite a bit.

But she could feel a barrier between them, something that had slipped into place quietly when she had said she didn't want to date.

That lay entirely at her door, and in one sense she didn't regret her decision. Her life had been jam-packed with changes, and she didn't want to make him a crutch, which she could have easily done, as helpful as he'd been. No, she'd been in no position then to even consider something as important as whether they should date.

While it was true that dating was a far cry from marriage, it carried certain obligations with it. And if it didn't work out, someone was bound to get hurt. So she guessed she'd been the one who'd raised the barrier, but he was definitely observing it.

What she hadn't expected was that with passing time, it didn't get easier. Far from it. She was beginning to hurt. But in no way did she get the sense from him that he felt the same. Except for his attention to Daphne, he appeared to have moved on and to be satisfied with friendship.

Well, why not? As he'd pointed out, they really hadn't had time to get to know one another. Not then. He'd proposed dating as a way to do that, and she'd shut him down. Worse, she'd probably made him feel the way Ailis or Alice had years ago. He'd reached out and been slapped away because of her stupid concern that she was in no position to make a decision yet.

But she hadn't needed to decide anything. All she had needed to do was date him, see how things went. He'd been frank about that.

He'd also been right that they'd started everything backward. Even now his description of putting the cart before the horse could amuse her.

Time had passed, however, and the feeling that she'd made an awful mistake kept growing. She began to lie awake at night, wondering if it was too late to change her mind.

It hardly seemed possible that autumn was nearly over. The leaves had lost their color, and most had fallen from the trees. In town, diligent people raked them into leaf bags or blew them away to somewhere.

She enjoyed some amusement when she was out walking Daph in her new stroller, to think of the chain link of leaf blowers sending the crackling debris on a steady trip out of town.

Daphne apparently hadn't reached an age yet where she was ready to be terrified by anything new, because she seemed to enjoy even the noisy leaf blowers or the occasional roar of a passing vehicle that needed a muffler job. Everything tickled her. She waved her hands and made happy sounds that came pretty close to giggles.

Diane wondered if she'd been this happy as a baby. Once she started growing up, she sure hadn't been. But she was determined that Daphne would be loved and appreciated in all the ways she herself hadn't been. One way to learn parenting was to learn all the things not to do, she thought wryly.

It was Sunday afternoon, and Blaine had called last night to ask if he could come over. That was making her uncomfortable, too, that he felt he needed permission to pop in. None of her other new friends seemed to feel that way.

He was sitting on a plastic chair on the porch, one of those molded things that were cheap and she'd figured would do for now. He stood up when he saw them coming and waved, smiling.

Damn, he looked good enough to eat. Feeling the pull toward him as strong as ever, maybe stronger, was like a wake-up call to her stubborn brain. She hadn't stopped wanting him, and her reasons had all been a sham. She was afraid she would fail, ruin any kind of relationship with Blaine. She didn't think she could stand that failure.

He came down the two steps and picked up the stroller, lifting it easily onto the porch, all the while talking to Daph in something approaching baby talk, which she had to admit sounded a wee bit strange emerging from a man whose voice rose from the bottom of his chest.

"I brought you a surprise, Daffodil," he was saying as he unbuckled her from her stroller. "I used to have one when I was little like you, but they're hard to find these days."

Diane couldn't help but smile as she watched the big man lift her daughter and watched Daphne smile and chortle in response to his voice. There was a bond there now, no two ways about it.

Inside, she offered him tea as he shed his jacket and began to remove Daphne's warm sack and knit cap from her. "She'll need mittens almost before you know it. Yes, I'd fancy that tea, if you don't mind. Everything still sailing smoothly for you?"

"Have you heard anything to the contrary?"

Blaine didn't immediately answer then said, "Is that sarcasm or a real question?"

"Probably both," she admitted as she grinned at him. In the kitchen she put the kettle on, and he sat at the table with Daphne on his thigh. "I've been digging into things. I'm not exactly sure of all I've found. Some of it feels a bit...archaeological."

That drew a crack of laughter from him. "That I can believe. No, I haven't heard a word against you, at all. You seemed to have buttered them up well."

"I hope so. We aren't going to get a damn thing done if they're mad at me. And you haven't really mentioned culverts, for all the times you've dropped by."

"We're fixing the ones that most need it. Take it from me, it's going to be a mess come spring. A lot of places don't have much life in them." He paused, then added, "I hope that one of these days soon you'll be able to do that historic district lookover with me. We really need to get that sorted."

She flushed faintly because she realized she'd been avoiding that—he'd asked her when she first got here. Yes, there were things she needed to settled with the city government, but she also needed some idea of what she needed to push for. "Soon," she heard herself promise.

"Good. Now the pressy for Miss Daffodil here." He reached into a deep pocket on his work shirt. In fact, the shirt had all kinds of pockets, looking more suited to a photographer of old, but most of the pockets appeared to contain something.

Out of one he pulled a small sheaf of cloths. Suddenly curious, Diane leaned closer. "Is that a cloth book? I don't think I've seen one in forever."

"It is, and I had to be ordering it online. Seemed strange to me. They were common enough when I was helping raise up the youngsters. Anyway, while you make us that tea, I'm going to read her first book to her."

Diane listened, charmed, as he read the very simple story to her, which included lifting flaps to reveal new objects. Daphne probably didn't understand a bit of it, but she enjoyed the colors, the changing scenery and…might as well face it, Blaine's attentions.

"I wouldn't leave her alone with it till she's older," he said when he finished and folded the book up, holding it so Daphne could explore it with her hands. "It's supposed to be safe, but I wouldn't be trusting that just yet."

"I agree," she answered and didn't resent the suggestion in the least. He seemed as much a part of Daph's life now as she did, and Diane felt not the least bit of possessiveness. Well, Blaine had been here almost from the very start.

She glanced toward the window and saw the early evening was beginning to shade the world. "I was going to make a small roast for dinner. Join us?" It was the first time she had asked him to stay for dinner since she'd dropped the hammer on him. Not even the next day when he'd assembled Daph's crib for her.

"I'd like that," he said, granting her a smile before returning his attention to the baby.

She stared glumly for a few moments, then started making the tea. He only came around for Daphne. He'd lost all interest in her, and she couldn't blame him for that.

When she'd set the mugs on the table, along with a saucer for the tea bags, she sat across from him and watched him tease Daphne by waggling his index finger around until she reached up and caught it. Then she didn't want to let go.

Oh, she had a way with him, she thought. A way with her, too. And now she wondered if she could even force the words past her dry mouth. But... she wanted him with an ache that was still growing rather than diminishing, and it was hard to accept the responsibility for having broken any chance they might have had. Fear, she thought. Fear of failing once again. Was that to hobble her entire life? It had certainly made a mess of this.

She rose and pulled the roast out of the refrigerator. A beef roast was an extravagance she seldom indulged, but every so often the serious carnivore in her emerged. She'd even bought an extra baking potato, too, so she had enough.

But it wasn't time to start cooking yet, she realized. She was just going to have to live with any awkwardness.

"That land you were wondering about?" she said as she sat at the table again.

"Which?"

"Alongside the road that the board suddenly wants paved with oil and gravel."

"A bad thing to be doing before late spring, and so I told them. They didn't like it, but they didn't want the problems I described, either. Did you learn something?"

"Yes. I went after it because of the new comprehensive plan. It's been subdivided. One of the county commissioners is part of an investment group that wants to build a strip mall there."

"There?" Disbelief edged his voice. She couldn't blame him. "Have they lost their bloody minds? The middle of nowhere?"

She had to smile, and in smiling let go of the tension that had tightened every nerve ending in her body. There were worse things than only being friends with this man, such as not being friends with him at all. "You said it joined two major roads, correct?"

"Ya. But it exists only so ranchers can move stock and supplies around. The master plan was totally vague on any other use."

"Well, it's not vague anymore." She sighed and leaned her elbows on the table. Boy, did Daph look happy on Blaine's lap, surrounded by one of his powerful arms. She made little noises and the waving of her arms had become more purposeful. She wanted that book.

"Meaning?" he asked.

"Apparently there aren't a whole lot of services on the northern road, and the southern road, well, you have to take some twists and turns to get to town. Somebody must think that a gas station, convenience store and small restaurant could make some money there as long as they have signs on the main roads giving directions. But of course they can't get the financing until they have a road in good enough condition to handle construction traffic. After it's all built, there's some hinting around that it could be paved into a two-lane."

He drummed the fingers of his free hand on the tabletop. The sound made Daphne giggle. "I'm quite certain that isn't in the current master plan."

"Nope," she answered. "But the pressure to get it into the one I'm working on is how I learned about it."

He frowned. "Did you just write it in?"

"Of course not, Blaine! I'm not the ruler of this county, and despite the pressure I started to feel, I pointed out that we needed to have a charette with all the affected property owners."

"Charette?"

"Public meeting. Everyone who'd be affected— we call them stakeholders—gets the opportunity to see the proposal and comment on it. That slowed down the push, I can tell you. But I didn't get the whole story until this past week. I've been edging around it, but I wasn't getting anywhere until I finally said I could see no point in turning that road into some kind of artery. Not enough traffic. Didn't your friends at the road department tell you we'd been taking a traffic count?"

He nodded. "But I didn't think much about it when I heard. I'd had my victory. No paving before spring. A strip mall? Where the devil did they find investors willing to go for that out there?"

"That I don't know. Their construction plans are my business only to a point. You know that. Providing a comprehensive plan gives me some input, but we won't be looking for grant money for something like this, so…" She shrugged. "I need to get everyone who'll be affected by this together before we write it into the plan. I think I ticked off at least one board member, but there's a lot in the scale now. They hired me because their plan was so outdated they couldn't get grants. Heck, it was in violation of more regulations than I can count. So they can't just sweep this under the rug. They might be able to push through their strip mall before the new plan is ready for a vote, but it won't help in the long run, because I suspect there'll be a lot of environmental concerns that will have to be addressed regardless."

He nodded slowly. "You mean that the environmental requirements can't be ignored simply because they're not in the old plan."

"Exactly. It's not like the regulations come into being only when they're written into the plan." She sighed. "I've spent the better part of a week trying to get that across."

"And you survived?" He looked faintly amused.

"You bet. I told them they'd better get an impact statement before anything is touched, signed or paid for."

"This whole thing still feels weird." Daphne had drooled on his forearm, and he took a napkin from the basket on the table to dab it away, then dab at her mouth. She gurgled and reached again for the book. "Maybe I should put this away for another time."

But he didn't move, and neither did she.

"I'm sorry," Diane said after a few moments. "Here it is the weekend and I'm talking about work."

"I don't mind, actually. I've been so busy running around putting out fires that I haven't been able to keep up. I'm glad you filled me in. But I still don't get this whole strip mall idea."

"Me neither. Would you have any idea why Sagebrush Ranch would want to sell off that parcel?"

"Money. Ranching is a tough business these days."

Daphne's head was nodding. Blaine rose. "Bed or playpen?"

"Either one. I doubt she'll sleep long. She's staying awake more in the daytime."

A significant change, Diane thought as she rose and went to look over her dinner choices. A three-pound beef roast was about as small as she could cook in the oven and hope to have it done just right. She hated when it grew so overcooked it tasted like cardboard. Plus, she loved cold roast beef sandwiches for lunch.

Then a wave of longing hit her so hard she gripped the edge of the counter and squeezed her eyes shut.

Her feelings about Blaine had only grown, she realized. The last month had fed them until there was no longer any doubt in her mind that she'd made the stupidest of decisions. It was probably too late now. The sense that she'd placed a barrier between them had grown, and he was observing it.

She heard his step as he returned to the kitchen.

She had to face this, settle this one way or another. She had to know if her hopes should be buried.

"Blaine?" Her voice cracked. She turned to face him and saw him wiping Daphne's drool from the book. To her surprise, he still carried a baby who had become suspiciously wide-awake.

He looked up immediately. "Is something wrong?"

Oh, man, those Irish blue eyes. She licked her lips.

"Well, go on," he said gruffly. "I haven't bitten anyone since I was two, I promise ya."

She squeezed her hands into fists, fearing she was about to experience the worst failure of her life, but knowing she had to take the risk. "You said…you asked… Can we start dating or is it too late?" The words came out on a hurried rush and she stared at him, feeling her heart begin to sink when all he did was look at her.

"Good God, woman," he said presently, "and just what d'ye think we've been doin' these past weeks?"

She froze. His words struck her as if he'd just spun her around and left her dizzy. She closed her eyes briefly, swallowing hard. "Maybe—maybe you should tell me."

A quiet chuckle escaped him. "First, Daffodil's nodding off again, so I think I'd best check her diaper and put her to bed. She woke up on my first try, and I didn't want to leave her to cry. My guess is she'll be waking soon to eat, anyway."

"Usually," Diane agreed, still trying to collect herself. "The fresh air from our walks makes her sleepy and then the book you brought—anyway, she'll be hungry soon. Well, I'm sure I don't have to tell you." Words grew less coherent as her mind struggled to make sense of what he'd said. She was chattering nonsense.

What did she think they'd been doing? Being friends, that was all. Nothing formal. He popped in and popped out whether at work or here. They'd had some great conversations, but he'd never tried to touch her again, not even to hold her hand.

What did she think they'd been doing?

He returned a short while later, smelling pleasantly of baby, and washed his hands at the sink.

"Your tea must be cold," she said quickly. "Let me make you some fresh."

But as she started to rise, he turned and his hand shot out, gripping her forearm gently but firmly. "I don't need tea, Diane. But I think we need a bit of conversation, if that's okay."

The way he held her arm, she could have tugged free with the least effort. He wasn't using force. But she didn't care, because her body was lighting up like the Fourth of July, sparklers spreading anywhere. Time had cured none of her attraction to him. If anything, it felt stronger than ever.

Confident that she wasn't leaving, he sat across from her.

"Now, I understood why you didn't want to date. I told you, I'm not good at that kind of thing. Ya want romance, call an actor—you'll get a better show. But

I understood, and my ham-fisted way of going about it made it seem like this dating thing was all fraught with danger and formality."

She started to open her mouth, but his entire face softened. "Di, be honest. When you heard that, did you kind of panic? Start to feel hemmed in? Like you were going to make a big mistake if you said yes?"

She sighed, lowered her head for a few seconds, then raised it. "I felt confused," she agreed. "I was also...afraid I'd fail."

He nodded. "I reckoned. Merely naming it made it a task you could either mess up or get right. I shouldn't have done that."

"So what have we been doing, Blaine?"

"We've been dating informally. Me dropping by, all that stuff. Bringing dinner over. Little things. And you haven't told me to get lost yet. So yes, if you've changed your mind, I'm agreeable. Seeing more of you would be a pleasure. But we don't have to press it. I don't want to press it. Slow and easy."

He looked away, staring out the window over the sink into the darkening evening. All anyone could see on the glass now was a reflection of this unin-spired kitchen.

"I've got me own problems, Di."

She caught her breath. "What do you mean?"

He shrugged one shoulder. "You're afraid of fail-ing, aren't you?"

Sadly, that was something she had no choice but to admit. "Yes. I told you about my mother."

"And your father, to be fair. You said he was a vet?"

She nodded, her insides flip-flopping. "Vietnam. When I was growing up, I sometimes felt…that he was empty inside. That all he wanted was to be left alone. But then there were times—"

"The times that make you keep that chair."

He was looking at her again, so she simply nodded.

"Poor man," he said. "He was the one who failed you, ya know." He held up a hand before she could speak. "I'm not condemning the man. God knows what he went through to leave him such a husk. But it remains, you needed some support to deal with your mother, and you weren't getting it. You felt like a failure because you couldn't please her, and he didn't stand up for you. But he was the failure because he wasn't there when he was needed. Not that it really matters now. Damage is done and all that."

She couldn't speak, had no idea what to say. He was making sense, but she wasn't sure she was ready to accept it. She'd made something of herself, yes, but it was almost in reaction to her mother, not because she was special in any way.

"Anyway, as I was sayin'. I have me own devils to deal with. I told you the story of Ailis, but I rather made light of it. She gave me a lesson and I still have the scars. I've never really let myself care. Too much danger there. But somehow, you're different. Maybe because of Daphne. I don't know how you got under my skin fast. So you're not the only one who's been a bit edgy about this."

He smiled. "I say we date and take it as slow as we need to. Because you're a special woman, Diane Finch, and I'm pretty well hooked. Fair enough?"

"Fair enough," she agreed, her heart beginning to rise like a helium balloon. So she hadn't lost him. And at some point, she hoped he would feel as sure as she was beginning to feel.

Right now, she couldn't ask for anything more.

He extended his hand across the table and she took it, closing her eyes with absolute pleasure as she felt the warmth of his skin once again.

"After we get the daffodil down for the night, or most of it," he said quietly, "I'd like to take you to bed."

"Oh, please," she whispered. "Please."

But then Daphne woke again, her cries sounding cranky. Blaine went to get her, and Diane started their dinner, turning on the oven and scrubbing potato skins.

There was still hope. Thank God. She couldn't believe she had almost thrown away her chance with a man like Blaine Harrigan.

A tear of happiness rolled down her cheek. They'd date. They'd see. And maybe heaven waited in the wings.

Epilogue

Daphne's cries woke Diane, and she looked at the bedside clock. "Three a.m.?" she asked under her breath.

"I'll get her," Blaine said groggily.

"No, I will. It's the cold, I'm sure of it."

But Blaine was already sitting up. "The medicine the doctor gave her isn't helping?"

"Not a whole lot. Besides, who isn't cranky with a cold?"

"Good question," he replied. "I'll check the humidifier then make us something warm to drink. This house is drafty."

"I definitely need to rent a better place," she agreed. Jamming her feet into slippers, wrapping herself in her warmest robe, she slid across the hallway and by the soft glow of the child's bedside lamp, decorated with images of stuffed animals, she found Daphne on her back, blankets kicked off and looking mad as hell.

Diane changed her swiftly, aware of the drafts in the room. That sure didn't make her daughter any happier. She heard Blaine behind her, fumbling with the humidifier, heard him pour more water and probably add more menthol to the cup. The place reeked of menthol right now.

Then she wrapped Daph snugly in a warm blanket and carried her out into the magic that had become her living room.

Blaine didn't believe in half measures. A large Christmas tree, covered with lights and ornaments, filled the front window. She flipped on the lights, and the twinkling and sparkling immediately seized Daph's attention. Her crying subsided to hiccups while Diane wiped her runny nose and wondered if she needed to use the suction bulb to clear her passageways.

At the moment, though, Daph didn't sound totally clogged. Maybe some of that baby ibuprofen for her misery? How she hated not even being able to tell if the girl had a headache or something. She felt warm, but Diane didn't want to undress her again to take her temperature.

Okay, then, she'd see how it went for a while before pulling out the medicine.

She heard the kettle whistle from the kitchen, announcing that tea or hot chocolate would soon arrive. She sat in her dad's old recliner, next to the new one that Blaine had bought. A beautiful Christmassy scene, utterly wasted on Daph.

Well, not entirely, because the girl had become fascinated with the twinkling lights. Her cries steadily diminished until they sounded almost like an afterthought.

Blaine appeared with two mugs of hot chocolate and a bottle. "Do you think she can drink? Or should we aspirate her nose?"

"I'm wondering. Right now I'm not even sure she's hungry."

Daph quieted, still fixated on the lights, evidently liking the display.

"Maybe I should sleep here with her," Diane suggested.

"Fine. I'll join you. If the lights make her happy, we can stay here as long as it takes."

She loved his generosity, his willingness to stay with her, the lack of cranky grumbling of his own as he shuffled back to bed. After all, there was no need for both of them to stay up.

She reached for her hot chocolate.

"Careful."

It was hot, but not too hot to drink. How had he managed that?

"Look," he whispered suddenly. "Me daffodil is nodding off."

"I hope so. She's been so miserable."

"And it's Christmas Eve," he remarked. "I hope next year it's better for her."

"Really? It's Christmas Eve?"

"We passed midnight a few hours ago, darlin'."

She almost laughed. Daph being so sick had evidently cost her her mind. "I forgot."

"I haven't. Think she'll sleep for a bit?"

"She seems comfortable now."

"Then there's something I wanted to do on Christmas Eve, and I don't see any reason to wait until tonight. Seems like with an infant you take your time where you find it."

"Ain't that the truth," she answered wryly.

There were wrapped packages under the tree, mostly toys and clothes for Daphne, but one or two surprises for the two of them. She'd been staring at a huge box with her name on it for days now, wondering what the red-and-gold foil wrapping concealed.

She'd tucked a few things for him under the tree, too. He was a man who didn't seem to want much, so she'd bought him a chamois shirt that nearly matched his eyes and a new set of double-layered gloves. And...well...she hoped he'd understand the Saint Brigid's medal.

He rose now and reached around the back of the tree. In his hand he held a small red box. "I know how you're liking small earrings, studs, right?"

"Right. I love studs because they don't catch on things. And Daph here isn't likely to yank one out of my ear. But that can wait, can't it?"

"No. This is special, and she might only sleep a few minutes, sick as the tyke is."

Then he knelt in front of her and passed her the

red box. "I hope you like my taste. I can always exchange…"

She didn't hear anything else he said, because she opened the box and found an absolutely beautiful ring, a diamond surrounded by tiny emeralds. "Blaine? Blaine?"

"I'm in the way of asking you to marry me, Diane Finch," he said quietly. "And I'm hoping you can answer me before I die of the suspense."

She lifted her gaze from the box and looked into the blue eyes of heaven. "Yes," she whispered, her heart swelling until it felt it would burst. "Oh, yes. I love you so…"

He took the box, removed the ring and slid it onto her left hand. Then he looked straight into her eyes. "I'll be loving you with my last breath, Diane Finch. You are the reason my heart beats. And I wouldn't mind hearing that again."

"I love you," she said more strongly, but any other words were suddenly buried against his shoulder. He wrapped his arm around her, holding her as close as he could without disturbing the baby.

"My heart," he said, and twisted enough to kiss her to the depths of her being.

Daphne decided to protest, but they looked at one another and laughed with joy. Perfect. Everything was perfect, including the cranky baby.

* * * * *